THE FEY

The story begins!

Claude Hall Crust

THE FEY

Claudia Hall Christian

Cook Street Publishing
Denver, CO

ISBN (*13 digits*) : 978-0-9822746-3-7
(*10 digits*) : 0-9822746-3-7
Library of Congress : 2009909008

PUBLISHER'S NOTE:
This is a work of fiction. Names, characters, places and incidents either are the product of the author's imagination or are used fictitiously.

Second edition © September, 2009
Cook Street Publishing
PO Box 18217
Denver, CO 80218

For the Silent Partner.
*If you were truly silent,
the Fey would never exist.*

PROLOGUE
October 8 – 12:42 P.M.
Paris, France

"This is it?"

"We thought you'd like to see a familiar face," her childhood friend said. His bright cricket smile flashed across his face.

"Well, they got it wrong in Catholic School."

His top hat bounced on his head when he nodded. Adjusting his ascot, he held a white-gloved hand out to her.

"Take my hand."

"What about the others?" She pulled her hand to her chest. "Don't you have to take them first?"

"Except for one, they have moved on," he said. "It's your time."

"I think I'll stay here."

Jiminy Cricket's head fell back in laughter. The buttons on his vest strained against the gale.

"I am thirty years old," she said through her teeth. "I am a Special Forces Intelligence Officer. I am a Sergeant in the United States Army. They call me the Fey. My name is...."

The lights came on. The cricket faded.

She was sitting cross-legged with her best friend's head in her lap. Touching his face, she confirmed what she already knew. Sergeant Jesse Abreu was dead. She collapsed back against the door to the limestone vault. She would join him soon.

Her heart jumped. There was movement to inside the vault. Someone survived! Shifting her torso toward the vault, Jesse's head ground further into the gaping wounds in her left hip. She clamped her mouth shut against the scream forming in her throat.

Overwhelmed with pain, her focus slipped. The cricket's smiling face came into view. She screwed up her face and squinted her eyes.

She was not dying.

Not yet.

Her beloved childhood friend laughed and fanned her with his umbrella. She was sitting in the doorway again.

"I wondered if you were alive," a slight dark-haired man said in Arabic. "Don't move."

Pressing the muzzle of a handgun against her forehead, he kneeled in front of her. His hand reached under her jacket. Pulling her dog tags from under her T-shirt, he jerked the secondary tag from the longer chain.

"From the look of things, you'll be dead soon enough."

He rummaged through Jesse's shirt ripping his secondary dog tag from its chain. The man held eleven dog tags in front of her face.

"You're quite valuable." Holstering the handgun, he stood and looked back into the vault. "Now, where can I find that security token? No token, no payment."

"Gosh, I wish I could help you." She replied in Hebrew knowing it would make him angry. She opened and closed her eyes in an attempt to bat her large brown eyes.

"Yes, fuck me." The man sneered then kicked Jesse's dead body. Continuing in Arabic, he said, "I'm not the one who is fucked. You should be grateful. Death is preferable to what is planned for you. Just give me the token, and we're even."

She glowered at him. Under Jesse's body, she slipped her hand into her pocket to find her Zippo lighter.

"No matter. You'll be dead in a few minutes."

Drawing on her deepest reserves, she jerked her torso left causing the man to look into the vault. With a quick flip of her right hand, the lighter bounced down the dark limestone hallway. When the man jumped after the lighter, she pulled a small journal from inside her jacket. Tucking the journal deep into the front pocket of Jesse's shirt, she sagged forward.

"Nice try, Fey. I have the token." The man bent and kissed her cheek. "Thanks. With this, I can afford that house in the South of France."

The man's expression turned to disgust when he noticed he was holding a St. Christopher medallion on a secondary dog tag. Spitting on the medallion, he threw it into the pool of blood forming around her. She grabbed for the St. Christopher, the only gift Jesse ever received from his mother. With his foot, he moved the medallion just out of her reach and smirked at her.

"I am sorry. I did like your team… and you."

"If you like me so much, why not just kill me now?" she asked in Hebrew.

"I am not a killer. I am merely a business man."

"You hire people to do your killing. You must have known that I would kill him."

"In fact, I predicted that if we left you alive, you would kill our associate. But you were to be left alive." He shrugged as if to say that the shooter's death was a reasonable business expense. Looking into the vault, he said, "Did you have to shoot him in the head? So messy."

Pulling a neck gaiter up over his mouth and nose, the man retreated into the blood-drenched vault. He glanced around the vault, and then began rummaging through a stack of clean clothing. Finding what he needed, he wrapped the shooter's head with T-shirts.

The man jerked to a stop.

Footsteps in the hallway!

Through drooping eyes, she watched him press into a dark corner of the vault.

"Take my hand," Jiminy Cricket said. "It is time."

She took the gloved hand and looked into the cricket's beloved face.

"Can we sing?" she asked.

"Of course," her cricket began singing her favorite song, "When you wish upon a star."

They sang as they rose through five floors of limestone tunnels and into the building above. They were floating through the bright fall Paris day when a male voice joined in their song.

"Max," she whispered the name of her identical twin.

A strong deep voice, with a distinctive London accent, joined the song.

"John," she whispered her husband's name.

Like a beacon, their voices called her home.

Turning to Jiminy Cricket, she let go of his hand. With death on her tail, she dove back to the pain. She leapt toward the horror. She pushed her spirit back into her broken body.

Feeling a brush across her lips, Alexandra "The Fey" Hargreaves opened her eyes.

CHAPTER ONE
Two weeks later
October 22 – 3:00 A.M.
Somewhere deep within the Pentagon
Arlington, Virginia

Sergeant Marcia Wizinski walked down the long dark corridor toward a conference room. For the last three hours, the men's angry voices echoed through the deserted halls. She tapped on the door to let them know that she was entering. When their voices dropped and the room became silent, Marcia opened the door.

"Sir?" Marcia looked for her boss, the Admiral in charge of Special Forces.

"Yes, Marcia?"

The Admiral was sitting at the end of the table facing the door. Marcia could tell he was angry. She noticed that three of the men had turned away from the door to avoid recognition. Stepping into the room, she kept her eyes on the Admiral.

"You asked me to let you know when they have landed."

"And?"

"The Air Force reports that the Fey has touched down." Marcia looked at a piece of paper in her hand. "Sir, um, the Jakker?"

"Sergeant Zack Jakkman?" the Admiral asked.

"Yes, Sir. Sergeant Jakkman insisted on taking her all the way to Walter Reed. Her husband and twin are with her in the Black Hawk. There is a Green Beret waiting for her.... A Sergeant Matthew Mac Clenaghan? The Army says that he is AWOL."

"She's alive?" a nondescript brown-eyed man near the middle of the table asked.

"Yes sir. She is alive. She remains in a medically induced coma."

The tension in the room dropped like the barometer before rain showers. A handsome man with caramel colored skin, broad shoulders and cropped hair stood and walked toward Marcia. Shifting her eyes toward the movement in the room, Marcia felt a jolt of attraction rush through her.

"Thank you, Marcia," the man said in a Queens accent. "May I walk you to your car?"

"I . . ." Marcia looked up into the man's grey-hazel eyes then blushed. She forced her eyes back toward the Admiral. "Sir? Will you need me any further?"

"No, Marcia. Thank you for staying. Please let Agent Rasmussen walk you to your car. Raz?"

"Yes Admiral?" Homeland Security Agent Arthur J. Rasmussen turned toward the Admiral.

"You'll report from Walter Reed?"

"Yes sir. And Sergeant Mac Clenaghan?"

"We'll take care of his status," the Secretary of Defense replied.

"Shall we?" Raz said. He moved through the door then held it for Marcia.

When the door closed, the men were silent. No one was quite sure what to say. In the single largest attack on a Special Forces team, ten soldiers were killed under the streets of Paris. Not just soldiers, these men made up the most successful and talented team in Special Forces. The very best of the very best were cut in two by AK-47 fire in a matter of minutes.

And, beyond all reason, the Fey clung to life.

"I need to get to Walter Reed," General, turned Senator, Patrick Hargreaves said breaking the silence. "As I see it, we have three remaining issues: maintaining our relationships with our allies in Europe, determining the cause of this action, and protecting the survivors. Have I missed anything?"

"I believe that covers it, Patrick," the Admiral said.

"When this gets out, our allies will be furious," the Secretary of State said. "Why was an unauthorized Special Forces team working in Europe?"

"They were authorized to operate in any country where someone was held hostage," the Admiral replied. "The Joint Chiefs, as well as NATO, gave them authority to go where they needed to go. You know their track record."

The Secretary of State shifted his watch to show a black scripted F tattooed to the inside of his right wrist.

"Yes, Admiral, I am aware of their success."

"I thought so," the Admiral said.

"There are no known hostages in Europe," the Secretary of Defense said. "And the Jakker is not talking. We have no idea why they were in Paris. We need a cover story."

"We've taken care of that. The French know the truth." The CIA Director shrugged. "The rest of the world believes that the team was killed in Afghanistan. But I'll tell you. In the last ten days, we've heard from almost every warlord in Afghanistan, including the Taliban. They are shocked, upset and not one claims responsibility for the attack. If Afghani warlords had Internet access? We'd be in big trouble."

"What do we do about the French?" the Secretary of State asked.

"My brother works in French government," the non-descript man said. He continued tapping a cigarette against the table. "He has smoothed any ruffled feathers. At this moment, there is no record that the Fey or her team were ever in Paris."

"I didn't know elite intelligence agents had brothers," the Secretary of Defense said looking at the non-descript man. "Well done, Ben."

"Thank you, sir," Ben replied. He set the cigarette down on the table. "Do we have any idea why they were...."

"Murdered?" the Admiral finished Ben's statement. "No. We have no idea. Who called you to warn you?"

"Someone who is no longer living."

The Admiral looked at Ben. His distaste for spies, CIA, FBI, Homeland Security, even Military Intelligence, showed on his face. Amused, Ben raised his eyebrows at the Admiral.

"And the vault?" Patrick Hargreaves asked. His voice broke the tension between his best friend and the head of Special Forces.

"We'll continue trying to get in, but it doesn't look good," the Secretary of Defense said. "There is a note in Captain O'Brien's file that says: 'Only the Fey has access to storage.'"

"The note was made by?"

"The notation was made five days prior to the assault. By the Fey."

"If she doesn't survive...." Patrick Hargreaves' voice caught with emotion.

"When Alexandra is well," Ben said, "she will stop at nothing to find out what happened."

"So we wait?" the Secretary of Defense asked.

"We already have a cover," the Admiral said. "We will stick with the story until we know one way or the other. I will not waste any more time on 'what ifs'. In the meantime, I've been authorized to create a memorial for the Fey Special Forces Team at Fort Logan National Cemetery. How will we protect the survivors?"

"Agent Rasmussen has created a new identity for the Fey," Ben said. "She is Alyssa Kreiger, orphan, married to John Drayson. Senator Hargreaves had a son named Alexander instead of a daughter named Alexandra. Alexander was killed in the assault."

"She'll work for me," Colonel Howard Gordon spoke for the first time, "at Military Intelligence in Colorado. We are creating a cartography team for her."

"She's already remapped most of Afghanistan," the Secretary of Defense said. His eyes flicked to her father.

"Alex likes to work with maps," Patrick said. "Ever since she was a small child, she's loved maps… stars… her twin…."

His voice caught. The great General Hargreaves gulped back his emotion.

"We agree then that she won't be discharged?" the Secretary of Defense asked.

"She is a welcome addition to our team," Colonel Gordon said. "We will do everything in our power to keep her safe."

"She is still contractually obligated to continue working in US Intelligence," the CIA director said.

"So you ARE holding her to that Goddamn contract." Patrick spit the words at the CIA Director. "You don't give a shit about her. You just want your prize."

"She is a valuable asset that we are extremely unwilling to…."

"Alexandra will continue working under me as Agent Rasmussen's partner," Ben said.

"And Captain Walter?" the Secretary of Defense asked. He tried veering away from the topic they had spent the last hour arguing about.

"Captain Walter is on six months leave," the Admiral said. "He was due to re-join the team in three weeks."

"Captain Walter and his family are in the process of being relocated to rural Colorado," the FBI Director said with force. While these men argued over details, his agents were doing the actual work. "They will be settled by the end of the week."

"And Robert Powell?" the Secretary of Defense asked.

"The Boy Scout?" The Admiral asked. "He was not with the team at the time of the assault. He is currently in Nicaragua."

"A guest of the CIA?" the Secretary of State asked.

The CIA Director nodded.

"Healing from his fictitious wounds. He was only with the team for a little more than five months," the Admiral said. "He will receive a long term assignment, probably in Northern Afghanistan."

"You're burying him in Afghanistan?" The Secretary of Defense asked.

"I prefer 'keeping an eye on,' but yes, we are burying the Boy Scout in Afghanistan."

"Anyone know where he was at the time of the assault?" Patrick asked.

"Ben?" The CIA Director asked.

"Rumors."

"Could he have done this?" The Secretary of Defense asked.

Everyone in the room turned to look at Ben. Ben's eyes focused on the cigarette which he was once again tapping against the table.

"Ben?" The Admiral asked.

Ben looked up and shrugged.

"Killed everyone? No. Involved? Probably." Ben nodded his head. "Yes, I believe he was involved."

The men digested the information in silence.

"What's left?" Patrick said moving to get up. "I need to be with my daughter, my family."

"One thing," the Admiral said. The scripted "F" tattoo on his right shoulder burned as if he received it yesterday.

"We protect the Fey. No matter what. We protect the Fey. With any luck, she'll return to what she does best. With any luck...."

The men nodded in unison.

ᔪᔪᔪᔪᔪᔪ
Three weeks later
November 12 – 12:15 P.M.
Walter Reed Hospital
Washington DC

"Go to lunch," Alex whispered to her worried husband.

Dr. John Drayson kneeled next to her bed. His cobalt blue eyes held her brown eyes while his hand stroked her face. He and her identical twin, Max Hargreaves, had been by her side since she arrived at Walter Reed.

The doctors' predictions were horrifying. Don't expect much. She may not recognize you. She won't be the person you knew. Five days ago she opened her eyes, looked into John and Max's worried faces and laughed. Beyond anyone's guess, she was her smart, funny, mischievous self.

She just didn't remember the last six months of her life.

"I..." he started.

"Trying to control everything?" she raised an eyebrow.

"Me?" he laughed. "Never."

"Come on, John," Max said. "She wants to play cards."

"How can you say that?" Alex exclaimed. Looking up at her twin, her eyes danced with laughter.

"Liar," Max replied.

"I.... I am a wounded veteran. Have some respect!"

At that moment, the door opened and Sergeant Matthew Mac Clenaghan came into the room. Tall and thin, his dark hair was shorn in a military haircut. He looked like an accountant or maybe a lawyer, not a Special Forces officer.

"Are you guys off to lunch?" Matthew asked.

"I guess so," John said. He ruffled his dark curly hair then leaned over the bed to kiss Alex on the lips. "Sixty minutes. Don't die."

"I can't move. There are guards with machine guns at my door. What could happen?"

"I'll walk you out," Matthew said. "I'll be right back, gimp."

Alex laughed.

Max held her hands for a moment. Their brown eyes held and they smiled matching smiles. Letting go of her hands, he followed John out of the room.

"She still doesn't know?" Matthew asked.

"No, she does not know that her team is dead," John said.

Matthew looked up to nod "Hello" to Sergeant Troy Olivas as he pushed open the door to Alex's hospital room.

"We need to tell her."

"When she's better," John said, "stronger. You will not tell her."

Matthew nodded.

"Enjoy your lunch."

"You'll call if…" John started.

"Of course," Matthew said giving his most reassuring smile.

Matthew waited until John and Max were down the hall before he returned to the room. He spoke with the two Army soldiers guarding the door then pushed the door open.

Sitting on Alex's bed, Troy entertained her with finger puppets. He was in the middle of a nonsensical love story about Enrique and Frieda. Alex giggled at his funny voices and the ridiculous story.

From the moment they met at Special Forces training, Troy and Matthew were best friends. They agreed on one thing. Neither Troy nor Matthew liked the woman in their midst. Less than two months later, Alex's easy smile, gentle wit, as well as her willingness to drag them through training, won them over. The three soldiers had been friends ever since.

"Is Jesse coming for cards?" Alex beamed at Matthew.

Troy caught her attention again with the squealing voice of Frieda the finger puppet. Frieda's heart was breaking and Enrique, the brute, did not care.

"You get us instead," Sergeant Andrew "Trece" Ramirez said coming through the door. "We're a poor substitute for Jesse but the White Boy never wins."

A muscular man with a barrel chest, twenty-inch arms and a small waist, Trece held the door for an equally large man with almost albino skin. Trece carried a white bakery box while the other man carried a dozen large sunflowers.

"We brought donuts and flowers," Sergeant Christopher "White Boy" Blanco said. "Trece? Can you get the china?"

Trece winked at Alex causing the empty teardrop tattoo under his left eye to fold into his coffee colored skin. Setting the donut box on Alex's bedside tray, he went into the bathroom for paper towels and Dixie cups. When the bathroom door swung closed, and Matthew bent to pick something up, the White Boy pulled a DVD case out of his inside jacket pocket.

"I got the movie," the White Boy whispered.

He gave her a copy of Walt Disney's *Pinocchio*. She tucked the movie under her sheets. The White Boy sneered at Troy who shrugged. Hearing Trece return, the White Boy became very busy setting the sunflowers into her plastic water pitcher.

"Oh gee, what shall we drink?" Matthew asked. He stood up holding up a bottle of Irish Whiskey. "But none for you, missy."

"You are so mean!" Alex exclaimed.

Crossing her arms across her chest, she pretended to pout. The men laughed at her efforts. Trece returned from the bathroom with Dixie cups and napkins. Matthew poured the whiskey.

"Can you help me sit up?" she asked.

"Sure. Get up Troy."

"We're in the middle of the story!" Troy exclaimed. "How will we know if Enrique and Frieda are meant for each other?"

"Oh God," Matthew said.

"Hey, if little Troy wants to put on a show, then I think we should watch," Trece said. He crossed his arms and leaned back on his hip. "Go ahead. We like to be entertained by the little people of the world."

Alex laughed at the idea of six foot tall Troy as a "little" person. Alex met Trece and the White Boy when they sat down next to Jesse in the dining hall in Bosnia. The four soldiers were inseparable the rest of the tour in Bosnia. Even after Alex and Jesse went on to be Green Berets, and Trece and the White Boy moved into a unit that worked in government security, they remained fast friends.

"Go ahead, little man," the White Boy said. He looked up from the donut box. "Alex, you want the chocolate sprinkle?"

Alex nodded and took the donut from the White Boy.

Troy, flustered by the attention, stood from the bed. Glancing back, he saw that Alex was laughing at him. He smiled in return and slipped the puppets into his pocket.

From the waist down, Alex was a freak show of gauze, tubes, tape and wire. Her left hip all but destroyed. No one knew if she would walk again.

Trece and Matthew, one on each side, lifted Alex to sitting. The men looked away when she grunted with pain. She smiled when she was situated. Then the DVD case fell on the floor.

"What's this?" Trece asked. He bent down to pick up the DVD case. "I love this movie. Shall I put it on?"

The White Boy looked at Alex who shrugged. Who knew that Trece loved *Pinocchio*? Trece put the DVD in the player and flipped the television so the movie played in the background.

"I was going to ask," the White Boy said. "Do you love Pinocchio because you want to be a boy? You know Pinocchio wanted to be a boy?"

"No, that's Max! I'm the blue fairy like my tattoo."

The men stared at Alex.

"What?" Matthew asked.

"Max and I were supposed to be this boy-girl deformed person but Max wanted to be a boy. So we're identical twins instead," Alex said. She looked from one confused face to the next. "John can explain the genetics if you want. But that's what happened."

"All right then. Anyone has to look at you to know that your identical twins, but... thanks for the clarification." Matthew said. "Can we play cards now?"

"Thanks. Oh, I might get a call," Alex said. "Would you mind bringing the phone over?"

"A call?" Matthew asked.

"Are you her personal secretary?" Trece asked. "Man, I would never let a woman push me around like that."

"Shut up, Trece," Alex said.

"Yes, ma'am," Trece replied. The men laughed.

"King Abdallah likes to call on his anniversary," Alex said. "I'm sorry Mattie. Do you mind?"

"I'm happy to help," Matthew said.

"Can we play?" the White Boy said passing cards to each of the men. "We only have fifty-one minutes before the clone and the cutie-pie husband return. I need to make some extra money."

"You're going to win?" Trece asked. The White Boy looked at him and they laughed.

Troy snatched his cards from the White Boy's hand. Plopping down in a chair near Alex's bed, he set his feet on her bed. Matthew pushed Troy's feet off the bed and sat down in their place. Like most experienced soldiers, they were seasoned poker players. They fell into the easy rhythm of playing poker, eating donuts and drinking whiskey.

Alex was about to win her second hand when the phone rang. She opened her mouth, but Trece beat her to it.

"Mattie," Trece said imitating her voice. "Would you mind getting the phone for me?"

Matthew shook his head at Trece. Walking across the room, Matthew picked up the telephone. Carrying the phone across the room, he lifted the receiver to his ear.

"Yes, sir," Matthew replied in Arabic. "She is right here. One moment."

Matthew gave Alex the telephone receiver. Alex set her cards face up showing her straight flush. The men groaned and threw their cards at her. She ducked to avoid the cards and took the telephone receiver from Matthew.

"As-Salamu `Alaykum," she said giving the standard Arabic greeting into the phone. She smiled at Troy's exaggerated response to her win. Even Enrique the finger puppet protested.

"Alaykum As-Salam, my dear," a man's voice said in Arabic. "How does it feel to have killed your entire team? Decorated soldiers with wives and families cut down in the prime of their lives because of you."

"What are you talking about?"

"They didn't tell you?" the man's voice purred in her ear. "They are all dead, Alexandra. And you are to blame. Charlie, Dwight, Paul, Nathan, Jax, Dean, Scott, Mike, and Tommy. That's not to mention Jesse Abreu. How does it feel to have killed your best friend?"

"Jesse?"

"You as good as put a gun to his head and pulled the trigger."

Troy nudged Matthew's arm and pointed at Alex. Her face had blanched white.

"Who is this?"

"My name is Eleazar. I want you to know my name so you will know precisely who did pull the trigger. Just in case you forget, I will call you every month at the exact time I was forced to kill your team. You will never forget what you have done."

"What have I done?"

"Forced me to kill the Fey Special Forces team. You better take a good look at what's left of your friends. Enjoy them while you can. I will kill every one of them while you watch until you give me what I want."

"What do you want?" she whispered into the phone.

"I want my property," the voice screamed into the phone.

Alex screamed. Dropping the telephone receiver, her hands covered her ears and a flood of tears poured from her eyes and nose. Her ears filled with the sound of ragged breathing. And panic set in. Desperate to get away, to get anywhere safe, she ripped the tubes, wires and IVs from her body.

Troy jumped from his chair. His arms went around her torso as he tried to stop her thrashing. Trece's hands went around her ankles to keep her legs still while the White Boy ran to get the doctor. Matthew dropped beside her into the bed.

But the damage was done. In her terror, she ripped the deep sutures in her hip. Her blood flowed freely from her femoral artery.

A nurse ran into the room followed by the White Boy. The nurse ran out of the room to get the doctor.

"Trece, put your hands on the wound," Matthew screamed.

The White Boy took Trece's place at Alex's ankles. Trece jumped to press his hands against her open wound.

"Yes, right there."

Despite their efforts to hold her still, she rocked back and forth in the bed.

"Everyone's dead. Everyone's dead. Everyone's dead. Everyone's dead." She whispered over and over again.

"Alex, honey, you have to stop moving," Matthew said. "Ah fuck."

The monitor screamed when her blood pressure plummeted. The doctor ran in with a nurse. Yelling orders to the nurse, the doctor fumbled with Alex's useless IV lines. He pointed to Alex's arm and the nurse shot Alex full of barbiturates. Within seconds, she fell back against the bed.

"Mattie?"

"I'm here," he said.

"I killed everyone." Alex dropped into drug-induced oblivion.

CHAPTER TWO
Fourteen months later
January 5 – 5:30 A.M.
Denver, Colorado

Alex lay somewhere between sleep and awake when John began stroking her naked body. She reached for him and he shifted on top of her. His lips brushed hers before moving to her chin. His tongue flicked the crease in her chin and his mouth began a biting, pulling journey down her neck. She giggled at the waves of goose bumps down her back and the rising warmth in her core.

She delighted at his weight, his lush male scent and shivered under his still moving mouth and skilled surgeon's hands. Shifting her hips, she drew him into her depths. At the moment of union, he pushed back to look into her brown eyes.

"Good morning," Alex whispered.

"And a very good morning to you," he replied in his wonderful London accent.

He began subtle waves of movement that brought them luscious warmth. With deliberate motion, he flipped her on top of him giving him access to her full breasts. Alex increased the pace, moving with purpose, against him while he rubbed, bit and tortured her nipples. When she dropped her head back, he sat up to meet her. With his strong arms around her, he moved on top of her again pressing forward. They rose in tempo and pace.

Feeling her close to the edge, he said, "Promise me…"

"Oh God, I hate it when you do this."

He kissed her lips.

"I'm going to buy a vibrator."

He laughed. He moved his hips causing her breath to catch.

"Yes my darling?" he said imitating her American accent.

"What?"

"You need to leave the house today," John said.

"I already promised to leave the house today," she said. She tugged at her dog tag hanging around his neck. She kissed him then bit his lip. "I need to buy a vibrator anyway."

Dropping his mouth to hers, he continued deep and slow movements until she gasped with pleasure and shuddered against him. He shifted their tempo then followed her in waves of blissful release. They held each other tight, face to face, heart to heart, entwined.

"I love you," he whispered in her ear.

"Not more than I love you."

He kissed her nose, nuzzled her neck, then slipped from the bed to begin his day. When he moved into his closet, she pulled the covers over her head. She was asleep by the time he left for his morning run.

He yanked the covers off her warm naked body when he returned. She played along and chatted with him until the moment he entered the shower. Flipping the covers over her head, she was asleep.

When she opened her eyes, he was dressed in blue scrubs, ready for another day as a resident in the Vascular Surgery program at the University of Colorado Health Sciences Center. Knowing her love of coffee, he waved a mug under her nose to wake her. When she reached for the coffee, he held the mug away from her.

"You've never broken a promise to me Alex."

"Not yet," she said.

"Not in twelve years," he said. "Come on, love, it's time to start living again."

"Yes, I'll begin with a purple vibrator," she said taking the cup from him. She sat up against the headboard. Wrapping both hands around the mug, she took a long drink of coffee.

"Why purple?" he asked.

"It's not your favorite color. You won't want to borrow it."

"Oh I might."

Moving his hand in quick motion, he made a buzzing sound and pressed his hand between her legs. She screamed and splashed the coffee on the covers. Laughing, he gave her a hand towel to mop up the mess.

"Would you like to take my car? It's easier to drive."

She smiled. John loved his Audi A8 like a child. The car's heated leather seats and plush interior was his daily confirmation that he was no longer a poor starving orphan. If he's offering his car, he must genuinely want her to leave the house.

"My mother's coming to get me," Alex said. She passed him the mug then, using her hands she pressed her left leg to the edge of the bed. He gave her a metal forearm crutch. She pushed herself to standing.

"You're taking your mother to purchase your first vibrator?" he asked.

Holding her bathrobe, he helped her slip into the warm terrycloth. He put the mug of coffee in her hand then watched her drain the mug. "You can get a shower? Get dressed?"

"I can," she said. She kissed him. "Thanks. My mother is taking me to her hairdresser to begin the transformation to Alyssa Kreiger. We have a makeup consultation, contact lenses, clothing, blah, blah, blah."

"No vibrator?"

"Sadly, I'll have to wait until tomorrow," she said. "Unless you'd like to pick one up."

"I won't pick out my replacement, love." He brushed his lips across her lips. Turning to leave the room, she caught his hand.

"Thanks," she said.

"You have to fight this depression Alexandra. It's eating you alive."

"When you see me next, I'll be a new woman."

"Thank God. I was getting a little bored."

She slapped at him and he laughed. With one last kiss, he scooted down the stairs, through the kitchen and out the back door to the garage. She listened for his car then got back in bed.

Staring at the ceiling, she wondered why she had promised to leave the house. She hadn't left the house since Zack the Jakker flew her home from Walter Reed. No amount of cajoling, threatening or begging could get her to leave the house once she was finally home. She even ignored a subpoena from the Senate Subcommittee on Personnel. She wanted to be right here, in this bed, in this house.

But today was THE DAY TO LEAVE THE HOUSE as determined by... everyone. Her family ganged up on her last weekend making her promise to get out of the house or go on antidepressants and get more counseling. Only John and Max knew that she took antidepressants and saw a counselor.

Not that it helped.

Well... she had cried all day and all night the first month. No, two months. She couldn't stem the flow of tears that started the moment Eleazar told her everyone was dead. Everyone was dead except Alex.

Enter pills and counselor. Exit hysteria. She pulled the covers over her head.

Eleazar. Two days and.... She used her fingers to count the hours until she had to speak to him again. Two days, three hours, and twenty-four minutes until his January call. Her mind went blank.

With a sigh, her internal review returned. Max kept her from killing herself. Like many twins, they were linked together mentally, emotionally, and psychically. She feared that he would die when she died. She rubbed her hands over her face.

No work today. Alex, now Alyssa, was a cartographer for the 734D Military Intelligence Division. Her interest in maps, and habit of annotating them with interesting details, became her career. She was even a Major with a department of her own. Of course, there was no one in her department. Just Alex. And her assistant. Some department.

She worked at home in her secure office with a video link to her assistant and command at Buckley Air Force Base. She had been to the base… see, she did leave the house… about three months ago. Alex rolled over.

There was no reason for her to leave the house today.

"I know you are thinking that there's no reason for you to leave the house today," Max said walking into her bedroom. He pulled the covers from her. "You're wrong."

"Ah Maxie," Alex said. She gave him her best "you have to understand" face but he was having none of it.

"Get up," Max said. "Moping around does you no good. Plus you're getting fat."

"WHAT??" Alex jumped from the bed. "What do you mean I'm getting fat? I've always been too thin. I'm still too thin. Last time I checked I was less than 15% body fat."

Max laughed. He had tricked her from the bed.

She plopped on the bed and he sat down next to her. Resting her head against his shoulder, he put his arm around her. The twins sat on the bed, in silent communion, until Alex's cell phone began vibrating in the pocket of her bathrobe.

"Love?" John asked. "I know you're still in bed."

"Actually your best friend is here berating me about how fat I've become."

John laughed.

"I just wanted to let you know that…"

The doorbell rang.

"I scheduled the cleaners this morning."

"You what?"

"Love you too," he said and hung up the phone.

"Go shower," Max said. Pulling and pushing, he got her into the shower. He went downstairs to let in the cleaning service.

She sighed.

Her mind flitted through John and Max's encouraging words. What do you have to lose? Try it for one day. You're just bored. You can always come home.

She sighed.

If I don't leave the house, how will I ever get my vibrator?

Smiling at the thought, she turned on the shower.

⚭⚭⚭

Six hours later
January 5 – 1:00 P.M.
Denver, Colorado

"Alex!"

Alex looked over at her petite little sister Erin. Erin's green eyes were wide with laughter. Alex blinked.

"What did I miss?"

Alex began singing songs in her head, a standard technique for surviving torture, during the two hour scalp scorching hairdressing episode. Transformed into Alyssa, Alex was now blonde, blue-eyed, and wearing an outfit that was fit for the matron's ball. That's not to mention the 'you-look-absolutely-fabulous' makeup mask. Alyssa Kreiger was a complete dud.

Erin laughed. She reached across the table to hold Alex's hands. Their mother, Rebecca Hargreaves, was talking to a friend at another table.

"I'm glad you left the house," Erin said. "I've looked forward to spending time with you since you returned to Denver."

"Bed ridden?" Alex asked.

"Yes, I was hoping to spend time in bed with you," Erin laughed. "I just thought that we could be friends now that we're grown up and stuff."

"That sounds nice," Alex said.

"First thing? I'm going to take you shopping for some... er... decent clothing!"

"If I had known that so much shopping was in my future? I'm fairly certain I wouldn't have fought so hard to survive."

"Alexandra!" Rebecca said sitting down next to Erin. Her hazel eyes were sparked in shock. "What are you saying?"

"I'm attempting a joke."

"It's not very funny," Rebecca said.

When Rebecca turned to order lunch, Erin flared her nostrils and winked at Alex. Alex laughed.

"I have some news," Erin said.

"Are you done with school?" Rebecca said. "Erin, that's wonderful! Will you look for a job at a pharmaceutical company?"

"Actually, mother, I quit school six months ago," Erin said.

Alex blinked. That got her attention. Erin had wanted to research infectious diseases since a friend of the family died of Hanta virus when she was ten years old. She was a year from finishing her Ph.D. Erin's thesis research project was underway.

"What are you saying?" Rebecca asked.

"I'm engaged," Erin said. The words seemed to drop onto the table.

Rebecca squealed and began peppering Erin with questions. Erin blushed, looked down and shifted in her seat. While Alex watched, Erin seemed to blossom and withdraw at the same time. Something was not quite right. Erin looked up at Alex with pleading eyes.

"How exciting. Have you set a date?" Alex asked.

"Not yet," Erin said. "I wanted to get married in twelve hours, but he wanted to wait."

"Thirteen hours," Alex laughed.

"Only Alex is crazy enough to marry someone she'd known for thirteen hours," Rebecca said.

"And keep it a secret for ten years," Erin said. "I thought I'd just put it right out there."

"And you are marrying....?" Alex asked.

"Christ Alex! Do you pay attention at all?" Rebecca asked. "Erin is marrying that nice boy Marcos Ruiz."

"I was just wondering because...." Alex nodded her head in the direction of Matthew, who was walking toward them.

Erin's head jerked around to see Matthew. She flushed bright red, then looked down, her hands moving instinctively through her red curly hair. Erin and Matthew dated off and on since she was sixteen years old. They were currently in an "off" phase while Matthew was out of the country.

"When did he get back?" Erin said between her teeth.

"Yesterday," Alex said. "He called me when we were at the old ladies' boutique."

"The fashion consultant?" Rebecca said.

"Hmm," Alex said. "He's in a martial arts tournament tomorrow and wants to spar. I invited him to lunch. I'm sorry. I didn't think it was a big deal. Have I met Marcos?"

"No," Erin said with a shake of her head. "No, you'd have to leave the house for that."

"Don't get up," Matthew said to Alex in Irish Gaelic.

"Hello ladies. May I join you for lunch?" he asked in English.

"Matthew, of course, please join us," Rebecca said.

He leaned to kiss Rebecca's cheek while he stroked Erin's neck with his fingers. Erin turned to look up at him. Erin's face flushed with longing, then something else, something foreign to her vibrant sister, crept into Erin's eyes. Her eyes flashed with fear. Matthew's eyes asked the question, but Erin shook her head and looked away. He gave Erin a peck on the cheek then sat next to Alex. Under the table, he reached for Alex's hand.

"What a surprise," Rebecca said. "Erin was just telling us that she's engaged."

"But it's not done," he asked Alex in Gaelic under his breath. Matthew nodded slightly. He smiled at Erin, continuing in English, "Congratulations Erin."

Erin squinted her eyes at Matthew then looked away.

"It's not done," Alex replied in Gaelic.

"So this is Alyssa?" Matthew said. He turned in his chair to get a better look at Alex.

"She's kind of a dud," Alex said.

Matthew laughed. Turning to Rebecca, he said, "God, the eyes creep me out. What do you think?"

"She's beautiful," Rebecca said. "But you're right. The blue eyes are a little disconcerting."

"And the hair?" Erin said.

Matthew touched Alex's blonde locks then laughed.

"What a difference a few years make," he said. "Did you even wash your hair in training?"

Alex laughed. She and Matthew met on a martial arts sparring mat during their Special Forces training. They became sparring partners and, prior to Alex's injuries, won every tournament they entered. Alex rotated in her chair to look at him. He was now competing, and winning, without her. Like so many things, life had moved on while she remained stuck in one place.

When the waiter cleared the plates, Alex asked Rebecca to help her to the bathroom giving Matthew and Erin a chance to talk. Even with Alex's slow movements across the restaurant, Matthew and Erin were arguing when they returned. Rebecca stopped for a loud conversation with an acquaintance to announce their arrival. Squeezing Alex's hand, Rebecca helped her sit then insisted on ordering desserts to celebrate the engagement.

Taking over the conversation, Rebecca chatted about their brother Colin and his wife Julie. Two years younger than Max and Alex, Colin was Rebecca's favorite child. His siblings called him the "Golden Child" as a reference to his white blonde hair and his special spot in Rebecca's heart. Also a Green Beret, Colin left the Army around the time of Alex's injury. He now had his own elementary school classroom.

Rebecca's chatter did nothing to decrease the tension at the table. Looking at Matthew's blank face, she knew that he was very upset. But her sister? She hadn't spent any time with her since she was seventeen years old. She had no idea what was going on between Matthew and Erin. She slipped her hand into Matthew's hand to encourage him.

The waiter was placing their desserts in front of them when a short, dark haired man stormed toward them. Catching the movement out of the corner of her eye, Alex's hand went to the handgun she wore in a holster at her sacrum. Reading Alex's gesture, Matthew shifted. He was ready for action.

Noticing the change in Matthew and Alex, Erin turned to see what they were looking at. Her back stiffened in surprise then she jumped from her chair. Almost running down the aisle, Erin used her hand to hold the man in place.

Alex flinched when he pushed Erin aside to move toward the table. Erin caught his hand and he turned to look at her. Alex couldn't see what he said. She only noticed the look of desperation on Erin's face.

Glancing at Alex then Matthew, Rebecca turned to see why they were staring.

"Erin?"

Erin's face shifted to a smile. The man turned to Rebecca. His plastic smile and cruel eyes were not lost on Rebecca. But Rebecca smiled.

"The groom is here," Rebecca said. "Oh Marcos, how nice to see you!"

Holding Erin's hand, Marcos came toward the table.

"This is my friend, Alyssa," Erin said, "and her boyfriend Matthew. This is my boyfriend...."

"Fiancé," Marcos interrupted.

"Right," Erin looked down. "Fiancé Marcos."

Towering over Marcos, Matthew leaned over a little in order to shake Marcos's hand.

"Nice to meet you. Please join us." Matthew retrieved a chair from another table and placed it at the end of the table. "Can you move over, darling?" he asked Alex.

She shook her head.

"I'll help," he said. Pulling her to standing, he moved her chair over, then helped her sit again. "Alyssa is recovering from an injury."

"You were in a road side bombing in Iraq. Erin told me about you. Nice to meet you. While I do not support the war, I believe it's important to support our troops. Of course, they need to be responsible for their own choices. Their choice to be in the military; their choice to be injured. It's really that simple. We both feel strongly about this."

Alex blinked at the underhanded insult. Prick.

"Nice to meet you," Alex said.

Glancing at Erin, Alex was surprised to see that Erin's eyes glazed over. Feeling Alex's gaze, Erin's blank eyes shifted to Alex.

"How long have you been together?" Marcos asked.

Matthew made a face then looked at Alex. They laughed.

"A long time," Alex said.

"About ten years," Rebecca added. "Didn't you meet at a training? Alyssa was dating Colin but one look at Matthew and…" Rebecca shrugged. "I had hoped to have Alyssa as a daughter-in-law."

Alex's eyes flicked to her mother. Rebecca was no fool. Her mother played along to insure that her daughters were not involved in a public drama.

"Why were you holding Erin's hand?" Marcos asked. "Just a minute ago. I could have sworn that you were holding hands."

"Were you hitting on Erin?" Alex asked. She mock hit Matthew. "A girl can't even go to the bathroom."

"I was asking Erin if she would keep a secret for me."

"A secret?" Alex asked.

"Alyssa," Erin said. Relief spread from her eyes through her body. "I promised not to tell."

"What's the secret?" Marcos asked.

"If you must know, I was asking Erin what kind of ring Alyssa might like. We bought that little band a while ago. I was thinking of making it legal."

Alex squealed and reached for Erin's hands.

"We'll both be brides!"

"Thanks for spoiling the surprise."

"I still don't get why you were holding Erin's hand," Marcos pressed.

"Erin was showing me on her hand a ring that Alyssa had admired. I don't think I held her hand as much as pointed to it while we discussed the ring. But from across the room, I can understand why you were confused."

"Oh Matthew," Alex said. She leaned against his shoulder and he kissed her head. He put his arm around her shoulder. "Let's get out of here."

Despite the tense situation, Matthew gave a genuine laugh at her suggestive tone.

"I don't want to miss my chance. Plus," Alex arched an eyebrow, "I have a surprise of my own."

Matthew opened his mouth at the suggestion, then moved to get up.

"Please stay for dessert," Erin said.

"Yes, stay for dessert at least," Rebecca said. She returned to her chatter about Colin's new classroom.

With Matthew's arm around Alex, they shared a dessert so that Marcos could have one of his own. Alex had no idea what this guy's problem was or why Erin introduced her as Alyssa, but she did not like this Marcos. As soon as she could, Alex was going to do a little spy work on this Marcos.

"I thought you were married to the big curly haired guy," Marcos asked

Alex as they said good-bye. "Erin has an old photo of you, her brother and that other guy. She's standing next to you and you're at Disneyland. She said he was your husband. Of course, your hair was dark."

"Are you sure it was me?" Alex asked. "Erin is friends with a girl named Alex. They are as close as sisters. People often get us confused because we're both tall and thin. But Alex has brown hair and brown eyes. She's married to a doctor in town. Mattie, honey, do you remember his name?"

Matthew made a face and shook his head.

"Brain on testosterone," Alex said. She shook Marcos' hand. "Very nice to meet you."

Leaning on the forearm crutch, Alex made slow progress through the restaurant and into her Jeep CJ-7 which Matthew drove to the restaurant. He helped her into the passenger seat, then jumped into the driver's seat. They were two blocks away before they started laughing.

"What the fuck was that?" Alex asked.

"He reminds me of my Dad," Matthew said.

"And that's not a good thing."

"No, it's not," Matthew said.

"What happened?"

"She flipped out. In a very low voice, she told me exactly how much I suck. I took her hand to try to comfort her. I don't think I've ever seen Erin that upset."

"It's not like that's new information."

"That I suck?" Matthew laughed. "No it's not news. What do you know about this guy?"

"I've been so caught up in myself that I.... No, I've never met him."

Matthew nodded. They drove out of the Cherry Creek shopping area and toward the highway. Flicking on the radio, Matthew picked a classic rock station. When "Sweet Home Alabama" came on, they sang along with Lynard Skynard. They were almost to the highway when Alex spoke.

"Will you take me to see Jesse?"

Matthew pulled the Jeep over to look at Alex. Their eyes held for a moment.

"Honey, Jesse's dead."

"I haven't been to the memorial. You went to the ceremony but I was in the hospital. I haven't been able to go because it wasn't safe. I'm all Alyssa-ed up today. Please Mattie. Please take me to see Jesse."

"Alex, it's your first day out of the house. Do you...."

She nodded.

"All right. But then we train."

"Then we train."

CHAPTER THREE
Five weeks later
February 8 – 11:45 A.M.
Denver, Colorado

Alex pressed the video link to her command and waited for her assistant to respond. She sat in her leather office chair in front of the red oak armoire that held her computers and the link to command.

"Name," her Sergeant said.

"Fey," Alex replied. She waited while security confirmed her face and voice imprint.

"Sir, you are amazingly popular today."

"Oh yeah?" Alex asked.

"Seven messages. Would you like me to read them to you?"

"Just send the emails," Alex said. "Is it...."

"Eleazar. There's new intel out of Iraq about him."

"We go through this every month. The eighth of the month rolls around and suddenly everyone has something to say about Eleazar. Anything I need to know?"

"Officially?"

She laughed at his sarcasm. She wasn't sure how they picked him to be her assistant, but he was a perfect counter balance. She was amazed at his ability to predict her mood then give her exactly what she needed. He even ran interference with brass.

"The Colonel would like to speak with you before you take the call."

"Can you connect me?"

"He's in a meeting but he said he would call you at 1200 hours."

"Anything else?"

"I'll email the messages. Do you know someone named Olivas?"

"Troy? I went to basic and Special Forces training with him. Why?"

"He's left three messages saying that he's at the Fort. He won't tell me what he wants. He just says, 'Tell the Fey that I'm at Fort Carson.' Sir, I ran his profile and.... Sir, he has a reputation for being wild."

Alex laughed.

"There's a new sim at Fort Carson. Afghanistan, I think. He wants me to beat it."

"Can you do that?" Her Sergeant's voice held a mixture of surprise and disbelief. "I mean, with your injuries, you can still beat the training simulations?"

"I've beaten every one so far." Alex shrugged. "I'll call him when I'm done with Eleazar. Have we heard from Trece or the White Boy?"

"They're off the radar. Last report, they were at working at Camp David."

Alex nodded. Her friends had a way of showing up on the eighth of the month.

"When Olivas calls again ask him about Trece. They're probably at the Fort."

Her Sergeant nodded.

"Maps? We're cartographers. And cartographers...."

"Work on maps," they said in unison.

"Yes sir. The Intelligence Center fixed the map phone."

When her team arrived in Afghanistan with only aged, inaccurate Russian maps, Alex fixed, redrew and annotated their maps out of habit. Her team passed their maps on to other teams. Soon soldiers were begging the Intelligence Center for copies of those 'fairy maps'.

After fielding international requests for the maps, the Intelligence Center began distributing the Fey map series. In turn, Alex requested a telephone line where soldiers could leave their feedback. Eleazar called the 'map phone' every month.

"Just in time to talk to Eleazar."

"The Intelligence Center expresses its profound apologies for any inconvenience the Fey might have experienced," her Sergeant read from a letter. "Sir, I've never known anyone who received an apology from the Intelligence Center."

"They make a bundle off the maps," Alex said.

"And then some. Do they...."

"Just doing my duty, Sergeant," Alex answered his unasked question. No they didn't pay her for the maps. They were considered intellectual property of the United States Army. Or something like that. "Iraq-Iran border?"

"The map of the Iraq-Iran border has been a great success. We've heard from three of the six teams. Their messages are waiting for you on the map phone. You can get them when Homeland returns the line."

Alex nodded.

"Sir, there's some question about quadrant four and sixteen. The overhang near the center of the quadrant four? It's about a foot wider and three feet deeper than marked. Quadrant sixteen has a well marker but there's no water there."

"Let me check," Alex said.

Alex looked at the quadrant in question on her computer then moved to wide table where she worked on her maps. She pulled out the hard copy of the map from black wood cubby tucked into the wall. Unrolling the map against the table, she noted the overhang change, then searched for the well.

"I made a note on the overhang. But I don't have a well on my hard or electronic copy."

"It shows on the GPS copy."

"God I hate GPS."

"It's an inanimate object, sir."

Looking up from the map, Alex caught his wry grin. She laughed when he wagged his eyebrows.

"Can you shoot a message that GPS is always behind? It's usually at least two months behind a map change."

"Yes sir," her Sergeant said.

"Anything else?"

"There's a new order to continue in Afghanistan," he said. "Um, three, no six identified zones that need remapping."

"Oil?"

"Probably," he said.

"All right," she said. "I've been working on refugee maps of Jordon and Syria. Do you have those changes?"

"Yes," he said.

"Thanks Sergeant."

Alex looked at the clock. She had an hour and four minutes before Eleazar phoned.

"Sir?"

"Yes Sergeant?"

"Good luck."

"Thanks."

Alex clicked the connection to standby. Pushing back her leather office chair, she wandered across the hardwood floors to the overstuffed green chair that sat in the corner of her secure office. She flicked a remote and the gas fireplace cast a dancing yellow glow onto the antique map of the world hanging on the opposite wall. Alex closed her eyes, resting for a moment, in the warm, safe room.

Sixty minutes to go.

When Alex traveled, Max, Alex and John lived in the house next door. After Alex was injured, Max and John purchased and remodeled this house with two guest bedrooms, a spa bathroom, an entertainment room, laundry and this secure office in the basement. Alex spent most of her time in the basement either working in the office or recovering from more than forty surgeries in one of the guest bedrooms. She felt safe and protected here.

Until Eleazar called.

She went to bed the seventh of every month knowing that she was hours away from speaking with Eleazar. The morning of the eighth evaporated into intelligence details and her own fear. What would he say this month? Would he tell her again about the powerful Mike begging for mercy? Would he laugh at Jax's futile efforts to save Nathan? Or would he repeat what he said over and over again: she killed her friends.

Alex leaned her head back against the chair. She despised the very timber of his voice, his heavily accented Hebrew or Arabic or Farsi and the distinctive cruel laugh that turned her stomach. He repulsed the very center of her being.

Not for the first time, she wondered what Jesse would say. Jesse, who happened to sit next to her in the mess tent a couple weeks into basic training. Jesse, who stood next to her when they received their Berets. Jesse, who slept next to her night after night in the field, celebrated her wedding and invited her into his family as the godmother to his children.

It was Jesse who forced her to get the tattoo that designated her as the Fey in name and legend. 'Just get your essential nature' he told her before whispering to the tattoo artist in Cairo that she was a fairy. The bright blue winking fairy tattoo under her left bicep was legendary in Special Forces. Jesse encouraged her to get her belly button pierced. Jesse also designed the green Vivaldi scripted"F" armband that designated the Fey Special Forces team. Many of the people they rescued wore, with immense pride, a black Vivaldi scripted"F" on their right arm or wrist.

"Eleazar killed Jesse," Alex said out loud. "He stole Jesse from Maria, from his babies, Jesse Jr. and Gabriella and from me."

Her eyes caught a glimmer of light dancing around her office. She said to the glimmer, "Eleazar killed Jesse. He wants to kill me. I will kill him."

She sighed.

"I'm just crazy."

"We knew that was true, love," John said.

He walked into the office. His curly hair was wet from the snow and his cobalt blue eyes flashed while his eyebrows worked at the insinuation. He bent to kiss her.

"Thank you for coming."

"I won't let you do it alone," he said. "I brought lunch–Chinese–if you'd like to come up."

"I have a quick call to command, then I'll be up."

Lifting her from the chair, he crushed her against him.

"Meet me upstairs," he said. His lips brushed across hers. "I love you Alex."

Her fake blue eyes searched his face. She flushed then nodded.

"Sir," her Sergeant called from the flat screen in the armoire.

"Yes, Sergeant," Alex turned to sit in her office chair. John kissed her neck, then went upstairs.

"The Colonel is on the line for you."

"Thanks," Alex said.

The screen flickered to the bushy hair, bushy eyebrows and round face of Colonel Howard Gordon. He was talking to someone just off screen, then turned.

"Major Drayson," Colonel Gordon said.

Alex saluted and he returned it.

"It's just strange to salute the computer screen. At ease, Alex. I wanted to check in to see how you're holding up. The CIA informs me that they believe they have some good information on Eleazar."

"They've said that before," Alex said. "I'll review the information when I'm done with the call. We're hoping to get another location on him. Our guess is that he's in Jordon."

"Major... Alex... I am going to request again that you don't take this telephone call. In sixteen months, we have learned very little except that you can tolerate psychological torture. You've proven your point. Let it be over."

"Sir, respectfully, we cannot stop him from coming after me. He is coming, sir. This is our opportunity to...."

"God damn it, Alex."

"Sir." She watched the Colonel, known for fighting for his people, fight with himself. There was a voice behind him and he turned.

"I was just informed that my job is to support you in the endeavor."

Alex raised her eyebrows and laughed.

"We'll go over the transcripts tomorrow in my office, Major."

"Yes, sir," Alex said.

The screen flashed dark when Colonel Gordon ended the conversation. Alex turned in her chair to get up when her Sergeant's face appeared on the screen.

"Sir there's a priority message coming in for you from someone named Anderson. It's nonmilitary but he has the code."

"Tom Anderson?"

"Yes sir."

"Can you patch him through?"

"Yes sir."

A moment before he realized the connection was made, Alex saw the flashing dark eyes and rumpled hair of Max's friend Tom.

"You'll just have to fucking shoot me then," he said to someone off screen.

"What's up Tom?"

"Holy fuck Alex. You have to believe me that I didn't have anything to do with this. Oh God Alex never, never would I… Homeland fucking Security has shut down our servers. There's fifty…sixty guys in the building with machine guns. Oh Alex, I'm so sorry. Oh fuck…"

"TOM! What are you…?"

There was movement on the stairs to the basement. Rolling her chair to the doorway, Alex saw Homeland Security Agent Arthur "Raz" Rasmussen and his boss, her mentor and the best intelligence agent in the world, Ben, take the stairs two at a time.

Tom continued his espresso fueled panic.

"Tell me what to do Alex. The geeks are freaking here. Your brother is going to fucking kill me."

"Who is that?" Raz said.

"Tom Anderson," Alex said. "He runs…"

"MySpace."

"Tom, Homeland just got here. I don't have any idea…"

"Alex," Tom leaned into the webcam. "I have been Max's friend for almost fifteen years. I would never endanger you, never. That's what I wanted you to hear. From me to you."

"Of course, Tom. Clearly something is going on. I need to get up to speed, but we're golden."

"We're golden. I will do whatever I have to do to make this right."

The muzzle of a machine gun moved into the screen and Tom swore at the person.

"I'm getting off the God damn…" Tom said and his screen went blank.

Alex's screen split as the image of her Sergeant and Colonel Gordon both joined her video feed.

"God damn it, Alex. Homeland…" Colonel Gordon said into the screen.

"They just arrived, sir."

"Then you know," he said.

"Know what?" Alex asked.

"Eleazar has a photo of you, Max, John and Erin," Ben said in slow even tones.

"WHAT?" Alex twirled around in her chair. She raised her finger to Ben. "Wait." She turned back to her screen.

"Sir, Ben is here to brief me. I..."

"We've got your back Alex," Colonel Gordon said clicking off.

"Major?" her Sergeant asked.

"Sergeant, I need five minutes."

"Yes, sir."

"What?" Alex turned to Ben.

"Your sister's fiancé Marcos Ruiz posted a photo of you to his MySpace page. It says, 'The Fey and family: The Fey, John Drayson, Max Hargreaves and Erin Hargreaves.' There another picture of you as Alyssa. It looks like it's taken from a cell phone. It says, 'The Fey is Alyssa Kreiger and Alexandra Hargreaves.'"

"One of my programs found them less than three minutes after they were posted," Raz said. "There were four hits before we took the servers down."

"Would you excuse me for a moment?" Alex asked.

Raz nodded.

Dragging her left leg behind her, she pulled herself to the bathroom just making it to the toilet before she threw up. Panic rose from the center of her being. Slow flashes of machine gun fire, splashing blood and the sound of ragged breathing dragged her mind beyond memory. She covered her ears with her hands as Eleazar's laughter echoed off the bathroom walls. She threw up again.

Panic turned to terror and she rocked herself. Her eyes focused on the toilet but her vision filled with death. Death everywhere. John... Max... Erin... Everyone she loved died. Everyone dead. Jiminy Cricket took them all to heaven while she lived alone in a blood red hell.

He appeared from nowhere. John dropped to his knees beside her. His strong arms slipped around her. She knew he was talking, saying something while he rocked her back and forth, but she only heard the ragged breathing brought on by panic. She buried her head into John's muscular chest.

Like a speaker being turned on, soft at first, then gradually louder, she heard John's voice.

"Shh, shh... We're in Denver. We're in our own safe home. Nothing's happening. You're safe. Shh."

"I'm in Denver, Colorado sitting in the basement bathroom on the floor," she said She forced her attention to the present. "You are my husband. You are John Drayson."

"You sure?" he chuckled.

They learned this technique when Alex was studying for her Ph.D. in psychology. What once was a joke, now served as the only thing that broke through the wall of sight and sound when her brain seized in flashback. John still laughed every time.

"What are you wearing?"

"I'm Alexandra Hargreaves Drayson. I'm sitting on the floor of the basement bathroom of my home in Denver, Colorado. I'm wearing blue jeans, body armor and a T-shirt."

"Ah love, did you forget panties again?" he laughed. He reached to flush the toilet.

"Yep, no bra either."

"That's odd because I can feel it right here." He flicked her bra strap through the arm holes in her body armor. He slipped his hands into the back of her pants. "Maybe you're flashing on not wearing the bra and panties last night. That's probably why you were moaning."

Alex smiled.

"Come on. The spies want to speak to you and you have a phone call in a few minutes."

She nodded.

"I can't get up," she said.

"Let me," he said.

John stood then lifted her to his arms. With his free hand, he opened the cabinet to retrieve a washcloth. At the sink, he wet the washcloth and she wiped her face and hands. He carried her back to the secure office where Raz was working on the computer and Ben was talking on his cell phone. They looked up when she returned.

"How much did they pay him?" Alex asked.

"Two hundred thousand dollars," Raz said. "How did you know?"

"Matthew said that he reminded him of his father. Mattie's father would sell his soul for a dollar."

"Matthew's father sold his soul for a lot less than a dollar," Ben said closing his cell phone. "We have fourteen minutes."

"Why is the photo a big deal, Ben?" John asked. He smiled at Alex, "Want down?"

She nodded. He nuzzled her neck then set her down.

"A picture is not such a big deal. He probably has a least one of Alex already. It's the combination of the picture and your names. It's only a matter of time before..."

"He's coming for me. That's what it means. And now he knows where and who. It's only a matter of when."

"But not today," John said.

Alex shot a look to him, then laughed.

"No," Ben said. "Not today. Today we need to get through the phone call. Alexandra, we need a strategy."

"What does that mean?" John asked.

"Alex is good at coming up with strategies. She's better than we are," Raz said.

Alex nodded.

"Shall we go upstairs?" Ben asked. "I believe your friend Ben left some espresso here."

"Then drank it all," Alex said. "Did you...?"

"I spoke with your Sergeant," Raz said. He kissed her cheek. "You OK?"

She nodded. "Go on. I'll close up."

While Alex closed the office, the men went upstairs. She heard Max in the entry way when she closed the door to the office. Checking her watch, she had eleven minutes. She took the stairs one at a time, pausing at the landing, then working her way up to the hallway and the main floor of the house. She saw the men talking in the kitchen, then made her way to the living room.

Clearing her head, Alex watched the snow fall in drifts through the living room window. She pressed all emotion out of her body. John floated in front of her eyes to light a fire in the fireplace. A cup of espresso appeared in her hand. Max's head rested on her shoulder some time after he sat almost on top of her on the couch. Her mind was silent. Her body clear. Somewhere in a corner of her mind a plan began to form. Keeping her attention on the blank space in her head, the plan grew.

"Alex, you have one minute," Raz said.

CHAPTER FOUR

She blinked but kept her focus.

"It's time," Raz said. Her cell phone rang. He answered the phone to her Sergeant. "Don't put him through yet."

Turning to Alex, he said again, "Alex, it's time."

She startled, then blinked.

"Tell my Sergeant that I'm not available."

Raz looked surprised, opened his mouth to say something, then nodded.

"Sergeant, please tell the caller that the Fey is no longer available. Yes, then lock it down. Yes, that's correct. The Fey is no longer available. Thank you."

Alex let out a breath.

"What's for lunch?" she asked.

The men, who had been tiptoeing around her silence, began laughing and talking at once. She laughed. John bent to kiss her.

"Who's working today?" she asked looking from face to face. "No one? Let's celebrate. No more phone calls."

"Champagne or whiskey?" John asked.

"Whiskey," Alex replied as if it was obvious.

She passed a bottle of Red Breast Irish Whiskey to Max and followed Raz into the kitchen. While Raz opened the containers of Chinese food, Alex explained her plan. Alex pulled plates from the cabinet and Raz drilled her with questions. She answered, then smiled. He nodded in agreement. They had a strategy. Raz carried the food out to the dining room.

Alex made three phone calls, clearing her schedule for the day, then joined the laughing, talking men in the dining room. As the snow fell, they ate, gossiped and celebrated the end of conversation with Eleazar.

❦❦❦

Nine hours later
February 8 – 9:30 P.M.
Piñon Canyon Maneuver Site, Southeastern Colorado

Sliding backwards in the dirt and snow with her legs in front of her, Alex fired her paintball pistols, one in each hand, at the targets. With her crutch hooked onto her forearm, she rolled under a bush for protection. She raised an eyebrow. Only two targets left.

She was in a simulation designed to train soldiers in warfare. Right at this moment, she was in the middle of a terrorist cell in the mock Afghanistan area of Piñon Canyon in Southeast Colorado. Her assignment was to take out the terrorist cell in the shortest amount of time with the least gunfire. The army estimated that a Green Beret should complete this task in two hours and seventeen minutes. A healthy Green Beret, that is. Alex checked her watch. If she finished in the next thirty-three minutes, she would beat the simulation time.

She had eliminated seventeen targets leaving only the main target and his bodyguard. He was hidden somewhere behind her. She rolled to her stomach and pulled her night vision binoculars from her backpack. Scanning the snow brushed tops of sage and prairie grass, she saw no one. It was even too cold for wild life.

She heard movement and turned to watch two men moving through the brush. They were looking for her but didn't know where she was. Her mind ran through the map of this area of the range.

Of course, Raz gave her a rundown of the simulation including its weak points. What did they expect? She was an intelligence officer after all. But intelligence only gives you an edge. She already looked at the places Raz believed they would stash the main target. She smiled. Every once in a while even Raz was wrong.

Using her forearm crutch, she moved across the landscape. Gunfire echoed through the canyon and she dove into a small ravine. She rolled forward coming to a stop next to a small pocket cave and the chief target's bodyguard. One swift kick knocked the weapon out of the bodyguard's hands. She tossed a paint balloon at the soldier and he mock died. The target was in the cave behind this guard or so they wanted her to think.

That meant that the primary target was right *here*.

Turning, she used her boot heel to dig into the dirt across from the pocket cave. She pulled her Bowie knife from the sheath strapped to her leg. Kicking and slicing into the earth, she reached the airspace of the man-made cave below. She widened the space with both feet then dropped into the cave. With her paintball pistols in front of her, she startled the soldier playing the target.

"You're supposed to come in the entrance," said the sandy haired soldier playing the target.

"Done," Alex said with twenty-four minutes to go.

"Done," the soldier target said. "You can lower your weapons, Major."

"There's another soldier here," she said. "I can smell him."

She grabbed the soldier target around the shoulders. Her paintball pistol pressed against his ribs.

"Show yourself or he dies. You are wearing body armor, aren't you?" she screamed.

"Yes Major," the young soldier said.

Two soldiers carrying paintball machine guns stepped forward. As part of the simulation, they began screaming butchered Arabic slogans. Pushing the target to the ground, she shot the two soldiers with her paint handguns. She rolled forward and shot another soldier hiding in the wings.

"Come on," Alex said.

Grabbing the target, she worked her way out of the cave. They reached the entrance to find what Alex expected: a group of soldiers pretending to be a tribe. With her paintball pistol at the head of the target, they made their way to the center of the tribal gathering.

Alex blinked her eyes.

Jesse?

Jesse Abreu stood on the edge of the gathering. He was pointing to something to her right. When she looked again, he was gone. Turning her head to where he pointed, she saw two men cresting a small hill carrying machine guns.

Live machine guns.

Ah crap.

"M-16." As he had for more than a decade, Jesse called the weapon.

"Live rounds," Alex screamed.

She tackled her target and, with her arms around him, rolled sideways. Machine gun rounds pummeled the dirt around them. Shards of dust and rock flew into the air. The soldier tribe ran toward a ravine to get away from the live rounds. Alex yanked the target back into the cave.

"Zack, get me out of here." Alex whispered into the microphone in her sleeve. "We have live M-16 fire. Two shooters."

The soldier playing the target screamed in pain. Pushing away from him to assess his injuries, she found his leg askew, broken when she tackled him. Alex covered his mouth with her hand and dug through her pack for a morphine auto-injector. She shot the soldier with the pain medication.

"You have to be quiet. Shhh."

His blue eyes wild with pain and fear, the soldier nodded.

Belly crawling to the entrance of the cave, she listened for movement. She saw and heard nothing but prepared for the worst. Pulling her handgun from its sacrum holster, she checked for live rounds. Ten 9 mm bullets. She opened the zippered compartment of her backpack to find another loaded clip. Saying a silent prayer of gratitude, she slipped the clip into the back pocket of her pants.

Hearing a sound behind her, she rolled over to point her handgun at the noise. The 'dead' soldiers came forward to see what was going on. With her hand on her lips for silence, she ordered them to carry the soldier with the broken leg deeper into the cave.

The sound of the nearing helicopter echoed through the dry terrain. Zack.

Rolling back to her belly, she scanned the area with her night vision binoculars.

Where had they gone?

Ah. Fuck. no.

The shooters ran toward the unarmed soldiers.

She unhooked her crutch then jumped from the cave. Dragging her leg, she ran toward the unarmed soldiers. With a solid leap into the air, she fired in quick succession at the shooters. One man screamed and dropped to the ground with a wound in his abdomen.

Upon landing, Alex rolled sideways. The other shooter fired in her direction. Shards of dirt exploded around her. Stopping her roll with her leg, she fired. The other shooter fell backwards with two bullets through his forehead.

Breathing hard, she collapsed back into the dirt.

"What was that?" a soldier near her asked.

"Death," Alex said. "Get the shooter. He still has a weapon."

A group of soldiers surrounded the shooter and took his weapon from him. She heard the sound of punching and kicking.

"Do not kill him. That's an order," Alex yelled.

Just then a Black Hawk Helicopter landed in the clearing. Trece and the White Boy jumped from the chopper screaming Alex's name.

"I'm here," she said. She pushed to sit up and wave. The soldiers around her stood to wave.

"Get the fuck down. On your faces." Trece fired above their heads. The soldiers dropped on their bellies.

"Alex," Matthew said. He reached the top of the hill followed by Troy.

"I'm all right," she said. "I just can't get up."

Laughing, Troy pulled her to standing, then held her tightly to him. He released her and Matthew hugged her.

"Where's your crutch?" Matthew asked.

"In the cave," she replied.

"Gentleman, the Fey would like her crutch," Matthew said to the soldiers.

The soldiers jumped into action to look for her crutch.

"Would you like a lift?" Matthew asked.

Alex shook her head. There was no way she was going to let these soldiers see that she couldn't get around.

"I need to speak to command," Alex said.

"Zack's on the radio. They're coming out. They requested that you stay here with the…"

"Bodies," she said. She nodded. "We need medics."

"On their way," Matthew said.

"We have coffee in the chopper," Troy said. "Congratulations."

"For what?"

"You beat another sim."

"And almost got killed. I need to speak with Colonel Gordon. We're due in Denver in a couple hours."

"Yes, we're very busy today," Troy laughed.

A soldier handed Alex her crutch and she made her way across the clearing. Matthew jumped into the helicopter then pulled Alex in behind him. Once in the chopper, she collapsed in pain.

"Where's your morphine?" Matthew asked.

"I gave it to a soldier in the cave," she said. "I broke his leg."

"Is there another on the chopper?"

"I don't think so." Alex shook her head. "I just need a minute, then we'll go back out like rock stars."

"Hey Fey," Trece yelled into the chopper. "These guys want to know if you're really the Fey or just the pretend Fey. I told them but you know how boys can be."

Alex laughed.

"Come on, honey, it'll take the edge off. These kids haven't been shot at before. They're freaked."

"It's time for the Fey to return," Matthew said.

Alex pulled off her long sleeved shirt to reveal a white tank, cream colored dragon body armor and the famous tattoos. Matthew dropped a blanket over her shoulders. Coming from the cockpit, Zack helped Alex to sit in the doorway of the chopper then poured cups of piping hot coffee and cream.

"That's them, isn't it?" a soldier said to Troy when he jumped from the helicopter.

"Who?" Troy asked.

"The Fey and the Jakker," another soldier said. He nodded his head toward the helicopter.

"I think it is," Troy said. Trece and the White Boy laughed their way to the cave.

"How does it feel to be the Fey again?" Zack asked in a low tone.

"Weird. Zack, someone tried to kill me tonight. If it hadn't been for Jesse, I..."

"Jesse's dead, Alex. You know that," Zack said.

Alex nodded. Everyone seemed to think that she forgot the single worst reality in her life. Alex flipped the blanket so that the fairy tattoo was visible.

"Thanks for coming to get me," she said.

"The Jakker flies the Fey," he said. "Looks like we're in business again."

Alex had no idea what that meant.

CHAPTER FIVE
Two hours later
February 9 – 12:05 A.M.
Lower Downtown Denver, Colorado

"This has not been my favorite day," Alex said.

They were standing in the hallway of Erin's loft. She looked down the grim line of men finishing with Trece and the White Boy. Inside the loft, they could hear Marcos screaming. They were waiting for Colin.

Homeland Security kept Marcos under surveillance all day. According to heat imaging, he and Erin had been arguing most of the evening. Homeland Security suggested that they wait until things cooled down a little bit. No one wanted to see Senator Hargreaves's youngest daughter on the cover of the Denver Post. The plan was to pick up Marcos in the quiet of two in the morning. Alex and Raz would attend but not participate.

But the couple continued to argue.

Alex was diagramming the shooting for Fort Carson Military Police when Raz called with the news. Marcos Ruiz was beating her sister. They flew as a team to the loft, landing on the roof of a nearby building. Max and John were waiting in the hallway when they arrived.

Marcos changed the locks when he moved into Erin's loft. Somehow, Erin managed to slip Colin a key. Colin, his blonde hair standing straight up and face marked by fury, ran down the hall. Two Homeland Security teams waited in the wings to take over when Erin was safe.

"Ready?" she asked.

The men nodded. They were tasked with subduing Marcos and retrieving Erin.

"Come up," John said.

She jumped into his arms. He held her with his arms around her hips. She wrapped her legs around his waist, hooking her feet together to hold her in place. Slipping her arms around his neck, she kissed him. Colin flipped open the door.

Alex and John crashed into the apartment. John set Alex down against a wall and lifted her arms above her head. He moved to pull her tank top off and she moaned. She caught his lips with her mouth. They consumed each other with palpable heat.

"What the hell is this?" Marcos yelled.

Ignoring him, they continued kissing. John popped open her pants.

Marcos stomped toward them. He pushed John off Alex. John's eyes stayed focused on Alex. With deliberate hesitation, he turned to Marcos.

"How embarrassing," John said his accent thick. "We were drinking in bar downstairs when Alex remembered that Erin moved in with you. You know how it is sometimes..."

"You fucking whore. I knew you were with this guy too. Get the fuck out of my house."

Marcos put his hand on Alex's shoulder to push her out the door. She threw him over her shoulder. He landed in a thud on his back. Alex moved into the apartment. Hearing Marcos move to his feet, she turned to punch him. But John had already done the honor. Marcos was on his knees rubbing his jaw.

"Erin?"

"I'm in here," Erin called from the bedroom area.

Alex let out a low whistle. Colin and Max moved to stand next to John.

"Your work?" Colin laughed at John.

Threading her way through broken furniture and glass, Alex heard Max tell Marcos that he needed to stay where he was. There was scuffling in the hall but Alex was too taken aback by Erin's appearrance to care what was happening somewhere else.

Erin sat on the bed in her panties. Her torso, arms and legs were covered with new and aging bruises. Alex gasped when Erin turned to look at her. Her nose was broken, her eyes blackened, her lips were swollen and at least one tooth was broken. Her beautiful green eyes pled with Alex for understanding. Erin tried to stand. Dropping back to the bed, she returned to staring in front of her.

"Get dressed," Alex said.

"I ... He'll..." Erin said.

"I'll find you some clothes. Get dressed," Alex said.

Alex kept her voice and manner stern. Any empathy would cause Erin to break down. She had to get Erin out of this loft. Alex found sweat pants in a pile of broken furniture and clothing on the floor. She helped Erin put them on, then found a T-shirt.

"Can you stand?"

"He'll kill me," Erin said.

"Not today," Alex said. She whistled twice. Then held Erin upright.

"What the fuck is he doing here?" Marcos yelled from the entryway.

Matthew scooped Erin into an embrace that lifted her off the ground. Pulling back, he searched her eyes.

"Oh God Erin," he whispered. Erin's thin control over her emotions dissolved and she wept into his shoulder. Alex put her hand on Erin's back. "Come on."

Erin pulled back from Matthew for a moment, then nodded. Matthew lifted her into his arms. As they turned the corner, Marcos screamed and lunged for them. Colin blocked Marcos's movement and Max let loose a swift punch to his throat. Wheezing, Marcos dropped to his knees. Matthew stepped over Marcos and carried Erin out of the apartment.

"Hi scumbag," Troy said walking into the apartment. "I'm Troy. This is Trece and this is the White Boy. We're here to subdue you."

The White Boy closed the door.

♂♂♂

Six hours later
February 9 – 6:34 A.M.
St. Joseph's Hospital, Denver, Colorado

Alex sat in a chair near the wall of the Intensive Care Unit.

Matthew carried Erin to the car before he realized she was in serious trouble. Somehow, he made it to the emergency room before her spleen ruptured. The doctors hoped that a series of medications would reduce her swelling but, according to John, Erin needed surgery today.

Erin had been in this emergency room before. Her file was thick with two years of broken bones, bumps and bruises. The social worker confided in Alex that she begged Erin to get help but Erin was terrified of Marcos. So terrified that Marcos was listed as her medical power of attorney.

Since Marcos was currently detained elsewhere, they were waiting for Erin to awaken to make decisions.

Erin's nose and cheekbone were broken. Her jaw was cracked. Her liver had lacerations. Her spleen was… Alex couldn't keep the list in her head without wishing she had put a bullet into Marcos's brain.

Nodding to herself, she was a little relieved that the Military Police had taken her handgun. They would keep her gun until they finished their inquiry into last night's shooting. If Colonel Howard hadn't intervened, she would still be at Fort Carson.

Marcos would have killed her sister.

Less than ten minutes into their interaction with Marcos, Matthew called from the emergency room begging Alex to come. She had to turn Marcos over to Homeland Security before any real justice was served. But Marcos was on his way to Guantanamo Bay where Fey friendly US Army soldiers guarded the nasties. Alex smiled at the thought.

With a gasp and a scream, Erin rose from the bed. Alex jumped from her seat and Matthew held Erin in his arms. The nurse came to check Erin's vitals. Matthew, kneeling down so his face was inches from hers, held Erin's eyes while the nurse worked. They whispered back and forth. Alex sat down on the other side of the bed when the nurse finished.

"Hi," Alex said.

"Oh Alex. I'm so sorry. I had no idea that he..."

"Shh," Alex said. "It doesn't matter. What matters is that you're safe. John will be here in a minute to talk to you about your options."

"Before... I mean..." Erin pressed her hand against her heart. She looked at Matthew then Alex. "I have to know..."

"Erin, we can talk about this when you're feeling better," Matthew said.

"I have to know."

"Know what?" Alex asked. She looked at Matthew who was shaking his head. "Erin, what do you need to know?"

"I need to know about you and Matt."

"What about me and Matt?" Alex asked.

"She thinks we're lovers because I was with you when you were injured. It's why we broke up... what we argued about at lunch."

"You broke up because Matthew stayed with me when I was unconscious?" Alex shook her head at the idea.

"He comes from God knows where, filthy, AWOL, to sleep in your bed then tells me that you aren't lovers. I... It's crazy but I have to know. I just need the truth. I need something to count on... something real."

Erin wept into her hands. When Matthew tried to comfort her, she shook him off.

Alex closed her eyes and sighed. Opening her eyes, she caught Matthew's eyes. He nodded slightly.

"OK, OK, Erin, it's okay," Alex said.

"You won't tell me." Erin's emotions rose into hysteria. "Even now, you won't tell me."

"I don't tell you because knowing will hurt you," Alex said.

"Because you are lovers... That's it. Isn't it? No matter how much I love Matt, no matter how much John loves you, Alex, you and Matt come first."

"Erin," Alex said. "We will tell you but you must calm down. Your body is broken and you're making it worse."

Alex looked up when John walked into the area.

"Erin wants to know about Matt and me," Alex said.

"Erin, you don't want to know," John said.

"So it's all right with you that they are lovers?"

"It looks like that but..."

"It's all right, John," Matthew said. He pulled his jacket off. "Erin, I'd do anything for you and anything to protect you. I'd even lose you to protect you. If you must know, and knowing will help you..."

"I'll start," Alex said. "Erin, you met Mattie just before he left for Afghanistan."

"Show her the marks," John said. Alex looked at him then nodded.

"You know that no one wanted me to be a Green Beret. I had to be better than everyone else."

"Alex was the best student in the history of Special Forces," Matthew said. "A lot better than me."

"Anyway, the last part of training is called S.E.R.E. The training is designed to teach you about torture."

"They torture the soldiers so that they will know how to handle it. Sometimes, they push well past the breaking point," John said. He pulled up Alex's sleeve to show the scars on her wrists. "She has these marks on her wrists and ankles."

"I was in the hospital for a week after we were done," Alex said. "It was their last chance to deny my Special Forces tab. They were brutal. But I was ready. You remember Dad and I practiced when I was in high school. But Matthew and Jesse... They went after them because they were my friends. I had to watch."

John lifted Alex's shirt to show a series of deep scars on her back. "Matt," he said.

Matthew pulled the back of his shirt up around his neck showing the same scarring.

"We were friends," Matthew said wagging his head. "You know buddies, sparring partners, whatever, until they locked us in that cold room. Your sister saved me... and then..."

"Show her," Alex said.

Matthew pointed to a black Vivaldi "F" then another in the armband tattoo on his right arm.

"He's branded with your mark!"

"It means..." John started. Alex put a hand on his arm to stop him from finishing.

"I'll do it," Alex said. "Matthew has been held hostage twice. I extracted him about six years ago and then again a couple months..."

"Seven," Matthew said.

"Seven months before I was shot."

"What are you saying?" Erin's hands flew to her face in horror. "You were a hostage?"

"The last time was bad, Erin, really bad. Mattie wasn't..."

"Sane. I lost it."

"The CIA put everyone in this super secret hospital in Costa Rica. Jesse and I went with the guys. There were six of them."

"I couldn't sleep," Matthew said. He pulled his shirt down and looked at the wall. "Fuck."

"Jesse stayed with him during the day and I stayed with him at night. At first I sat in a chair but in the dark, his mind... went. I started sleeping with him in his bed. Just having me there was enough that he could sleep... recover. We slept next to each other most of training. It wasn't much different."

"Erin, your sister saved my life three times, then saved my mind. When I found out she was injured, I had to be there, right there, with her. You have to believe that I've never been Alex's lover. Even before they were married, before I knew you, we weren't lovers. But you're right. We are a lot closer than friends."

"Does that help?" Alex asked.

"I don't know what's real... Everything is upside down. I..."

"How can we help?"

"Marcos told me that..." Erin wept into her hands. "I... Oh God..."

Matthew lifted her from the bed to his lap and into his arms, "Shhh... Shhh... This is what it was like for me. Just what you're going through." He rocked her gently. Petite Erin sobbed into his chest.

"I'm sorry Erin but we have to make some decisions," Alex said. "Matthew has to get back to base. He wanted to be here to help you decide."

Erin nodded. Sticking her bruised chin out, she shifted her shoulders back to bravely deal with the issues at hand. Her eyes casually shifted to Matthew and she softened. He winked at her and they entwined hands.

"What should I do, John?" Erin asked.

"We need to operate on your spleen and check your liver. We've arranged for a plastic surgeon to fix your nose, cheekbone and jaw this afternoon. Then we'd like to move you to our home since we're set up for injured people. We can take you to your appointments and make sure you're cared for. We think you'll recover there faster than in the hospital or alone. Plus, it's easier for Matthew to get away to see the Major than to come see you."

"What major?" Erin asked.

"I'm a Major," Alex said. "What about Mom? Would you like.. uh... Colin to call her?"

Erin smiled at Alex's joke. "When I'm settled. You're sure about me..."

"Of course," Alex said. "It will be fun to have you around."

"Will you stay with me in the operations, John?" Erin asked. "I know you have to work but... I'd feel a lot better if you were there."

"Of course," John said. "It's already arranged. If you're ready, we can start straight away."

"Can I..." Erin looked at Matthew.

Alex bent to kiss her cheek.

"We'll see you when you wake up," she said. "Come on doc."

Holding hands, she and John walked out into the hall. John wrapped her in his arms.

"You're filthy," he said.

"Rolling around in the dirt," she said. She kissed him. "I killed someone last night in the simulation. Oh God. John..."

"You need to get some surgery yourself," he said.

"But not today," she said. "Today, I want to cry my eyes out."

"Good plan. She'll be out for the rest of the day. Just come back around five."

"I have to take Mattie back to the Fort and the MPs want to see me. I don't know how long that will take."

"After you see Jesse," John said.

Alex held John's eyes for a moment, then looked down.

"It's all right, love. Hey," he pushed her chin up so he could look in her eyes. "I miss him too."

"Wanna make out?" she asked raising an eyebrow.

"I want more than that." He pressed her against him so that she could feel his rising interest.

She laughed.

"Here they come," John said. He nodded his head in the direction of the anesthesiologist.

With a quick kiss, he went to make the introductions. Alex waiting in the hall until Matthew came from the ICU. Holding hands, they walked to her Jeep.

CHAPTER SIX

Nine hours later
February 9 – 3:25 P.M.
Fort Logan National Cemetery, Colorado

Alex's Jeep crept past a large funeral party. Standing in the cold February morning, a family said their final good-bye to a son or daughter. She had been to so many of these funerals that she could almost hear the minister's words in her head: "ashes to ashes," "gone to a better place," "it's the very best of us that die young."

Words.

Nothing eased the pain or the loss. As she watched, a pregnant woman collapsed onto the casket only to be pulled off by a brother or friend. The honor guard raised their rifles and twenty-one shots echoed through Fort Logan National Cemetery. Another soldier was finally home.

Alex drove to a small cul-de-sac where she parked the Jeep. Using two crutches against the uneven ground, she worked her way over to a memorial twenty feet away.

Eleven black granite stones placed in an arch and a black granite obelisk created a monument to the soldiers that died October eighth on a hilltop in Afghanistan. She closed her eyes. Somewhere inside, she remembered what happened. Her only true memory was of the ragged breath and the devastating knowledge that the breathing would end.

Eleazar gave her graphic details about what happened, who was killed first, how they screamed and begged for their lives. The Army told her that they died within minutes of each other and that no one suffered. Ben just shook his head, lit a cigarette, and said that she would remember when she was ready.

Looking at the memorial, she read the polite, sanitized version scratched into the granite obelisk. Alex covered the words with her mittened hand.

Would she ever know the truth?

Taking a package of incense from her pocket, she placed a stick at each stone. She stopped, as she always did, at the last marker. Under the twelve pedaled sunflower, which graced every grave, the stone read: "Alexander Hargreaves, Beloved Brother and Son." They placed this stone, over the grave that should be her own, in the hope that the people who wished her dead would believe they had succeeded.

It was smart espionage.

But Eleazar knew she survived the assault. And, now, he knew where she lived. Alex bent to touch Alexander's stone. What he didn't know, and couldn't conceive, was how many times she longed to be in this grave. They asked to be buried together, spend eternity together, and she belonged with them. No amount of antidepressant pills or counseling changed that reality.

Starting at one end, she clicked her Zippo lighter. Charlie O'Brien, their Commanding Officer, purchased these Zippos to commemorate the medals they won for rescuing five journalists from Central Mexico.

Their first assignment as a team.

Alex looked at the lighter. In the jumble of death and destruction, somehow she wound up with Jesse's lighter in her pocket. Her lighter was lost somewhere in Afghanistan. Maria insisted that Alex keep Jesse's lighter. She flicked the lighter again and went down the row lighting the incense.

She promised herself that she would be strong today. She would light the incense, say a few words of thanks for Jesse's help then go home.

But the tears came. Standing back to evaluate her work, she watched the fragrant smoke blow on the wind. Then, as if yanked by a rope through her abdomen, she fell forward onto Jesse's grave and wept.

Racked with sobs, she lay against the granite markings in a heap. Her heart opened and her grief poured out onto the stone.

"Maxie, I have a friend," she glowed to Max in their weekly phone call.

"A friend?" Max asked. "You've never had a friend before."

"I know. His name is Jesse. I told you about him before. I met him in basic and now we're assigned to the same unit in Bosnia. Oh Maxie you would like him so much."

"He wants to get in your pants."

"Max! He's married to his soulmate Maria," she said. "You're just jealous 'cuz I have a friend."

"I have a friend," Max said. "I'm friends with my roommate, John Drayson."

"Now we both have friends," Alex said.

"You're still my best friend."

"You're better than my best friend. You're my twin."

"I'm still your friend."

Alex heard Jesse's voice speaking Spanish. Gasping, she wiped her face with her mittens and looked around the monument. She saw no one. She blinked, then rested her head against the granite. Her fingers traced the familiar sunflower carved into the granite. She lay staring straight ahead until she heard the cars moving from the funeral. Gathering her strength, she moved to get up.

"Pumpkin, let me help." A male voice came from behind her.

Alex turned her head to see her father move across the grass to her. He lifted her from the ground then helped her with her crutches.

"What are you doing here?"

"I try to make it to the funerals for the soldiers from Colorado," he said. "More than fifty so far. It's the least I can do."

He put his right arm around her as they faced the memorial. He was tall enough to play college basketball and trim from a lifetime in the US Army. When Patrick Hargreaves stood with his favorite child in front of the grave that should be her own, he was all father.

"We aren't supposed to be seen together," Alex said.

"I asked the press for some time alone at my son's grave," he said. "I came over after they left. How are you feeling?"

"I'm all right," she said. "I over did it last night."

He laughed. "Most father's worry about their thirty-year-old daughters over doing it on a Friday night."

"Simulation," she said.

"I heard. I also heard about Erin. How is she?"

"They removed her spleen and a part of her liver," Alex said. "She should be out of surgery in a couple hours. Ben?"

"He called."

"Does Mom know?"

"No. I thought that Erin would tell her when she wanted her to know. Was it . . ."

"Awful. I should have killed him."

"One death a night is probably a good number for a cartographer."

"There's no flies on you," Alex said.

"Two men, M-16s with two loaded clips, live ammo. They hiked ten rugged miles into the range through the adjacent National grasslands. No one saw them in the dark. Alexandra, someone wants you dead."

"You think?"

Despite himself, he laughed. She laughed in response.

"I received three phone calls and two email informing me that the Fey has returned," he said.

"It's not like you to believe the press," she said.

He laughed.

"It's more like make way for the gimp," she added.

"It's difficult to survive. Have you considered joining another team?"

"I like being a cartographer. It's interesting and creative. I'm good at it. I get to come home every night."

Patrick looked at Alex's blonde head and wondered if she believed what she said.

"Yes, the risk of living again," he said.

She looked up at him. When their eyes caught, she looked away. How did he always know the truth?

"I come here every time I'm at Fort Logan. I stand right here and watch Alexander's stone." He paused for a moment. His baby blue eyes searched her face. "I know that a part of you is buried here."

She nodded.

"Sir," a male voice said from the road. "We are running short on time."

"Thank you Justin," Patrick said to his intern. "I need a few more minutes."

"Intern?" Alex asked.

Patrick nodded.

"He looks like he's twelve years old."

"I think he is twelve years old," Patrick laughed.

"Did you ever think that you saw or heard any of your friends, you know, after they died?"

"Never," he said. "Why?"

"Oh nothing," she said

"When's your next surgery?"

"It's scheduled for this week but I want to make sure Erin's all right first. I mean who would have thought that Erin would be in a relationship like that? Erin? I've been so focused on my own crap that I haven't even considered her or really anyone in a long time."

"You are the very heart of everyone who knows you, Alex. You'll sort it out."

Patrick leaned to kiss her cheek then walked across the grass without saying another word. Alex turned back to the monument while his limousine passed behind her. With a sigh, she made her way across the uneven grass.

CHAPTER SEVEN
Four weeks later
March 8 – 6:35 A.M.
Denver, Colorado

Three weeks after a full hip replacement, Alex was running on a treadmill between Max and Erin. They made a pact to workout every morning at six-thirty. So far, despite injuries, they had been successful.

And they had fun. Erin was treated to an inside view of the delightful insanity of the twins. In their funny, friendly company, she began growing into herself again. Right now, she was making faces at Alex while Alex told her about peeing from a helicopter. Max laughed so hard that he had to turn his treadmill off.

"Hey you have a text," Max said pointing to Alex's fanny pack.

"You're the only one who texts me, Text Boy."

Max snatched her fanny pack from the floor then pulled out the phone.

"Ten bucks it's an ad," Alex said.

Max opened the phone then puzzled at the message.

"Well?" Alex asked. She turned off her treadmill to see what was going on.

"It says, 'You have six hours before they die.'"

"It does not say that."

Alex grabbed the phone from him. Staring at the phone, Alex's heart sank inside her chest. As if responding to her stare, her phone rang. Walking away from her siblings, she answered the phone to her Sergeant.

"Fey," she said. "Hey I just…"

"You have to wait," her Sergeant said. "Okay, go ahead."

"I just received a text message that says…"

"You have six hours before they die. That's 1230 hours our time."

"Right," Alex said.

"At approximately 1230 hours, Afghanistan, three soldiers disappeared."

"That's…"

"Four hours ago. We were notified about a potential map issue because the soldiers walked into a GPS dead zone. Then…"

"What is today's date?"

"It's March eighth."

"I'll call you back."

Alex jogged to the bathroom. She just made the handicap toilet before throwing up. Wiping her mouth with the back of her hand, she focused on tile in an effort to stay present. Four blue tiles. Six green tiles. She threw up again. The walls are made of white tile with blue and green tiles in a diagonal line.

"Alex?" Erin asked.

"I'm here," she said.

Erin rattled the door to the handicap stall where Alex was standing. Alex flipped open the lock. Erin looked at Alex's white face and the toilet. Reaching past Alex, she flushed the toilet.

"I didn't know you still did this," Erin said. "I thought that being a Green Beret…"

"Some habits die hard," Alex said. "I usually don't eat when I'm working. It's why I get so thin."

"What happened?" Erin asked.

Matthew and Troy are in Afghanistan. Ah fuck. Alex raised her finger to Erin. She dialed her Sergeant.

"Who is lost? Who is it?"

"You have to go through voice security."

"Fuck security. Sergeant who is it?"

"Sergeant First Class Fred Rhine, Sergeant First Class Stuart Quinn, Sergeant First Class Kenneth Boransky."

"Thank God."

Alex snapped her phone closed. Pressing her phone against her forehead, she squeezed her eyes against the panic and despair.

"Alex, what happened?" Erin asked.

"Some soldiers are missing in Afghanistan," she said.

"So what?"

"I have six hours to find them," Alex said.

"Or what?"

"Or they die."

"Matt's in Afghanistan," Erin said.

Alex nodded. "Matthew and Troy. That's what I just checked. It's not them. I won't know if they are safe until I get home."

Erin hugged Alex.

"If anyone can fix this, you can. I believe in you, Alex."

"Thanks," she said. "Come on."

Max waited for them outside the bathroom. He took one look at Alex and they ran through the gym to his Jeep Cherokee. On the short ride, the tension in the car was palpable.

"I'm sorry, but I need to do this alone." Alex jumped out of the car. She ran to the side door and down the stairs to the basement.

"Alexandra Hargreaves Drayson," she said into the voice imprint.

A scanning pad opened in the wall and she scanned her left hand. A key pad opened and she entered a series of numbers.

"Code," a mechanical voice said.

Alex whistled the first verse of "When you wish upon a star" and the door to her secure office clicked open. Flicking on the lights, she opened another key pad to the armoire and punched in another series of numbers, then scanned her right thumb. The armoire clicked open. With a flip, she turned on her computers and signaled command.

"Fey," Alex said, then waited.

"There you are," her Sergeant said.

"I turned the phone off until I got to the office," she said. "Sorry I hung up on you."

"Sergeant Mac Clenaghan and Sergeant Olivas are in the air to the dead zone."

"God damn it," Alex said. "Who authorized that? They're supposed to be working on a map and under my command."

Her Sergeant shook his head.

"Find out."

"Sir, we don't..."

"This is Eleazar. He said he would come for my friends first. Who's flying them?"

"Sergeant..."

"Jakkman" they said together.

Alex let out a string of curses.

"Sir," her Sergeant started.

"I don't want to know."

"Sergeant Ramirez and Blanco are with them."

"Of course they are." She blew out a breath. "Can you set up a direct link?"

"Yes Major," he said. "Let me work on that. You have a message from Agent Rasmussen."

Alex nodded.

"Sir, we have five hours and forty-two minutes. Can you find them?"

"I know where they are," she said. "Map 75-1090, quadrant fourteen, fifteen or part of thirteen."

"That's one of the maps we're supposed to work on."

"Those quadrants are GPS black out zones. There's an old Russian military compound smack dab in the middle of those quadrants. They've tried sending drones, but they crash on the site. That's why Matthew and Troy were supposed to look into sending a team there."

"Well, they're on their way."

"Don't remind me. Can you collect the Dragon Lady imaging?"

"I have it already," he said. "There isn't much but I'll send it to your computer."

"Thanks. Let me know when I'm connected to Matthew."

"Yes, sir."

Alex dropped her head in her hands.

"He thinks that killing them will destroy you," Ben said walking into her office.

She turned to look at him.

"He is correct in that assumption," she said. "Do you live here now?"

Ben laughed. "I'm your father's best friend. I took his key."

"It's pretty good service for Homeland Security," she said.

"We arrived last night. I expected that he would do something to get your attention. I want to pay attention to what he wants you to ignore."

"Like what?"

Ben shrugged.

"Raz?"

"Making breakfast for your sister and brother. John's upstairs showering."

"He said…"

"I know. We don't believe he's in the country. You were right. It will take him months to make his move here. I think we still have time. It's a little different in Afghanistan."

"How…"

"Who knows? He may have had this plan lined up all along. Our intel, which you know is crap, says that he's holed up in Jerusalem."

"New baby," Alex said.

"New bouncing terrorist baby boy," Ben said attempting a joke. "I'm going to smoke. You may as well come up."

"I'm going to check the maps."

"Who would have thought that you would be a cartographer?" Laughing, he walked up the stairs.

Alex set to work. As the clock counted down to 12:30 p.m. Mountain Time, Alex memorized the contours of the map, reviewed the surveillance data, then read through the reports. Closing her eyes, she remembered the area where almost twelve years ago, she and her team dropped Matthew for a two year assignment with an Afghani warlord.

Charlie agreed to drop Matthew because the village was only slightly out of their way. Or so he thought. They were ten hours into an uphill hike when they realized they were lost. Their ancient Russian map was wrong. They were too far away for a pick up and turning around would put them behind their extraction timetable.

When the team settled for the night, Alex, Jesse and Matthew hiked to a nearby ridge. Lying on her back between Jesse and Matthew, Alex watched the stars and her watch. When the sun rose that morning, she checked her measurements and went to work on the map. By the time the team was ready to travel, she completed the changes. As a joke, Alex stamped the map with a tiny fairy rubber stamp that Erin had given her that Thanksgiving.

The Fey was born.

Everyone knew that story. Alex blinked at the surveillance data. What they didn't know is that the Russian map was intentionally wrong to cover a sprawling compound cut into the mountain of Afghanistan. The deserted compound, hidden from the world by the mountains, was not only a GPS dead zone but a complete electromagnetic nightmare. Compasses went haywire. Radio transmissions failed. Instrumentation went out. The team crept through the compound on full alert then swore they would never go back. Clearly Eleazar had better intelligence than the Special Forces grapevine.

"Sir?"

"I'm here," Alex said.

"I have the link to Sergeant Mac Clenaghan and a radio link to the cockpit," her Sergeant said. "The Jakker says... well, you should talk to him. I've tracked the order. It looks as if it was generated from our office. I've checked with everyone and..."

"No one sent the order."

"Right," he said. "Colonel Gordon is furious. He wants them back in Kabul. Be glad you aren't on site today."

Alex smiled.

"The lost soldiers' CO requested a communication regarding the whereabouts and..." Her Sergeant wrinkled his nose. "He wants to talk to the Fey."

"Fine."

"Who would you like first?"

"I'd like to speak with Matthew."

"Here you go."

"Hey Alex, whatcha doing?" Matthew asked. He was laughing at something Trece said behind him. "What's the story with rounding up all your friends then going incommunicado?"

"What do you mean?"

"I've been trying to call you since we got orders. I think I left about forty messages, well four, on your cell phone."

Alex held her cell phone up to the webcam.

"What?"

"I never got them Mattie," Alex said. "I didn't send these orders. It's Eleazar."

"What? Zack too? He had orders. We thought it was weird but we couldn't get a hold of you. What about the soldiers?"

"Eleazar snatched three soldiers. We don't think they're hostages. We actually think they're lost in that Russian compound."

"The one we found when you were dropped me off?" Matthew asked.

Alex nodded.

"Don't fuck with me, Alex."

"I'm not. Ben's upstairs. Eleazar told me that he would come for my friends first and that I would watch them die."

"Trece said it was the eighth. I didn't put it together. Fuck. What do you want us to do?"

"Colonel Gordon has requested that you return to Kabul."

"And leave the soldiers there? No way."

"Matthew, he will kill you."

"Fuck him. God damn it."

Matthew turned from the laptop computers. Alex heard him tell the others the news. She heard moaning. Matthew turned back to the computer.

"You have a mutiny. We're not going back to Kabul."

"Matthew! God damn it."

"Before you go all 'you do this because I'm female,' we're doing this because that mother fucker killed our friends and got away with it. We're not going to let him take three more soldiers."

"I would like a vote. I'm not going to send anyone to their death without letting them choose."

"Fine," Matthew said. Turning the laptop, he said, "She wants to hear from each of you."

"Hey Alex," Troy said. "This kind of crazy shit is my specialty."

"I've been lost in Afghanistan," Trece said.

"And I was with him," the White Boy added. "We were saved by one of your maps."

"It sucked. We want to get the soldiers. We also know that you're smarter than some terrorist prick. Do your intelligence thing and figure it out."

"I wasn't smart enough a year and five months ago."

"You're smarter now," Trece said. "Get to work and save our asses. That's what you intelligence pricks do. We'll take care of the boys on the ground."

Matthew's smug face came back on the screen.

"Get to work Alex," Matthew said. "Do your job."

"You need to tell Zack," Alex said.

"I will. This is a direct connection?"

Alex nodded.

"You'll be in touch then." Matthew clicked off.

Fuck. Alex rubbed her forehead.

"Sir?"

"Sergeant, I need about fifteen minutes. Then I'd like to speak with the CO."

"They aren't returning to Kabul."

"No," Alex said.

The Sergeant nodded. "I'd do the same thing. Your friends are very brave."

"Or stupid."

CHAPTER EIGHT

"Brave. That's why they're your friends."

Her whirling mind came to a halt at his comment.

"What?"

"You are incredibly brave, sir. Most people would hide in a hole after what you've been through. It's an honor to know you."

"Thanks, I think. Fifteen minutes."

"Yes, sir."

Alex jogged up the stairs to find Ben and Raz working on laptop computers at the dining room table. Her family had already left for work. Pouring herself a cup of coffee, she took a seat. The men listened to the entire situation, from the Russian compound to Eleazar's threats, without interruption. When she was done, Ben spoke. Raz followed with his thoughts and she listened. Raz and Ben agreed to work their contacts to find answers to her questions. Alex jogged down the stairs with a better, broader perspective.

Still Alex felt as though she was missing something. Something big.

The conversation with the Commanding Officer went as expected. The soldiers dropped off the map after following what they thought was a high level Al Qaeda target. The CO was in contact with the soldiers until 1230 hours then communication ended. He didn't report the outage right away because he was sure they would turn up. After an hour, his intelligence officer insisted on calling Military Intelligence.

Of course, he was delighted to get a chance to work with the infamous Fey. If he had known he would get to work with the Fey, he would have called immediately. Alex tried for professional but she laughed when she clicked off the connection.

Looking at her watch, her heart clenched with anxiety. Two hours to go. Christ.

She had no idea what to do next. She had no idea where to even start. Without direction, she could not even start creating a strategy. Maybe if she let her mind wander, some brilliance might rise to the surface.

Closing her office door, she sat down in the overstuffed green chair. Her finger caressed the green fabric of the chair. John bought this green chair for their bedroom in their apartment in Santa Monica. Alex smiled at the happy memories.

It was a two bedroom apartment with a small yard and gleaming hardwood floors. Max, John and Alex moved in at Thanksgiving, the weekend Matthew and Erin met.

God, her mother had been angry that she was moving in with her twin. 'You'll never find a husband now,' she insisted. Alex sighed. She could have told her mother that she and John were married six weeks earlier. Even all these years later, Alex shuddered to think of her mother's hysterical, 'it doesn't look right.'

The apartment was perfect. And so was John.

She smiled remembering John. He'd sit in this chair surrounded by books. His blue eyes vague while his mind worked to memorize another scientific fact. His hair askew. He usually had a pencil stuck behind his ear or in his mouth. He would look up just before she landed in his arms.

From the moment she laid eyes on that man, his gravitational pull was more than she could withstand. She had to be near him, in his arms and touching his skin. She would throw money at the cab driver then fly past the bubbling fountain and blooming roses through the apartment to his arms. Every single time....

Except the time she broke her thumb.

Holy crap.

Alex sat up in the chair. She forgot about breaking her thumb.

She never thought to tell John that her thumb was broken or the subsequent surgery to fix the break. Standing at the apartment door, she realized he would be furious. Her ears resonated with his imagined: 'and you never thought to tell me?!" She dropped her duffle at the door and ran away. John found her sitting on the swings of a nearby playground. Their first Christmas together…

She broke her thumb when they were dropping Matthew off in Afghanistan. They found the Russian compound that trip.

She lay between Jesse and Matthew focused on the world of stars and the calculations in her head. They were lost and she had to find their location. Still the new 'girl,' she had to get this right. Her stomach rumbled with nausea. Letting out a breath, she turned on her head lamp to check the map one more time.

They were attacked by four Afghani men. Throwing a man over her head, she caught her thumb on the strap of his AK-47. She broke her thumb and a bone in her hand. She worked that entire trip with a broken left thumb. Jax, their medic, wrapped her hand every morning.

Just before they were attacked, Jesse said something. What did he say? Alex's core burned hot. This was the piece she was missing.

If only Jesse was here. Fuck.

"I said that we don't know how big this blackout area is."

Alex's mouth fell open. The full apparition of Jesse Abreu appeared in her office. He was wearing digital fatigues pushed up over his forearms and his dog tags hanging outside his T-shirt. His pocket read "ABREU" in block letters. As she watched, the apparition began to fill in. The tattoo of an angel, Jesse's essential nature as defined by the Cairo tattoo artist, flashed on his forearm.

"Who did you think you were talking to?" Jesse continued speaking in Spanish. They spoke to each other in Spanish. "I've been trying to do this for a long time. You know, being a ghost doesn't come with a manual."

"Jesse," she said in an exhale of breath.

"Hiya, Alexandra. I hate that blonde hair."

"Jesse, you're dead," she said continuing in Spanish.

Jesse laughed. "I've heard at least four people tell you that."

"You were there... at Piñon Canyon. I saw you there."

"It was my first time like this," Jesse faded for a second. "I just freaked and it happened."

"The guy who killed everybody? Eleazar? He's got some soldiers in Afghanistan."

"He didn't kill me."

"What?"

"You heard me. He wants to get to you. He's going to kill Mattie and the boys today. Did you ever forgive Zack?"

"No," Alex said.

"It's good that some things don't change." He faded out.

"Jesse," Alex said. "Please don't go Jesse."

"Jeez, I'm not any good at this ghost crap," Jesse said. The outline of his form appeared, then in a flash, his body appeared. "Listen we never mapped the edges of that GPS zone."

"Right. Matthew's going to the compound."

"The soldiers are twenty miles south of the compound. The dead zone is huge, Alexandra. They're about four miles into the area."

"Thank God we have some time."

"Why would you think that he would keep to a time table?" Jesse disappeared.

Stunned, Alex fell back in the chair.

"Get to work, lazy butt," Jesse's voice said.

Alex jumped to her desk just as the video link clicked showing Matthew's face.

"Hey Alex," Matthew said. "We're about five miles out from the compound. Zack says that the instruments are going crazy. I wanted to check in before we got cut off."

There was a knock at her door. Without looking, she reached behind her to open the door to Ben and Raz.

"Mattie, you have to turn back. Jesse said..."

"Honey, Jesse's dead."

"Do you think I'm fucking stupid? I know that Jesse's dead. The soldier's aren't at the compound. They're planning..."

"Hey Zack can you hold," Matthew called through the intercom to Zack. Alex heard Zack laughing. "Let us check it out. We'll be careful. We're all wearing..."

"They don't have any intention of letting you land."

Alex clicked her computer to connect with Zack's radio feed.

"Zack?"

"Hey Alex, we're way ahead of schedule. We've got at least an hour before..."

"Listen you've got to head back. Eleazar doesn't intend for you to land."

"Have a feeling?"

"Something like that," Alex said.

"That's enough for me. One-eighty time."

Alex closed her eyes for a moment. Zack was the only one who had experience working with her. She let out a breath and said a silent prayer for patience. But the familiar longing for "normal"–a team that listened and responded, her Fey team–rose from inside. Opening her eyes, she saw Matthew discussing the change with the men.

"Ah crap," Zack said.

"What happened?"

"We picked up a couple of Grails. Missiles," Zack said. "Four."

"Have they locked?"

"Not yet," Zack replied.

"Can you evade?" Matthew said.

"Does shit stink? You'd better hang on," Zack said. "Release the chaff. Hey Matthew, can you get your guys..."

"We're on it," Matthew said.

Glued to the screen, Alex watched as Matthew and Troy threw open the helicopter doors and began shooting at the missiles with machine guns. Trece and the White Boy used their bulk to hold the men in the weaving helicopter.

"Troy?" Trece gave Troy a Barrett .416 longrange rifle. Throwing his machine gun to the side, Troy fired in quick succession.

"Hey! That boy can shoot." Zack's echoing voice through the radio feed created commentary for the riveting scene in front of her. "Troy's hit two of them with that .416. My gunner's hit another. One more to go. Now this shit is just pissing me off. Hang on."

"We picked up two more," Matthew yelled.

Troy threw the empty rifle at Trece and picked up the machine gun. Trece worked to load the weapon. The screen jerked as the helicopter evaded the missiles. Flares, designed to draw the Grail heat-seeking missiles away from the helicopter, sparkled outside the helicopter doors. Trece gave the loaded Barrett back to Troy. Troy picked up the rifle and fired in quick succession.

"He hit another. Where'd you pick up this guy, Alex?" Zack asked.

"Basic."

There were voices in the background. "The gunner hit another missile. FUCK! We picked up another one. They must have watched us go over. Alex, you know this area. Where can we go to get away from these missiles?"

"What's your exact location?" Alex asked.

"Command just linked to your Sergeant. You should have it on your screen."

Alex tabbed her second computer screen as her Sergeant flicked onto the video link.

"Fey?"

"Sergeant? Can you contact the CO and tell him that he needs to get moving? Tell him it's orders."

"You have the…"

"I'm looking at the coordinates right now."

Alex walked to her table to review her maps of Afghanistan. Nodding her head, she returned to the armoire.

"Zack."

"Alex, you should leave the Englishman and marry me."

"You're very funny. Listen if you make a quick right turn." The men clung to the helicopter as it swung around. "Ten kilometers that's all, then left. Good job Zack. Now head South. Right. Your engineer is good. But don't stay there too long. You'll pick up another tribe in fifty kilometers. I don't think they're hostile but I wouldn't risk it."

"Got it," Zack said.

"Grails?" Alex asked. The video feed continued to jump and dodge as Zack maneuvered the helicopter to evade.

"Still have two on us."

"Locked?"

"One," Zack said. "Ah fuck. Hold on."

"Got it," Troy screamed.

Trece and the White Boy pushed the doors closed as a missile exploded within feet of the helicopter. Through the small window, they watched the fireball of light and shrapnel explode, then explode again. Zack maneuvered the helicopter away from the worst of the fire.

"Hey," Zack said. "We're clear. My gunner got the last one."

Alex watched the men cheer and laugh.

"I'm sending your engineer the coordinates to get you back to Kabul," Alex said.

"What about the soldiers?" Matthew said. "We're here to get the soldiers."

"It's too dangerous."

"Alex, where are the soldiers?" Zack asked.

"We came to do a job," Matthew said. "God damn it, Alex. Those men are out there. Alone."

Alex closed her eyes for a moment. Two years ago, she would have laughed, celebrated and sent them on to do their job. But today? When she closed her eyes she saw their death in bright blood red Technicolor.

"A terrorist succeeds when you are afraid," Ben said.

Alex startled when he spoke. She had forgotten he and Raz were there.

"Where are the soldiers?" Raz asked. He was standing next to her map table looking that the maps.

"Hang on, Matthew," Alex said.

She pointed to an area of the map.

"They started here." She pointed to an area to the left margin of the area. "Assuming they walked three or maybe five miles an hour at the maximum, they should have made it here." She pointed to a ridge line. "According to their CO, they said they were in a flat, dry spot, which is not this location. The U-2 data shows a series of caves under here."

Alex pointed to an area that looked like a flat open valley between the squiggly lines of the topological map.

"I thought you knew that tribe," Ben said. "Isn't the guy who controls that whole area a friend of the Fey's?"

"I'm not there," Alex said.

"Where's the rest of the team?" Ben asked.

"Here," Alex pointed to a spot near the edge of the map. "I ordered them to get moving."

"Eleazar's going to roll on them," Raz said.

Ben pointed to the map.

"You're thinking they have Grails in the caves or that the helicopter won't be able to land."

Alex nodded.

"You have no contact with the three soldiers."

"According to the CO," Alex said.

Ben raised just a small corner of his mouth.

"What?" Alex asked.

"Would you mind if I used your computer?" Raz asked plopping down in her chair.

Standing behind him, she watched him log through the Homeland Security server then through to a world network. He clicked in a series of codes and they were looking at satellite feed.

"Is that the soldiers?"

"Let's see."

Alex peered at the computer. Three soldiers lay in individual sleeping trenches. Their faces were covered in digital camouflage. They seemed to be asleep.

"I think so."

He clicked a series of buttons and they were looking at heat-seeking imaging.

"You're right," Raz said. "There's at least three guys, maybe more, on the ground here. I would say tunnels, not caves. There's also a grouping of people just over this ridge."

He clicked the buttons again to look at a picture of twelve armed men, Eleazar's men.

"Can you see into the compound?"

"No, the mountains get in the way." Raz reoriented the satellite to the area of the compound with little success.

"Hey Alex," Zack said. "We need a decision."

Alex raised her eyebrows to Ben and Raz. "What does he not expect us to do?"

"Reinforcements?"

"He'll have planned for that," Ben said.

"Leave them there?"

"Expected."

"Alex," Zack's voice sang over the radio feed.

"Hang on Zack," Alex said.

"Drones?"

"They crash at the sight. These guys," she pointed to the sleeping lost soldiers, "are dead either way. Those guys," Alex pointed to Eleazar's twelve armed men, "will kill our lost soldiers if the guys in the tunnel don't."

"So we give up on the strangers?" Ben asked.

Alex laughed.

"That's my girl," Ben said. "I'm going to smoke."

"What was that?" Raz asked.

"There's no record of the Fey every being in this region of Afghanistan."

CHAPTER NINE

"What about the map?"

"Myth and legend. He clearly knows that my team went through the Russian compound. But in Afghanistan? Twenty miles away is new country."

"He doesn't know about the extraction."

"The story is that we were dropping off a Green Beret, not that we were extracting a doctor." She smiled. "Eleazar will never expect that I have friends in this region."

She went to the map and marked the location of the soldiers, the armed men and the tunnels. Tapping her yellow pencil on the table, she chewed the inside of her mouth. Her mind laid out a strategy. Blowing out a breath, she hoped she was right.

"Can you see what the Special Forces team is doing?" Alex asked.

Raz reoriented the satellite picture. They watched the team packing their gear and moving out of their location.

"Sergeant," Alex clicked the video feed. "Can you set a secure link to the CO in Afghanistan? Let me know when it's set."

Turning to Raz, she said, "Can you relay all this information to Zack?"

While Raz updated Zack and Matthew, Alex sat down at her map table and began making calculations. Reaching into another cubbyhole, she pulled out a stack of rolled up maps. Under the rolled maps, toward the back of the cubby, she found what she was looking for–a filthy tattered map. Unfolding the map on the table, she compared the original map, the Russian map, to the more recent map.

"Can I have my chair?"

"What's that?" Raz asked. "Oh you're shitting me. This is the original map."

Alex nodded. "The only copy."

"Sergeant?" Alex asked clicking the feed.

"Fey? I have the CO but he's a little prickly."

"That's fine. Can you send two drones to these exact coordinates?" she sent him the coordinates by instant message. "I want the controls. Also, can you put this set of coordinates through to Zack's engineer? I don't want to risk the radio. Make sure he confirms the altitude."

"Got it."

She waited for a minute while the Sergeant made the call. She heard voices behind the Sergeant.

"You have an audience?"

"You have an audience. All right, Army command says that the drones will hover at that location in fifteen minutes. They asked me to remind you that the drones become disabled less than two feet from that location."

"Yes, thank you for the reminder."

"I have confirmation from the engineer as well."

"Great. I need a secure line, then I'll talk to the CO."

"Who are you calling?"

Alex looked at the video controller.

"I need it for the log," he continued.

"Dead soldiers or log," Alex said.

"You'll initial this or it's my ass."

Alex nodded. The phone rang twice indicating that it was secure. Alex reached up to a small shelf near the top of the armoire and pulled down an address book. Time to call some friends.

"Can I have that?" Raz asked looking over her shoulder.

"When I die," she said.

He laughed.

Alex flipped open the address book that contained coded telephone numbers, birthdays, addresses and personal information from every person she had extracted. This tiny book held confidential personal information on some of the world's most powerful people.

She began dialing, laughing and chatting with people whose lives she saved. Even the prickly CO was laughing when they disconnected. By the time the drones arrived, a plan was underway. When she looked up, Raz was shaking his head from the overstuffed green chair.

"Friends?"

"The most unpredictable force in intelligence," Alex said. "And something I'm good at."

Alex slipped the address book back onto the shelf of the armoire.

"In case you are wondering, this book is resting on a light-sensitive scanning device. The book will be set on fire if someone other than me takes it down."

"I don't remember setting that up," Raz said.

"You're not my only friend," Alex replied.

Raz laughed. Ben came jogging down the stairs with a bottle of cold water which he gave to Alex. She smiled her thanks and took a drink.

"Shall we watch?" Ben asked.

Alex stood to allow Raz to take her position.

"Lost soldiers first," Alex said.

Raz clicked the satellite photo back to the three lost soldiers. While they watched, a large herd of goats moved through the valley followed by a small boy. He moved in such a way that by the time he reached the soldiers, the goats had spread out covering the flat valley. Standing a few feet from the soldiers, the boy spoke. The soldiers startled, pulled their weapons, then seemed to understand what the boy was saying. When the soldiers moved, three men raced out of the caves. Tripping on the goats, the men screamed and fell to the ground. They fired their machine guns in the direction of the soldiers.

"Troy?"

"Got it," Troy said.

From almost two miles above the valley, Troy fired the Barrett .416. The terrorists fell to the dirt. Following the boy, the soldiers ran out of the valley.

Alex fired a missile from a drone into the area where the twelve armed men waited to down the helicopter and kill the soldiers.

"Zack? Move before they fire. Raz? Can we see the other location?"

He switched the screen to the area where the armed men waited. As planned, the drone missile dropped close enough to Eleazar's men to cause them to scramble. Two men raised Grail missiles to their shoulders and Alex fired the second drone's missile. The drone missile hit the men. The Grail missiles exploded in their hands.

"Captain? You can go in now," Alex said to the Commanding Officer.

The Special Forces team engaged Eleazar's armed men in a quick firefight. Eleazar's men surrendered and were rounded up by Special Forces.

"We've got the soldiers, uh, Quinn, Rhine and Boransky." Matthew's face flashed onto the computer screen causing Alex to jump. "Surprised you?"

Alex laughed.

"Should we get the others?"

"Army command has sent a unit and a couple choppers. Take the men back to Kabul. Get them checked through medical. No fucking around this time. Get back to Kabul. That's an order."

Matthew laughed. "The boys want to say, 'Hi' to the Fey."

He pressed the laptop to show the soldiers they had just picked up.

"That's the Fey?"

Alex waved.

"That hot chick is the Fey?"

Trece made a face and stood to block the computer.

"We have some important drinking to do, then we'll be back stateside," he said. "Anyone have anything interesting to say?"

"Is she available? Have you..."

"That's a 'No'," Trece said. "See ya."

The screen went dark and Alex leaned back in her chair.

"Thirty minutes," Ben said. "It's just twelve now."

"Let's send him a message," Alex said.

Ben smiled. "I've got just the thing. Close up and we'll buy lunch."

Alex nodded.

A half hour later, a large bouquet of flowers was delivered to a small residence in Jerusalem. The card read simply: "Congratulations on the new baby. With Love, the Fey." No tricks, no games, just congratulations. Eleazar screamed and ripped the flowers from their stems.

In Denver, the day dissolved into lunch and paperwork. With kisses all around, Ben and Raz left in their government vehicle and Alex retired to the hundred-year-old claw foot tub in the upstairs bathroom. Turning the water on, she put a little bubble bath, lavender oil and Epsom salts in the tub. She wandered, lost in thought, into her walk-in closet to undress. Naked, she startled to see John leaning against the doorway.

"I wondered when you'd notice me," he said.

"What are you doing here?" she asked.

"I thought we could celebrate," he said. He stepped forward to hold her. "I assume you've saved the universe again."

"The universe?"

His hands stroked her naked body. "You always inspire and impress me."

Her face broke into a wide smile. She helped him take his clothing off. They walked into the bathroom where they stepped into the fragrant water. Tucked into his shoulder, she relaxed against him in the claw foot tub.

"Oh, I forgot to tell you," John said.

"Yes."

"We're booked to Mexico in a couple hours. Colonel Gordon said 'get the hell out of town' or something like that."

Alex laughed. He kissed her head then pushed her back to his shoulder.

"Max, too?"

"He's meeting us there. I have you to myself for a day and a half," John said.

"Nice. What's the occasion?"

John shifted so he could look in her eyes.

"We are celebrating that you're alive."

"Hmm," she said.

"Hmm?"

"I'm just wondering if I can wait that long."

He stepped out of the tub. Laughing, she joined him in bed to begin the celebration.

♂♂♂

They spent four days in the sun around March eighth. Four days of great food followed by great sex and great conversation. For the first time in almost two years, Alex was laughing, available and present.

She hadn't realized how much she missed her gorgeous husband. Like a famine victim, she gorged on the very sight of him. She watched him move his hands when he talked, his intense cobalt blue eyes flashing as the generous curve of his mouth formed around words.

In the candlelight, their final night in Cabo San Lucas, John unwound his experience of the assault. He described waking to Max singing "When you wish upon a star" at the top of his lungs. John's eyes clouded, his brow furrowed and his breath stopped.

She was dead. He just knew it.

He sang with Max because he didn't know what else to do. When the phone rang a few minutes later, they let the answering machine pick it up. They couldn't bear to hear the words: "Alex is dead." John will never forget Ben's words on the answering machine: "She's alive. Get to Washington."

Blowing out a breath, his blue eyes held her eyes. He pulled out the dog tag bearing her name from under his shirt. Running his fingers over the indentations, he told her that the medics threw the tag at him when they unloaded her from Germany. Did she mind that he wore it? She put her hand over the tag and pressed it to his heart, the heart that she owned. This simple gesture launched him from his seat. He carried her to the bed where they consumed each other in unabated heat and passion.

They celebrated the eighth day of every month that spring and summer. They were riding their bikes through downtown Denver to a Colorado Rockies game on April eighth at twelve-thirty. The baseball game started at one o'clock and Max's law firm had season tickets. John, Alex and Max ate hot dogs and drank beer in the sunshine of their baseball team's opening week. With sunburned noses, they moved down Blake Street to a bar where they joined Erin and Matthew for dinner, drinks and dancing.

John and Max were flyfishing in the middle of the Arkansas River on June eighth. At twelve-thirty, a large brown trout rose from the bottom of the river to snatch at the fly Alex had cast from the banks. Screaming and laughing at her success, the men took a quick picture of Alex and the fish before returning the fish to the river. They ate dinner in Buena Vista then soaked in the Cottonwood Hot Springs. On the drive back to Denver, Max slept in the back seat of John's Audi while Alex and John whispered back and forth. John pulled into a turn off near Kenosha Pass. They cuddled on the hood of his Audi A8 and watched the moon rise to brighten the high plains valley below.

The entire day of July eighth was spent in the honeybee hives. Max and Alex went frame by frame through their five hives checking the health of their queenbees and the growing supply of honey. The hot, detailed work absorbed their entire attention. Twelve-thirty came and went almost without notice. Hanging their bee suits in the shed around four in the afternoon, the twins discovered a mini-party forming in the house. Samantha, their oldest sister, was visiting from Washington DC. John lit the barbeque just as Colin and Julie arrived. They laughed their way through barbequed salmon and bottles of red wine.

They were uneventful days that started when Alex opened her eyes to John's face and ended when she closed her eyes nestled under John's arm. Simple, boring, mundane days. But for Alex, who had been in the military since she was seventeen years old, every day sparkled with the brilliance of the Hope diamond. Plain living—dinner at home, trimming the roses, checking the bees, bubble baths—was new, special and perfect. Day after day, Alex woke up at home, ate at home, worked at home, played at home, laughed at home. Home. The very thought of home made her smile.

Near the end of July, Alex stood at Alexander's grave. For the first time in almost two years, she no longer yearned to lay under that stone.

Rebecca arrived in Denver near the middle of July with a clear agenda: get Erin's life back on track. Refusing to utter Marcos's name, Rebecca moved through Erin's broken life like a gale force wind picking up the clutter and leaving only bright sparkling possibility in its wake. Erin re-enrolled in school. The cosmetic dentist finished Erin's teeth. A long visit with the family lawyer was celebrated with a new hairstyle and a complete new wardrobe. Erin was poised to flourish.

Matthew surprised Erin with a two week vacation to the Outer Banks and the family began work on the loft. Patrick, Max and Colin spent three entire days clearing everything out of the loft. The Denver Post ran a picture of a filthy Patrick, standing next to a dumpster filled with broken glass and furniture, with the heading: 'There are some things a father must do himself.' A team of plaster experts repaired the holes, chips and splatter in almost every wall. After the walls were painted bright happy colors, the hardwood floors were sanded and varnished.

John and Max spent a weekend moving furniture from this spot to that spot, as Rebecca tried to make the loft just right. Alex sat on the floor and assembled lamps, small tables and whatever else was in the trunk of her mother's Mercedes. Colin and Julie made the bed, set out linens, and unpacked glassware while Patrick 'helped' Max connect the Internet and cable. Samantha arrived with a variety of rugs then escaped for a 'meeting' leaving their placement to Rebecca and her boys.

At twelve-thirty on August eighth, Alex was arranging a dozen orange roses when Matthew called from the airport. The entire family waited. Erin gave a small scream and burst into tears when she saw the loft. She floated like a worker bee touching one thing then the next. She hugged each person and returned to the warm embrace of Matthew's arms. Alex couldn't remember a time when Erin seemed happier. She watched her sister look up into Matthew's face and smiled at the love that passed between them.

Erin was moving forward in her life too.

CHAPTER TEN

Ten days later
August 18 – 5:30 P.M.
Denver, Colorado

"You look nice," John said coming up the stairs. Alex was adjusting her fake blonde hair in front of the full length mirror. She wore only a lace thong. "Is this what you're wearing tonight?"

Alex laughed. He ran his hand across her belly while his fingers played with the large round diamond she wore in her belly button. He kissed her neck before tugging her toward him. She leaned her head back against his shoulder and they watched themselves in the mirror.

"Have I mentioned that I love you recently?" he asked.

"I'm not sure," she said catching his eyes in the mirror.

"Oh love." He dropped his mouth to her neck again. "When are we due at dinner?"

"In a half hour," she said.

"Hmm," he said.

She smiled at him.

"What would you say to a..."

"Hey!" Max called from downstairs.

John spun Alex around and kissed her with such intense passion that she was out of breath and melting to his touch.

"Later," he said.

John moved into the bathroom to take a shower.

Alex was almost dressed when Max came into the bedroom. Screaming that she was wearing old lady clothing, he dug into her closet and handed her a tiny red strapless metallic stretch nylon dress hiding in the back. They argued back and forth until Max convinced her to try it on.

"Where did that come from?" John came into the bedroom with a towel around his waist.

"Max bought this dress online. He's become very interested in slutting Alyssa's dress code."

John raised his eyebrows to Max.

"Thanks man," he said as he walked into his closet to change.

Alex watched herself in the mirror. The dress was just long enough to cover the scarring on her left leg and hip. The skintight red metallic fabric covered from the top edge of her breasts to just below her hips. Turning sideways, she made a face and tugged the fabric down. Max handed her a pair of four-inch red patent leather stiletto pumps. She slipped them on then watched herself in the mirror again. When she looked up, John was staring at her, the blue of his eyes virtually consumed by his black pupils. Max looked over at John then laughed.

"It's unanimous," Max said.

"Can you help me with this?" Alex asked.

She gave Max a tube of concealer. Together, the twins covered the fairy tattoo.

"No Fey today?" John asked coming out of the bedroom dressed all in black.

Alex shrugged. "I went with Erin today to get her black 'F' tattoo and saw this concealer. Alyssa shouldn't be so tattooed."

"Weapon?" John asked.

"Yes, that too," Alex said.

She went into the bedroom. When she came out, the men shook their heads.

"Where is it?" Max asked.

"What?"

"Your gun?" John asked.

"Ah, some things are better left to the imagination," she said.

Laughing, she went down the stairs. They walked a few blocks to a trendy restaurant where they met Erin and Matthew, Colin and Julie, and Samantha. The siblings laughed through dinner then took a cab to a nightclub on South Broadway. Despite the long line, they were waved into a dance club by a bouncer Matthew knew. They danced until they were thirsty and drank until they were dancing again. As the night wore on, Colin and Julie made an early exit. Samantha slipped into a reserved section with a handsome professional football player. With a wink to Alex, Max disappeared with a beauty.

When Matthew and Erin went to the rooftop to dance under the stars, John took Alex's hand and led her off the dance floor. Pressing her into a dark corner, he kissed her lips. His hands ran over the tight dress and her responsive flesh. Alex burned with rising desire. She held him in a tight embrace as his lips worked down her neck and shoulders. He let out a breath.

"Let's go home," she said into his ear.

"Just one more." He took her lips with his lips.

"Ah Johnny," a voice said over the music.

John stiffened at the voice.

"I didn't expect you to be an exhibitionist," the man's voice continued in some form of Gaelic.

John pushed Alex from him. Two slight men grabbed him by the shoulder.

"Not so fast."

John's eyes filled with desperation. Shaking his head, he continued to push Alex toward the corner.

"She's not a part of this," John replied in the same language.

"Oh yes, she is," a bright red haired man said speaking the same Gaelic.

"Let's go for a little drive?" the dark haired man said to John.

The red haired man grabbed Alex by the arm and pressed a handgun into her ribs. She was about to take the weapon away from the man when she caught John's eyes. He shook his head 'No.' His eyes pleaded with her to go along. Alex looked down at the ground. She would bide her time in this made-for-television kidnapping.

At gunpoint, the men escorted them through the club. They were near the door when Matthew came flying down the stairs. Without looking at him directly, Alex raised her left hand and he stopped in his tracks. She moved her hand horizontally and he nodded. They walked past him and out the door into the deserted alley behind the club. The men tied Alex and John's hands behind their back then shoved them into the back of an SUV.

"I realize we are in the middle of a made-for-TV movie," Alex said in English. "But I'd like to know what's going on."

She wasn't sure what form of Gaelic they were speaking. It was similar to Irish Gaelic which she spoke fluently. She wasn't about to let them know that she spoke any form of Gaelic.

"Listen, maybe you should be more choosey about the married men you pick up in clubs."

"He's..."

John fell into her. He murmured in English, "Whatever they say, remember that you are now and have always been my only love."

Alex turned to him as if she was stung.

"What? You didn't know he was married?" the dark haired man asked in accented English. Irish?

"Fuck you," John said.

"Ah, yes, fuck me. Johnny, your family's missed you all these years."

Alex closed her eyes for a moment. She felt a spinning sensation in her head. She bit the inside of her mouth to stay present. Tasting her own blood in her mouth, she pushed her emotions away. When she opened her eyes, she felt nothing. She would deal with John later. She saw the glimmer of Jesse in the car. At least she wasn't alone.

They drove in silence until the SUV slowed at a warehouse. The men dragged John and Alex from the SUV. When they stopped to open the door, John attempted to protect Alex with his body. The men laughed. They pushed John through the door and into the empty warehouse.

Alex followed John into the warehouse without a word. She was relaxed and calm. Just waiting for action. After all, it was only two small men. Irish? Maybe Scottish. She shrugged. Either way they weren't much.

After tying them to chairs, the men went to the edge of the open space to make phone calls and Alex began to undo her ropes. Working with the spike of her stiletto heel, she loosened the knot. Her ropes fell to the ground. Standing barefoot on the concrete floor, she jumped rotating her hands from behind her back to in front of her. With her hands in front of her, she untied John's ropes then he untied her hands. When the men returned, John and Alex were standing near the chairs.

"I'm a Homeland Security agent," Alex said.

"And I'm Father Christmas," the dark haired man said holding the handgun on Alex. "I don't know how you did that but..."

"I won't kill you if you let us go" Alex had to work to keep the amusement from her voice.

"Why would I let you go?" the dark haired man continued. "I've wanted to talk to your boyfriend for over twenty years."

"All right," Alex said. "We talk then we walk."

"Who the fuck are you? I have a gun!"

Shifting to the left, Alex kicked the gun from the man's hands. The gun skittered into a far corner of the warehouse.

"Now you don't."

"Will you shoot them?" the dark haired man said to the red haired man.

"I don't know, Cian. This isn't going very well," the red haired man replied.

"Holy fuck. Cian?" John asked.

"Johnny. It's a big Kelly family reunion. Now shut the fuck up," Cian said.

"You're John Kelly," Alex said with more breath than sound.

John's head wrenched toward her. His face flushed with emotion while his mouth moved. Without saying a word, he dropped his head.

"That makes you Cian Kelly," Alex said in clear Irish Gaelic. "You're Irish Republican Volunteers."

"Now we have to kill her," the red haired man said. His arms dropping to his side. "Fuck Cian, we didn't even know if they needed killing. I told you we should have left her at the club."

"Who's in charge?" Alex asked.

"I am," Cian said.

Alex reviewed the man's curly dark hair and blue eyes, not quite John's cobalt, but deep blue anyway. He was smaller and older than John. She shook her head.

"No you're not," Alex said. She sat down in the chair she had been tied to. "Call whoever is in charge and tell them this: 'I captured the blue fairy.'"

"I'm not going to..."

"You better do it," she said. "I'll wait here."

She made a movement with her hand.

"Go on."

Cian Kelly gave Alex an aggravated look then turned his back on them. Walking away, he dialed his cell phone.

"Sit down," Alex said to John.

"Alex... I..."

Her heart flashed with emotion. She shook her head and pushed the emotion away.

"You may as well get comfortable," she said then yawned.

Cian Kelly was yelling into the telephone. Storming back to the chairs, John moved to cover Alex with his body, but Cian punched the phone in her direction.

"He wants to talk to you," Cian said. "Where's your fucking tattoo?"

"Have a tissue?" she asked reaching for the phone.

The red haired man ran to the bathroom and returned with toilet paper. She wiped off the concealer from her fairy tattoo.

"Oh fuck Cian, do you know who that is?" the red haired man wheeled back from Alex as if he was hit.

She waved at the red head then began speaking into the telephone.

"Dia duit," she said.

"You are with John Kelly," the voice said in Irish Gaelic.

"I just found that out," Alex said continuing in Gaelic. "How are you?"

"I'm well. I have three more grandchildren since you were here last," the elderly man's voice said. "How is your health, dear? I hear you're walking... kicking guns from people."

"I'm much better than when we spoke last. Did you hear the Fey is back?"

"I did hear that but I prefer to see it with my own eyes."

"Why are you here?" Alex asked.

"As you know, John Kelly is a curiosity of mine. I received this photo of him with a group of people and, things being what they are, I thought I'd send a few boys to talk to him."

"His wife? Where is she?"

"Yes, his wife. Why are you with John Kelly? The boys said you were pretty hot at it."

"He's my husband," Alex said.

The man laughed. "John Kelly is your John? The John that taught you Gaelic? Wait… Oh my God, this is a picture of you. Christ, you're wearing mouse ears."

"That's what you do at Disneyland," she said. "Where did you get the photo?"

"It came in our direction. I'm not sure."

"But you'll find out."

"Yes, lass. We have a few questions," he said.

"Fine. Then we go home."

"I don't care where the questions get answered."

"Great," she said. "He wants to talk to you."

Alex passed the phone to Cian. She stepped into her shoes then stood.

"Come on John," she said. She held her hand out to him. "Let's go home."

"Wait a minute," the red haired man said. "We need to talk."

"You'll be much more comfortable at our house," Alex said. "I can call a cab or…"

"I'll drive," Cian said stomping over to them. "You know it's not very fair to cover that tattoo. How the fuck are we supposed to know who you are?"

"Right, I could just be some other girl you are holding at gunpoint," Alex said.

"Shut up," Cian said. "Get in back."

They drove in silence. John reached and entwined his fingers with Alex's fingers. When she turned to look at him, he saw that she had placed herself somewhere far away from him. He kissed her hand. Closing his eyes, he prayed to a God that he was certain had abandoned him years ago. He prayed that Alex, the only thing that mattered to him in this whole world, would possibly understand. When the car stopped at their house, Alex got out.

Turning back into the SUV, she said, "There are some people here to see you."

The car was surrounded by Homeland Security agents. Raz jumped from the porch of the house and swept Alex into a hug. John stood behind Alex, not sure if he should touch her.

"We got the call from Matthew and tracked you with the GPS locater in your hip. We thought it was Eleazar."

"I'm sorry to have worried you," Alex said. "We got picked up by the PIRA."

Raz made a face.

"Yeah. I'm sorry. I need to go to bed. Can you hold these guys? Just hold them. They didn't do anything."

"Got it," Raz said.

Alex walked up the porch to where Ben stood smoking a cigarette. She searched the face of her mentor and saw what she expected.

"Why didn't you tell me?"

"Because it doesn't matter," he said.

She gave a curt nod and moved to follow John into the house. Ben touched her arm.

"Remember. He's a psychological terrorist."

Hearing his words, Alex's eyes shifted to look at Ben but her mind was already slipping down the familiar path of depression. She followed John into the house. Moving like a person in a trance, Alex walked up the stairs. Each step brought her further into the depressive fog that blanketed her for the last two years. Rather than walking into their bedroom, she turned into the guest bedroom and closed the door. John stood on the landing staring at the door.

"You have to talk to me," John said to the door.

Standing on the other side of the door, Alex turned the lock of the door. She didn't have to talk to him tonight. Pulling off the tight red dress, she threw it on the ground and kicked the pumps under the night table. She went to the closet and put on a battered marathon gimme shirt. Sitting on the side of the bed, she heard John sit down in the hall.

"I know you are just sitting there, Alex," he said. "Will you hear me out?"

"Why?" she asked. "You've had twelve years to be honest, to tell me that you were already married. Ah fuck."

She pressed her hand against the pain and anger that lived in her heart. Rolling onto her side, her heart away from John, she pulled the covers over her head. Unbidden, her mind began to walk the trail toward death. Now that John wasn't her husband, she could just go and be with her team.

With a sigh, she closed her eyes and fell into a dream.

She was walking down a familiar white tunnel. As she walked, round fluorescent ceiling lights flickered on. She had the sensation that she was walking out of the light and into the dark over and over again. She heard laughter. Mike, their operations officer, was teasing Jax, their medic, about placing third in the hundred and thirty-five mile Badwater Ultramarathon. Alex smiled. If she hurried, she would spend the night playing in Paris. She began to jog, running mostly in the dark now, as the lights flickering on behind her.

But the faster she ran the farther away they seemed.

Jesse was laughing with Dwight, the other weapons officer, about something the engineer Paul was doing. She beamed with expectation and turned into the room. Sliding on a pool of blood, her vision filled with the horror of her beloved friends' bodies in pieces, bleeding onto the floor.

Screaming, she collapsed to the floor.

CHAPTER ELEVEN

John kicked the door open. Pulling Alex from the bed, he held her to him until she stopped screaming. He moved to her to his lap. His hands pressed her head against his muscular chest while he caressed her hair. She knew he was talking but her ears heard only the ragged breathing to a backbeat of blood dripping onto the white floor.

"Oh John," she said when terror shifted to sadness. Weeping against his shoulder, he rocked her back and forth until her ears heard what he was saying: "Oh my God, I love you so very much. You have to believe me. You are the very heart of me."

He pulled her face away from him. Looking into her eyes to see if she was present, he said, "Please hear me out."

"I can't. I can't. I can't." She pressed her palms to her ears and shook her head.

"Oh love."

He lifted her from the bed and carried her to the bathroom. Sitting with her on his lap, he filled the tub with water and bubble bath. Then, undressing her like a child, he placed her in the bath before joining her there. She lay with her head against his shoulder and his arms wrapped around her. While the warm fragrant water worked to calm her fear, she cried into his chest. He said nothing, caressing her skin, waiting for the storm of emotion to pass. When she was silent and breathing deeply, he moved to look at her face. Her eyes stared straight forward, glazed as if she was in shock.

"I'm sorry," he said.

"Me too," she said.

"I've never known how to speak to you about this. I've spent the last two hours racking my brain as to how to say everything."

She shifted away from him.

"Why were you screaming?"

"I saw them dead." Tears seeped from her eyes. "Blood everywhere... dripping on the floor."

"The shock of my crap has stirred things around in your brain," he said.

"I loved you."

He jerked up to look at her. "Loved?"

She moved out of the tub. Grabbing a towel from the rack, she went into their bedroom. She threw on comfortable sweats and a T-shirt then began to pack. When John came to the door, he nodded his head.

"You're leaving."

"You're married to someone else, John. You should live with your wife."

"Stop. Alexandra, please stop." He fell to his knees before her. "I beg you."

Alex blinked at him. She felt nothing—not calm or sad or angry or afraid—just blank. Looking down at John, she heard Ben's voice, 'He's a psychological terrorist.'

Rage ignited deep within her belly. Fuck Eleazar. This is my life. I've fought for my country. I've fought for my friends. I will fight for my own God damn life.

"All right. I'll listen."

John nodded. While she watched, he dressed in jeans and a T-shirt. He led her downstairs to the living room couch, then went to the kitchen for a bottle of wine. When he returned, Alex had closed the living room drapes and lit a fire. He opened the wine then gave her a glass.

"I don't know where to start," he said.

"Ok, I'll start. What language were they speaking?"

"Ulster Gaelic. The language of my youth. They spoke and I responded without thinking. I guess some things never leave you. How do you know the PIRA?" he asked.

"You remember we extracted that Irish singer?"

"The tabloid picture of you making out with him is right there," he said. He pointed to a grainy picture of Alex kissing the rock star on the balcony of his hotel room. "Some old friends thought they could make some cash by holding him hostage. Charlie liked the band and knew their manager. You went to get him then couldn't get him back to his life. So you pretended to be his lover."

"We spent an entire week with him," Alex said. "He's very into a united Ireland. As you can imagine, I was incredibly bored and wanted to go home. He said that if I wanted something to do, I should find this girl, PIRA, who disappeared the year before. No one knew what happened to her. Jesse and I checked around and found this whole messy drama involving... Anyway, it's not important. We were able to find her and get her home. Somehow, both sides were satisfied. It's one of the only times they agreed on anything. It turns out that her father is a big deal. I spoke Gaelic so he kind of adopted me. He's really a great guy–kind, funny, very grandfatherly. He told me that if I could find his daughter, maybe I could find John Kelly."

"Why did he want me?"

"He said that John Kelly disappeared as a child and they thought he was taken by the British. I looked into it but never got very far. Well, that's not true. I have a lot of information–sightings, contact, pictures and all the police documents. I never found John Kelly."

"Until tonight."

"Right under my nose," she said.

She took a drink of wine then shifted to look at him. "Your turn."

"I don't know where to start," he said.

"John Kelly was standing next to his father when a bomb exploded. It's believed that Ronan Kelly set the blast then stopped for a smoke. The bomb exploded early due to a faulty switch. Fairly common for that kind of device," Alex said. "Ronan Kelly died and John Kelly disappeared.

"I have a crime scene photo of him…you… covered in blood… in shock. Ronan Kelly's carotid was punctured by a knife or stiletto. The police report says that a Catholic nun came to take you to an orphanage but they never found the nun or the orphanage."

"I have eleven siblings," John said.

"John Kelly is the youngest of twelve," Alex said.

"My sister Rita, she's just younger than Cian, was the nun. She walked me to her church, cleaned me up, then we caught a ferry to England. We reached London by rail."

"Huh. Why did she take you?"

"I'm not sure. It's a little fuzzy. We hid from the IRA at a church in Central London. The priest gave us a small room and Rita worked as the church secretary. She met her husband the week we moved to London. They were married about six months later. He adopted me. He's called Tom Drayson. That's why I'm John Drayson."

Alex watched the fire burn in the fireplace. Her mind jumped from facts about this person John Kelly and the man sitting next to her. She remembered his face, full of passion and love, the heat and desire in her belly, the cool sand in her toes and his words: "Marry me Alex. Marry me tonight".

"Please say something," John said.

"Why did you ask me to marry you when you were already married?" she asked. "Do you live with your wife? Do you have children? How come Max doesn't know?"

She watched him stand to place another log on the fire. Walking to the window, he shifted the drapes to look out at the night. He turned back to her. He opened his mouth, then closed it. Shaking his head, he returned to the couch.

Alex pulled her knees against her chest and turned to face him.

"It's a complicated question." He paused for a moment. "I asked you to marry me because I was inexplicably in love with you. I wanted you in a way that I can hardly express, even now, twelve years later. I had this overwhelming feeling that if I didn't act, at that moment, I would lose you forever."

"But you were already married. You belong to someone else."

John closed his eyes. "I... It's complicated."

She looked at the small gold band on her left hand. They bought these bands three days after they were married. He put it on her finger that day and she never took it off. With a sigh, she pulled the ring from her finger and dropped it into his hand.

"Complicated?" A bubble of sadness burst the moment the ring left her finger.

She wasn't married anymore.

She looked over to John to see his eyes squeezed shut in pain. His hand closed around the ring. When he opened his eyes, their eyes held. Sliding her ring onto the pinkie of his right hand, he spoke in a torrent of words.

"I was fifteen when they found me. Is that in your records? They found me in church. Two IRA soldiers. I was an alter boy helping with mass. They attended the mass then... They knew who I was immediately. I tried to escape but.... They caught me... Beat me. Bad. Tom found me where they dumped me... broken... bleeding. He hid me at home. Rita was pregnant with their second. She was so upset about me that the doctor was called. They thought she might lose the baby."

"I... I was terrified. They came to the house about a week later. The IRA was desperate for money then, absolutely desperate. They said that I had to marry this girl... Eimilie... then work in America. She would give the money to them. Tom... I... told them whatever they wanted to hear. I never... They dragged me to a church where they forced this ancient priest to... I married this girl... woman... I think I kissed her." He shrugged. "I never thought it was legal because we didn't..."

"Consummate?"

"She was dating one of the IRA guys. They took me back to some apartment where she had a fine time with one of the other guys while they made the husband watch. They got very drunk... very dangerous. I escaped when they passed out. Tom was waiting for me at a pre-arranged meet up spot... an underground station. We always knew they might come for me.

"Tom sent me to this farm in Scotland where his Grandparents lived. I don't know who they were. They weren't his grandparents that's for sure, but they were very kind to me. They kept me safe, helped me with this great London accent and sent me to school. When I—John Drayson—passed my O levels, they put me on a plane to America.

"I didn't marry her Alex. John Kelly married her. John Kelly is married to Eimilie."

"You're John Kelly."

He was silent for a while then poured the rest of the wine in their glasses.

"I thought it was over, you know. I almost forgot it even happened until I started at UCLA. I received this letter from Eimilie telling me that she was pregnant with my child. She was going to garnish my wages for the baby. I... I hadn't seen her but the one time. I had no idea what to do. I worked for everything and if she took the money, I'd have to leave school. I was sitting in my dorm room, you know, the one I shared with Max, trying to decide what to do when Ben showed up. He said that your father, having grown up with Irish people, thought I seemed Irish, not English. Patrick asked Ben to check it out. How would I like to go for a walk?

"He knew who I was and about Eimilie." John snorted remembering. "He even knew about the farm in Scotland. He asked me questions, bought me lunch, and listened to what I had to say. I mean he listened to everything from my terror for Fionn, that's Rita's second son, to the days on the farm. It was as if he knew all the players, but Rita says that she's never met Ben."

"You have contact with Rita? Tom?"

"We speak about once a month. They've come to see me in Edinburgh when I've been coming or going to see you. They live in Scotland now."

"And Eimilie?"

"She receives benefits for John Kelly. He's classified as missing, presumed dead. I don't know. Her benefits have something to do with the Belfast agreement. Ben told me but I don't remember. I don't care."

"And you never... I mean, you were very promiscuous at UCLA. Why didn't you..."

"I was fifteen, Alexandra. I wasn't a lady killer until I was fifteen and a half at least." He smiled at his attempted joke.

"And later?"

"I never saw her again." He paused for a moment. "Well, that's not true. She came here... to this house when you were just out of hospital. I couldn't believe the nerve. I didn't recognize her until she introduced herself as my wife. We argued on the porch. She wanted money, of course. I gave her what I had in my wallet then she went away. I called Ben. He was at your parents' house. I think he had her deported but I don't really know."

"Why didn't everyone know about it?"

"Your family was upset about our marriage. It was like an explosion for them. Ben and I agreed not to add to the drama with this crap."

Alex watched the glimmer of Jesse move into the room.

"Jesse says there's something else... something you're not saying."

"Jesse's dead, love."

Alex glowered at John. "What are you not telling me?"

"She had pictures of her and me... you know... together. I'm wearing my wedding ring, but I never... ever... never. I gave them to Ben. He says that I must have... bedded her when I was at UCLA and they superimposed the ring."

"The photos were altered?"

"He said it was definitely me but that it's possible the ring was added. He was as confident as I am that I hadn't... been with her, or anyone for that matter, after we were married. I assume they keep track."

"Standard protocol for high level agents."

"I only remember seeing her twice—once in London and once on our porch. She says that one of the children is mine."

Alex startled.

"I was very careful. I always, always used protection, every single time. I didn't want a disease or a baby to get in the way of my plan to be a doctor. The only time I didn't was..."

"With her?"

"With you. I was intoxicated by you. I think you'll remember that we barely made it to the apartment. I've never felt that way about anyone... ever. I had to have you." He shrugged. "I'm still that way."

Alex's lips turned up in a smile then pressed into a tight line. She digested what he had said.

"Have you check the DNA on the child?"

"I couldn't do that without you knowing, right?"

"She's blackmailed you?"

"That's what Ben calls it. I... I guess I understand."

"What?"

"My mother died when I was a baby, maybe two years old. My father was in Maze Prison. We lived on the streets. We had neither clothing nor food. And when someone took us in? We were literally taking food out of someone else's mouth. The poverty in Belfast was incredible. Ben says it's better now, but there isn't much industry or jobs. I've never given her that much money... a couple thousand dollars total."

Alex nodded. "It sounds like you don't mind being married to her."

"I don't think of myself as married to her," John said. "I am married to you."

Alex turned to look at him. Her eyes searched his face.

"No, you're not."

Standing from the couch, she went into the kitchen. She flicked on the coffee maker and poured breakfast cereal into a bowl. John stood in the doorway of the kitchen.

"That's all you have to say?"

"Guess I don't need the vibrator," she said pouring milk on her cereal.

"And why is that?"

"Because if I'm not married to you? I'm going to have some fun."

John's mouth fell open.

"You can go be with your wife and children," Alex said. She poured herself a cup of coffee then added some milk. "Maybe she'll support you while you finish your residency."

Taking her cereal and coffee, Alex walked past John to the dining room and sat down at a chair just as her cell phone rang.

"Hey, did you know I'm not married? Yeah, he's married to someone else. Kids and everything. I know! Oh that sounds fun, I need to change. No, I'll meet you there."

"Who was that?"

"What's it to you?"

"Alexandra."

Her eyes followed him but her mind and heart were miles away. She would move into Max's house. They would sell this house. John could just move back to Belfast to be with his family. She nodded. She was going be all right.

"Stop."

"Stop what?" she asked.

"You're planning your life without me."

"There was never any you in my life. Only dreams and lies. You're married. Go be with your wife."

"YOU are my wife."

"No, I'm not. Jeez, I wish I had known that. I would have had a lot more fun as a Green Beret."

He dropped to his knees next to her chair.

"Don't do this."

"What did you expect would happen John Kelly? You've lied for over a decade. You thought you'd just reveal the truth and we'd go on our merry way. What about your child? Or children? Or fuck…"

In a breath, she was overcome with sorrow. Like walking under a waterfall, her sadness dropped into her mind and body. She pressed her hands against her eyes and cried. He moved to put his arms around her but she shrugged him off. Jumping from her seat at the table, she ran upstairs to their bedroom and slammed the door. She threw herself on the bed and sobbed. He followed her into the bedroom and sat on a corner of the bed. Alex's cell phone rang again.

"Bring them here in three hours," she said. She wiped her nose with her arm. "Yeah."

She closed the phone and moved to get up. John stood before her.

"Get out of my way," she said.

"No, I'm not going to let you go off with some guy just because you're mad at me."

"What's it to you? What I do, or don't do, is none of your business."

John sat down on the bed.

"You're just going off with some guy. Just like that. You can't have loved me very much."

"I need to make up for lost time," she said. "Twelve years of being faithful to a married man can really make a girl... I don' t know... horny. Now, if you'll excuse me, Mr. Kelly. I need to get dressed for my date."

She made it to her closet before she fell to the ground crying. He came behind her to hold her but she pushed him away. He held her firm and kissed her. Between sobs, she tore his clothing from him while he pulled at her clothing. She was weeping when they joined. Pressing against him, she moved to be on top then, in her sorrow, she collapsed against his chest. They fought against each other, pressing and pulling, rising in pitch and tempo. In one blinding moment, they slipped over the cliff together in release.

"You're not mine. You're not mine. You're not mine." Shaking her head, her tears dropped from her eyes.

"I'm only yours. I belonged to you the moment, the very moment, I saw your crooked smile in that terrible bathroom all those years ago. Oh God Alex."

Wrapping his arms around her, he carried her to the bed. He slipped her between the sheets then lay beside her. She wrapped herself around him, holding him tight around the waist. Her head rested on his chest.

"What about your date?"

She looked up into his face then shook her head.

"Marry me Alex."

She groaned.

"I'll get this sorted. I promise. I'll take a DNA test. I'll deal with Eimilie. Marry me Alex."

"You've had twelve years to work this out. Instead you've just given her money, my money, no less."

John shifted so that he was on top of her. He kissed her.

"Our money. Marry me."

"No."

"Your mouth says 'no' but your body says 'yes.'"

Alex pushed at him and slipped from under him. He held her in place. They lay face to face staring at each other. Alex searched his eyes, his face, and his heart for answers.

Should she hold on, fight for him, for herself or run away from the betrayal? He was right. Her mind said run away but her hands and arms held onto him, unwilling to let go of what had been hers for twelve years.

When he pulled her back to him, she succumbed to the overwhelming desire to have him, at least one more time, before she had to let him go. Pressing her arms above her head, his mouth worked down the sides of her neck and to her shoulders. She gasped when he caught her nipple in his mouth. Arching her back slightly, he began to move his hips against her. She rose again to his insistent press.

"Marry me Alex."

"No." She slipped just over the edge.

He moved with increasing pitch as her climax spread throughout her body. She began to rise again. He plundered her mouth with his teeth and tongue. They crested releasing in waves of intensity and bliss until they slipped off the edge.

"Marry me."

"No."

"Why? Alex, give me one reason why?"

"Because I'm already married to you," she said.

He laughed. Wrapping her in his arms, he rocked her with his laughter.

"I love you Alex."

"You'd better."

CHAPTER TWELVE
August 19 – 6:17 A.M.
Denver, Colorado

"They are here," John said.

"Cool," Alex said. She hopped to the entry way of their home where she hugged Raz. "Good morning."

"Still unmarried?" he asked.

"Sort of. How was the shooting range?"

"We worked on this stuff instead." Raz caught her eyes then kissed her cheek. "Are you all right?"

Alex shrugged.

"Thanks for taking care of this crap."

"It's my job." Raz scooped her into a hug. "I'm so sorry."

Alex took a breath and nodded. He stepped back and touched her face. She smiled.

"I brought some bagels," he said. "We made them sit handcuffed in the car while I went in. They are not very cheerful."

"Great. John made some fruit salad. I can make..."

"That's all right. I'll make breakfast," Raz said. "I'd rather not die today."

"I'm not that bad. I took that class you gave me for Christmas. I can..."

He raised an eyebrow and she pretended to punch him. He laughed.

"How about if I take care of the PIRA and you get breakfast?"

"Good," Raz said. "Hey John."

The men hugged in greeting.

Alex walked out to the SUV where three Homeland Security agents waited with Cian Kelly and his red haired friend. The IRA members were sitting in the back seat with black hoods, their heads and their hands cuffed in front of them. When Alex approached the vehicle, two agents stepped out of the SUV and dragged the men from the vehicle. Alex walked with the men up the porch and into the house. With a nod, the Homeland Security agents unlocked their handcuffs and left the house. Alex waited until the SUV pulled away before removing their hoods.

"Welcome to our home," she said.

Ben walked in the door. He leaned in to give her a kiss on the cheek, then squeezed her arm. He moved past them into the kitchen for a cup of coffee.

"Breakfast is almost ready," Alex continued. "Would you like some tea?"

"What the fuck is this?" Cian Kelly asked.

"In this country, when family comes for a visit, we invite them to a meal," Alex said.

The red haired man laughed. "That's it then. Spend some time terrified by the American government, then it's come in. Have a cup of tea."

Alex raised her eyebrows.

"Do come in," John said. He came and put his arm around Alex. She looked at him and he kissed her nose. "We understand that you'd like to talk."

"What the fuck? I was just in handcuffs," Cian said.

Alex smiled.

"Come on, Cian. I'm hungry and the food smells delicious," the red haired man said. "I'm Eoin Mac Kinney."

"I'm Alex Drayson. Nice to meet you. This is my husband, John Drayson. And my brother Max Hargreaves." Max was walking down the hall from the kitchen. He hugged Alex then they pressed their foreheads together. "Max, this is John's brother Cian."

"Hey, nice to meet you. Come in. " Max led Cian and Eoin to the dining room table. "Make yourself at home. I'll get some tea."

"Please have a seat," Alex said.

Cian made a face then sat down.

"I can always send you back," she said.

"We're happy to be here, Mrs. Fey. Thank you for having us to breakfast," Eoin said with a laugh.

Max brought a pot of Irish Breakfast tea and set it in front of Cian. Eoin poured himself a cup of tea.

"How do we know it's not drugged?" Cian sniffed at the pot of tea.

Raz came in carrying a plate of eggs and sausages.

"And the Homeland guy is making breakfast?" Cian pushed himself away from the table.

"I don't know what your problem is, brother, but please, eat with us," John said.

"Hey, don't start without me," Matthew said coming in the front door. Alex stood to greet him in the entry. She hugged him 'hello'. "Sorry I'm late. I was..." he cleared his throat and shrugged his eyebrows, "detained."

"Sounds like you are enjoying your new off-base status," Alex said.

"I love my new job pleasing your sister. I mean, working with you," he said.

Alex kissed his cheek. "Come meet John's brother and his friend."

Matthew reached for her hand. "You OK?"

Alex nodded. Holding hands, they walked into the dining room.

"Hey, I want to be greeted like that," Eoin said.

Cian rolled his eyes at Eoin. "They're trying to fool us into revealing more than we want to. Well you won't get anything from me."

Alex laughed. "I don't need to get anything from you. I know everything there is to know about Cian Kelly. It's my understanding that you have some questions for us. That's why we are here. To answer your questions."

Alex and Matthew sat down. Breakfast was passed around the table. Ben came in from the back deck and sat in the chair next to Cian. Alex passed the coffee in Ben's direction. They chatted and ate while Cian and Eoin watched them. Finally, Eoin put some eggs on his plate and began to eat. Cian watched Eoin, then filled his plate as well.

"Would you like to ask your questions?" Alex asked.

Cian's eyes shot over to her. He swallowed the food in his mouth, then cleared his throat.

"Before you start, we already talked to the IRA. If there's something you want to know, you can ask. Then we have a problem that we think you can help us with."

"Who are these guys?" Eoin asked.

"To me?" Alex asked. "That's Arthur Rasmussen. We call him 'Raz'. He's my partner when I work for Homeland Security and our boss is called Ben. My mother calls him Benjamin. He trained me. This is my twin Max. And this is my old friend Matthew. He's just started working with me."

"Why are they here?" Eoin continued.

"Curiosity," Ben said. "I've known John since he was Max's roommate at university. We have a couple questions to ask."

"And you?"

"My boss told me to be here," Matthew said.

Alex laughed.

Cian Kelly looked at Alex, holding her eyes for a full minute, then nodded slightly. He glanced at John, then looked down at his plate.

"You sorted this with..."

"Yes," Alex said. "John spoke with him this morning. He is satisfied."

"What did you tell him?" Cian's voice shifted in a way that made Alex look up. Cian saw her look and added, "He's my brother first."

Alex smiled.

"He asked about Da, mostly," John said. "He wanted to know about me–

what I was doing, what kind of a person I am. I guess because of Alex. Then he told me that some of the people I used to interact with would be happier if I didn't remember those interactions."

"The troubles are over, Johnny," Cian said. "It's strange for us natives, but many of our old friends are legitimate business people now."

"Native?" John asked.

Cian, Alex, and Raz opened their mouths to reply, but Ben spoke first.

"Native IRA. You and Cian were born into the high ranks of the Provincial Irish Republican Army."

"Some groups you can join," Raz added. "The upper ranks of the IRA? You have to be born into that."

"We take care of our own, Johnny," Cian said. "What about Eimilie?"

"It's one of the questions we have for you and Eoin," Alex said.

She nodded to Raz. Raz reached into his bag and pulled out a stack of photos.

"Who is this man?" Alex asked.

Raz handed the photos one at a time to Eoin who passed them to Cian.

"Isn't that Johnny?" Cian asked. "It looks like him."

"It's not him," Alex said.

"How can you be certain?" Eoin said.

Alex looked up to see Ben watching her. He smiled then nodded to encourage her to proceed.

"I've been John's lover for more than twelve years. This is not John," Alex said. She picked up a photo. "You might have to be a woman to notice it but John is right-handed and this man is left-handed."

"The rings are the same," Cian said.

Alex pulled John's wedding ring from the middle finger on her right hand and passed the gold band to Cian.

"This man is wearing a plain gold wedding band and John wore a plain gold wedding band."

"Look at that," Eoin said. "The rings are the same, but different. Cian I think this is…"

Eoin looked at Cian. Cian shook his head slightly.

"No holding out," Ben said in even tones. "You are free men at the will of an upper level Homeland Security agent. It's wise to be forthright."

"The man you spoke with? He has a son called Néall," Eoin said. "Néall is very… active."

"Does he look like John?" Alex asked.

Eoin and Cian shared another look.

"I've known Cian since primary. We grew up together but Néall… he's…."

"There's a rumor that Johnny has a different Da," Cian said. "Da was in Maze for most of the year before Johnny was born. Ma visited, but…" Cian shrugged.

John looked at Cian, then Ben. Ben did not look up from his coffee cup. Ben's lack of eye contact told John all he needed to know.

"That's why they thought I killed Da?" John asked. "That's why they beat me. They said I killed our father."

"Did you?" Cian asked.

"I don't think so," John said. "No. It's not that I didn't want to kill him. He could be…"

"Cruel. He was especially cruel to you," Cian said.

John looked over to Alex. Holding her eyes, he said, "I was capable of killing him, but… I mean, I think he was dead… I know I did not set that bomb. Alex said that intelligence believes that Da set the bomb. But bombs were also your work, Cian."

Cian nodded.

"Why would Néall blackmail John?" Alex asked.

"It's probably just Eimilie," Eoin said. "She probably tried to catch Néall but Néall couldn't give a crap. His wife would just point her toward the back of the line."

"Of lovers?" Raz asked.

Eoin nodded. "He's a busy boy."

"It's a small island," Cian said. "We all share a look. Johnny and Néall look a bit alike. Johnny is taller than all of us…"

"Combined," Eoin added

"He was always more aggressive, smarter. Ma used to say that he was the best of all of us, which is probably why he's supposed to have a different father."

Alex began clearing plates from the table. Raz took the stack of plates from her and they walked into the kitchen. Alex set to making a pot of coffee.

"What do you think?" Raz asked.

"We either kill them or invite them into our lives. With Eleazar breathing down my neck, we don't have a choice to wait and see or get to know them slowly over time. And we can't risk sending them back. They know too much." Alex shrugged. "We've done the intel. They seem to be good guys. I think we should go ahead."

"I agree," Raz said.

When Alex returned to the dining room, they were talking about Eimilie. John's face was flushed red. He looked down when she came into the room. Matthew stood, blocking Alex's access to the room, then took her hand. He shot John a disgusted look.

"Come on, let's get some coffee," he said. Before he left the room, he turned to look at John. "I told you what would happen if you fucked up."

John looked up at Matthew then looked away.

"What happened?" Alex asked.

"They were talking about John's wife. I thought they were talking about you. I was getting offended when..."

Raz came touched her shoulder then moved into the dining room.

"I just found out," she said.

"Thank God Jesse's dead. He would have killed John," Matthew said.

"Actually, he's all right about the whole thing. He thinks John's going to make it right." Alex shrugged.

Matthew crushed her in a hug. "Honey, Jesse's dead."

"Mattie, he's still here. He's the one who told me where the soldiers were. He says that you hear him in your head and even talk to him in your head, but you pretend it's not him."

Matthew startled.

"I'm sorry about all of this."

"Oh Mattie, me too," Alex said. "Every single thing I depended on is gone. I mean, what's next? Max isn't my twin?"

"I'm here now," Matthew said. "And Troy will be here as soon as he finishes up."

Alex nodded. "Thanks."

"For what?" Matthew asked pouring a cup of coffee.

"For being my friend," she said. "You know, I went from Basic training to Bosnia then Bosnia to Special Forces training. I married John, or thought I did, the day I left training. I don't really know what to do. Should I move out? Date other people? Maybe we should get re-married but..."

Raising her shoulders in a shrug, she looked away from him.

"Alex, you and John have something rare and very special."

"It was all a lie."

Shaking her head, she began to cry. Matthew swept her into his arms, catching her. After a few moments, she pushed the pain back into its tight box. She let out a breath, kissed his cheek and stepped back.

"We have to finish this," Alex said.

"What can I do?"

"You've already done it." Alex arched one eyebrow. "My sister is very hard to please."

He burst out laughing.

Alex winked at him then carried the coffee pot back into the dining room. She caught John's eyes then looked away to cover her sadness. John took her hand when she sat down next to him.

"What happens to us?" Cian asked.

"I'm glad you brought that up," Raz said. "We've spoken to your associates in Ireland. They are willing to let you move to Denver, if you would like to."

Ben tapped two pieces of paper on the table. "These are work visas. They are good for the next year. We believe that a year is a long enough time for you to sort out what you would like to do with your lives."

"And what do you want in exchange for all of this?" Cian asked.

"I'm going to need help sorting all of this out," John said.

"I'd do that anyway," Cian said.

"My brother, Max, is John's best friend," Alex said. "He has offered space in his home with a few conditions."

"You must find work. Everyone works at our house," Max said. "You must be wiling to join the family which means that you make efforts to make seven o'clock dinner and you help out around the house. "

"More than anything," Raz said. "You must be loyal to us. We are not asking that you give up your other loyalties, just that you are loyal to us."

"Who's in this family?" Eoin looked at Raz.

"Everyone in this room," Alex said.

"You mean, we get to move here, have a place to live, find work in America and join you guys?" Eoin looked at Cian and laughed.

"I haven't worked in a long time," Cian started. He shrugged then looked down.

"I always wanted to own a bakery," Eoin said.

Cian looked at Eoin's excited face. "How are you going to do that?"

"We can talk about that as well," John said.

"Everyone sitting in this room had someone step in to help them at one time or another," Max said. "We'd like to extend a little luck in your direction."

"Why don't you think about it?" Alex asked. "I hate to eat and run, but I'm supposed to meet my family at Mass in," Alex looked at her watch, "crap, forty minutes. I need to get Alyssa-ed up."

"You're welcome to join us for Mass," Max said. Wrinkling his nose, he added, "Maybe after a shower."

"We don't have any midget clothing here," John said.

"I brought their suitcases," Raz said.

"Then we're set," Alex said.

She ran up the stairs to the bathroom. Standing under the warm shower, her sadness rushed forward and tears dropped from her eyes. Her mind repeated the logic—you're married to John Drayson, not John Kelly—but her heart only felt the betrayal of his lie. When she felt the water pressure shift with someone taking a shower in the basement, she knew she needed to keep moving. Wiping her eyes, she pushed her emotions away again and stepped out of the shower.

One thing was true: Eleazar was good at his job. He was destroying the very fabric of her life.

CHAPTER THIRTEEN
Three hours later
August 19 – 11:24 A.M.
Cherry Hills Estates, Denver, Colorado

"Pumpkin, I need to speak with you," Patrick Hargreaves said.

Alex was standing on their back deck of her parents' Cherry Hills home. When her parents were in town, the family met at their home after Sunday Mass.

Today, Alex and Max were inseparable. Where one went, the other followed. John was Max's best friend, the best friend he had lied to for fourteen years. Max might have let it go, but he felt Alex's struggle in a deep visceral way. When Alex withdrew into her connection with Max, everyone was locked out of the twins' world.

Alex turned to look at her father.

"Why?" she asked.

"Ben suggested that you and I discuss something," he said, "in private."

Alex looked at Max then two alike faces turned to look at their father.

"No thanks," Max replied. They turned their backs to their father.

"Alexandra," Patrick said.

Alex turned her head toward Patrick.

"I've had a very difficult night and no sleep. I don't think I can do any more."

"You don't have a choice," Ben said. He walked to stand next to Patrick. "I'm sorry Alex, but after last night, we must clear the closet."

"What does that mean?" Max asked.

Ben looked at Max and shook his head. "Our closet."

"Why do I care about the skeletons that lie in your closet?" Alex asked.

"Because they involve you," Rebecca said. She moved across the deck to Ben and Patrick. Patrick put his arm around Rebecca and she smiled up at him.

"What? Max's not really my twin?" Alex asked. Her squinted eyes reflected her anger. "Why do we look exactly alike?"

Ben laughed at Alex. "Picked the worst thing?"

"I picked the only thing left that matters to me," Alex said. "Screw this. Come on Max. Let's go home."

"Alex, he will use the truth to destroy you again," Ben said.

"Fine, spill it, then we leave," Alex said.

"We're adopted," Max asked.

"You found us on the doorstep," Alex said.

"We're aliens," Max said.

"Worse, we're illegal aliens," Alex said. She made a face at Patrick's latest political drama.

"I was a girl," Max said.

"I was a boy."

"We don't actually exist," Max said.

"We were conjoined."

"We only have one brain," Max said.

"Hey, that's good." Alex and Max looked at each other and laughed.

"You're not going to intervene?" She looked at Patrick then Ben.

"They're pretty funny," Ben said. Switching to French, he said to Alex and Max, "Nothing pains me more than to cause you misery, especially today. After Walter Reed, you made me promise to never keep an important truth from you. There's an important truth you do not know."

"We'll do it together," Max replied in French.

"Fine," Ben replied. Turning to Rebecca and Patrick, "They are willing to listen if they do it together."

Patrick nodded. "Let's go to my office."

Alex and Max followed their parents and Ben into the house and upstairs to Patrick's home office. As they walked passed, their siblings turned to watch the glum parade. John moved to follow Alex and Max but Alex shook her head. Standing at the bottom of the stairs, he watched them until they were out of sight.

Patrick flipped on the office lights. He gestured toward the leather furniture grouped around his gas fireplace. Alex and Max pressed against each other in a leather armchair. Ben took the armchair opposite to them. Rebecca and Patrick sat together on the couch. They sat in silence.

Alex made a face, then looked at Max. The twins moved to leave.

"Please sit down," Rebecca said. "I'm sorry. I can't imagine what you think."

Alex and Max looked at each other again, then sat down. The silence continued.

"Who would like to go first?" Alex asked. Her scowl and sarcastic tone expressed her disgust.

"I'm your father," Ben said.

"Benjamin, God damn it," Rebecca said. "There are better ways to..."

Alex's fake blue eyes held Ben's brown.

"Metaphorically? Biologically? Spiritually? Intellectually?"

"Biologically," Patrick said.

"Is that all?" Max asked.

Alex and Max walked from the room. Alex heard their parents voices behind them but she didn't care. They walked down the stairs and out of the house to Max's car. John ran after them.

"We need some twin time," Max said closing his door.

"I'll wait for you at home."

Alex raised her hand to wave good-bye but when he caught her eyes, she was somewhere else. John closed his eyes and touched her dog tag around his neck. His mind filled with the horror that he had lost her forever. When he opened his eyes, Patrick was standing next to him.

"I..." Patrick started.

"You are not putting me in the middle. My allegiance is with them. Period. I'm going home."

"What did you do?" Erin screamed at her father.

"It's none of your business, Erin. Go back inside," Patrick said.

"Oh no. I let you push Alex away once before and did nothing. I'm an adult now and you will not push my sister out of my life again. I'm leaving. Come on Matt," Erin said.

Matthew raised his eyebrows. Turning into the house for their jackets, he ran into Colin.

"What's going on?" Colin asked.

"Dad pushed Alex and Max away again. They're really gone this time."

Colin shook his head.

"You never understood, did you Dad?" Colin said. "They don't need us. They never needed us. We need them. This family can't survive without them."

Turning, Colin walked into the house passing Matthew on his way out of the house with their jackets and Erin's purse. Without another word, Matthew and Erin got in the car. They followed John's car out of the driveway. Colin and Julie came out of the house.

Colin put a hand on his father's arm, "You'd better fix this." They climbed into their car and drove out of the driveway.

Samantha stood in the doorway. With a flip of her hair, she walked to her car.

Patrick turned to see Rebecca come from the house.

"Where did everyone go?" Rebecca said.

"They left with Alex and Max," Patrick said.

"I guess it's clear where the children stand," Ben said.

"They can't be serious," Rebecca said.

"You've never understood them, have you Becky?" Ben shook his head. "Colin's right. Those two don't need anyone. They never did. It wouldn't surprise me if you never heard from them again."

"What about you?" Rebecca asked.

"They'll speak with me when they are ready," Ben said.

"You lied to them as well," Patrick said.

"Only because it's what Becky wanted."

"It was for the best," Rebecca said.

"How you can say that? You've lied to them for more than thirty years. A moment ago, you had the chance to be honest, to tell your story, and you refused to speak. You broke their hearts and it's for the best?"

"Benjamin," Rebecca said. She furrowed her brow. "Please."

"You never care who you hurt, Becky, just as long as everything looks right. I wonder how much comfort you will get from everything looking right when your children don't speak to you. Those are great kids—better than you, better than me. You've been so ashamed at how they came to be that you don't even know them."

"And I suppose you do?"

"Alex was married for ten years and you had no idea, not even a clue. You know why she didn't tell you? They got married so fast it wouldn't look right to you. That's what our daughter told me two days after she married John Drayson. Mom won't think it looks right."

"Getting married in thirteen hours doesn't look right," Rebecca said.

"And not knowing about it for ten years does?" Ben asked. "God Becky, have you truly turned into the bitter old witch that your mother was?"

"Ben" Patrick gave a low warning.

"You never knew her, Patrick. That woman was evil. Becky, you used to say that she was evil. Now without hesitation, you lay the same crap on your children."

Ben and Rebecca glowered at each other.

"I'm sorry. I need to leave before I say something I regret."

He walked to his Government issue car. Patrick and Rebecca stood on their porch.

Alone.

❦❦❦
August 19

Alex and Max went to the only place they could think of—the archery range. They learned to shoot with a longbow when they were nine years old. Alex moved on to shooting handguns while Max continued with archery. He won a variety of competitions in the way Alex had won awards with her Glock 9 mm handguns.

Max drove to a members-only archery range in the foothills of the Rocky Mountains. They unpacked his long and short bow, as well as a micro-compound bow he was experimenting with, from the back of his Cherokee. Without saying a word to each other, they found a lane under the shade of a large Cottonwood tree. They took turns shooting and retrieving arrows in silence.

After all, what was there to say?

Everything they thought was true about them was false. Alex replayed in her head all the times she had said, 'It's a Hargreaves thing.' She wasn't a Hargreaves. She had no idea what a Hargreaves was or wasn't.

But hell, she wasn't married either.

Some super spy. How could she have missed it? Samantha, Colin and Erin look like each other. They look like Patrick and Rebecca. Alex and Max only look like each other.

And John?

She has more information on John Kelly than any person on the planet but she had no idea that her precious John was John Kelly. Or that John Kelly was married. She held the tidal wave of overwhelm at bay by placing another arrow in her bow and letting it fly.

"We should eat," she said. She retrieved an arrow in the deepening night.

Max packed their gear.

The streets were Sunday quiet as they drove through Morrison, Colorado. Near the edge of town, they stopped at a small local's bar. Pushing baseball caps low over their eyes, they went in one at a time to avoid the "Are you identical twins?" crap. They hid at a booth near the back. Max ordered burgers, french fries and beer. They drank their beer in silence. Neither Max nor Alex wanted to break the silence, the surface of their calm. When their burgers arrived, they looked at each other then ate them in silence.

"What do you think?" Alex asked. She pushed her fries across the table to Max.

"A lot of different things. You?"

"Me too. Plus my feelings are hurt," she said.

"Yeah."

"I'd like to say that I don't know who I am and get all dramatic. But I'm still Max's twin. That's who I am."

"And I'm Alex's twin."

"I don't know how to express how I feel."

"Me too."

"In the course of twenty-four hours, I lost my husband and my family."

"Misplaced."

"Right," Alex said. "Like I misplaced them somewhere and can't find them. I feel…"

"Ashamed," Max replied. "It's like Ben gave voice to something that's always been there. I mean Mom isn't exactly nice to you."

"Or you."

"They're also great parents. They love us and we love them."

"I love Ben too."

Max shook his head.

"What?"

"I love Ben too. He's been very kind to me over the years. I'd be in Paris… Like when I was starting as a lawyer? Ben would stop by the apartment just to say 'Hi.' He'd stay just to talk to me. I mean really talk to me, like I mattered to him. I always knew Dad loved me, but I'm not sure I mattered that much."

"It's not like there's a set of good parents and another set of bad parents. We've been lucky."

"Very lucky."

"I still want to cry my eyes out," Alex said.

"Me too."

"John's not my husband. Erin's not my little sister. Sam's not my big sister. And Col…"

"I hear you say that, 'John's not my husband', and I…" Max pressed a hand against his heart.

"Me too."

They fell silent.

"Do you want to go home?" Max asked.

Alex shook her head.

"What home?"

Max reached across the table to grasp her hands. They held each other's eyes.

"When I was in the field, I used to stay up to watch the stars after everyone was asleep. We'd be in the middle of no-where-stan and I'd imagine being at home. Home with you. Home with John. I could hardly wait to get there. I always jumped up and down on the plane wanting it to go faster so I could be home. I wished on a thousand stars that I could blink and be home. Home."

Alex stopped talking while the waitress cleared their plates and brought another round of beer.

"I had a home built with walls of lies. My parents aren't my parents. My husband isn't my husband. My siblings aren't even really my siblings."

"I'm still your twin," Max said.

"God, I hope so. Maxie, what do we do?"

"I don't know," he said.

"I don't want to see them."

"Mom and Dad?"

"Rebecca and Patrick. We should call them that now."

Max nodded.

"Patrick is going to want to talk to you. You're his favorite."

"I'm not his child," Alex said. "Why would he want to talk to me?"

"There's more to parenting than biology."

"Well, he's going to have to get in line behind my used-to-be husband."

They fell silent. The waitress came around to see if they wanted another round. Alex never looked at her. She was just a voice in the middle of the storm.

"I felt like I belonged to Dad. You know," she looked up at Max. "I was General Hargreaves's daughter. I belonged to him."

"Now we don't belong anywhere," Max said.

"Right," Alex said. "That's the best way to say it. We don't belong anywhere. Except..."

"To each other," Max finished.

Alex nodded.

"Do you want to go back to Denver?"

"I need to deal with John. What do you want to do?"

"John's my best friend, Alex." Max tried to come up with words for himself and his soft hearted twin. "I don't really care if he's from Ireland or is in the IRA or whatever. He's stood by me, and you, for a long time."

"He's a good friend," Alex said. "Yeah, I get that. In some ways, it's not a big deal. I mean, I married him and stayed married to him, right? It doesn't really matter that we aren't married officially. I'm not embarrassed or ashamed or feel some moral dilemma of sleeping with him for all these years. I love him."

"Even now?" Max asked.

"More than I can express. Yes, I love him. That's why all of this is so hard."

"It's the lie," Max said.

"It's the lie."

"I think he was ashamed of being victimized."

"Like Mattie is ashamed of being a hostage?" Alex nodded. "I get that here." She pointed to her head. "But here?" She pointed to her heart and shook her head.

"Let's go back," Max said.

"We gain nothing by postponing the inevitable," they said Patrick's favorite saying together then laughed.

"Should we turn on our phones?"

"No," Alex said. "I don't want to hear it."

They drove to Denver in silence.

CHAPTER FOURTEEN
August 20 – 2 A.M.
Denver, Colorado

Alex crept into the quiet house then stood in the entry. Max gave her one more hug for courage and left her at the front door. Switching off the entry light, she climbed the stairs. Unsure of what to do, she paused at the landing wondering if she should sleep in the guest room. When she turned, John was standing in the doorway to their bedroom. He was wearing his pajamas and his curly dark hair was sleep tousled, but his eyes scoured her with alert intensity. She took his extended hand and they stood looking at each other.

"Would you mind…" John broke the silence then stopped. "I'd like to see your real eyes."

She nodded and went into the bathroom to remove the blue contact lenses. John stood in the bathroom doorway. She turned to look at him and he smiled.

"Much better," he said.

"I…" they said at the same time.

Alex looked down at the ground.

"I'm sorry," John said. "Sorry is not really enough, I know, but I am sorry. Ben told me what happened and I… You've had an awful day."

She nodded.

"You said this thing to me, the morning after we were married. You said, 'As long as we don't feel like we've made a huge mistake, we'll figure it out as we go.' Do you feel like you've made a mistake?"

"It's the lie, John. The lie hurts… bad."

John closed his eyes against the pain he placed in her heart.

"Before you start explaining or telling me why you've lied to me for all this time, I think you should answer your own question. Do you feel like you made a mistake?"

"In marrying you? Never. In not telling you? Oh Alex, I know you don't want to hear excuses but I… I couldn't have had this conversation at twenty years old. I was so overcome by you. I wouldn't have risked it."

"I wouldn't have cared."

"Why do you care now?"

"You really don't know?" Alex asked. "Two years ago, I worked as an intelligence officer nestled in arguably the best team in Special Forces. I had this amazing marriage to this British guy. I was General Patrick Hargreaves's daughter. None of that is true today. Everyone is dead. You aren't my husband and I'm not Patrick Hargreaves' anything."

"Our relationship is still amazing. I'm still here, just the details are different."

Alex closed her eyes and sagged. She was too exhausted to explain and too heart broken to fight it out.

"I understand. I do," John said.

Alex opened her eyes to look at him.

"You feel as if every single thing that was true about you has disappeared and you're just you."

Alex felt a rush of relief for the words, the sounds that made sense out of the whirlwind of her emotions.

"I've felt that way. You probably felt like that when you entered the Army."

"Except that there was a reason and path—start here and move to there. Today? There's no reason and certainly no path. Every answer to the question 'Who am I?' has shifted. I feel stripped naked and very alone."

"But inside, you're still the same. Yes."

He took her hand and led her past the bathroom to the loveseat in the tiny room he used as his study. He pulled her onto his lap. Tucking her head under his chin, his arms held her close.

Alex felt as if they were in a small quiet bubble while chaos swirled around them. She closed her eyes drawing him in through her senses. He felt the same, smelled the same. He was the same and different.

"Misplaced," Alex said. "Max used the word misplaced."

"Yes. It's as if you misplaced your life, yourself."

"When did you feel like that?"

"When we moved to London, then again in Scotland. I spoke Ulster Gaelic. I had heard English, but never spoke it. I could read English but I hadn't been to school... probably ever. My life was all family, all the time. Suddenly, I'm in this English-language-only Catholic school in the middle of London with no Irish people around. Rita worked to support us. She was busy and bereft for herself. I was basically alone. It was like being an apple plucked from a tree filled with apples to sit amongst a bushel of peaches."

Alex's eyes watched his face. He never talked about his childhood. She wondered why she hadn't noticed.

"I did well in school because I was desperate to create some traction, some definition of myself–I'm a student; I'll be a doctor; I'll make a lot of money. I could not tolerate living in that vast unknown."

He looked into her face. "Is that how you feel?"

Alex nodded. He caressed her face.

"And yet, the phone has rung off the hook for you. Erin and Matthew waited for you until ten o'clock tonight. I guess, she had it out with your father. Raz left his date early to come home. He's asleep in the basement. Ben's rang from the airport, from the plane and from France. Colin wants me to tell you to ring him. Your father came by this evening. Your mother rang. She's very upset, by the way. Even Sam rang. And you were off shooting arrows?"

Alex nodded.

"With your twin. That's not to mention me. I've been here waiting for you to return to our home, our life and my love."

"It sounds stupid or selfish, but in some ways that makes it harder."

"Why?"

Alex closed her eyes for a moment trying to collect her thoughts.

"To use your metaphor, I guess because the peaches expect me to be an apple. I just found out that I'm not an apple, I'm an orange. I don't know how I feel about being an orange."

"I think it takes time. Do you feel like you made an awful mistake?"

"I love you more than I have breath to express."

He held her tight against his chest.

"Good answer," he said. "I rang in sick tomorrow. I also spoke with your command. Colonel Gordon would like a conversation. Otherwise, you are free for the day. I made some arrangements."

"Arrangements?"

"I scheduled a massage for you first thing, then I thought we could spend the day together in the mountains. I booked lunch at your favorite restaurant in Aspen. Maybe we can figure out what is next for us."

"What about the flock of people?"

"They'll be peachy."

Alex smiled at his joke. "You hurt Max too."

"Yes, I did," John said. "But Max has a hearing tomorrow. He'll be in court most of the day. We can get together tomorrow evening. I made reservations at Sushi Sasa for dinner."

"What about your brother?"

"My brother," John said. He laughed at the sound of the words. "He has a lot to attend to. We'll leave him with the peaches."

Alex nodded.

"Come to bed, love. You need rest."

He took her hand and led her to the bedroom. One piece at a time, he carefully removed her clothing then helped her into bed. He plucked his pajamas off, then laying face to face, he rested on his side.

Her eyes watched his face while he stroked her hair with delicate care. She ran her fingers over the curves of his familiar face. He kissed the palm of her hand then closed his eyes. She watched him fall asleep then, rolling onto her back, she released into peaceful sleep.

Some time before dawn, she opened her eyes to find John watching her. Not quite awake, she smiled and turned to her side to look at him.

"Will you marry me, Alex?"

"Of course."

CHAPTER FIFTEEN
Three weeks later
September 8 – 10:15 A.M.
Denver, Colorado

"I'm sorry to bother you. I'm looking for Alex Hargreaves," a medium sized muscular man said when Cian opened the front door.

"And who might you be?" Cian said.

It was the eight of September and everyone was on edge. Well, Cian was always on edge having not quite settled to living in Denver. He said that the altitude kept him agitated but Alex thought his agitation was just part of his personality.

"Who are you?"

"Joseph! Get in the house. Oh my God, what are you doing here?" Alex asked. "It's not safe to be here."

She pulled him into the house then held him to her. They stood in the entry way hugging until Alex wiped the tears from her eyes and stepped back.

"It's great to see you," she said taking his hand.

Captain Joseph Walter nodded, working to control his emotions, then smiled at her beaming face.

"You too," he said.

"This is John's brother, Cian Kelly," Alex said. "This is my Captain, Cian. Joseph Walter."

Joseph shook Cian's hand and Alex led him into the living room.

"So you know," Joseph said under his breath.

"I found out a couple weeks ago. How did you know?"

"Remember all that trouble you got into after marrying John?"

"I was almost kicked out of the Army," Alex said.

"John's IRA connections made for a good excuse to kick you out," Joseph said. "Ben vouched for you and Charlie…" Joseph's eyes filled and he cleared his throat. "I still can't say his name without…"

"He was your best friend for more than twenty years. It's

understandable."

Alex hugged him.

"Cian? Would you mind closing the drapes?" Alex asked.

After closing the living drapes, Cian returned to the kitchen where he and Eoin were working on possible recipes for their probable bakery. Joseph took one end of the couch and Alex sat facing him from the other end. As if he wasn't real, she scanned his face, his hands and the casual T-shirt and jeans.

"How are you?" Alex asked.

Joseph turned to look at Alex when she asked the question. Their eyes held for a moment. He nodded then looked away.

"There are a lot of answers to that question, Alexandra," he said. "Our Alex is doing well. He started the third grade a couple weeks ago."

"Wow, the third grade."

"Yeah, the time flies."

"And the girls?" Alex asked.

"Wanna see pictures?"

"You know I do," Alex said taking Joseph's wallet from him. The picture showed two adorable girls' faces under matching hats and a picture of a beaming boy in a Pop Warner uniform.

"Alex is nine years old and the twins turned two years old in June," he said looking at the picture. "Here's another. They are amazing Alex. I. . ."

Joseph looked at the picture of his three children. Glancing to Alex, he held out a beefy hand out to her. She grabbed onto his hand.

"I would have never survived this without them," he said.

"I know," Alex said. "Do you like living in Crested Butte? It's pretty remote."

Joseph reflected for a moment on his life in hiding.

"It was a hard transition. Nancy wasn't able to find a job for a while. We can make it on my pension but hanging around her grief stricken husband was pretty trying for my Nancy. When they sold the ski resort to that corporation, she was able to get a Controller job. She seems happy there. I think we both miss living in Denver." He shrugged. "We have a lovely home tucked into the side of a mountain. We ski in the winter and hike in the summer. I finally have time to work out every single day. I try to really live, every day, because I know. . ." He cleared his throat.

"Me too," Alex said.

"How are you feeling?"

"I'm not a hundred percent but getting around without a crutch is pure bliss," she said.

"I bet."

"Why are you here? It's a tremendous risk."

"I received a telephone call from the President," Joseph said.

He stopped talking when Cian came into the room with a plate of Snicker Doodle cookies and two cups of Irish Breakfast Tea.

"Would you like to try a biscuit?" Cian said. He handed Alex a cup of tea then gave the second to Joseph. "We thought they were pretty good but you can tell us."

"They are trying out recipes for a bakery," Alex said.

"A PIRA bakery?" Joseph laughed.

Cian startled. Shaking his head, Cian's eyes went wide. "We're out of all of that."

"He's kidding Cian. I guess he and our Commanding Officer knew about John."

Cian smiled. "So I don't have to pretend to be normal? I didn't want your friend to think..."

"Normal?" Alex laughed.

"Drink your tea," Cian sneered. They heard Cian telling Eoin in Irish Gaelic about their response. Eoin laughed and mocked Cian.

"Why would the President call you?" Alex asked.

"He wants to have a ceremony on the second anniversary of..."

"What?"

"Yeah. He wants me to attend. He said that I'm no longer at risk and that he would like me to come to the ceremony as the only survivor of the Fey Special Forces team."

"Huh," Alex said.

"Exactly. Nancy and I were up all night talking about it. Nancy wanted me to talk with you. You're still my intelligence officer to Nancy... and me. I didn't want to risk the telephone so I came down the mountain."

"I'm glad you did. It's wonderful to see you."

"We don't believe that I'm no longer a target. Have you heard that?"

"As far as I know, nothing has changed. We don't know why everyone was killed so we don't know if someone wants to kill you."

"Do you still get those phone calls?"

"Not for six months." Alex shook her head. "It's complicated but we believe he's coming for me... probably next month. He tried to kill Matthew, Troy, Andy, Chris and Zack in Afghanistan on March eighth."

"Your friends," Joseph said. "That's what he said he would do right? He said he would kill your friends while you watch."

Alex nodded.

Joseph was silent for a moment. "I haven't left Crested Butte in over a year."

"And the house?"

Joseph looked at Alex. "Not much. You?"

"My family forced me out just after the New Year. I've been... It's nice not to get those phone calls."

"I bet," Joseph said. "I just..." His eyes filled with tears and he stopped talking.

"Have you been to the memorial?"

"Not since the funeral," he said. "Do you think Eleazar will kill me?"

"I don't know," Alex said. "Let me do some research. At this moment, I'm not sure why the President thinks that you aren't at risk. What do you want to do?"

"I'm a patriot, Alex. My President personally asked me to do this one simple thing. How can I say no?"

"What does Nancy say?"

"Where was the President when your team was cut in two by an AK47? He wouldn't give two shits if you were dead right along with them."

"Sounds like Nancy," Alex said. "She loves you."

Joseph smiled. "I'm very lucky and so are you. How are you and John?"

Alex shrugged. "It's been an interesting couple of weeks."

"I like the ring," Joseph said. He touched the three carat round diamond surrounded by two heart shaped sapphires on Alex's left ring finger.

"My engagement ring. It turns out that this is the proper ring for a doctor's wife."

Joseph burst out laughing. "We created a monster."

"Yes, one time humble army husband turned flashy rich surgeon."

Joseph jostled Alex and she laughed.

"He wants to get married again," Alex said. "John Kelly is married to someone in Belfast. It's just..."

Laughing, Joseph shook his head.

"What?" Alex asked.

"You intelligence folks despise secrets and that's a doozie."

Alex smiled.

"Can I come to this one?" Joseph asked.

"If we get it all worked out. There's a question of a child."

Joseph knocked Alex with his shoulder.

"You can't believe that John cheated on you. You guys have that one and only true love."

"I don't really know what I believe," Alex said. "I'm just trying to follow my heart."

"I've never known your heart to lead you wrong. We wouldn't have Alex if you hadn't followed your heart in Lebanon."

Alex smiled. Joseph adopted the baby who had been at the center of a complicated hostage situation in Lebanon. Called the 'Beirut solution,' that extraction was currently used as a training exercise for Special Forces intelligence officers. So far, no one had worked out the solution.

"I heard they asked you to teach," Alex said.

Joseph nodded.

"You'd make a great teacher, Joseph."

"I'd like to do it but…"

"You'd have to leave the house," Alex said. "I've felt like that."

"Maybe when the girls are a little older." Joseph bit into a cookie. "These are pretty good. I bet the kids would love them."

"I'm certain you can bring a dozen or three home."

Joseph smiled at her.

"I was thinking about going to the memorial while I was here. Will you come with me?"

"Of course. I need to change, then we can go. We'll bring these IRA guys to guard us."

Joseph stood when Alex did. Alex ran upstairs changing into her Alyssa clothing and eyes. She heard the men laughing in the kitchen. The entire team learned Irish Gaelic as a way of communicating privately in the Middle East. She smiled to herself. She was jogging down the stairs when John came in the front door.

John caught her in his arms at the bottom of the stairs and kissed her. He swung her around then kissed her again. She giggled and hid her head in his shoulder.

"I have some news," he said.

Alex raised her eyebrows.

"DNA samples from all parties were submitted today. Ben thinks we'll have the results by the end of the month."

Alex smiled.

"Kiss me again," John said and she did.

"DNA? How did you get it from Néall?" Cian said coming down the hallway from the kitchen.

"His father," Alex said.

"And Eimilie?" Eoin asked following behind Cian.

"The police arrived at her door with a subpoena. She wasn't happy about it but what could she really say?"

"Hey Joseph," John said when he spotted Joseph behind Eoin.

"John," Joseph said.

Joseph held his hand out for John to shake. John took his hand then hugged Joseph.

"It's great to see you. Have you met Alyssa?"

"Holy crap Alex," Joseph said. Pressing a hand to his heart, he stepped back from the blue eyed Alyssa. "When you said you needed to change I had no idea."

"Sorry, I should have warned you. This is Alyssa. She's kind of a washout."

"I see that," Joseph said. "Did you actually gain weight?"

"It's padding." Alex lifted her shirt to show the body padding. "I've been so anxious that I've been losing weight again."

Joseph nodded his head. His intelligence officer's struggle with anxiety always kept her thin.

"We were going to visit the memorial," Alex said to John. "Wanna come? These guys said they would guard me today. I figured we could all go."

"Where's Max?" John asked.

"Paris. Things are starting to come apart with Fran."

"Again?" John asked

Alex shrugged. "He's taking some time to see if they can work it out. He left an hour ago with Delores."

"Delores?"

"Our next door neighbor?"

"Oh right."

"He's probably at DIA if you want to catch him."

"Let's take his car," John said. "I think we'll fit better."

"I can drive," Joseph said. "We'll fit in my Durango."

"Sounds good. Do you have your incense?" John asked.

Alex nodded.

"I brought my lighter," Joseph said.

Alex smiled at Joseph and he hugged her.

"It's really good to see you," Joseph said.

"You too."

They checked weapons. Everyone except John carried a loaded handgun. They left the house in a laughing group. John sat in the front to catch up with Joseph. Eoin brought a bag of Snicker Doodle cookies. Joseph stopped at the drive thru Starbucks for coffee. They laughed, ate cookies and drank coffee on their journey to Fort Logan Cemetery. Arriving at the cemetery, Cian and Eoin were wide-eyed at the fields of white markers.

"This is a military cemetery," Cian said.

"Yes," Alex said.

"I'd want to be buried with my brothers in arms."

Alex touched his arm.

"By the time we bury you, you'll have other brothers in arms," she said.

Cian's eyes flicked in her direction then returned to watch the green grass and white markers.

"It's just hard to imagine so many people," Cian said almost under his breath.

"I know," Alex replied.

At twelve-thirty on September eighth, Joseph pulled up to the memorial. Cian and Eoin had never been to the memorial before. While Alex took Joseph's hand, John walked with Eoin and Cian to the obelisk.

Holding hands, Alex and Joseph walked to Alexander's grave. One stone at a time, one dear friend at a time, Alex placed the incense and Joseph flicked his Zippo. They were weeping, tears seeping from guarded eyes, after Alexander's stone. As John, Cian and Eoin stayed out of the way, the two friends moved arm in arm from stone to stone. Lighting the last incense at Charles O'Brien's grave, Joseph spoke of forming the team, how they chose each person and how, risking everything, they selected a woman, Alexandra Hargreaves, for their intelligence officer.

Alex and Joseph were holding each other when, in unison, their cell phones rang. Stepping back to answer the phone, Alex's gaze shot toward John when his phone rang.

"Holy fuck Alex, where are you?" Raz screamed into the phone. "Talk to me. Alex say something."

"Raz, I'm at the Cemetery. Joseph came for a visit so we decided to see the team."

"Oh my God," Raz said.

She could hear him working to control his emotions when her phone beeped that there was an incoming call.

"Raz, I'm all right. Ben's on the other line. Do you mind if I click over?"

"No. Alex… you know I …"

"I do," she said. "I do. Just hang on for me. Okay."

Clicking over to Ben.

"Hey sperm donor, what's up?"

"Oh my God Alex. Where are you?"

"I'm at Fort Logan. Raz is on the other line."

"And Max? Alex, where's Max?"

"At DIA."

"Oh my God." She heard Ben, the super spy, weeping into the phone. "I thought…"

Alex shook her head and looked over to Joseph. His face blanched white as he spoke into the telephone. She glanced over to John. Noticing John's distress, Cian came over to stand next to his brother. John spoke in a staccato flood.

Alex's phone beeped again. Her Sergeant was on the line.

"Can you hang on?" Alex said to Ben.

"Yeah," Ben said.

She clicked over to her Sergeant.

"Fey"

"Major?!? You're alive?!?"

"Yes, can you hold on? I have Homeland on the other line."

She clicked over to Raz.

"What happened?" she asked.

"There's been an explosion. Max's car and John's car were rigged with C-4. VBIEDs. They both went off at twelve-thirty. The homes are... I'm sorry, Alex. I never expected anything like this."

"Like what?"

"Our home is destroyed."

CHAPTER SIXTEEN

Alex breath caught. The words—our home is destroyed—ripped through her. Her sanctuary, her one safe place, her home was gone forever. She siphoned out a breath.

"Our neighbors?"

"The bombs were designed to have full impact on our homes. Your neighbors have some damage but no one was home. Oh my God, Alex, where's Max?"

"He's on his way to Paris," Alex said. She looked over at John. "I think he's on the phone with John. Are you still in Atlanta?"

"Yes," Raz said. "I'll be there tonight. Alex… I… I'm just glad you're all right."

"I love you too," Alex said.

"Oh God," Raz said. She heard him sniff in the background. With a gust of wind, he blew out a breath.

"Do you want to hold or just come here?" Alex asked.

"I'm on my way," Raz said. "We'll buy another, Alexandra. We'll rebuild. At least…"

"We're alive to do it. Yes," Alex said.

"Yes. I'll call you when I get there." Raz clicked off the phone. Alex pressed a button and her Sergeant was on the phone.

"Sergeant? I just heard the news."

"Call me when you can."

"I will. Please let Colonel Gordon know that I am all right."

"Yes sir," her Sergeant said clicking off the line. Alex clicked the phone again connecting to Ben.

"Ben?"

"Claire says to tell you that you must come for a visit before you get blown up." Ben's humor helped him gain some control over his emotions.

"I need a dress for my wedding. Would she make one for me?"

"She'd be honored," Ben said. "Alexandra…"

"I'm all right," Alex said. "He fucked up."

"Yes, it looks that way, " Ben said. "Let's hope that's true. Are you armed?"

"Yes, we're driving Joseph's car. Should we return home?"

"Go home. The police are looking for you. Then…"

"We'll stay downtown tonight. Don't worry. Would you mind…?"

"Alexandra, what can I do?"

"Will you call my Dad? I haven't talked to them since… He'll be crazy and Mom…"

"I'll take care of it. Just… be safe," Ben said.

"Always," she said.

She looked down at Charlie's grave. For a moment, the world seemed to stand completely still. Her eyes traced the sunflower carved into the stone. Twelve petals, a stem, two leaves… The words, "Captain Charles O'Brien, Loving father and husband. The very best of the very best" echoed through her head. As if the world stopped moving, in that moment she felt nothing and heard only silence.

In a rush of sensation and sound, like the bomb that destroyed her home, sadness and loss overwhelmed her. In front of Charlie's grave, she fell to her knees and wept into her hands. John came behind her, pulling her from the grave, to hold her in his arms. She clutched at him, burying her head in his shoulder, her tears falling unnoticed from her eyes. She felt a hand at her back, and turned to see Cian standing behind her.

"We need to leave," Cian said. "It's not safe to stay in one location for too long."

"Was it IRA?" Alex asked. She swiped at her eyes with her hand.

"No," Cian said. "When the news goes International, you'll get confirmation of that. But it wouldn't surprise me if it looked IRA."

"Why?" John asked.

"It's additive, brother. Someone is trying to break Alex's mind."

Alex nodded. She looked over at Joseph who was still on his cell phone.

"Did you speak to Max?" she asked John.

"Yes," John said. "He was at DIA and saw the news bulletin. I told him to go to France. He should be on the plane."

"Ben will check on him," Alex said.

John nodded. "We're alive."

"For now," Alex said.

"We'll stay downtown." John pulled her back into his arms and whispered into her ear. "It will be great fun. We'll call room service, drink all of those little bottles of alcohol and I will make love to you all night, cherishing every single moment I have you alive and in my arms."

Alex closed her eyes and rested her head against his chest. Then, with a jerk, she remembered his betrayal and pushed away from him. Their eyes held for a moment. She shook her head.

"My safe place…"

"Has always been with me," John said. "And when we rebuild, we'll make a place for Raz to live, a place for our bees and a place for our love."

"The future," Alex said.

"Yes."

"Our future?" Her mind reeled with doubt.

"Of course."

Alex's eyes held John's eyes. She opened her mouth but he kissed her quiet.

"Let's see what's left of our home," John said.

Alex nodded. She held out her hand to Joseph. Taking his hand, they walked to the Durango where Cian and Eoin were under the car checking for explosives. They rose, shaking their heads, and got in the car. Without saying a word, Joseph started the car and drove through Fort Logan Cemetery.

The devastation of their homes wiped clean any memory of the silent drive. Even the chaos of news reporters, helicopters and police disappeared from memory. Alex's Homeland Security badge allowed them to walk past the police barricade to the edge of their South City Park homes. They stood, stunned, at the wreckage.

The hundred-year-old Craftsman, where Alex, John and Max lived until she was injured, was leveled. Standing at the edge of the home, they could see into the basement. One and a half stories, and eight years of their lives, lay in tiny pieces on the ground.

Next door, the hundred-year-old Denver Square, where Alex and John had created a home, was destroyed. Most likely due to the reinforcements from the secure office, part of the front wall and the sub-floor covering the basement remained. The water streaming in from the Denver Fire Department would destroy anything that remained. Two stories of love, laughter, and brick disappeared in the explosion and subsequent fire. The garage was flattened.

Looking past the house, Alex saw that the bricks and fire had destroyed all but one beehive. Frantic bees flew back and forth looking for a place to call home. At the end of the day, the surviving bees would assimilate into the remaining hive. Bees were like that.

Where would she assimilate?

She closed her eyes for a moment touching the place where Max lived inside her. At least they were alive. Opening her eyes, she saw that Homeland Security was taking over from the Denver Police. With another flash of badges, she and the men escaped to a coffee shop a block away. They sat in shocked silence while the people around them gossiped about the neighborhood bombing.

"You need to go home to your family," Alex said to Joseph. "Nancy must be crazy with worry."

"She is," Joseph said. "I... You'll let me know about the other stuff?"

"Of course," Alex said. "Go home."

"How will you get around?"

"We can take a cab," Alex said. "My Jeep was parked on the corner. We can go and get it if we need it."

"I'm sorry Alex," Joseph said standing. Alex hugged him.

"I know," Alex said. "We..."

"You'll work this out, Alex. I know you will," Joseph said. "You'll do it."

"I'd like to get through today first," she said and kissed his cheek.

Joseph nodded. John hugged him good-bye. After shaking Cian and Eoin's hand, Joseph walked out of the coffee shop.

"I wouldn't get the Jeep," Cian said. "If it was me? I would set up all three cars. I bet the CJ will go off if it's started."

"Always good to have a Volunteer around," Alex said attempting a joke.

"I turned the oven off. I'm certain of it. It wasn't me," Eoin said.

Alex and John laughed at the absurdity of Eoin's comment.

"Can you find us a place to stay John?" Alex asked.

John pulled his cell phone from his pocket. In a matter of moments, he arranged for a suite where everyone could stay. As the news of the bombing reached the airwaves, Alex fielded phone calls from her friends and siblings, while deftly avoiding her parents. Her parents told Erin that they would return to Denver by nightfall.

Two hours later, a Homeland Security team arrived to escort them to their hotel suite. When the hotel door swung shut, John and Alex were finally alone. Lifting her from standing, he made good on his promise to make love to her all night.

✧✧✧

The next morning
September 9 – 9:30 A.M.
Denver, Colorado

"Of course, you will move into our house," Rebecca said.

Rebecca Hargreaves shook the ash off the bent head of a lone giant sunflower that somehow missed the blast. Three inches smaller than Alex, Rebecca's perfect hair, makeup and clothing gave her an almost regal air, even among the broken brick, glass and wreckage of their homes.

"I'm not moving into your house," Alex said.

They were standing in the front yard of what had been Max's home. John had to work, so Alex agreed to meet the insurance adjuster. Somehow, her mother got wind that she would be alone and decided that this was the moment for them to talk. Alex made a mental note to scream at her siblings or let Max do it. She smiled at the thought of Max yelling at their siblings.

The insurance adjuster picked his way through the debris in order to take pictures of the wreckage. He had been there for two hours wandering the building with the fire inspector and the Denver Police Department explosive expert.

Alex put her hand under her mother's arm to stabilize her, "Watch out Rebecca."

"Do not call me that. You only call me that to punish me. I am your mother. God damn it. You are the most infuriating child on the planet."

"You told Max he was the most infuriating child yesterday. So which is it? Bastard number one or bastard number two?"

"Alexandra!"

"What do you want, Rebecca?" Alex asked. She stared down at her mother.

"Don't call me that," Rebecca said.

Alex dropped her head back to implore the heavens for patience.

"Why won't you move in to our home? We are in Washington until Thanksgiving. The house is large enough for you and all of your friends."

"Because I am angry with you."

"Well get over it. You and Max are being petty and childish."

"Why do you have such a hard time believing that Max and I are struggling with this? You were so ashamed of our pedigree that you didn't tell us… for thirty-two years, you didn't tell us. Finding out about our pedigree creates the same awful hole in my life as destroying my home. Don't you get that?"

"Oh," Rebecca said. She softened for the first time. She shrugged. "I guess I feel guilty."

"Well you should," Alex replied.

Rebecca stepped back as if she was bitten.

Alex shook her head. "I'm sorry, Mom. My life is falling apart. I'm not very nice right now."

Rebecca nodded.

"Erin tells me you're getting married again," Rebecca said.

"Erin talks too much."

"I would like to be involved in this wedding," Rebecca said.

"We have to dispose of the other wife and child first."

"Benjamin tells me that there is no legal record of John Kelly marrying anyone."

"They found a church record. For whatever reason, the priest didn't file the paperwork with the government."

"Benjamin also told me that the child is not John's."

Alex turned to look at her mother. She bit her tongue against the harsh words that sprung from the awful despair of seeing her home in pieces.

"You and the sperm donor talk quite a bit."

"Alexandra. My God. Do you have to be so crude?"

Alex looked out across the two lots that were their homes. Everything disintegrated in the blast. Every piece of paper—mailers, recycling, bills, books, even recipes—burned in the fire. Every photograph, token of affection, journal or memory vanished. For a hundred years these homes stood, for almost ten years they lived in one or the other of these homes, and in one instant everything was gone.

Alex looked down at the heat register in her hand. The neighbor who lived behind them, across the alley, called to say that she found a heat register in her elm tree. Alex stopped by this morning to pick it up. This ten pound cast iron heat register, and the clothing on their backs, was all they had left.

"I'd like to throw a proper wedding for you and John," Rebecca said.

Alex grit her teeth.

"You can't, Rebecca. Remember? Your son Alexander is dead. You never had a daughter named Alexandra. Fuck. Where have you been?"

"You will not swear in my presence."

Alex let out a string of curses causing her mother to laugh.

"We're standing next to the crater that was my home and you're concerned about my language? I think you should go."

"I'm not going to let you do this alone," Rebecca said.

"Then stop being such a pain in the ass," Alex said.

"It just doesn't..."

"AGGGGHHH!" Alex screamed.

She stomped away from her mother rather than hear one more time that something didn't look right. Peering over the edge of the pit that was Max's home, she noticed that his stacked washer and dryer were still there. Surrounded by pieces of bright red brick, blackened on one side by the fire, the appliances stood like white pillars in a field of black stone. That didn't look right either. She turned, feeling her mother's hand on her arm.

"I'm sorry," Rebecca said.

"I know," Alex said. "You can't help it. We've known that for a long time. It doesn't mean we like it."

"We? You and Max? Or all of your siblings?"

"We agree that there are worse things a parent can be than obsessed with how things look."

Rebecca's hazel eyes searched Alex's face. Alex was such a foreign creature to Rebecca that she had no idea if Alex was joking or serious. She saw only kindness in her daughter's face.

"Let's get out of here," Alex said.

She raised her hand to the insurance adjuster. Walking through the rubble to him, he shook his head. He would be there for a few more hours. She told him that they were going to the coffee shop a block away. He promised to call when he was done. Alex held out an elbow to her mother, which she took, and they walked toward the coffee shop.

"Where will you stay?" Rebecca asked.

"We'll stay at the hotel for a while. Did you know that if you drink all the little bottles of alcohol, they will replace them?"

"It's a good way to spend your inheritance."

Alex laughed. "The insurance company is paying for the hotel or some of the hotel." She yawned. "Sorry, I didn't get much sleep."

"I bet," Rebecca said. "Listen Alex, I know this isn't the best timing, but we have to talk about this."

"What?"

"Your parentage."

"Why?" Alex asked. "You cheated on Dad with Ben. What's left to tell?"

"Alexandra."

"Can I at least get some coffee before you lay bullshit on me?"

Rebecca smiled. Alex could be so like Patrick. Biological child or not, this daughter could pass for Patrick Hargreaves any day of the week. Alex ordered a Macchiato then made fun of Rebecca when she ordered a low fat, low foam, half-caffeinated latte. Rebecca made faces at Alex. While Rebecca paid for their drinks, Alex walked away to take a call from her Sergeant. She was off the phone by the time Rebecca walked over with the drinks. Setting the heat register next to a tattered gray armchair near the store front window, Alex sat down. Rebecca sat in a matching chair next to it.

Alex took a sip of her delicious espresso and milk foam mixture and smiled.

"I love coffee," Alex said.

"I know," Rebecca said. "May I put on your wedding?"

"How are you going to do that?"

"I told Page 6 that I am working through my grief over the loss of Alexander by throwing a large wedding for my son's college roommate. He is like a son to me, you know."

"Yeah, an Irish Volunteer son," Alex said. Rebecca laughed. "We don't have anything set because we're waiting..."

"I was able to arrange for Father Seamus and I booked the Cathedral for October twenty-second. That's your anniversary, isn't it? It's a Sunday this year. They had a cancellation in the evening. We were lucky because usually you have to schedule a year in advance for the Cathedral. Father Seamus said you were married around eleven at night, but that's too late for a formal wedding. We have the Cathedral from four to sixish. There's a Mass at six-thirty."

Alex stared at her mother. While she was angry at the nerve of her mother for scheduling her wedding without asking, she couldn't help but be impressed. Rebecca could make almost anything happen when she set her mind to it.

"I thought we could have a reception at the Denver Country Club, but I remembered how much you hate the Country Club. So I booked the Natural History Museum."

"The Museum of Nature and Science?"

"Whatever they are calling it these days. The atrium. You can see the stars under the glass ceiling. I thought you would like that."

Alex couldn't think of anything to say.

"Well say something."

"Thanks. I think."

"What are you doing about a dress?"

"Claire said she would make one for me but the timing is tight," Alex said.

"Claire makes beautiful dresses. I've noticed a few of her gowns at the President's functions. I'm sure you saw that one of her dresses was 'Best Dressed' for the Oscars."

Alex raised her eyebrows. "The Oscars? Who's Oscar?"

"I guess you missed that. I've invited them to stay with us."

"How does that work? Your boyfriend and his wife stay with you and your husband?"

Rebecca looked at her latte and took a drink to stall for time. In one quick movement, she set the drink down determined to deal with this once and for all. But when she looked into her daughter's blank face, she chickened out. Picking up her latte, she took another drink. She closed her eyes and said a silent prayer for courage. When she opened her eyes, Alex was watching her mother.

"You can be very intimidating," Rebecca said.

"That's what it means to be a Green Beret," Alex said. She looked away from her mother to collect her thoughts. Looking back, she said, "Listen, we went to the Cemetery with Joseph yesterday. We had planned to be at home. You know Cian and Eoin are working on their recipes. But Joseph came for a visit and at the last moment we decided to visit the team. That's why I'm sitting here in this shop and not blown to bits."

Rebecca nodded.

"You should go ahead and speak your mind. There's no way to know how long I'll be around. One of these days, he's going to succeed. It's just a matter of time, really."

Rebecca reached for Alex's hand and held it tight.

"I always wonder what he wants."

CHAPTER SEVENTEEN

"What do you mean? He wants me dead."

"Probably. Do you remember the first phone call?"

"Not really, why?"

"I came in the room while you were on the phone, just before he screamed at you."

"Screamed at me?"

"He yelled at you and you dropped the phone," Rebecca looked over at Alex. "I thought you knew this."

"No, I only remember him telling me that the team was dead." Alex gulped back the grief which rose with the words.

"Yes. You were upset by that but you didn't start..."

"Ripping at myself?"

"Writhing, until he told you he wanted something."

"What?"

"I don't know. Some land... no property. He wanted his property."

"Really."

"You became very agitated and ripped your stitches. Matthew and those big guys were trying to keep you still. They had to put you out."

Alex looked at her ridiculous, superficial mother with new eyes. Maybe her mother wasn't a complete idiot. Alex nodded.

"Thanks."

"For what?" Rebecca said.

"I don't remember the call. Mattie and the guys only remember how upset I was. That's really good information, Mom."

"You mean your mother isn't a complete idiot?"

"Something like that."

Rebecca laughed.

"Will you listen to me now?"

"Can we get more coffee first?" Alex raised her eyebrows showing a true addict's appreciation for her favorite drug.

Rebecca laughed. "We have to counterbalance those little bottles of alcohol."

While Alex ordered more coffee and a couple of scones, Rebecca watched the people and cars moving on the street. She collected her thoughts like beach glass from a sandy shore. When Alex gave her another latte, she realized that she needed to tell this story as much as Alex needed to hear it. Rebecca was ready to begin.

"It's a long story. Do you mind?"

"Let's see. I was in the middle of running a load of laundry. Oh that's right, my house was blown up."

"That was your house?" asked the man sitting behind them.

Alex looked at him and nodded.

"Oh my God," he started. He opened his mouth to gossip, then noticed her "get out of my face" look. Shutting his paper, he stood. Mumbling, "I'm sorry for your loss," he left the shop.

"Fucking paparazzi," Alex said.

Rebecca laughed.

"Maybe this isn't the best place to talk," Rebecca said.

"He left," Alex said. "Go ahead."

"I think the story starts with my mother. She was a person who liked everything 'just so.' If anything was out of place, she was upset. My brothers had free reign, because they were boys. But she controlled every single thing that I did. Everything: what I wore, who I was friends with, the boys I dated, where I went to school, everything. I know that you think I am controlling, but she was…

"After having children of my own, I cannot imagine the amount of energy she spent managing the details of my life. As you know, my brothers left as soon as they could and never came back. I haven't seen any of them in over thirty years. My father was like a ghost in the house, then he had the nerve to die when I was eighteen years old.

"After that Mom and I lived in this Chicago mansion. We had help. 'Servants'. That's what we called them in those days. And lots of money. I was incredibly dependant on my mother. My best friend in the whole entire world, since we were three or something, was Benjamin's youngest brother Philippe. Philippe was funny, crazy and always up for some wild adventure. He'd drag me along… Anyway, my mother thought I would marry Philippe but he… Philippe was a homosexual."

Rebecca stopped talking for a moment. She looked out the window lost in thought. Alex touched her arm and Rebecca turned back to Alex.

"He killed himself about six months after my father died. The priest wouldn't give him Last Rites because he killed himself." Rebecca fell silent again. She lifted her shoulders then dropped them. "I miss him. He would have loved you and Max, understood you in a way that I... struggle. Patrick never met him but... he arranged for Philippe to be re-buried with blessings in consecrated soil... here, in Denver, so that I can go and visit him. Your father is a wonderful person."

Alex was silent while her mother struggled for words. As she watched, a wave of emotion moved across her mother's face. Alex waited.

"I didn't really know Benjamin. He was older than Philippe and I by four, maybe five years. I knew about him, but I never really spent time with him until Philippe died. Benjamin came home from who-knows-where to attend to his parents and take care of Philippe's funeral. He's the oldest in his family and very responsible.

"Philippe was my only friend. We were inseparable, like you and Max. When he died... I had no one. Benjamin was destroyed over his brother and so was I. We dated. I should say that he took me out. I was really a girl, very naïve. He was world-traveled, very experienced and so suave with his cigarettes and French accent. He could order dinner in at least four languages. That was very sexy for a simple girl like me."

"I bet," Alex said.

"He left about six months later and I was alone trying to please my iceberg mother. He... Benjamin... reminded me last month that I used to say that my mother was evil. She *was* evil. Alexandra, she was nasty and when she wasn't nasty? She was vicious. I did every single thing to please her until I met your father... Patrick.

"I guess, well, my mother thought I would marry Benjamin," Rebecca turned to look at Alex. Rebecca smiled. "She also thought he was a lawyer."

"He's 'the lawyer from a good family' your mother wanted you to marry?"

Rebecca nodded.

Alex laughed. She knew that Ben was recruited to work for the CIA right out of college. He must have been a field agent when he dated Rebecca.

"Are you bored yet?" Rebecca asked.

"No. But the whole mandatory individualization thing makes a little more sense," Alex said.

"How? What an awful thing. Forcing you into the Army two days after you graduated from high school is the meanest thing I've ever done. You were not to have any contact with Max or the family for four years. God. I am my mother."

Alex put her hand on her mother's arm. "We survived."

"Max would not leave your room all summer. When he left for college, he wouldn't speak to me. It was like a death. Everyone grieved the loss of you. Patrick walked around the house like a zombie. But the therapist said that you had to individuate."

"He was a quack and a jerk and," Alex shook her head, "unimportant. What I'm trying to say is that you didn't want Max and me to end up like you were when Philippe died."

Rebecca's hazel eyes shifted to look into Alex's fake blue eyes. Rebecca felt a surge of relief as the wall of guilt and remorse melted in the warmth of her daughter's understanding.

"I've never thought of that. Maybe. I was trying to do what I thought was best of you. But it wasn't best for me or anyone in the family. And you were gone for almost thirteen years. You were married for ten of those years and I had no idea. You're only sitting here because you were injured."

"What does this have to do with you cheating on Patrick and getting sperminated by Ben?"

"You are so crude!" Rebecca's hazel eyes were wide with shock. "I sent you to finishing school so you would not be so crude."

"Talk about a waste of the old inheritance."

"You know the story of Patrick and I?" Rebecca asked.

"You were walking down the stairs of your mother's home and saw him standing in the dining room. He attended a charity function at your mother's house in place of his General. His baby blues caught your eyes and it was love at first sight. You were married three days later."

"I was dating Benjamin at the time. My mother was planning on marrying me off to Benjamin within the year. I just… I'd never been with a man. I'd never slept even a night away from the house. I did every single thing my mother wanted me to do. Until I saw Patrick. And that was that. She… Would you mind if we walked for a while?"

"Let's go to the park."

Alex picked up her heat register. They walked a couple blocks down Colfax Avenue to avoid the hole that replaced Alex's home. Turning down a side street, they walked toward the park.

The day was warm and they walked in silence, each caught up in her own thoughts. Alex smiled remembering John the night before. He was amazing. He drank champagne around the diamond in her belly button, fed her chocolate strawberries and rubbed her feet. He touched, bit, pulled at, pressed on and loved every piece of her flesh as if he was an explorer on a new continent. Alex shivered remembering his touch.

"This is such a beautiful park," Rebecca said. They walked across Seventeenth Street to enter City Park, Denver's three hundred acre park in the middle of the city.

"We've talked about getting a dog but…" Alex sighed. "I guess it depends on where we end up living."

"Will you rebuild?"

"I..." Alex shrugged her shoulders and shook her head. "We don't know. Max is in Paris. We'll decide when he gets back."

They walked along the flagstone path. In the shade of the tall trees, they passed large grass soccer fields where children were playing soccer. While Alex's eyes watched the laughing children, her thoughts returned to the brick and mortar hole that was her home, her life.

"My mother disowned me," Rebecca said.

Alex was so lost in her own world that she startled when Rebecca spoke.

"Sorry, I didn't mean to startle you."

"It's all right. Please go on."

"She didn't approve of Patrick. He was too old for me or so she said. I think she was angry that she didn't hand pick him. And she was furious. I'd never seen her that angry. She threw us out of her house. I thought she would come around but... I guess she was so angry that she had a small stroke. I heard through my grandmother that she wasn't doing well. But I didn't really care. I was angry too... and distracted. Patrick and I lived in this bubble of love. We were completely obsessed with each other. When Patrick was promoted, we moved to North Carolina. We had this tiny house. I'd never cooked a meal or cleaned a toilet. Patrick taught me how to do everything. We..."

Rebecca smiled softly remembering.

"I got pregnant right away which was probably a mistake. I see how much fun you and John have without children and wonder what it would have been like. But I do love babies. Anyway, you've heard me gush over babies before."

"I have," Alex said. She touched her mother's arm and they turned onto a path through the deep shade cast by a grove of trees.

"A couple hours after Sam was born, I called my aunt, hoping she would tell mother about Sam and everything would be all right. My aunt told me that mother was dying. Cancer. She only had a few months to live and she did not want to see me or Sam.

"I... just lost it." Rebecca looked over at Alex. Alex's face was blank as she listened intently to what her mother was saying. Rebecca continued her story.

"Your father thought that I was complete now that I had the baby. He kind of retreated into work to give me space to enjoy the baby. He'll tell you that we were inseparable and so happy. And we were deliciously happy. Sam is a beautiful woman. She was a gorgeous baby. I would sit and watch her for hours. Mother died when Samantha was seven months old... to the day. Then bit-by-bit, piece-by-piece, everything fell apart for me. Was it like that for you? Your depression?"

"No. It's like walking into a fog or under a waterfall. We can talk about it later. What happened?"

"They call it post-partum depression these days. I left the house one day to go to the grocery store. Sam was napping. The next door neighbor also had a little girl and she agreed to watch Sam while I did both of our grocery shopping. I came to myself outside of West Virginia. I was driving home."

"Wow," Alex said. She couldn't remember a time that her mother had done anything irresponsible or, for that matter, on the spur of the moment. "You must have been crazy."

"Thank you for that," Rebecca said. "I was crazy… and very young. I was twenty-four years old going on twelve years old. I stopped at a gas station and called your father. He begged me to return but I had to go home. I just had to do it.

"I stayed with my grandmother. She was kind but had no idea what to do with me. I spent every day at my mother's home, the home I grew up in, going through my mother's things. My brothers appeared for the lawyer's appointment then disappeared as soon as they learned that mother had no money in her own right. Everything reverted to grandmother."

"That must have been a shock," Alex said wryly. Unbeknownst to Rebecca, Alex had first-hand experience with her scumbag uncles.

"They were furious. My grandfather had given mother the house as a wedding present. So she owned the house. My brothers wanted to throw mother's things in the trash and sell the house. I couldn't do it. I had to go through everything. I was under constant pressure from my brothers and…"

Rebecca fell silent.

"And?"

"I was very depressed. I ached for Patrick and Sam… but I couldn't make myself go back. It's funny too. Patrick would never let me do something like that alone now. No matter what was going on in his work or the world, he would insist on helping. When my grandmother died, then left us all that money, he was by my side every step of the way. He dealt with my brothers, the lawyers, the probate, the trusts, everything. But when my mother died? He didn't know to insist and I didn't know I could even ask for his help. We had no idea how to have a relationship then."

They stopped at the edge of a large grass field to watch a man play with his Border Collie. The man threw a Frisbee and the dog would wait until the Frisbee had almost landed before he took off to catch it. Then, proud of his catch, the black and white dog raced back to his owner. Alex touched Rebecca's arm and they continued walking.

"Please go on," Alex said.

"My grandmother arranged a little dinner party for my twenty-fifth birthday," Rebecca sighed. "Benjamin was there. I didn't make it through dinner. When I started crying at the dinner table, he offered to take me out. It was the first time I'd been out in the world in almost two years.

"Charming, sophisticated Benjamin and I went out on the town. We laughed, listened to music, and drank. I felt like I was eighteen again—my father was still alive, Philippe was by my side and my whole life was in front of me. I was certain, utterly certain that Patrick was with...well, any number of woman who hung on him all the time. He wasn't."

"Of course."

"Benjamin and I... we had a wonderful, absolutely wonderful time. It was one of those nights, I'm sure you've had them, where the stars line up and every single thing is memorable. The food was wonderful. The wine was superb. We saw, if you can believe it, Miles Davis in this tiny jazz bar." Rebecca smiled. "I've never had a night like it—before or since. Certainly there are moments in time that stand out, but there was something about that night that was special, star struck almost. He took me back to his apartment. We hadn't intended to... but one thing led to another. I mean, it was the seventies and everyone was sleeping with everyone."

Rebecca smiled at the wry look on Alex's face.

"I guess that's an excuse. The truth is that it was all wrong—for me and for him. I think we noticed how wrong it was because everything else that night was so perfect. I ached for Patrick and he wasn't Patrick. He wanted... well, probably Claire. Of course, she was six years old or something then. Anyway, we were good enough friends that it wasn't weird and like I said, it was free love everywhere. We got dressed and he took me to another bar where we saw another amazing jazz act." Rebecca smiled. "We saw another trumpet player. Benjamin loves trumpet players. He became really famous, uh, Marsalis? Something like that."

"You saw Wynton Marsalis?"

"He was just a kid," Rebecca nodded. "See what I mean? It was a very special night. We stayed out all night going from one club to the next. And the sex in the middle? If I wasn't married? If I didn't get pregnant? Nothing against Ben, but I don't know that I would have remembered it."

Rebecca stopped walking to look at her daughter. She smiled. Of course it was a special night. It was the night that brought her Alex and Max, her male-female identical twins. Alex smiled at Rebecca.

"The very next day, I put mother's house on the market and went home," Rebecca said. "I was probably gone... I don't know three weeks, maybe a month total."

Rebecca fell silent as they walked. Turning the corner, they walked along the Park Hill Golf Course. The shade was deepening as the short Fall day retreated into afternoon.

"That sounds very hard," Alex said.

"Going home? It was hard," Rebecca continued. "Patrick wasn't as mad as he was heart broken. He'd never loved anyone before me, and I broke his heart. We talked about getting a divorce and slept in separate bedrooms. Then I realized I was pregnant. He was furious, absolutely furious. He felt trapped by the baby. He'd never leave me while I was pregnant, but he did not want to be with me or my ill begotten child. Then the baby was twins— you and Max. Well, we expected boys. But you know that.

"I went into labor after a little more than seven months. He took me to the hospital then went back to work. He was mad and I deserved it. When they called him to tell him you were born, he felt obligated to see you... you know, to put on the show." Rebecca chuckled a little and shook her head. "He took one look at you guys and that was that. You'll have to ask him about it.

"We've told you this part. The hospital separated you. You would not eat or sleep. You just cried. After three days, Max began to fail... probably that hole in his heart they found when he was five years old. We didn't expect him to last the night. I was absolutely hysterical. I'd lost my husband and now was losing my babies. They sedated me."

Rebecca pressed her hand to her heart where the intense feelings still lingered.

"You were lying on Patrick's lap. You opened your eyes and growled at him. Growled! You made this gesture with your hand. I've seen you make the same gesture when you're coming out of anesthesia. You reached for him, for Max. Patrick says that he heard you say, clear as day, 'I want Max.'"

Rebecca smiled.

"You and your father shared this connection from the very start of your life."

Alex smiled, not sure of what to say. How could they share a connection when they weren't flesh and blood?

"Anyway, he jumped up, putting you on his shoulder, and started arguing with the nurse then the doctor then the hospital administrator. They were firm. You might fail like Max was failing. When they left the room, he put you in the incubator with Max.

"You were tiny...a little more than five pounds... and you reached for him. Max knew you were there the moment you were together. He opened his eyes, the first time he had, and took your hand. You made that face that you make when you greet each other and suddenly he was better. He was hungry! You were hungry! Patrick made the nurse bring me back to the nursery. I held you and Patrick held Max. You both ate, a little bit, then slept wrapped up in each other.

"I don't know what happened or how it happened but we started talking while you slept. For the first time in our relationship, we just talked. You would wake up, eat, then sleep and we talked... for weeks. Months really. Sami never left our side so we played and laughed with her. And we talked.

"I had loved Patrick," Rebecca paused trying to put the experience into words, "but I didn't know him very well. In those days and weeks, I learned a lot about him and loved him even more. Ben came to see the babies, you and Max. He and Patrick stayed up talking three or four nights in a row. They weren't best friends before that but somehow you guys brought everyone together. It was a miracle.

"So that's it. That's the story of how Ben is your father and Patrick is your father."

"Thank you for telling me."

"You'll tell Max."

Alex nodded.

They cut across the grass to the rose garden near the Museum of Nature and Science. Alex stopped to smell one red rose then touch a pink flower. She moved to a sunflower bush covered with yellow blossoms. Alex laughed, reaching over her head to touch the flowers that grew at least six feet off the ground.

Rebecca watched her daughter mourning the loss of her own roses and sunflowers that once lived in her own yard outside her safe home.

"It's going to be all right," Rebecca said.

Alex's head jerked to her mother. Her hand closed over a dark red blossom while she hid her leaking eyes behind the hand holding the cast iron heat register.

CHAPTER EIGHTEEN
Five hours later
September 9 – 5:13 P.M.
Denver, Colorado

"I'm not going to call you Papa," Alex said answering her cell phone. She was standing at the window of their hotel room with the door open to the suite sitting room.

"I'd be a little offended if you did. It would be nice to not be the sperm donor anymore."

"I'll think about it," Alex said disagreeably. "Why didn't you use protection?"

"Because I planned on marrying your mother. I thought..." Ben blew out a breath. "It was my last chance at a normal life. She was gracious enough to want to be with Patrick instead of me. She saved us both from a real mess."

"Hmm," Alex said.

"Property?"

"Yes, let's move on," she said.

"There's nothing in any of the transcripts about a land or property of any kind. Raz ran one of his programs and came up with nothing. You don't remember the call."

"I remember Eleazar telling me that everyone was dead. I have this vague impression that he screamed at me." She shook her head and rubbed her eyes.

"Focus on the vague impression."

She sighed.

"Ok... The feeling is that he knew I tricked him."

"Tricked him?'

"I mean, I wasn't surprised that he wanted this thing or that he was angry. And at the same time..."

"What?"

"I felt like I lost something important. Not lost, I put something somewhere but I couldn't remember where."

"What do you mean?"

"I don't know what I mean. I was distraught, bleeding, in tremendous pain and he was yelling at me. I'm not very good when people yell."

"Let's back up. Is it some *thing* or something."

"Thing. Some object."

"This property exists."

"But I don't have it. Yes, that's right."

"I wonder what it is," Ben said.

"Who knows? Listen, this bombing is the first time he actually tried to kill me," Alex said. "I spoke with the IRA. It has all the hallmarks of an IRA bombing but they swear they weren't involved."

"I've never known them to not take credit for something."

"They are credit hounds," Alex said.

"Go through it for me. Start at the beginning of the day."

"We got up about five o'clock. Max and I took my jeep to the gym where we met Erin. John went to the hospital for rounds and was due home before noon. Max was at the house answering email in John's office when he got a phone call from Fran."

"When was that?"

"Eight? Maybe eight-thirty."

"Okay, go on."

"Fran, as you know, is a complete freak. She was very upset."

"They've been on the verge of break up for..."

"A year at least. Anyway, Max thought he should be there, in Paris, with her, in case this was the end. I was at home hanging out with Cian and Eoin so I told him to go."

"He bought the plane ticket at the airport," Ben said confirming what he knew.

"Yes. He took a cab... no that's not true. He was going to take a cab but found out our next door neighbor, Delores was on her way to the airport. He went with her."

"Delores Mendes, the bartender?"

"Yes. She subleases the house from a girlfriend who is living with her boyfriend. I don't think there's even a paper lease. The girls are just friends. Raz checked her out when she moved in. She seems clean."

"There's no way anyone could have known that Max was gone."

"Or who he went with. Right. We planned to make cookies and hang out. John's been teaching Cian how to play this video game. I was going to check the bees."

"Did John drive his car to the hospital?"

"Yes. And I took mine to the gym. Cian says that it takes at least a fifteen minutes to set up a bomb like that."

"Per car?"

"Yes, per car and that's assuming you are good at it."

"So we have to assume that the cars were rigged the previous night."

"Right. The demo team says that they were on a timer but also..."

"Your cars should have gone off when you were driving them."

"Yeah," Alex said. "The VBIEDs had mercury tilt switches. Standard IRA issue. The Jeep was set up the same way. The Denver Police demo team sent the entire thing to Homeland. Maybe they'll find something. Denver PD said the VBIEDs might have been timer sensitive but no one has seen or heard of a timer sensitive mercury tilt switch. I have a call into my Navy SEAL friend Vince Hutchins. He's a munitions expert."

"The guy who shared your room at Walter Reed?"

"Yeah," she said.

"So far, we've worked on the assumption that Eleazar is trying to mentally wear you down."

"Cian suggested that the IRA style bombing was to add to the IRA news of the last couple weeks."

"Maybe... also takes away your home. It's one of the few things left on the 'what's important to Alex' list."

"Friends, husband, home..."

"He doesn't know that you know about your parentage."

"Family."

"We must assume he's going to go after Max."

"Right. But he tried to kill all of us—John, me, Max, Cian and Eoin."

"It's pretty dumb for someone to go after the three native IRA... huh..."

"What?" she asked.

"The IRA would respond immediately, and in-kind, to anyone who killed three of their own. Cease fire or no, the Irish Republican Army takes care of its own."

"Maybe he thinks he's doing them a favor, misinterpreting their interest in John Kelly as a desire to kill him. Cian and Eoin had a 'talk or a hit' contract."

"I hadn't thought of that. Maybe. Why did you leave the house?" Ben asked.

"Joseph hadn't been to the memorial since the ceremony. We decided to go on the spur of the moment."

"Why did he come down?"

"He received a call from the President. He decided to come down after talking to Nancy all night. There's no way anyone could have known that. Number one, Joseph has been in hiding. I might be wrong, but I haven't heard even a murmur that Joseph has been located. He's underground. Number two, no one knows what this President will or won't do. Plus Joseph said that he decided to come down about an hour before he left the house."

"He didn't call before hand?"

"No, he just came down," Alex said.

"When did he get there?"

"About ten, ten fifteen."

"And it's a four hour drive?"

"Little more that that," Alex said. "Do you think the bombs were planted while he was on the road?"

"Who knows? How did he know you would be at home?"

"He didn't. He said that if I wasn't here, he would spend the day in Denver shopping. Joseph never trusted the telephones, radios, computers, or any transmission really. He felt that they were too easily monitored. He used to say that secure lines are always monitored by the people who secure them. It's why we traveled so much."

"Odd that the President would call on the seventh of the month," Ben said.

"It's a month before his big event. He wanted to land Joseph in his corner."

"Raz is there, right?" Ben asked.

"He's in Denver. Denver PD says that we can go into the secure office this evening. We've rented a truck and lined up a platoon of soldiers. We're going to get everything tonight."

"Before we ring off," Ben said, "I want you to know that I've never regretted that night with your mother. She probably told you that we weren't great. We were awkward at best. But that night was truly one of the best nights of my life. Every single thing was perfect, well except…"

"She said that you knew it wasn't right because the night was so magical."

"We had male-female identical twins, Alexandra. It's very rare and completely wonderful. I'm so glad, so blessed, to know you and Max."

"We feel the same about you, Ben."

She heard him let out a breath.

"Thanks. That means a lot to me. You'll be careful?"

"Of course."

"Philippe used to call me 'Benji'. Just a thought."

"I'll talk to Max."

Ben hung up the phone.

She dropped into a chair near a window looking out over the Rocky Mountains. The suite was large and comfortable but it wasn't home. With a sigh, she checked to see if housekeeping had replaced the bottles of alcohol. She was squatting in front of the tiny refrigerator when John came in the door. Holding a bouquet of two dozen white roses and another bottle of Cristal champagne, his eyes flashed with desire.

Chuckling, she stood to greet him.

ᕤᕤᕤ

Two hours later
September 9 – 7:46 P.M.
Denver, Colorado

"And who the fuck are you?" Troy Olivas asked the young sandy haired soldier.

"Sergeant Lawrence Flagg, sir," the boy said.

"And why do I want to talk to you?" Troy asked.

Troy and the Sergeant were standing in what was left of the basement of Alex and John's house. Up to his knees in black water, Troy blocked the young man's entrance to the secure office.

"I'm a Green Beret, sir."

"Good for you," Troy said.

Sticking his head in the door where Alex and Raz were packing the electronic gear into boxes, Troy said: "Some kid wants to talk to the Fey."

Alex gave Troy a pained look.

"He has a familiar name. What's your name again?"

"Lawrence Flagg, sir."

"You mean the commander of the GI Joe team is standing out there with you?" Raz asked. "Well by all means send him in."

"Hey that's right. He was killed by…"

"Major Bludd," Raz said. He and Troy laughed.

"You really want him in here?"

"No," Raz said.

"Troy, can you do me a huge favor?" Alex asked.

"Besides standing in disgusting dendrites?"

"Ooh big words make me hot," Alex said.

Troy blushed and looked down. "What?"

Alex reached into the gun locker and pulled out a rifle wrapped in a blanket.

"Will you give this to my brother Colin? Only Colin."

"A Winchester Repeater Rifle? Holy crap Alex. Where did you get this?" Troy ratcheted the metal lever.

"It's a Henry and it's…"

"This is an original Henry .44 caliber repeating rifle?!?"

Troy spoke in reverential tones. Looking up from the box he was packing, Raz laughed at Troy.

"Do you know what this is?" Troy asked Raz.

"Manufactured by the New Haven Arms company, the Henry was designed by Benjamin Tyler Henry in the late 1850s," said the young man standing behind Troy. "Does it work?"

"Who cares?" Troy asked.

Alex covered the rifle with the blanket.

"The Henry works and belongs to the General," Alex said.

"Can I use it?" Troy asked

"Ask the General."

Carrying the rifle in front of him, Troy ran up the stairs. The young man stood in the doorway of the secure office.

"Sir, Sergeant Lawrence Flagg, sir," the young man saluted.

Alex looked up from the box she was packing. Looking at the young man's sandy hair and his blue eyes, she furrowed her brow.

"At ease, Sergeant. Do I know you?"

"He looks just like Howdy Doody," Raz said.

"You broke my leg, sir."

Raz looked up at Alex and laughed. "How did you break his leg?"

"In the sim, remember?" Alex bumped Raz's arm.

"Ah, yes, the simulation in which I was wrong, wrong, wrong."

Alex laughed.

"Sergeant, this is Homeland Security Agent Arthur Rasmussen."

"Really? You're Art Rasmussen?"

"I am," Raz said. "Why?"

"You're the best profiler in the business. I'm an intelligence officer. Even the Fey, I mean, ma'am…"

Alex looked at Larry then Raz and laughed.

"You have a fan," Alex said.

"Where's the Jakker?"

"With his children," Alex said. "He's on Daddy duty all September. He was supposed to bring pizza about ten minutes ago."

"I'll get to meet the Jakker?"

"If you're lucky," Alex said.

"I…" The Sergeant swallowed. "Wow."

"Sergeant. We are standing in what used to be my home. We need to finish this task and get out of here before the rest of the building comes down. I don't mean to be rude, but what do you want?"

"Well, I want to help."

"Great," Alex said. "Can you take this chair and give it to my husband? Do you know who that is?'

Larry nodded his head.

"I realize it doesn't seem important, but I've owned this chair for a long time. My husband will probably cry when he sees it. Please take very good care of it."

Alex handed Larry the overstuffed green chair which somehow managed to miss the water, fire, and blast. Her thumb ran over the green fabric as Larry took hold of the chair.

"Special care."

"Yes, Major."

With serious intent marked on his face, Sergeant Flagg carried the chair up the seven remaining stairs and into the night. They heard Max call for John then John scream when he saw the chair. Alex smiled and looked toward the sound just as her Sergeant came running down the stairs.

"Sir, the Denver Police are saying that we need to finish up. The engineer says that the building is beginning to shift. The ground continues to be unstable. He thinks it's only a matter of minutes before the rest of the building collapses."

Alex nodded.

"What can I do?"

"Will you pack the gun locker? There isn't space in here but you can get a couple soldiers to carry them upstairs. Please inventory the weapons and then lock them tight. The locker holds most of my family's weapons. We don't want to lose anything."

"Yes sir," the Sergeant said. "Sir, Captain Jakkman is here with pizza, a keg of beer and three kids. The men are wondering if you might authorize…"

"Of course," Alex said. "Can you ask one of the soldiers to watch the kids?"

"Sir, Captain Jakkman has already done that."

"Great. Thank you. Would you mind…" Alex saw Zack walking down the stairs. "Never mind."

"Oh Alex," Zack said.

He walked into the secure office and hugged Alex.

"I'm so sorry."

"Me too," Alex said.

"What can I do?"

"We're almost done, actually. I was wondering if you might keep a couple things for me."

"Of course," he said.

Alex reached into a cubby and pulled out twenty folded maps and a small wooden backed rubber stamp. She held the stack out to Zack. Their eyes held for a moment. Alex gave him the last remaining original Fey maps and the Fey rubber stamp.

"Would you mind locking these in the car then get Max and John to help move the armoire?"

Zack leaned forward and kissed her cheek.

"Thank you for trusting me."

She nodded.

"Hey Alex," Max called from the landing of the stairs. He moved aside so Zack could get by. "Maria is here."

"Can you bring her down?"

Alex stepped aside as a soldier came to remove the weapons from the weapon safe. He picked up five handguns and walked up the stairs. Another soldier picked up two rifles in each hand and went up the stairs.

Maria and Max pushed past the soldiers. Maria Abreu's eyes were luminous at the wreckage. She held Max's elbow as he helped her with the stairs. Seeing Alex, Maria ran down the stairs. Max raised a hand to Alex then returned to packing the truck.

Speaking in a flood of Spanish, Maria clutched Alex to her. Hearing Jesse Jr. scream, they turned to see him chase Zack's oldest son, Teddy, in a game of freeze tag. The boys screamed and laughed at the same time.

"I need a huge favor," Alex said in Spanish.

"Anything," Maria said continuing in Spanish.

"Jesse told me that you have a special secret place where you keep important things."

Alex pulled the address book from her back pocket. Her eyes held Raz's for a moment then she turned back to Maria.

"Would you put this in that place?"

"Of course," Maria said. "I will keep it until you ask for it. Does this put us at risk?"

"No one knows that this book exists except for Mr. Rasmussen here."

Maria looked over at Raz. He winked at her.

"He's very cute. Can he be trusted, Alexandra?"

Alex turned to look at him. Raz opened his mouth to say something then laughed.

"I hope so," Alex replied.

"I will take care of this for you."

Alex hugged Maria and kissed her cheek.

"We need to talk about the President's circus next month," Maria said. "I would invite you to lunch but my boss is in town."

Alex laughed. Out of kindness, when Jesse died, Patrick gave Maria a receptionist position in his office. Within six months, she had reorganized his office and his life. Patrick called her his 'life manager', swearing he could not survive without her.

"I have an in with the boss man," Alex said.

"Let's have lunch then," Maria said.

Alex walked Maria up the stairs. Standing in the night air, Alex's eyes followed the activity: the children chased each other in delight; a group of five or six soldiers drank beer and laughed; a soldier moved past her to remove the last of the weapons; John, sitting in the green overstuffed chair, laughed at Zack; Troy and Colin argued over the Henry rifle; Matthew tried to make space for the last of the boxes and the armoire inside the truck; and this woman, Jesse's soul mate, stood beside her.

"This is crazier than that New Year's Day party you have," Maria said.

"Had."

Maria laughed. "I don't believe for one minute that you won't have that crazy party this year." She kissed Alex's cheek. "I'm going to take care of this."

"Thanks Maria."

Alex watched Maria thread her way through the chaos and call to Jesse Jr. and Gabriella. The children ran to their mother. Pleading and begging, Jesse Jr. and Gabriella worked on Maria until she relented. All five children cheered. After a quick conversation with Zack, the children scooted into Maria's car. They waved to Alex when they drove by.

Alex jogged back to the office to find Raz closing the last box. He gave the box to the soldier checking to make sure the gun locker was empty. Zack, Max and John came to get the armoire. With care, the four men carried the oak furniture to the truck.

Alex stood in the office by herself. She touched one spot then the next. She looked in the map cubby holes. She touched the broken gas fireplace. Closing the empty weapon vault, she removed the antique map that hung over its opening. She bent down to pick up a shred of paper which she crumpled and stuffed into her pocket.

"Sir, the engineer says that the building is coming down. NOW. You need to get out of here."

Alex turned to her Sergeant. She gave a slight nod. Looking at the walls that had been her sanctuary for almost two years, she didn't notice John when he entered the space. He touched her shoulder, then pulled her to him. They held each other in the crumbling office.

"Sir, that crack wasn't there a minute ago," her Sergeant said.

"Yes," Alex said. "We'll follow you."

The Sergeant ran up the stairs with Alex and John close on his heels.

They reached the last step when the basement fell into itself. The Sergeant jumped forward to avoid being pulled into the basement. Alex threw the antique map onto the grass and lunged for solid ground. John and Alex slid backward into the basement. Soldiers grabbed at their arms and legs to keep them on solid ground.

With a deafening noise, the earth swallowed what was left of the house.

CHAPTER NINETEEN

A week later
September 16 – 8 A.M.
Denver, Colorado

"I call to order the meeting of JAM properties," Max said.

"Do you have to say that every time?" Alex whined.

Max laughed at Alex's distress. They sat together in a chair in the hotel suite's sitting area. John looked up from a stack of papers to watch the twins make faces at each other. He sat in the middle of the couch.

"Let the notes reflect that we have guests. Cian Kelly and Eoin Mac Kinney are here to discuss a project," Max said.

"Who keeps these notes?" Alex asked.

"We tape the meetings, love. We have for the last three years," John said. He had to work to keep the exasperation from this voice. Alex attended their monthly financial meetings but never paid attention.

"He's not a guest then?" Cian asked. He pointed to Raz, who sat down in a chair across from John.

"He's a member of the corporation," John said. "He joined a couple years ago."

"There's no 'R'," Eoin said. "John, Alex and Max, I get that."

"They call him Art," Cian said to Eoin. "Do you share our Alex's 'A'?"

"Something like that," Raz said.

"Ew, Rasmussen is not his real name," Eoin said.

He and Cian shared a look.

"What was that?" John asked.

"We're just with the big boys…" Cian started.

"…and girl…" Eoin added

"Now," Cian finished. "Cloak and dagger."

"Spooks."

Alex furrowed her brow at Cian and Eoin, then laughed.

"Are you going to pay attention this time?" John asked Alex.

She nodded setting her eyes to her most sincere look. Raz and Max handed John five dollar bills.

"Betting?" Alex asked. She gauged her voice for offended rather than amused.

"It would be a first, love," John said.

Alex rolled her eyes at the men.

"Will you two sit down?" John asked.

"We're a bit nervous, Johnny," Cian said. "Do you want to try our cookies now?"

"Sure," John said.

"You said, Johnny, that if we came up with five recipes we could talk about a bakery. We have ten different kinds of cookies here."

"We made them at an industrial bakery," Eoin said. "No explosions. Very safe. Very sanitary."

"I made some special coffee for my favorite sister-in-law," Cian said. "We think that coffee and pastries in the morning could be a good thing for us. Lots of people around the building in the mornings... Foot traffic it's called."

Alex smacked her lips like a child when Eoin handed her a cup of coffee. Alex took away the cup Eoin gave to Max.

"You can't have coffee," Alex said. "It's hard on your heart."

"You put your God damn finger in my heart so you could drink all the coffee." Max laughed.

When the surgeon came to talk to the family after Max's heart surgery, he told Patrick that the hole in Max's heart was the size of a small child's finger. Of course, the entire family assumed that it was Alex's finger made the hole in Max's heart.

"Give me that." Max snatched the cup back from her.

Alex lifted her index finger and pointed it devilishly at his chest. Max put a hand on his chest to protect his heart.

"How long does this go on?" Eoin asked under his breath to John.

John looked from Alex to Max.

"A lifetime, if I'm lucky," John replied. "Alex. Max. Our Irish friends would like you to settle down."

Alex and Max, with matching looks on their faces, turned to Cian and Eoin and stuck their tongues out at them. Raz started laughing so hard that he had to stand up to keep from choking.

"You better give us your proposal," John said laughing.

"We'd like to open a bakery in Denver," Eoin said. "We..." He looked at Cian then stopped talking. "I..."

"We need some financial help getting started. We also don't know how to..."

"We need help with the forms," Eoin said. "We got confused and fucked them up."

"The truth is that we don't know anything, but we'll work hard and we can learn." Cian's face blushed bright red and he looked away.

John's cobalt eyes searched Cian's face then Eoin's face.

"We have already decided to help you," John said. "Raz?"

"I completed the start of business forms," he said. He handed Eoin a couple of forms then sat down in his chair. "When you pick a name for the bakery, we'll file for trademark and create the corporation."

"The point is this," Max said. "If you are willing to do the work, we are willing to invest in your bakery, teach you how to run it and, when or if the time is right, sell it back to you."

Cian's mouth fell open. He looked at Eoin and the men shared an awkward hug.

"I've reviewed the property you selected. It has an apartment over the store front. Who will live there?" John asked.

"Eoin," Cian said. "I like being with family. If it's all right, that is."

"Of course," Max and Alex said in unison.

"Eoin's already... well..."

"I'm going to find myself a wife," Eoin said. "A bakery and a wife. That's my dream. Well, kids too."

Alex took in his bright face, bright red hair and sparkling eyes. She laughed and everyone followed.

"I put an offer in on the building," John said. "We are waiting to hear from the owner. I believe, with the renovations, the space will be ready before the end of the year. Will you be ready?"

"Yes, Johnny," Cian said. His smile seemed to emanate from the very center of his being.

"We'll meet every week—you and me—to take care of paperwork and financing. My schedule is tight but I'll make time," John said. "You'll also need to meet with Max to learn about employment laws. I set an appointment with the Small Business Administration for you and I tomorrow."

"Yes, Johnny," Cian said. "Thank you."

John looked up at his older brother and smiled.

"It's our pleasure. Now sit down while we figure out what to do about the house."

"He's is very aggressive," Eoin said to Cian.

"And smart. Mum was right," Cian replied.

John moved over and Cian and Eoin sat down.

"I have received three offers on our houses," John said. He passed pieces of paper to Raz and Max. "A developer offered us three times what the homes are worth for the property. He has some in with the city and wants to build six walk ups... What do you call them here?"

"Townhouses?" Alex asked.

"Right. The neighborhood is a historic district so there's no building there."

"Unless for some reason the building comes down," Max said. He passed the paper to Alex, who glanced at the offer and set it down on the coffee table down.

"I have also heard from two builders who would like to rebuild the houses. One is an expert in historic homes and would rebuild them down to the details."

"You mean the details that were sold out of the houses in the 1940s?" Raz asked.

"Exactly," John said. "The other builder is a 'green' builder and would like to re-build the homes as a showcase for his work. He said, he is willing to donate his time and do the work for cost and materials."

"And advertising," Max added.

"Exactly. Our homes would be showcased in the paper and magazines."

"How is that going to work?" Alex asked. "Oh, Colorado Homes and Gardens, this is the super secret secure, but green, office that belongs to my spy wife. That? That's where expert profiler Rasmussen keeps his computers. Of course he won't mind if you take pictures."

Raz and Alex looked at each other and laughed.

"Right," John said. "You looked at houses at Lowry and Stapleton?"

The twins nodded their heads in unison.

"And?" Raz asked.

"The realtor got mad at us and won't show us any more," Alex said.

"That happens every single time," John said.

"What happens?" Raz asked.

"When we get around people we don't know, we tend to clam up. And realtors don't like it," Max said.

John laughed again. "They talk to each other silently and creep out the realtors."

"Ah," Raz said. "Did you see anything that would work?"

"I don't know," Alex said. "We can live in one large house with space for everyone but... I don't know. Everything is so..."

"...modern," Max said.

"We looked at the old base housing at Lowry. But..."

"That's like the house we lived in when we were kids," Max finished. "Too weird."

"We looked at condos," Alex said. She and Max shrugged their shoulders in unison.

"We looked at townhouses," Max said. He and Alex shrugged their shoulders in unison.

"We looked at lofts," Alex said. She and Max shrugged their shoulders in unison. "Speaking of lofts, Matthew would like to purchase Erin's loft from the corporation."

"Tell him to call me," John said. "We spent a small fortune fixing it up after the rampage. I'd like to wait until the loft increases in value a bit."

"Makes sense," Raz said.

"So you didn't find anything," Eoin said.

Alex and Max shook their heads.

"Not that we liked. If we're desperate to get out of the hotel, we saw things that would work, but…"

"I'm not here full time," Raz said, "but I want to be comfortable when I'm here. I'd rather wait until we find something that works."

"I agree," John said. "Cian? Eoin?"

"Oh, we get a vote?" Cian said. "Um, whatever you say Johnny."

Eoin laughed. "We've always lived where ever."

"Emily Lamberton's father called the General and offered us apartments in the Beauvallon."

"Beauvallon?"

"That luxury condo thing up the street from the dance club these guys picked us up from," Alex said. "Raz, are you still dating Emily?"

"No," Raz said. "Vince finally asked her out."

"It's about time," Alex said. "Anyway, the General… uh … Patrick, said that her father said to say 'hello' to you."

"That's a generous fourth offer," John said. "Do we have any decisions?" He looked from face to face. "No decisions. Let the record show that we are tabling the 'where shall we live' question."

"Max and I will go look at the Beauvallon. If it's big enough for all of us, then we can move out of the hotel until we decide. Patrick said Emily's dad offered one of the penthouse apartments, I guess, near where Emily and Amelia live. You've been there Raz, what's it like?"

"It's very plush," Raz said. "Pool on the roof."

"Won't it be weird to live there now that your girl is dating someone else?" Eoin asked.

"No," Raz said. "Vince is the love of Emily's life. They have a child together. I only hope they can make it work.."

"And you're cool with that?" Eoin pressed.

"I can't really do love now, Eoin. It's not in the cards," Raz said.

"Raz has ladies all over the world," Alex said.

"Really??" Eoin asked. "You'll have to tell me how you do that."

"A man who wants a wife doesn't need that information." Raz shook his head slightly.

"True," Eoin said. His face broke into a big smile. "Who would have thought it Cian? We're really doing this!"

Cian turned to Eoin and smiled.

"If that's it, I need to get to the hospital," John said. Turning to Alex, he asked, "What's on your agenda today?"

There was a knock at the door. Max stood to open the door for Samantha. Alex crossed the room to answer John's question.

"Sam is here to help us get some clothes. Raz and I are going with her. I have a list of what everyone needs."

"What about these guys?" John asked. He pointed to Eoin and Cian who were wide eyed at the beautiful Samantha. Max was attempting introductions but the men could barely speak.

"Vince Hutchins," Alex said. There was another knock on the door. She watched Raz open the door. "Vince is a munitions expert. He drooled all over himself that he might actually be able to speak with someone who knew something about VBIEDs, uh, car bombs particularly PIRA."

She noted Vince shift away from Raz. He must have know about Raz and Emily. Turning back to John, she smiled at the grin on his face. Max held his hand out to John who placed the fifteen dollar bet into it.

"Max won the bet?" Alex asked.

"I knew you'd pay attention." Max laughed and let himself out of the suite.

"Oh no you don't," Sam said as John and Alex moved to their bedroom. "I'm not sitting here with your…" She looked Raz up and down and curled her lip in disgust. "…friends while you slip off."

"I'm going to chat with him while he changes into scrubs. He has surgery in less than an hour," Alex said. "Ten minutes won't kill you, Sami. Just be pleasant. You can do that."

Samantha made a face at Alex and opened her mouth to say something snide.

"You can practice your secret Navy hand shake with Vince." Alex spoke first.. "You remember him. He shared my room at Walter Reed?"

Sam squinted her eyes at Alex then spotted Vince Hutchins. Vince flushed at the look the beautiful Samantha gave him.

Laughing at Samantha, Alex closed the room door then leaned against it. John had removed his T-shirt revealing his muscular chest. He was unbuttoning his jeans. Alex watched as one button at a time he revealed his cropped pubic hair.

"You're not wearing underwear?"

"I hoped you'd notice," he said.

She raised her eyebrows as his interest became apparent. Her lips turned upward into a crooked smiled and he pulled her to him. He plucked off her clothing. Taking her mouth, conquering the territory with his own receptive mouth, he mumbled, "Come up."

She jumped into his arms. With her legs wrapped around his hips, he pressed her into the wall away from the suite sitting room. His lips moved down her neck returning to her lavish mouth. He shifted his hips until he hit exactly the right spot. Alex's breath caught with the intensity of sensation. He pushed forward until she broke off from his lips. Rising together in fast, silent lovemaking, they let go in a breath.

Laughing, he pulled her into the shower. They rushed through soap and shampoo then dressed together. They shared one last pulling kiss before Alex left for the other room.

"See. Ten minutes," Alex said coming out of their bedroom.

"Twelve," Samantha replied. "Did you shower?"

"I had to change into my Alyssa clothing," Alex said. John came up behind her. He gave her a chaste peck on the cheek then left for work.

"Alyssa's boring. You don't expect me to continue… this… do you?"

"Let's hope not," Alex said.

"Is this creature coming with us?" Sam flipped her hand toward Raz.

"Yes. He lives with us" Alex held her hand to Raz. "His clothing was blown up as well."

"Fine. You're lucky that I do charity work."

Sitting in the back seat of Sam's silver Mercedes Benz convertible, Alex watched Raz win over Samantha. For the first hour or so, he subtly watched Sam in silence. When he spoke, he asked Sam thoughtful questions. His eyes never left her face when she spoke. He even went out of his way to ignore the women who bumped into him, winked at him and otherwise threw themselves in his direction. He gave the impression that for this afternoon, he belonged solely to Samantha.

And he was the perfect gentleman. He held the door for them, helped Sam out of the car and carried all of their bags. He encouraged Sam to try on a pair of super sexy Christian Louboutin heels, then insisted on paying for them. He waited for her when she fell behind and included her in every conversation. While he never went out of his way to touch Sam, his hand accidentally brushed her hip in one store and stroked her hand when he reached for the radio.

In return Sam warmed in a way that Alex had never seen. Sam's defensive snapping style slipped away. She chatted about whatever came up in the conversation. Like watching a flower blossom, Sam unfolded with gentle radiance that made her natural beauty glow. She laughed at jokes, asked questions and, to Alex's surprise, shared a little of herself. She even paid for lunch.

Late in the day, when Raz was trying on a pair of jeans and a stack of shirts, she asked Alex about Raz.

"So what's your relationship with Art?"

"He's been my partner for five or six years. We consider him family."

"Are you sleeping with him?"

"I've slept in the same bed with him more than once. He doesn't snore and I don't think he ever stole the covers. Is that what you are asking?"

Sam made a face at Alex.

"No Samantha, I'm married? Remember? Raz and I are close friends." Alex shrugged. "What about the Senator?"

Sam shrugged. Sadness crept across Samantha's face. Samantha had been having an affair with a married Senator for the last three years. Working as his lawyer by day, she was his bed partner by night. Sam defended her relationship with the Senator saying that she was a modern woman who didn't want to be held down by a man. But over the last year the family, Colin especially, saw the relationship begin to tear Sam apart.

At that moment, Raz came out of the dressing room. Alex hugged Sam, whispering in her ear, "He's a wonderful person—funny, interesting, very loyal. I've heard that he's amazing in bed. You should go for it. Have a good time."

Sam's cheeks were pink when she hugged Alex close.

"This has been fun," Sam said. "It's nice to spend some time with you. I've missed you."

"For me too," Alex said. "Oh God, please don't tell Mom that I like shopping. Please."

Sam laughed.

An hour later, Raz and Alex were sitting across from each other in a booth waiting for the waitress to bring their beer. Sam was in the Ladies Room "freshening up" and checking her messages.

"Would you mind if I took your sister out?"

"Erin's probably going to marry Matthew. You'd have to talk to him."

"This sister," Raz said. The waitress deposited their beer. "Thank you."

"You bet," the waitress said batting her dark eyes at Raz. He winked at her.

"Sam is very soft hearted."

"More than you?"

"Yes," Alex said. "She's mean and ornery because she's so soft at heart. I've never known her to get close to anyone. Will you promise to be extra kind? Extra clear?"

Raz smiled over his Heineken. Raising an eyebrow to Alex, he turned to watch Sam walk across the floor. Sam, absorbed in her own thoughts, was looking down at the Mexican tile floor. She blushed bright red when she realized Raz was watching her. Holding his eyes, she sat next to him in the booth.

They drank beer and discussed what was left on their shopping list. Alex groaned. She was tired and sore. Whimper, blah, ache, blah, moan, Alex went on and on. Finally, she turned sideways in the booth, tucked her legs into her chest and closed her eyes. She knew that Raz wasn't fooled by her act, but she didn't care. How else could she listen in?

"I'd like to take you out, but you need to know that I can't have anything serious in my life right now," Raz said in quiet tones. Covering Sam's hand with his large hand, his thumb stroked the back of her hand. "I travel almost every week of the year. It makes love impossible. I'm simply unable to do that."

"What does that mean?" Sam asked.

"We'd go out, have a good time, but I can't settle down, get married, or even be exclusive. If you want any of that then we shouldn't start. I'm simply not that guy."

"So I'd have to see you with other people," Sam said.

"You would never see me with anyone else." He paused for a moment, then added, "Anything is possible. You could see me with someone else, by accident. That could happen. It's just unlikely. There would be other women in other places at other times."

"And I could have other men?" Sam asked.

"You are incredibly beautiful and charming. I would be surprised if you didn't have other men," Raz said. "Of course, there is a level of care that an adult takes in modern times."

"Of course," Sam said.

They were silent for a while.

"You should know that I'm seeing someone in Washington," Sam said.

"And?"

Sam laughed. "I'd like to go out with you."

"Let's get Alex back to the hotel then see what might be fun."

Alex's eyes bounced open. "Boy I don't feel good. Sami, would you mind taking me back to the hotel?"

"We need to stop and pick up socks," Sam said.

Alex made a face. "Tomorrow? Please Sam. I need your help but I can't do anymore today."

Stifling a smile, Raz held Sam's hand in his own.

"Let's take the veteran back for her rest."

"Thank you," Alex said.

CHAPTER TWENTY

Two weeks later
September 28 – 10 A.M.
Paris, France

"Remind me again why I cannot come with you?" John asked. He moved to stand behind her.

"It's a tradition for the groom not to see the bride's dress until she walks down the aisle," Alex said. She made a face then adjusted her fake blond hair in the full length mirror. "Don't you want to be surprised?"

"Oh love," John said. He pulled her toward him. "Every moment is a surprise."

They stood looking at each other through the mirror. They were staying in Max's apartment in Paris. In a move that made more sense now, Ben sold his family's Paris apartment to JAM properties when Max started working in Europe. The apartment, which had been in Ben's family for over seventy years, was small, two tiny bedrooms and a bathroom, but had a priceless balcony overlooking the Seine from the tenth floor. Max was staying with Fran so they took his apartment.

"Plus you have your tailoring appointment," Alex said. "Dr. Drayson can't live in scrubs alone. Max ordered a couple of suits for you. You need to get them fitted."

"Hmm." He kissed her neck. "Why does Max get to go to your fitting? Doesn't he need to replace his suits too?"

"He did that when he was here last. He wants to meet..." she turned to look at him, "our siblings."

"He's never met them?"

"When we're in Paris together, we want to be together. I've spent a lot of time with Ben's family, but he's never met them."

Alex kissed John then held him to her.

"You seem nervous," John said.

"I guess I am." Alex turned back to the mirror. "It's the first time I've seen Ben since we found out."

John kissed her nose. "And?"

"And… I'm having trouble rearranging myself. My father, Patrick, is County Cork Irish, first generation American, a General turned Senator in the United States Senate. My father, Ben, is French, well, French-born, American-raised, and a spy. He can trace his family… no, my family. See it's confusing. Ben's family is from Paris since the cavemen or something like that. His father worked in Chicago, so Ben and his brothers grew up there."

"You're not Irish, you're French," John said. "Half Irish."

"On my mom's side. Potato famine Irish," Alex said. "I'm not a Senator's daughter. I'm a spy's daughter."

"It is a big shift," John said.

Alex moved away from him to finish dressing. She slipped on a pair of comfortable walking shoes and picked up her jacket.

"Kind of like finding out my husband is Irish, the elusive John Kelly no less," she said. She shook her head and shivered. "It's been an interesting few months."

John wrapped his arms around her.

"Still love me?"

"Oddly, yes, I do love you," Alex said. "Would you like to see Rita and Tom this trip?"

"I think we have enough to deal with. Your mom invited them to the wedding."

"I know," Alex said. She kissed him. "Come on. Max is waiting for us."

Shutting the apartment door, they took the elevator to the lobby where Max was chatting with the concierge while he waited for them. Looking up, Max caught Alex's eyes. They were both nervous. The twins hugged in greeting. Pressing their foreheads together, the twins felt immediate relief.

No matter what happened, at least they had each other.

With Max leading the way, they took a quick Metro stop. Alex and Max walked John to the tailor shop. Agreeing to meet him in an hour, the twins took the Metro to the heart of Paris. Alex and Max walked hand-in-hand down a long narrow street until they stood at the entrance to a small shop. Alex let out a breath and raised her hand to knock on the door.

Before she could knock, Ben opened the door with a lit cigarette in his hand. Max and Alex stood on the doorstep looking at Ben. He hugged Alex then Max. With an awkward gesture into the shop, Ben pulled the cigarette from his mouth to say something. A five-year-old boy sped out from behind him. Scooping up the little boy, Alex began a loud recitation of his favorite nonsense poem in French as she moved into the shop. The boy squealed with laughter.

Near the end of a hallway, Alex turned to look at Max. Their eyes held for a moment. Alex encouraged him to come in with a nod of her head. Max shook his head slightly and looked at Ben.

A medium-sized woman came from the back of the shop. Touching Alex's arm as she past, the woman moved to stand next to Ben. Looking up at Max with bright blue eyes, she smiled.

"Claire," Ben said in French. "This is my son, Max. Max, this is my wife, Claire."

Max startled at the introduction then looked down with nervous embarrassment. Claire rushed forward. Taking both of Max's hands, she kissed each of his cheeks.

"I've wanted to meet you for a long time. It is very much my pleasure to meet Max Hargreaves," Claire said in English. "Please come into our home. We've been so excited to have you here that… We're all crazy with nerves."

Max nodded.

"You and Alex are so similar," Claire continued in English. "Except for the new hair and eyes."

"Yes, we're identical twins," Max replied in French. He followed her into the shop.

"We're excited for Alexandra to celebrate her marriage," Claire said in French. "Who can believe they've been married thirteen years in a couple weeks? You are good friends with her husband?"

"Yes," Max said. Alex turned and caught his eyes. He smiled.

"We will meet him today as well." Claire's hand moved along the long black braid down her back. "It's a big day."

Max nodded.

"I would like it if you felt like this was your home," Claire said.

"In time," Max replied.

"Alexandra, you must undress. Take that fat suit off. You look awful."

Alex looked over at Max. Their eyes held for a moment as they assessed each other. With a smile and a nod, Alex set the boy down.

"Your lingerie and heels are in the changing room."

Alex moved behind the curtain. She came out in a small silk robe and cream pumps.

"Come here dear," Claire said.

Claire indicated that Alex should stand on a small raised platform surrounded by mirrors.

"I feel a little weird…" Alex said.

"Ben, Eugene, go on," Claire said. Ben picked up the boy and went up the stairs. Claire turned to a corner of the room where a small girl was hiding. "Camille."

"But Alex didn't say hello to me," Camille said in French.

Her large blue eyes glistened with tears behind black ringlets of hair. She was not quite three years old. Alex picked up Camille and carried her into the dressing room. Digging through her jacket, she found the Tootsie Roll sucker she had placed in her pocket. Camille squealed when she saw the orange candy.

"Maman?" Camille said.

"Yes," Claire said.

Claire shook her head and laughed at her daughter's ability to get her favorite treat. A black haired teenaged boy flew down the stairs.

"Papa said you were here," the boy said in English.

"Frederec, this is Alexandra's brother Max."

"Hey," Frederec said to Max. "Alex, did you bring it?"

"Max has it," Alex said replied in English. "He put a bunch of his favorite Alternative music on it for you."

Max pulled an iPOD from his pocket and gave it to Frederec.

"Thanks," Frederec said. "Alex says that you have good..."

"Taste?" Max asked.

"No, relationship with music?" Frederec said.

"I know a lot about music," Max said. "I like Alternative. Let me know what you think."

"Cool," Frederec said. "Have you seen the dress?"

"You have your gadget. Can you get out of here?" Claire said in French.

"Alex!" A young woman with curly brown hair ran down the stairs.

"Helene!" Alex turned to the young woman.

"Did Maman tell you that we get to come to the wedding? I'm going to look at University," Helene said continuing in English. "Papa said that we could look at school while we are there. Can you come with us?"

"I'm not sure," Alex said. "I hope so sweetie."

"No matter," Helene said beaming. "I'm hoping to go to the school in Boulder so we can be close."

"I'd like that," Alex said hugging Helene with her free arm.

"Helene, Frederec, go upstairs. Take Camille," Claire said in French. "Alexandra wants to try on her dress."

"We can't watch?" Helene asked in French. Helene lifted Camille from Alex's arms.

"Not unless you want to see all of my Frankenstein scars," Alex said in French.

"Cool," Frederec said in English.

"Maman, can I die my hair like Alex's?" Helene said in French.

"Children," Claire all but screamed in French.

Ben came out on the walkway upstairs and glowered down at his children. Helene and Frederec looked from Claire to Ben. Helene returned her father's look as she stomped up the steps. Stuffing the iPOD ear buds into his ears, Frederec followed his sister up the stairs.

"Sorry about that," Claire said in French to Max. "Now you've met the whole family."

"They are excited," Alex said in French. "It's pretty exciting to come to the States. Is it safe?"

"We won't live in fear," Claire shrugged. "Stand there."

She went to a corner of the shop and held up what looked like loose cream colored silk fabric. She returned with a strip of fabric.

"Since you are such a cheater, I am going to put this over your eyes," Claire said. "Don't peek."

Alex felt a brush of air as Claire removed the small robe.

"Those are gruesome scars, Alexandra," Claire said. "I am so sorry. We went to the church every day to pray for you. We practically wore out a bench."

Alex felt the drape of silk, soft against her skin, and Claire's professional tugging, pulling and finally buttons fastening in the back. Alex shifted her head and shoulders, feeling the weight of the dress. She took a breath and her ribs pressed against the tight fabric.

"Oh Alex," Max said. "You're beautiful."

"It looks nice. Doesn't it?" Claire said. "I have a little adjusting. You are a little bigger in the bust than you were."

"I've gained a little weight since I've been home" Alex said.

"And lost it again," Max said.

"Well, the weight looks good on you," Claire said. "You've been too thin."

"My mother says the same thing," Alex said.

"Well, pardon me," Claire said. "I'd hate to sound like Rebecca."

They laughed.

"One more thing," Claire said. "Can you bend down?"

Alex felt hair combs scrape against her scalp and the silk slipped from her eyes.

Alex gasped. The sleeveless butter cream satin silk dress was snug from her breasts to her hips. Its draped V-neckline and dropped waist accentuated Alex's breasts, wide shoulders and small waist. Alex turned to see inverted pleats creating a full skirt and chapel train. The bodice was covered in an intricate pattern of cultured pearls. The pearls continued on the inch wide straps. The pattern of pearls was repeated along the edges of the dress and train. She wore a tulle veil with the same pattern of pearls on the edge of the veil.

"She's speechless," Ben said from upstairs. Looking up, she smiled at Ben and the children standing on the passageway upstairs. "That's a first."

Claire buzzed around her making measurements for the alterations.

"Say something, Alex," Max said. "You have to talk."

"Wow," Alex said. "It's more spectacular than anything I could have ever imagined. Did you do all this bead work?"

"Helene and Frederec helped," Claire said. "Frederec has a real knack for bead work."

"Of course he does," Alex said. "Thank you for this."

"Oh dear," Claire said. "You are so welcome. Thank you for letting me create a dress for you. I hope this John will appreciate it."

"He will," Max said.

Claire looked at Max then looked up at Ben, who laughed.

"She hasn't seen Alex and John together," Ben said to Max.

Max laughed.

"Now out of the dress," Claire said. "I will make these alterations. Benjamin will bring the dress to you. You need to get it pressed."

Alex stepped out of the dress. Claire helped her into the silk robe.

"I will be there to help you get dressed," Claire said.

"What about my mother?" Alex asked.

"Rebecca will have to live with it. What is past is done. There's no changing it. Plus with such wonderful outcomes," Claire looked from Alex to Max, "who'd want to?"

Max blushed and held his hand out to Alex. The twins held hands, feeling the pulse of each other, then smiled in unison.

"At least you know, now, and we can be more of a family."

"Thank you," Alex said and hugged Claire.

"I put a little pocket in it so you can wear a pistol if you feel you need to," Claire said. "Let's hope you don't."

Alex went to change. When she came out, Max was chatting with Frederec about his new gadget while Helene pretended not to listen. Alex wasn't sure if the children knew that they were siblings. It never occurred to her to ask. Embarrassed, she withdrew into herself.

Feeling a bump against her leg, she looked down to see Camille's bright blue eyes. Camille lifted her arms and Alex picked her up. Alex kissed Camille's plump cheek, taking in her baby scent, and felt less strange. Camille's little fist reached around Alex's neck. When Alex looked up Max had picked up Eugene.

As Claire shooed them out of the shop, Max and Alex shared a look. At least they could be family. Alex and Max followed Helene out the door. The family laughed and talked through the narrow streets to the Metro station.

They took a few short Metro stops. They found John waiting for them on the platform.

"He's very handsome," Helene whispered in French.

"Yes, he is."

With Helene leading the way, the family wandered into a small bistro along a side street. Helene said hello to a couple handsome young men as they walked into the bistro. Alex watched the girl flip her hair, press her chest forward and wag her hips. Shaking her head slightly, her Goddaughter… no… sister?… was growing up. She looked up to catch Ben's eyes. Holding the door for Alex, he smiled and took Camille from her arms. Then, almost on impulse, he kissed Alex's cheek. Their eyes held for a moment and Alex smiled.

Alex watched everything from the sidelines. Naturally suspicious of a handsome Englishman, Claire peppered John with questions. She was perfectly clear. She was certain he was not good enough to be Alex's husband. Knowing how important Claire was to Alex, John gave Claire his full attention. By the time the waiter brought their lunch, John and Claire were sharing stories about Alex.

Sitting with Camille on his lap, Max chatted with Frederec. Alex watched one brother then the other brother. She was surprised that she never noticed how similar Frederec and Max were. She shook her head at her own confusion. Nothing had changed and everything was different. They had been dear friends. Now they were family.

Feeling a hand on her shoulder, Alex looked up into Helene's impatient face. The young woman's eyes were wide as she nodded her head toward the table of young men. Alex smiled at Helene's impatience. Raising a finger, Alex drank the last of her French press coffee then she kissed John. He stroked her hip when she stood to follow Helene.

Arriving at a table of five young men, one handsome man, Michel, shifted his knee sideways and Helene sat down in his lap. Helene flirted, blushed and worked her way through introductions. Alex had to look away when the young man's hands began moving along Helene's body. She had to bite her lip to keep from saying: "Get your filthy hands of my Helene!"

Chuckling at her own reaction, her eyes drifted across the street where she noticed Jesse standing under a green awning near the corner. Alex smiled at Jesse then looked back to Helene.

Helene moved her lips, saying something, but Alex's couldn't hear her. Alex opened her mouth to say something but found words beyond her capacity. Alex shook her head and Helene repeated herself. Alex had no idea what the girl said. Blinking her eyes, she realized that all sound was gone. Alex pressed her fingers to her ears in an attempt to clear them. Her face marked with concern, Helene put a hand on Alex's arm. Alex smiled, wagged her head then indicated with her hands that Helene should stay with her friends.

Jesse appeared next to the table.

"Follow me," Jesse said.

With one last smile to Helene, Alex followed Jesse across the street. They walked together in companionable silence until they came to the green awning. Alex looked up, reading, 'Le Fee Verte,' the Green Fairy, Paris' euphuism for absinthe.

"In here," Jesse said.

Glancing back at the bistro, Alex noticed that Ben was standing at the door. He opened his mouth and said something, but Alex couldn't hear him. Smiling, she raised her hand to wave to Ben then stepped into the busy shop.

Sound returned to Alex in a blaze of music, conversation, and clinking of china. Dazed by the noise, Alex stood at the entrance.

"Alexandra! How are you?" a tall blonde clerk said in French. She was standing behind a bar where three customers were drinking absinthe. "Where have you been?"

"It's been a while," Alex replied. She moved into the shop. Although she had no memory of the woman or this place, she played along because Jesse waved her into the shop.

"We haven't seen you in years. I was beginning to think you weren't coming back. Would you like your regular?"

"Sure," Alex said.

The clerk poured absinthe into a reservoir glass. Laughing at something the customer in front of her said, the woman rested a slotted spoon on the rim of the glass and placed a sugar cube on the spoon.

"You look good dear," the clerk said. "I like the hair."

Jesse stood near a door in the back.

"You can go downstairs, dear. I'll have this ready for you when you come up," the clerk said. "My God, Alex, you look like you've seen a ghost. Are you all right?"

CHAPTER TWENTY-ONE

"It's a little weird to be here," Alex said.

"It has been a while," the clerk said. She turned to speak to another customer.

Stepping aside so that a customer could move by her to the bar, Alex walked through the shop to where Jesse was standing.

"This is it," Jesse said.

Alex opened the door and jogged down a series of wooden steps into the labyrinth of limestone tunnels that run beneath Paris. Five steps, turn, five steps, turn. In the dim light, she counted the steps in her head. Even though the stairs continued into the darkness, she walked forward off the stairs into the fifth passageway and froze.

This was the passageway from her nightmare.

Her heart raced and her stomach lurched into her throat. Looking up the stairs, she longed to return to the busy shop. But the passageway called to her. Blowing out her feelings of dread, she stepped forward.

She heard the door open above her.

"Alex?" Ben called.

Jesse beckoned her forward into the dark limestone passageway. Round fluorescent ceiling lights flickered then came on as she walked under them. Each time she stepped into the dark, a light began to flicker over head. Counting her steps, fifty-seven, she turned at an unmarked door on her right.

No door knob. No hinges. Just a vague outline of a door cut into the limestone.

Placing her hand on the limestone, a green light scanned her palm. There was a soft click and a key pad emerged.

Alex looked at Jesse and he nodded.

Her fingers moved in an automatic rhythm across the key pad. There was a pop and the door opened a crack. Alex pushed the door open.

The smell hit her like a tidal wave.

Dried blood and death. Blood dried in thick pools on the floor. The white limestone walls were patterned with splattered blood. Crates and boxes around the room bore scars made by violent death. The sound of ragged breathing and dripping blood pounded her ears.

In a series of flashes, she watched it happen.

She stood in front of ten years of her mission journals tucked in a wall compartment. Holding her journal, the large one she carried in her pack, she laughed at Mike. He was bragging about his latest conquest . From his position at the door, Jesse encouraged Mike's exaggerations with provocative questions. Alex shared a look with Jesse and they laughed.

Jax, the medic, was changing into his running gear for his first long run since competing in the one hundred and thirty five mile Badwater Ultramarathon. Charlie O'Brien and Dwight Harris, the weapon's officer, were arguing about the outcome of the last Broncos vs. Raiders football game.

Alex glanced at Scott, the engineer, who was sitting on a crate talking to Tommy, the communications officer. When she looked away, Scott threw a piece of ice at her. Laughing, Alex caught the ice in her right hand. She threw the ice at Scott and hit him in the head.

Paul, the second engineer, was standing in his boxers displaying his new dance moves to Dean, the other medic. Laughing at Dean and Paul, Nathan had his foot on a crate so he could tie his shoes.

They were laughing and loose. Having finished their work early, they were ready to play. Their body armor was stacked in a corner. Alex tossed her body armor onto the stack then turned to put the journal in the compartment. Impatient and ready to go, Nathan started jumping up and down.

Hearing a sound in the hallway, she cast a glace at Jesse. Jesse screamed. Falling against the door, his body jerked as a round of machine gun fired hit him in the chest. Reaching for her handgun, Alex's abdomen and hip exploded. Dazed, she flew backwards and landed on a crate. Round after agonizing round, a machine gun cut into her screaming friends.

Sitting up, she fired in the direction of the shooter but was unable to stabilize against the gun's recoil. The shot went wild.

The shooter laughed, then turned to shoot Dwight in the head.

Alex ground her teeth together. Using her free hand to stabilize, she fired twice in quick succession.

Her shots knocked the shooter backward. The shooter sneered. Taunting Alex, he pointed to the spot where her shots hit his body armor. With a cruel laugh, he raised his AK-47 to fire at Alex again.

She pulled one shot, hitting him in the forehead. The shooter fell backward to the floor.

Bleeding heavily, she dropped to the blood slick floor. Sobbing and unable to stand or walk, she pulled herself from one friend to the next. Their bodies lay in pieces on the limestone. She fell forward over Charlie.

Then she heard the ragged breath. Jesse's alive.

"Don't die. Don't die. Jesse, don't you dare die. Please. Jesse. Please don't die. Jesse," echoed off the limestone walls.

Pushing and pulling herself along the floor, she fell forward in front of his broken body.

Jesse smiled.

Laying on her stomach, she pressed her hands into his wounds trying to stem the flow of blood.

Jesse shook his head.

She dragged her hips around and moved to sitting. She pulled his head on to her lap.

"I'm dying," he whispered.

"Please don't go. Please Jesse. Please…" Alex sobbed.

Jesse reached for her hands. Holding her hands, he looked into her eyes.

"Tell Maria that I love her," he whispered.

He drew in a ragged breath. With his exhale, he said, "We'll be friends forever."

"No, Jesse. No!"

Alex screamed and shook his body trying to make him take another breath. Overcome with grief, she rocked him in her lap.

She began to fade. With each beat of her heart, her life spilled into the pool of blood on the limestone floor. Closing her eyes, she let go, then jerked alert. Someone ran down the wooden stairs.

Looking around, she noticed the team journal. She propped the journal against the door when she tried to stop Jesse's bleeding. When she fell over sideways to grab the journal, Jessie's head pressed deep into her wounds.

She screamed in pain.

With all the strength left in her body, she lifted the nearest crate a tiny crack and stuffed the journal underneath. Righting herself, she kissed Jesse's forehead and surrendered to the dark.

The next thing she remembered was being carried by Raz through a room of people. She heard her voice begging Raz not to leave her but she wasn't sure she said a word.

Alex blinked until the memory receded.

She was standing in the team's storage vault. Glancing around the room, she saw the stack of body armor, weapons and various supplies the team used.

Closing and opening her eyes, she tried to clear her vertigo.

The journal compartment was empty. Someone had taken her mission journals. Dropping to her knees, she reached under the crate next to the door. Her fingers felt the binding of a journal.

Hearing movement in the hall, she rolled over and pulled her weapon.

"Alex," Ben appeared in the doorway. He was sweating and breathing hard. Noticing her handgun, he held his hands up. "Alex, what the fuck?"

Alex shook her head and blinked. Was this really Ben? He made an impatient sound. This was Ben.

Holstering her gun, she stood.

"What do you know?"

"I received a telephone call about a hit scheduled on... on my daughter and her team at twelve-thirty. It was a courtesy call, you know, designed to warn me but not give me enough time to change the outcome of the hit."

"Who called you?"

"Someone who is no longer living."

Alex jerked her head in a nod. Her eyes flitted from one spot to the next both taking in and avoiding the horror at the same time.

"We looked for you everywhere, everywhere. I couldn't find you. No one had seen you in hours. Zack was on his way to Afghanistan. You checked out of base at eleven. I called your cell phone but you were down here. Out of range."

"Where were you?"

Alex's eyes detected something shiny on the floor. Using a fingernail, she pried Jesse's St. Christopher medallion from the blood encrusted floor.

"London. Claire called to remind me that it was Helene's sixteenth birthday. She mentioned that you had stopped by around noon. She said you were going for absinthe then would meet them for a birthday dinner."

"I wanted to be here for her big birthday," Alex said. Pieces of the memory began to click into place. She wiped Jesse's medallion on her jeans in an effort to clean off the dried blood. "I remember that. How did you find me?"

"I have no idea. Angels? God? I don't know." Ben looked around the room. "I could see you from the landing, sitting here, in the doorway, with Jesse's head in your lap. I checked your pulse but I was so freaked out that I must have missed your low pulse. We assumed you were dead. I was in the room... Everyone was... cut in two by machine gun fire... dead. Raz realized you were alive. I guess Jesse's head stemmed your bleeding. Raz picked you up and ran out of here."

"I killed the shooter," Alex said. She slipping Jesse's St. Christopher into her pocket.

"Yes, his body was right here," Ben said. He moved to the space where the shooter's body had been. "When we got here his head was wrapped in T-shirts."

"You interrupted someone."

"Probably. By the time the Army arrived, the shooter's body was gone. What did you keep here?"

"We kept everything we needed here—cash, random tools, clothing, weapons or whatever. We kept my journals, the big ones that held our plans, schedules, ideas and notes, in that vault. We kept our Christmas presents and stuff like that here too."

"And the small journals? The ones you carried in your pocket?" Ben asked.

"Here," Alex said. She walked to another portion of the limestone walls and pressed on the wall. With a loud click, the wall opened showing a line of pocketsized notebooks. Looking around the room, she grabbed a large empty duffle bag and began dropping the journals into the bag.

"Who knew about this place?" Ben asked.

"No one knew it was ours. The shop upstairs rented the space and Charlie paid for ten years in advance. Cash."

"Just the team. Does Max know about this?"

"No," Alex said. "Max knew that I was in Paris for work a lot, but not why or what I was doing. You know Max. He couldn't care less about that kind of thing."

"Did the Boy Scout know about the vault?" Ben said.

"I don't think so," Alex said. "We never trusted him. We were going to meet him in Afghanistan after a night in Paris. Isn't that where he was? Afghanistan?"

Ben shook his head.

"No one is quite sure where he was that day. He was on leave. The Army wasn't tracking him. I've heard that he was in Paris."

Alex walked toward the door.

"Why the cover up? Why say we were killed in Afghanistan?"

"No one knew what you were doing here. It breaks about a dozen treaties to have an unauthorized Special Forces mission in Europe."

"We were here all the time."

"Europe wasn't your assigned area. Was it?"

"We rescued hostages in every country."

"There were no known hostages in Europe at that time."

"No known... Huh," Alex shrugged. "Can you lift this crate?"

Ben lifted the crate and Alex pulled the journal from under the crate. Although the journal was marked with bloody handprints, the crate had channeled the blood away from the journal. She flipped through the dry pages.

"I heard footsteps," she said. "I protected this journal for some reason."

"Alex, we have to get out of here," Ben said. "There's no way to know what events were set off by your presence in this vault."

Alex startled then moved into action. She stuck the journal into the duffle bag.

"I need a couple things," Alex said. She walked around the storage unit. "The cash is gone, but that's not too surprising. We were on our way to Afghanistan. We never needed cash there."

Smiling, she pulled a ten-inch square jewelry box from the floor. The outside of the box stuck to the floor, but the box held its shape. She tucked it into the duffle bag. She went to the wall and pushed open another cabinet that held a small box. She put it in the bag.

"We need to go," Ben said. Holding a handgun, he looked down the hall.

"Here," Alex said. She tossed Ben a body armor vest and pulled on another vest. "Army issue."

"Thanks," he said. "What about the property?"

Alex looked around the room.

"Nothing stands out. Who knows?"

She slipped her arms through the duffle bag handles. The bag rested on her back. She pushed the door to midway open causing the door to swing shut. The gears of the lock engaged.

She ran after Ben. Reaching the landing of the stairs, they heard the door open above them. Two people pounded down the wooden stairs toward them.

Following Ben, Alex flew down the stairs into the tunnels below.

CHAPTER TWENTY-TWO

"Count," Jesse said.

Alex counted the steps out loud, "One, two, three, four, five", turn, "one, two, three four, five." They stopped on a landing where a long set of stairs continued straight forward into the darkness.

"No. Keep your count," Jesse said.

On her left, Alex noticed a set of stairs which continued the five stair count.

"This way," Alex said. She pushed by Ben. Turning left, she continued down the short flights of stairs, "one, two, three, four, five", turn, "one, two, three, four, five."

"Jump," Jesse said.

Alex hurled herself forward over a five feet wide broken landing to a step below.

"Jump Ben," Alex said.

"I heard him," Ben said.

He leapt forward toward the step. Alex grabbed his waist as his feet slipped on the edge of a step. They stood for a moment, breathing hard, holding each other, then Alex turned and continued down the stairs.

"One, two, three, four, five", turn right, "one, two, three, four, five," turn left.

"Did they make it?" Alex asked Jesse.

"You lost one," Jesse said.

"That's Jesse Abreu." Ben said.

"What is?"

Jesse stood to the side of the next landing. Alex grabbed Ben's hand and yanked him into a limestone tunnel. As they raced through the dark, their surroundings began to change. The tunnel transitioned into well lit, clean storage areas. Passing wine racks, storage boxes, bikes and household items, they could hear someone chasing them.

Jesse stood at the corner of a cross tunnel.

"Behind you," he said.

Using her shoulder, Alex knocked Ben around the corner. Turning, she raised her handgun.

"Show yourself," Alex demanded.

The figure responded by firing a weapon.

"Smith and Wesson, 38 Special," Jesse said.

Two bullets smashed into Alex's body armor near her heart. The force of the bullets sent her a couple steps back. She took off running away from the shooter. Pushing Ben further down the corridor, she turned sideways and fired her handgun. The figure fell backward, shot through the forehead.

"Go," Jesse said.

They ran down the semi-lit corridor. At another juncture of tunnels, Alex stopped to get a reading from the compass on her watch.

"Get going, lazy bones." Jesse yelled over the sound of two pairs of feet running down a set of wooden stairs along the edge of the tunnel.

Alex turned to fight.

"No here," Jesse said. "Get going."

Ben grabbed her hand and pulled her down the passageway. Pursued by the two men, they ran down the tunnel.

"This way," Jesse said.

They turned down a poorly lit passage where naked light bulbs, hanging from the limestone ceiling by electric wire, created bright circles of light surrounded by deep shadow.

"Now," Jesse said.

Alex slammed Ben against the wall next to a stack of wine casks. Turning back, she dropped the duffle from her back. Two men were standing under a circle of bright light. They peered into the dark tunnel with their handguns raised.

Alex ran toward the men.

Jumping in the air, she rotated. With a powerful flying back kick, she caught a man in the upper chest. He fell backward into the hallway. Before the second man could react, Alex landed. She kicked him with a high reverse roundhouse kick catching him in the face with the ball of her foot. He dropped to the ground.

The first man grabbed her by the shoulders and threw her into a rack of boxes. Pressing off the boxes, Alex raised her leg in a front kick catching the man's solar plexus. He dropped to the ground. Breathing hard, she stood over him expecting him to get up from the ground. The man moaned, shaking his head, and Alex punched him unconscious.

Setting their weapons beside their feet, she motioned for Ben to come forward. With quick professional motions, they removed the men's identification and stuffed them into their pockets.

Hearing movement in the tunnel, Alex jumped up to assess the danger.

"This way," Jesse said.

He pointed to a tunnel, less than three feet wide, cut into the limestone. Alex moved a large box out of the way and pulled Ben into the tunnel. Once he was in the tunnel, she covered the tunnel entrance with the large box.

Holding the duffle in one hand, she mimicked Ben's sideways motion through the tight passageway. Within forty feet, they reached a four foot wall of human femurs. Ben stepped over the wall. Alex passed him the duffle bag then stepped over the wall. They stood in an open passageway surrounded by the bones of fourteenth century plague victims. Alex threw the duffle bag on her shoulders and they took off running. They past human femurs stacked in a perfect five foot wall adorned with a cross made of human skulls. Continuing straight forward, they threaded their way through rooms filled to the ceiling with human bones.

"This way," Ben said.

Alex followed him up a set of twenty white wooden stairs. Pulling his keys from his pocket, he unlocked the locked door at the top. He flew through the door and Alex followed. She shut the door and turned the bolt. They went down a narrow limestone hallway, passing bolted doors, to a door near the end of the hallway. Ben unlocked the door, let Alex through then used his key to relock the door. They climbed up three flights of stairs until they came to a door.

Out of breath, Ben ruffled his salt and pepper hair, then turned to Alex.

"My in-laws' home," he said. Alex nodded. "You must speak French."

"What language have we been speaking?" Alex asked.

"Spanish," Ben said.

He pushed the door open to reveal a tidy basement. Alex took off her body armor then held her hand out for Ben's body armor. Pulling a cell phone from his pocket, he slipped off his body armor while he dialed the phone.

"Claire?" Ben said. He continued in French. "Alex and I were in the tunnels then decided to visit your parents'. Would you mind asking Max and John to meet us here?"

Alex heard Claire's flood of confused words.

"Yes," Ben said. "I'm sorry. Please ask Helene to take the children home. Yes, come to your parents' as well. I…"

There was another flood of words from Claire.

"I love you," he said. Closing his phone, he turned to look at Alex. "We must clean up."

Alex nodded then crammed the body armor into the duffel bag.

"I don't feel well," Alex said. "Dizzy."

"Do you think it's..."

He fell silent when they heard footsteps above them. Alex pulled her handgun, but Ben pushed the gun down with his hand. They heard a lock click open.

"Benjamin," a woman's voice called from the top of the stairs.

"Yes Noémi," Ben replied in French. "I am here with my daughter, Alexandra. I was showing her the catacombs when I remembered that you have your own entrance."

The woman laughed.

"Claire called. Come up. Come up."

A small thin woman came half way down the stairs to greet them. She turned and led the way up the stairs. Ben followed and Alex came last carrying the duffle bag.

In the light, Alex noticed the blood on her hands and jeans. Claire's mother looked at her and raised her eyebrows.

"You better clean up, chérie, or no one is going to believe your story," she said. "There is a shower in there. Give me your pants. Hurry, chérie, your family will be here in a moment. Benjamin, you can clean up in the kitchen."

Too intimidated to argue, Alex pulled off her pants. She emptied the pockets into the duffle bag then gave the pants to Claire's mother. She carried the duffle into the bathroom and locked the door.

Leaning against the bathroom door, Alex closed her eyes and slid down to the ground. She pressed her eyes against her knees to keep from crying. With her arms wrapped around her knees, she held herself in a ball. She whispered the words: "My name is Alexandra Hargreaves. I'm in Paris. My brother is Maxwell. We have the same middle name but it's spelled differently."

The words had no impact on the spinning sensation in her head.

Pushing herself to standing, she caught her reflection in the mirror. Her face and lips were drained of all color and her eyes were round and gleaming.

Fuck.

I've been drugged.

CHAPTER TWENTY-THREE

She turned the shower to cold. Holding her breath, she stepped under the frigid water stream of water. She continued: "I'm Alexandra Hargreaves. I'm married to... well... I think I'm... no... I was married to... no... I'm going to marry... What's his name?"

She giggled.

Oh crap. This is Ketamine.

She stepped out of the shower to avoid collapsing. She needed to get situated before the Ketamine took full effect. A light tap at the door produced Claire's mother's hand holding Alex's pants. Alex took the damp pants and put her clothing on. She pulled her wet hair into a ponytail.

Stepping into the hallway, Claire's mother looked her up and down. She nodded, "Much better. I'm Noémi. You are Rebecca's daughter, no?"

"Yes, ma'am. I'm Alex."

"I've known your father Patrick most of my adult life," Noémi said. "Let me get you something to drink. You don't look like you are feeling very good."

"Special K. I think it's hitting me now that we're not moving."

"Hmm," Noémi said coming into the kitchen. "Benjamin, you were right. She has been drugged. She says it's Ketamine."

Ben's head jerked up. He was sitting at a wooden block table looking at the identification papers they had taken from the men in the tunnels. Searching Alex's face, he gave a curt nod.

"What's the name of the guy I'm marrying?" Alex asked.

Ben opened his mouth then laughed.

"It's John something. I can't remember."

"Yes, John something," Ben said.

"She needs a doctor," Noémi said. "I'll call. Can you make her an espresso?"

Ben moved to make the coffee.

"Sit down Alex," Ben said. "Sit down before you fall down."

Dropping the duffle bag on the floor, Alex plopped into a chair. She rested her head on her hands.

"You have to talk Ben or I'm going into a k-hole."

"Fair enough." He poured water into the espresso maker. "Claire's family was in the resistance. Her mother was in intelligence. That is how I met Claire. I was working with Noémi on a project that included Patrick when I met this staggering sixteen year old girl. I didn't, I mean, we didn't do anything but my God… I thought of nothing else for years. Drink this."

He placed a glass of water in front of Alex. With her head propped by one hand, she drained the glass of water then slapped the glass onto the wooden table.

"Anyway, that's why I went to bat for you and John," he said. "I knew what it was like to have your socks knocked off."

"You and Claire?" Alex slurred.

"I avoided Paris for a couple years. I had plenty of women, so it wasn't like I was alone. My father, your grandfather, died. He wanted to be buried in the family mausoleum in Paris. I'll have to show it to you. Introduce you to the extended family."

He looked up to see if Alex was laughing at his joke. With her head in her hands, she rotated her head back and forth in an attempt to clear her mind. He smiled wondering if she would remember any of this.

"I held a service for my father here, in Paris. Noémi and her husband, Jean, helped with the details. They insisted I come for dinner the night before the service. I arrived as Claire was leaving for a date. You would have laughed. We stood in the entryway staring at each other. The boy had to drag her out the door. I looked up and Noémi was laughing at me."

"You were pathetic." Noémi stood in the doorway to the kitchen. "The great super spy was at a complete loss for words over a mere girl. She returned from her date and they've been together ever since."

Alex smiled.

"Chérie," Noémi said. "The doctor will be here in a few minutes. Drink this before your husband gets here."

"I blame Patrick," Ben said. "He's the first man I ever met who says straight out that he fell in love at first sight. He planted the possibility in my head."

Alex drank the espresso down in one gulp. Setting the cup down, she picked up a second espresso and drank it down. Ben handed her another cup of water, which she drank. She stuck out her tongue causing Noémi and Ben to laugh.

The doorbell rang.

"What are we telling them?" Noémi asked.

"The truth," Alex said. "No more lies."

"Are you sure?" Ben asked.

She flopped her head up and down in a nod.

"Oh, not another one." She whimpered when Ben set another espresso in front of her. "Daddy..."

"Do not call me that," Ben laughed.

"Drink your espresso," Noémi said. She left to answer the door.

They heard talking at the front door. Turning in the kitchen chair, Alex watched Max and John talking and moving toward her. She attempted to stand but fell back into the chair. Speaking in a rush of Gaelic, John lifted her into his arms, but Alex was limp against him.

"What did you do to her?" John asked Ben in English.

"She's been drugged," Noémi said in English. "It seems like the drugs are affecting her now that the adrenalin is wearing off."

Shaking her head, Claire came into the kitchen giving Ben a dirty look.

"It wasn't me," Ben replied in English.

Leaning against the sink, Ben pulled a cigarette from his pocket. Bowing his head to light it, Claire pulled the cigarette from his mouth. He kissed her. She held him for a moment then put the cigarette back in his mouth. He smiled. Taking the cigarette from his mouth, he kissed her again.

"What's your name?" Alex asked looking up at John. He held her up with an arm around her waist.

John looked at Alex then at Ben.

"I remember that I was married... no I'm going to get married... Are we still married?"

"I hope so," John said.

"What's your name?" she asked.

"Keep working on it, love." John kissed her forehead.

"You're Max." Alex beamed as if she had discovered a special present at Christmas.

"I am," Max replied.

"He doesn't want us to call him Daddy," Alex whispered in a loud voice causing everyone to laugh.

The doorbell rang, announcing the doctor and Noémi went to answer the door. The doctor arrived in a flurry of French that Alex couldn't follow. She stood smiling at this gorgeous John. Noémi led John, Alex and the doctor into a small front room where the doctor examined Alex. With Noémi translating, the doctor conferred with John while Alex rested against his shoulder.

"What is it?" Max asked.

"She's been drugged," John said. "He thinks she should shake it. He took a blood sample to make sure it's Ketamine."

"How? What?" Max asked.

"I had something… Sorry I have to keep my eyes closed." Alex was silent for a moment. "My coffee was very bitter at the bistro. It tasted funny but I love coffee so I drank… three cups? It was a French Press. Maxie, what is this guy's name?"

Max laughed.

"Maxie?" Alex asked. "I'm going into a k-hole."

She sagged. John caught her before she hit the floor. He lifted her to his arms.

"What does that mean?" Max asked.

"She's tripping," Ben said. "Noémi, can she lie down in the guest bedroom?"

"Of course," Noémi said.

"You'll stay with her?" Ben asked John. "If it's a k-hole, she'll start hallucinating and having flashbacks."

John nodded.

"Max, you better go too."

"Bag?" Alex asked.

"I'll take care of that," Ben said.

"Come on, chérie," Noémi said. "You can lay down in here."

Noémi led the way down the hall to their guest bedroom. John laid her on the bed then sat in a chair next to the bed. Max sat down on the bed to hold Alex's other hand. After more than an hour of flashbacks and hallucinations, Alex fell into a sound sleep.

❦❦❦

Five hours later
September 28 – 1 P.M. MST
Somewhere between Paris, France and
Buckley Air Force Base, Colorado

"Wake up, Alex," Raz said. He shook her Alex's shoulder.

Alex opened her eyes, then closed them again.

"Come on, Alex. You're coming off Ketamine," he said. "You've got to wake up now."

"Leave me alone, Josh," Alex said. "I wanna sleep."

"You can't call me that," Raz said. He glanced around the military shuttle. If anyone heard his real name, they made no indication.

They had decided the best way to protect Alex was to stick her on a military shuttle back to Denver. Raz had agreed to accompany her and the duffle bag. John and Max would follow in a day as originally planned.

She spent most of the trip sound asleep against Raz's arm. But the doctor had been very clear. Alex needed to wake up within five hours. She has been through too much trauma, the doctor said. Her mind will crack, overwhelmed with the trauma, if she doesn't return to the present. You must wake her.

"Open your eyes," Raz said.

"I'm sorry. Can you talk to me? It will help me come back," Alex said.

"All right," Raz said. He put his arm around Alex's shoulder and spoke into her ear. "I had a delightful time in Paris."

"How is Clarissa?" Alex asked moving her eyes in an effort to wake up.

"Oh Clarissa. She is so blonde, beautiful and very fun."

"Are you actually smacking your lips?"

"You're hallucinating," Raz said smiling.

"Did you go dancing?" Alex asked.

"With you and John. You don't remember?" Raz asked.

"What is John's last name?" Alex asked. "I keep asking people but no one will tell me. Am I married to you?"

"Kind of," Raz laughed. "Open your eyes Alex."

"How can I kind of be married to you?" Alex said. She opened her eyes and felt a blast of pain from the light. She closed her eyes again. "Ouch."

"We're partners."

"Oh right, we're partners. We are very close. I know where you are at all times. You know where I am at all times. How come we don't have sex?"

"That's a very good question," Raz laughed.

Alex opened her eyes to look at him then laughed at the look on his face.

"It would be like having sex with my sister."

"You are having sex with my sister," Alex said.

Raz burst out laughing. "They told me you were very high, I just didn't believe it. I've seen you drink bottles of whiskey and not get this stoned. Come on, let's get up and walk around."

"What about our possessions?" Alex asked in a loud whisper.

"They are locked away."

"Oh great," Alex said.

Raz pulled her to standing and they began walking up and down the aisle of the jet.

"You know, when Jesse was on Ketamine, he became crazy angry." Alex said. She weaved down in the aisle at Raz's side. "He'd stomp around screaming and swearing at the walls. Matthew? He'd roll up in a ball and giggle, like a little kid being tickled. I'd tell you what Troy does, but I promised him on pain of death that I would never tell a soul. Me? I'd hallucinate for a while, usually about Minnie and Mickey Mouse, then fell asleep."

"I've wondered if someone had your file," Raz said. He snatched at her shirt to keep her from walking into the wall. "When was the last time your reaction to Ketamine was tested?"

"Three years ago? I think my tolerance has changed after all those surgeries."

They walked in silence down to the cockpit then turned and walked back. Gasping, Alex stopped walking. She put her hands to her face as her eyes welled with tears.

"Honey, what happened? What's wrong? He pulled her into his arms.

"I had this dream that Claire made the most beautiful dress for me," she said into his shoulder. "I've never seen anything so beautiful."

"I think that happened," Raz said.

"Oh," Alex said. "That means... Oh... I think I'd rather go back to sleep."

Breaking from his embrace, she plopped back down in her seat, crossed her arms, and closed her eyes. Raz made a face and pulled her to standing again.

"Let's keep walking," he said. "We can handle everything if we're awake."

"How many people did I kill?" Alex asked.

"Two not counting the guy who fell off the stairs," Raz replied. "You shot one in the forehead and broke the other's neck. Ben said you did it Chuck Norris style—reverse roundhouse kick."

"Chuck Norris's victims get up at the end of the work day and go home."

"Ben gave the police your body armor and explained what happened. There will be an inquiry, and we'll have to spend some more time in Paris to clear it up..."

"Now you are smacking your lips."

"I've become very fond of the flavor of chocolate crepes," Raz said, "and Clarissa."

Alex laughed.

"Ben said it's no big deal. The men are non-nationals, no passports, Interpol most wanted list, exactly what we expected."

"Well, hopefully they get their virgins."

"I've never understood the draw," Raz said. He steered Alex away from another wall. They walked back down the aisle.

"Thank you for saving my life."

"I don't have any idea how we found that hallway. Maybe it's not me you should thank."

"That's what Ben said."

"We ran down the hall. You were so pale... and your secondary ID tag was gone. Everyone's secondary tag was gone. We thought you were dead. Ben couldn't feel your pulse. We were...upset. Ben went into the room to see if anyone was alive. I was standing guard in the doorway when I thought at least I can bring your body home to the family. I kneeled down and kissed you. You opened your eyes then said my name. Do you remember?"

"I only remember you carrying me through the room full of people. Where was that?"

"The police were at Le Fee Verte when we arrived. Someone killed the clerk and a few of the patrons who tried to help her."

"What? I had a conversation with the clerk a few hours ago. She was making me an absinthe."

Raz shook his head.

"Today? The blonde clerk? Tall? I'm sorry, Alex, that was a hallucination. She was killed, stabbed, two years ago. I carried you through the shop then you begged me to stay with you. You kept saying 'he'll take me if you leave'. Any idea who 'he' is?"

They were at the end of the hallway again, near the cockpit. Alex began visibly shaking. The information triggered a physical flashback, Alex stopped walking. Holding her close, Raz pressed her against the wall and whispered, 'just breathe, just breathe.' She stood shaking in his safe arms until she caught her breath and nodded. He stepped back. Taking her hand, he led her back down the aisle.

"I stayed with you until you went into surgery in Germany. Then the Army made me leave. The Admiral locked security down tight. They wouldn't even let your father see you. They barely let Zack fly you. I met your helicopter when you arrived at Walter Reed. But after the first surgery, you never awakened."

"Thank you for taking such special care of me," she said.

Looking deep into her eyes, he smiled then stroked her face.

"Tell me about Samantha." Alex tried for a neutral topic.

"I like Samantha," he said. "We're just getting to know each other which is fun. It's fun to have the desire to get to know someone, you know?"

Alex nodded.

"I think she likes me. We enjoy similar things and know different things. She spent an entire day showing me around the Denver Art Museum and I spent a day touring her through the Smithsonian."

"In Washington?"

Raz nodded. "We're meeting in New York City for a show in a month or so. I'm her date to the Fey Team anniversary ceremony. She's such an adult, your sister. She expects me to be available when we schedule time and otherwise knows that I'm doing other things. It's nice."

"But not love," Alex said.

"No, it's not love," Raz said. He held her eyes again. "And that's nice too."

They walked down to the end then turned.

"How are you feeling?"

"Crappy. I'd like nothing more than to go to my home, take a bath in my bathtub and sleep in my bed."

"I know," he said. "We have to run you through medical at Buckley then we'll head back to the hotel for a bath."

She nodded then sighed.

"It's a lot," he said. "Why do you think this hasn't broken you? I went through less than this and completely fell apart."

"You watched your wife and her lover jump from the North World Trade Center Tower on 9-11. You were less than fifty-feet from where they hit the pavement. That's a bit more than losing your home..."

"And family and husband and job and team and health and..."

"Bees. That's what makes me the most mad. They killed four of my beehives."

Raz smiled.

"I guess I'm still Max's twin. That's who I am."

"They're coming for Max."

Alex nodded then smiled. "It will be interesting to watch them try."

"There isn't a file on Max Hargreaves."

Alex nodded.

"Let's get steaks tonight."

"I'll take you anywhere you'd like to go." He caught her hand and turned her toward him. Holding her eyes, he added, "my love."

He raised his eyebrows and Alex laughed.

CHAPTER TWENTY-FOUR
Nine hours later
September 29 – 3:21 A.M.
Downtown Denver, Colorado

Alex woke with a start. Her heart pounded against her rib cage. She had no idea where she was or what woke her. She was simply awake in the dark. Sitting up, she noticed that she was in a hotel room. She patted the bed next to her. John wasn't there. Moving to sit on the side of the bed, she heard the sound again.

The phone was ringing.

She reached to turn on a bedside lamp then realized she didn't know where the light switch was located. Her hand fumbled around for a few moments before she gave up. Standing up, she moved toward the light under the hall door and clicked on the light.

Ah shit. The light brought a round of Ketamine induced nausea and head splitting pain. There's got to be coffee here somewhere. She wandered into the bathroom, then heard the phone ring again.

Ah well, they'll call back.

Turning on the bathroom light, she blinked at the bright light and grimaced at her reflection. She was wearing panties and someone's big T-shirt. Her fake hair was crumpled, standing straight up in some places and flat in others. It looked like she had gone to sleep with wet hair...

Oh right. Alex remembered that she was at the hotel in downtown Denver. Her one bag of clothing was in Paris. Glancing at the half open suite door, Raz was across the suite. She nodded at her reflection. Turning on the faucet, she wet her hair trying to flatten it out.

She and Raz went to dinner at Elway's. They ate steak, drank wine and laughed. Alex insisted they eat some salad which they fed to each other. Raz ordered every chocolate dessert on the menu. Groaning and laughing, they managed to eat them. She smiled. She had such a good time with Raz.

When they returned, he ran a bath for her, set his T-shirt on bed, then left for a date. She scratched her head trying to remember who he saw last night. She could probably just go across the suite to find out who was there. She chuckled to herself.

The phone started ringing again.

Fuck.

Getting up from the commode, she went back into the hotel room to look for the telephone. She had never used the phone in this room. The clock's red digital letters cast light on the phone sitting on top of the desk . The phone's over there! Feeling like she had accomplished something, Alex picked up the phone.

"Hello?"

"Hello my dear," Eleazar's voice purred in Hebrew.

Alex set the phone down. Dropping into the chair next to the desk, Alex stared at the telephone. She hadn't expected that.

She knew she should get Raz. She knew she should call into command. She knew she should have the call traced. She knew that she should not pick up the telephone.

But when the phone rang again, she picked it up.

"What do you want?" Alex asked in Hebrew.

"Now is that anyway to speak to an old friend?" Eleazar purred.

"You are no friend of mine," she said.

"How are you feeling?"

"What do you want?" Alex yelled into the phone.

The door to the suite banged opened and Raz stood in the doorway wearing white boxer shorts. Walking over to her, he wrenched the phone from her hand. He listened at the ear piece then slammed the receiver down into the phone.

"What the fuck are you doing?" he said. "That was Eleazar. God damn it Alex. What are you thinking?"

Leaning her elbows on her knees, Alex shook her head.

"Your mind is fragile from the Ketamine."

The phone rang and Raz pulled the phone line from the wall. Alex looked up at him and blinked. She had no idea why he was so angry.

"I can't help myself," she said. "I feel compelled to speak with him, to find out what exactly it is that he wants."

"Alex, he planted that in your mind. All of those phone calls conditioned you to want to speak to him again. It's classic psychological programming. You know that."

Alex nodded. Her cell phone began ringing. She put her hands over her ears.

Realizing that his anger was also hitting her fragile mind, he pulled her up into his arms. "Oh honey, I'm sorry. Let's do it together. Give me two minutes."

When he released her from the hug, Alex plopped back into the chair. Dropping her head into her hands, she rubbed her forehead back and forth against her hands. She looked up to see Raz return wearing blue jeans and talking on his cell phone. She watched the muscles in his taut abdomen move side to side as he walked toward her.

Sensing movement in the sitting area, Alex looked past Raz to see a woman moving across the suite. That's our server from Elway's. Alex raised a hand to say, "hello" to the woman. She winked at Alex then let herself out of the suite.

"I'm sorry Raz. Your date just left."

Raz looked down at her and nodded, "I need your phone."

Alex dug around in her clothing, piled next to the bathroom, to find her cell phone. She gave him the phone.

"What did you tell her?"

"Cops," he said. He put his hand over the mouth piece of his cell phone. "I asked her if she would mind leaving. She was delightful." Turning his attention to the phone, he said: "That's what I thought. Can you check on that?"

With the phone propped against his chin, he said to Alex, "We're looking for terrorists. She didn't want to get involved."

"Will you see her again?"

"Probably," he said. "I seem to be in Denver a lot these days."

Alex smiled. There was a tap on the door.

"I ordered some coffee for you," he said.

Alex brightened which made him laugh. She answered the door for room service then stood by the door drinking a cup of coffee with a little cream.

"All right, thank you," Raz said disconnecting his telephone. He looked at Alex, who was completely absorbed by her coffee, and laughed. "Happy?"

"Very." She poured herself another cup of coffee.

"Let's go into the suite," he said then answered his cell phone.

Alex moved into the sitting area and he followed. Sitting down on the couch, she remembered that the coffee was in the other room. She jumped up and ran back into the bedroom where she grabbed the thermos of coffee, a cup and raw sugar for Raz, and returned to the sitting area.

"What's going on?" Alex asked. She poured a cup of coffee for him then stirred in the raw sugar.

Disconnecting from his phone, he took the cup and smiled at her generosity. Alex would never think to keep something for herself. He took a long drink of the warm coffee fixed exactly as he liked it.

"Eleazar went underground last month. He's been in Jordan, visiting his mother, as King Abdullah told you. Rather than returning to Jerusalem, he seems to be traveling through the Middle East. We believe he's been recruiting people for an operation here in the States, but we don't really know."

"How did you know he was on the phone?"

"Ben said that Eleazar would try to get to you before the Ketamine wore off. Prior to viewing the vault... Do you remember the vault?"

Alex nodded.

"You believed Eleazar killed your team. He wants you to believe that he killed your team. Ben thought he would contact you to clarify or convince you that your memory was wrong."

"That Ben is a smart guy."

"Like his daughter," Raz said.

Alex's cell phone began to ring again.

"Go ahead," Raz said. He waited until she answered the phone then connected through his cell phone. He would listen to the conversation while tracing the call.

"Hello?"

"You are hard to get a hold of," Eleazar said in English.

"A girl's got to keep her distance from all the handsome men who want to talk with her," Alex said. "What is it that you want?"

"I wanted to hear your lovely voice," he said. "You want to tell me how to get into the vault."

"I do?"

"You'll tell me how to get into the vault." Eleazar's voice was silky smooth.

"What do you know about that vault?" Alex asked.

"Why?"

"I'm the only one who can get in that vault. I can give you a code but you won't be able to open the door. Why don't you tell me what you want and I'll retrieve your property for you?"

Eleazar clicked off the telephone and Alex threw the cell phone from her.

"I feel dirty," she said.

"I bet," Raz said. "Is that true about the vault?"

Alex nodded. "Charlie could get in too."

"The Army tried for a month to get inside."

"Who closed the door?"

"They removed Jesse last. The door has on some automatic mechanism. As soon as Jesse was moved, the door swung closed. There was a guy inside who just managed to squeak out."

"Huh," Alex shrugged.

"They tried to force the door…"

"You can't do that," she said.

"Why so much security?"

"I was usually there by myself. I felt like that vault was the safest place on the planet but Charlie worried. I was supposed to close the door when I was there alone."

"Did you do that?"

"Mostly," Alex said. "Sometimes I was running in to drop cash or a book and I'd leave the door open but usually I closed the door. That's what's weird, Raz. What could possibly be in there? I was there every single time the vault was opened."

"And why didn't they get what they wanted after they killed everyone?" Raz asked.

"I wish I knew," Alex said.

"How does the lock work?"

"There are four spots that scan for hand prints. One spot for each of my hands and each of Charlie's hands. If I put my hand in the wrong spot, Charlie's spot for example, the door cannot be opened for seven days. Mess up more than once and the security has to be over ridden."

"How?"

"In a long and very painful process. The keypad is a complicated mechanism of fingerprint scanning and code. The codes are sort of random. Charlie had the system made some place in Asia… Laos I think."

"I've never even heard of such a thing."

"Yeah?" Alex asked. "The door used to just have the keypad lock but around the time Joseph left, Charlie changed the door. He set the codes to random and added the hand print scans. He also added a bunch of security inside the vault. There are compartments in the floor that only I can get into."

"Why did he do that?"

"I don't really know," Alex said. "Joseph and Charlie had been friends for more than twenty years. When Joseph left, Charlie became increasingly anxious. He would stay up after everyone went to bed as if he was guarding us. He didn't want anyone to go anywhere alone. I guess that's why we were in the vault. We usually roamed Paris then met at the apartment to change and stuff."

"I remember. And you don't have any idea what was going on?"

"With Charlie? No. I asked him, more than once, but he would just assure me that everything was all right. Joseph told me that he noticed the change in Charlie too."

"When did Joseph see Charlie?"

"We routed through Denver to meet his twins after they were born. Joseph said he asked Charlie what was wrong. Charlie made an excuse and changed the subject."

"Was that like Charlie?"

"Charlie? Oh yeah." Alex looked over at Raz. "Charlie was like a big Dad. He took care of every worry, every problem. He said our work was hard enough to have to worry about bullshit."

"Maybe the journals will give you some clues," Raz said then yawned.

"Maybe. I'm going to need help transcribing them."

"Transcribing?

"They are in a code based in Navajo."

"You mean that someone has ten years of your journals in a code? In Navajo?"

Alex nodded. Raz laughed then yawned.

"Are you going back to bed?" she asked.

"I didn't get much sleep."

"I'm glad."

Raz smiled. "Wanna snuggle?"

"That sounds very nice, but I should work on maps for a while. I haven't listened to the map phone messages in at least a week. The Intelligence Center added video so that should be interesting."

"Will you wake me if anything…?"

"Of course," she said.

She stood and hugged him. "Thanks."

He kissed her cheek then went into his bedroom.

With her cup and pot of coffee, Alex went back into her bedroom. She closed the door then sat down in an armchair by the window. Lost in thought, remembering and reliving, she watched the night turn into day. As the sun began to reflect off the mountains, Alex promised herself that no one else would be injured by Eleazar.

Not again.

Never again.

CHAPTER TWENTY-FIVE

The next night
September 29
Downtown Denver, Colorado

After spending a gutwrenching day documenting everything that happened in Paris, Alex excused herself from an afternoon meeting and a working dinner. She wanted to take a long bath.

When Raz came to check on her, she was sound asleep in the tub. He helped her out of the tub and got her into bed before he left for their working dinner. Concerned about leaving her alone, and exhausted himself, he promised to return early. He peeked in around nine o'clock and she was curled up in a ball sound asleep. With a sigh of relief, he was asleep in ten minutes.

Max and John arrived from Paris around midnight. Peeking into the rooms, they found Alex and Raz sound asleep with their doors open to the suite. John pulled Raz's door closed then, raising a hand in good-bye to Max, he went into Alex's room. Max returned to the room he had been using.

Pulling off his clothing, John slipped under the covers. He lay watching Alex sleep for a few moments. Drawn, as if by a magnet, his lips brushed her cheek then her ear. When she moved her hand, as if to bat at a fly, he put her fingers into his mouth. She sighed, rolling onto her back, and he slipped on top of her. She smiled slightly in her sleep then opened and shut her eyes. Her arms went around him.

His lips caught hers, pulling at her tongue, while his hands drew the T-shirt over her head. His mouth moved along her neck then took her nipple, flicking his tongue across its rising focus. She opened her eyes, looking down at him, as his mouth moved across her belly. His teeth pulled at the diamond in her belly button then his tongue explored the contours behind the gem. His fingers grasped her behind, slipping off her panties while his mouth worked along her fleshy contours and sensitive soft folds. She gasped in pleasure, wide awake, holding his head in place.

He chuckled, "Welcome home?"

She shifted her hips, rocking to his attention, until she moaned in rising intensity. She pulled him up toward her and he plowed into her moist depth. As she shuddered against him, he pressed forward. She wrapped her legs around his hips, giving him access to her deepest zones. He worked his hips against her while his mouth tortured her neck and nipples, then returned to plundering her mouth. She clutched at him lost in sensation. They began releasing in together in waves of intense pleasure, rising and falling, until he let go deep within her.

Resting with his head on her shoulder, he said, "I have some news."

"Uh huh," she said. Her fingers played with the curls in his hair.

"I'm not a father," John said.

Alex lifted her head to look at him. He nodded.

"Ben gave me the DNA results before we left Paris."

"Who is?"

"Néall. He's also my brother."

Alex smiled, "Bastard."

"Yes, one more thing we have in common," he said.

"Hmm." Alex shifted slightly and John moved to the bed. He stroked her warm body.

"I've only been married one time."

"To Eimilie?" she kissed his lips.

"To you. I am your lawfully wedded husband."

"I was having so much fun as the other woman."

"Our international lawyer spent the day in London. He was able to confirm that the records were not filed and that the notation by the priest in London does not constitute a legal marriage. The priest, who is no longer living, cannot verify the written account. You know that Father Seamus has confirmed with Rome that our marriage is valid."

"That is good news," she said. "How shall we celebrate?"

"I have an idea," John said.

Alex giggled when he pulled her on top of him.

෴෴෴෴෴

One week later
October 8 – 4:30 A.M.
Fort Logan National Cemetery, Colorado

"That's the best we could do." Trece turned around in the front seat of an armored black Expedition. "The area is clear by satellite and heat. You have a half hour to yourselves."

Joseph and Alex were sitting in the middle seat of the car with Matthew and Troy in the back. Joseph nodded to Trece. They were parked by the Memorial to the Fey Special Forces team at Fort Logan National Cemetery.

"We'll talk about the Circus when you're done," the White Boy said from the driver's seat.

"We can't leave you here alone," Matthew said. He put a hand on Alex's shoulder and the other on Joseph's shoulder. "I'm sorry."

Alex turned to look at him, "Thanks for doing this."

"I'm on watch," Troy said.

Glancing at the rifle and scope in Troy's hand, Joseph nodded.

"You're burning time," Trece said.

Alex opened the door to the Expedition. Stepping into the cold the October pre-dawn, she held her hand out to Joseph. They walked around the Expedition to the Memorial and Troy stood in the doorway of the truck. Alex turned one last time, catching the watchful eyes of her friends, then walked to the Memorial. As they approached, they saw that the families had decorated the graves for the anniversary.

Starting at Alexander's grave, adorned with a large bouquet of sunflowers, Joseph set a votive candle and a stick of incense. Together, they clicked their lighters touching the flame to the candle first, then the incense. They moved in silence to Nathan's grave.

A picture of Nathan and his teenage son hugging was stuck in the grass next to the grave. Making a space for the candle, Alex pointed to a picture of a baby, Nathan's first grandchild. Joseph kneeled to pick up the pictures. Ripping a plastic picture holder from his wallet, Joseph slipped the pictures into the holder and placed them near the top of the grave. Nathan talked about his son all the time. Alex touched the baby's picture with her index finger. She could almost hear him brag about the baby. Sniffing back their tears, they lit the candle and incense.

Paul's grave had a bright red bouquet of Gerbera daisies on top. Alex saw a drop of water on the flowers and looked to the sky to see if it was raining. Unable to see the clear sky through her clouded eyes, she realized that she was crying. As they touched flame to the votive candle and incense, she saw tears dropping from Joseph's eyes as well.

Alex fingered Jax's tattered Badwater Ultramarathon T-shirt, his lucky shirt from his first Badwater. Joseph pointed to the stethoscope near the top of Jax's grave.

"He would have been such a great doctor," Joseph whispered.

Alex nodded. Bending together, they lit the candle and incense at Jax's grave.

Dean's grave was covered with crayon drawings. Alex touched a plastic wrapped crayon picture of Dean. Joseph held up a crayon picture of a red girl and purple boy with their green mother. In block blue letters, the child had written: "WHERE ARE YOU DADDY?" Alex covered her mouth to stifle a sob. Joseph moved the pictures away from the flames and they lit the candle and incense.

Scott's grave was clean and polished. Andi, his flower child wife, had painstakingly clipped the grass around the granite stone. A tidy and precise person, this is exactly how Scott would have wanted his grave. Joseph and Alex placed the candle and incense away from the stone as to not disrupt the precision.

"Andi misses him horribly," Alex said.

"Me too," Joseph nodded.

Alex looked up to see Jesse standing next to Tommy's grave.

"Get down," Jesse said. "M21, longrange rifle."

Alex tackled Joseph just before two shots rang out across the Memorial. Jumping from the Expedition, Trece and the White Boy ran to Alex and Joseph while Matthew took off running across the grass.

"Are you all right?" Trece pulled Alex to standing.

"We're fine." Joseph took the White Boy's offered hand.

"Finish up," Trece said. "We'll take care of this."

Tommy's stone was covered with sayings written in white wax pencil. Tommy loved language, words and communication. A variety of hands had written his favorite sayings on the black granite with his favorite saying, 'Only the mediocre are always at their best,' under his name. Alex smiled touching the 'I love you' written in a teenage girl's hearts and curls. They lit the candle and incense for Tommy the communicator.

Alex touched the Pyrex cooking dish sitting on Dwight's grave. Raised by his grandmother after his mother over-dosed on heroin, Dwight's grandmother brought his favorite meal to his grave every Sunday. The groundskeepers asked her to stop. She told them that she made her baby Sunday dinner every week for almost forty years. She was not going to stop because of some groundskeeper. Joseph made a face when he opened the lid. They placed the candle and lit the incense against the smell as much as to remember their friend.

Overcome with sadness, Alex fell to her knees in front of Jesse's grave. Even with the apparition of her friend floating nearby, she felt Jesse's loss like a hole in her heart and her life. Reaching in her pocket, she intended to leave the St. Christopher medallion among the bright pink and blue blossoms which she and Maria painstakingly lay on top of his granite marker.

"What's that?" Joseph asked.

"I found Jesse's St. Christopher in the vault. It was the only gift he ever received from his mother. I was going to leave it here."

"I think Jesse would want you to keep it," Joseph said.

"I keep telling you that," Jesse said.

Alex nodded and placed the medallion back in her pocket. Joseph dropped to his knees to hug her. With an arm around each other, they lit the candle and incense.

Alex wiped her face with her hands then still on her knees, she placed a piece of incense at Mike's grave. She flicked a leaf off the top of the grave, then wiped the dust with the arm of her jacket. Joseph gave her his handkerchief and she cleaned the granite.

"She's with a woman now," Joseph said of Mike's wife.

Alex nodded. Married on paper only, Mike and his wife stayed together for their three children. Alex's heart broke to see that powerful, funny, quick to temper, loveable Mike received as little from his wife in death as he had in life. She promised herself to look after his grave. Lighting the incense and candle at Mike's grave from her kneeling position, she looked around for Joseph.

Joseph was standing, sobbing into his hands, at the end of Charlie's grave. Alex stood to hug Joseph. He pushed her away then dropped his head to her shoulder and wept. He had no words to express his loss, a sadness that never seemed to lessen.

They stood crying in each other's arms at the end of Charlie's grave until, hearing cars driving into the Memorial, they knew their time was up. They bent to light the candle and incense for Charlie together. Joseph collapsed against her in grief. Alex held him up with an arm around his waist.

Trece and the White Boy, armed with M-16 machine guns, came forward again to escort them to the Expedition. Once in the car, Troy pressed Joseph and Alex's heads into their lap. The Expedition slowed to pick up Matthew then drove out of the cemetery.

"Can we get up yet?" Alex asked.

"You're so beautiful like that," Trece said. "I thought we'd just leave you there."

Alex laughed and sat up.

"Snooze?" she asked. They had planned on meeting Max, John and Erin for breakfast at their favorite breakfast restaurant.

"I going to have the pineapple upside down pancakes," Trece said.

"You're off carbs, Trece," the White Boy said.

"That's right, I'm not eating carbs right now. My percent fat is up a half point."

"It's a celebration of life," Joseph said. "Pineapple upside down pancakes sound perfect."

"Oh sure, you want me to get fat. Just because I'm at four and a half percent fat and you are not, doesn't mean I should get fatter. Jeez. Alex, you didn't tell me that your Captain was a food enabler."

"A what?" Alex asked. "WAIT, I don't want…"

"Someone who encourages people to eat food that's not good for them. Honestly Alex, I thought you knew that. I mean…"

"Andy!"

"Oh right, I'm supposed to be quiet so you can reflect. You have to admit. I've been doing a good job keeping quiet."

"I think you've been doing a great job, Trece," the White Boy said.

"I am trying to be respectful. I've lost friends. Hell, I lost Jesse. I might not have spent every day with Jesse, but I loved him. Losing friends is like a wound that never ever heals. Sure, you feel guilty that you survived, especially when you see the families. I mean…"

"ANDY!" Alex, Joseph, Matthew and Troy said in unison.

"You guys sound pretty good. Oh, all right. I'm going to be quiet now."

Trece zipped his lips with his hand then looked out the window. They drove to the edge of Fort Logan National Cemetery.

"Where are we going?" Trece asked.

Everyone laughed.

CHAPTER TWENTY-SIX

Three hours later
October 8 – 9:00 A.M.
Downtown Denver, Colorado

Alex stood near the edge of the crowded room. The families of the Fey Special Forces Team planned a very small, family only, ceremony for the two year anniversary. They would meet at ten o'clock at Alex and John's home, then make their way to Fort Logan together. Alex had even arranged for a Denver Police escort.

What a difference two months makes.

Alex and John's house was gone.

Their private ceremony became a large public event where every politician and all of the military brass would be in attendance. The Secret Service expected at least four hundred people and every media outlet. The families were cajoled, begged and manipulated into attending with their children.

But the desire to be together, on this day of all days, was greater than the President or something as insignificant as a home explosion. Max found the largest and nicest meeting room in the Cash Register building where his international law firm rented three floors. Rebecca arranged for caterers and decorators. Everything was beautiful.

"Major Alex?" Dwight's grandmother asked coming over to Alex.

"Yes, Mrs. Harris," Alex said. She took the elderly woman's hands in her own. A small woman, with deep creases in her skin, Mrs. Harris looked up at Alex through the mesh of her black hat.

"I wanted to thank you for my necklace." Mrs. Harris put her gloved hand to the diamond encrusted platinum cross around her neck. "Dwight told me you each received a diamond. It never occurred to me that he would have made something for me."

Alex smiled. She spent the last week with the team's families. She wanted to tell them in person what happened and give them the diamond jewelry she retrieved from the vault. Each team member received their choice of diamonds after they rescued the board of directors of a large diamond corporation. No one knew what to pick, so Alex called Raz. The ex-New York City cop helped them choose diamonds. He also arranged for a jeweler in Paris. Raz picked a large diamond for Alex then convinced her to wear it in her belly button.

"Dwight was very clear. He wanted you to have something you would wear," Alex said with a smile.

"I have another question for you."

"Yes, ma'am."

"My Dwight was shot in the head. I wasn't able to have the casket open at the funeral. The other men weren't … disfigured in this way."

Alex's eyes glistened with tears as she searched Dwight's grandmother's face.

"Did they mutilate my baby because he was Negro?"

"Dwight was shot in the chest, the abdomen and the legs."

"Yes, ma'am. Seventeen bullets. The doctor said 'enough bullets to down an elephant.'"

"We kept our weapons in an area of the vault. One person stood guard…"

"Jesse Abreu was on guard," Mrs. Harris said. "You said there was no way for him to see what was coming. Professional killers."

"Yes, ma'am." Alex nodded her head. "It was our habit to drop our weapons in a particular area then go about our business. After Dwight was shot…". Alex paused and searched the elderly woman's face again.

"You can tell me anything, Major Alex. Nothing in this whole world is worse than my baby's dying before me."

"The shooter shot from left to right, then back right to left. Somehow, Dwight was still alive. He pulled himself along the floor with his arms toward the weapons. I fired at the shooter…"

"With that handgun you always carry."

"Yes, ma'am."

They were silent for a moment as the information and inference lingered in the air.

"You're saying that my boy was a hero."

Tears sprung from Alex's eyes, "Yes ma'am. Your boy was a hero."

Mrs. Harris pulled Alex into a hug. The women stood together for a moment. Stepping back, Mrs. Harris passed Alex a tissue she had tucked up her sleeve then used one herself.

"I said to my boy, 'There'll be no end of trouble if you have a woman on your team.' He said, 'Momma, you of all people should not be prejudice.' Over the years, you would pull them out of one crazy situation after another and Dwight would say, 'See Momma. You were wrong.' Alexandra, I'm sorry I misjudged you."

Alex smiled. "I miss him too."

"For the rest of our lives," Mrs. Harris said looking at the families. "We will miss them for the rest of our lives."

There was a lot of excited talking near the door, and Alex turned to see who had arrived. Mrs. Harris put her hand on Alex's arm.

"You're going to find the people who did this," she said. "I know it."

Alex nodded and Mrs. Harris hugged her again. John came over to the women.

"I'm sorry to interrupt but Paul's girlfriend, Greta, is here. She brought her baby. She wants to speak to you."

"Go on dear," Mrs. Harris said.

Maria touched Alex's arm as she moved to speak with Mrs. Harris. John led Alex to Greta. The young woman was standing with her back to Alex talking to Max and Rebecca held a child in her arms. When the baby turned to look at her, Alex gasped. The little girl smiled, her dark eyes sparkling with laughter, and she reached toward Alex. She was the spitting image of Paul.

"She likes you Alex," Rebecca said.

Alex touched the child's hand. She wrapped her fingers around Alex's index finger.

"Mrs. Hargreaves, would you mind watching Mindy?" Greta asked. She gave her diaper bag to Max.

"I'd love to! She is absolutely precious," Rebecca said. "How old is she?"

"She'll be fifteen months tomorrow."

"Greta!" Joseph's wife Nancy hugged the young woman. "I'm so glad you made it. Is this yours? Oh my God, Greta, she looks just like Paul."

Greta blushed, pushing a piece of light brown hair behind her ear, and nodded.

"Rebecca, you cannot hog her to yourself," Nancy said. She reach out to take Mindy from Rebecca.

"Come on." Alex led Greta away from the women. "You'll be lucky if you get her back from those two."

Alex found a quiet corner of the room where they sat down in two high backed chairs.

"She is beautiful."

Greta blushed again. "Like Paul. She's beautiful like Paul was."

They sat together in silence for a moment taking in the conversation and movement of the room.

"I'm sorry I wouldn't talk to you this week," Greta said. "I... It's been very difficult for me."

Alex nodded.

"Can you tell me about this?" Greta said.

She held her left hand where a three carat radiant cut diamond on a simple yellow gold band fit perfectly on her ring finger. Standing on Greta's mother's doorstep, Alex had pressed the ring box into Greta's hand saying, 'When you want to talk to me about this, I'm here for you.'

"We did a job for some diamond people and they gave us diamonds as a 'thank you.'"

"That's not what I meant," Greta said. "They found him in his boxer shorts. He was..."

"Dancing," Alex said. "We were all together in the vault in Paris. Did he tell you about the vault?"

"He said that you had a storage place in Paris but that's all."

"That's where the assault took place. Not in Afghanistan."

"I knew that he didn't die in Afghanistan. I knew it. I thought... Is this a secret?"

"For now."

Greta nodded.

"Paul took dancing lessons so that he could dance with you on your wedding night. He planned to ask you when the divorce was final then drag you off to Las Vegas. He wanted everything to be perfect. He was changing when Dean asked him about his dance moves. Paul was demonstrating. You remember how Dean and Nathan egged Paul on."

Greta's lips were pressed together in a tight line.

"He wasn't with a woman? I thought..."

"Never," Alex said. "He had been separated for six or seven years. He saw women in that time but once he met you... I could tell you about your first date, your second date, when you moved in together, everything." Alex chuckled. "I even know what you look like when you first open your eyes in the morning. Paul talked about you non-stop."

Greta began to weep. Alex put her hand on the girl's arm.

"His mother..."

"She's the only person on the planet who is fond of his Paul's ex-wife. You know that he didn't file for the divorce only because that woman is so unpleasant. Paul just didn't want to deal with the conflict. Greta you have to know that."

Greta nodded, wiping her eyes.

"We were together before you left. He... I met him in Colorado Springs. He left base for two hours and met me at the La Quinta. He wanted a baby so bad that he didn't want to miss a chance." Greta blushed. "You must think I'm a complete slut. They weren't even officially divorced."

"Trust me. If we could have snuck away for even a half hour, we would have," Alex said. "I gave Paul the pass. He took Jesse's Jeep."

"Then he died and... I was pregnant. His family won't have anything to do with Mindy or me. I've been living with my mother."

Alex nodded. "They are here. Paul's parents. I bet my mother will work this out. It's the kind of thing she's good at. She'll probably tell them they are being petty and childish." Alex smiled to herself.

"Did Paul..." Greta's eyes searched Alex's face. "Did Paul love me?"

"Yes Greta, Paul loved you."

"Thanks," Greta said.

"I know the others will want to see you and meet Mindy. Do you feel up to it?"

Greta nodded. "If Paul loved me, I can do anything."

"He did." Alex stood to hug Greta.

"Greta! I didn't know you were here!" Dean's wife Jennifer exclaimed. "Alex, have you been hiding Greta?"

"Greta has been hiding something." Alex nodded her head toward the door.

Jennifer gasped when she saw baby Mindy. "It's Paul. Oh Greta, you poor thing."

Alex moved away from the women as they hugged. Moving across the room, she walked right into a big redheaded US Army Sergeant.

"Sir," Mike's oldest son saluted her.

"Hi Michael. Oh, uh, at ease soldier," she said. She hugged the boy. "Thanks for bringing your brother and sister. It's great to see them."

Mike's bright redheaded children were mixing with the other families.

"Yes sir," he said. "Sir..."

"What's up?" Alex asked.

"I am currently in Special Forces training."

"Good for you. Isn't it fun?"

"Fun?" Michael asked. Was the Major making fun of him? He looked into Alex's smiling face trying to determine how he should respond. Taking a breath for courage, he continued, "I'm applying to a specialty and I wondered if you might give me a recommendation. I've heard that soldiers who have parents who were not held in high regard have a harder time moving forward."

"Speak freely, Michael. What are you saying?"

"My understanding is that my father will be an impediment to my career."

Alex burst out laughing. "Are you serious?"

"Sir."

"Your father was a decorated soldier, one of the best in his class. They asked him, more than once, to teach at Fort Bragg. He liked being with us, our team, in the field. Don't you have his medals?"

"No sir. I am not aware of my father ever receiving any medals."

"I'll see if I can find a list," Alex said. "Do you know who that guy is?"

"Your father, sir. General Patrick Hargreaves."

"Go tell him that you are Mike's son and listen to what he has to say about Mike. You should be very proud of your father. He was a wonderful person, a dear friend and a great soldier."

Michael's eyes glistened. He looked away from Alex in an effort to control his emotions.

"Sir, the recommendation?"

"Of course," Alex said. "Anyone would be lucky to have you on their team."

Alex took him by the arm and led him over to her father.

"Dad, this is Mike's son Michael."

"You're Mike's son? I could have guessed that." Patrick eyes brightened. "What a guy. He went through training just before we left Fort Bragg. I could tell you stories…"

Alex put her hand on her father's arm.

"Michael's been told that his father will be an impediment to his career."

Patrick laughed and put his arm around the young man's shoulders.

"Let me tell you about your father…"

Alex smiled leaving them to talk. Moving toward the center of the room, she found herself watching people talk and laugh. Last year, the loss was too fresh and the pain too extreme. This year, they were ready to connect, to remember. She saw the diamond earrings sparkle in Nathan's son's ears as he lifted his baby in the air, the dancing light along Maria's chin from the pear shaped diamond pendant that hung around her neck and the flash from Jennifer's tennis bracelet as she reached around Andi to hug her.

This year they could reflect the light.

❧❧❧

One hour later
October 8 – 11:00 A.M.
Downtown Denver, Colorado

Alex looked up to see a short small man jamming his index finger into Trece's chest. As she approached, she could hear the man screaming. Short man in a cheap suit. He must be a part of the President's event planning team. For all his good natured charm, and experience dealing with the public, the huge Trece was about to pounce on the man when Alex said,

"Can I help you?"

"Where are the children?" the man turned to glower at Alex.

"What children?" Alex asked.

Under the nose's of the President's event team, they slipped the team's children to Patrick and Rebecca's home. Alex would be damned before pictures of her friend's weeping children were splashed all over the media. That was not going to happen.

"The families were specifically instructed to bring their children to the event. The President has a few special words to say to the children of the Fey Special Forces Team. Who the fuck are you anyway?"

Trece moved his shoulder an inch, knocking the man onto his behind.

"That is assault. I will not hesitate to report you to your superiors, " the little man screamed jumping to his feet.

"That would be me. Report duly noted," Alex said. "I'm Major Drayson."

"This Neanderthal assaulted me," the little man screamed. "Where the fuck are the children?"

Trece moved forward, but Alex put a hand on his chest.

"Captain Ramirez? Will you collect your team? The families are ready."

"Yes sir," Trece said. He loomed over the little man and he stepped back. Trece stalked off.

"You do not seem to understand what I am saying to you," the little man started in on Alex. "Do you even know what the Fey was? What this team accomplished in their ten years together?"

"I have some idea, sir."

"Then you understand the importance of celebrating their accomplishments."

"Yes sir," Alex said.

"If you were half the soldier that this Special Forces team was…" The man scanned Alex. Seeing that he gained some purchase, he continued, "you would handle this ceremony with greater delicacy and much less incompetence."

"You're absolutely right. If you will excuse me, I need to attend to the security detail."

Alex turned her back on the little man and began to walk off. Unable to leave it alone, the man put his hand on her shoulder to turn her back to him. The next thing he knew, he was laying on his back, his breath knocked out of him and Alex's foot on his chest. She kept her foot on his chest while the parents, wives and families, dressed in body armor and sporting armored hats that read 'In Memoriam of the Fey Special Forces Team,' left with the security team. Every time he tried to get up, she pushed him back down with her foot.

"Who is that?" Colonel Gordon asked.

"Event team, sir. I detained him to keep him from harm's way."

"Harm's way?"

"I was going to kill him, sir," Alex said.

"Ah. Let him up and I'll take care of him," Colonel Gordon said. "You're needed upstairs."

"Thank you sir," she said.

She removed her foot from the little man's chest. Leaving the room, she heard the man start in on his diatribe with Colonel Gordon. In the elevator, Alex took long slow breaths to calm down.

Max held a side entrance to his international law office suite open for her. The twins pressed they foreheads together in silent greeting.

"Nice throw. Trece said that guy was from the President's event team," Matthew said. He and Troy were standing in the hall waiting for Alex.

"I was simply keeping him from harm's way."

"We need to compete again," Matthew said.

Alex nodded. She raised a hand to say 'hello' to Troy and walked back to the small conference room next to Max's office.

"Hi." She closed the door. "I understand you wanted to see me."

John turned from the plate glass window he had been looking out. In a step, he lifted her off the ground. She giggled.

"I love you so much I can barely hold all the feelings in my body."

She kissed his lips.

"I do not want to be away from you today, not any day, but especially not today. I can't lose..."

Alex kissed him quiet.

"Today marks the worst day, the very worst day of my life." His lip moved against her lips.

"Me too." She rested her head on his shoulder.

"What is your plan?" John asked.

"We are going to the Irish Snug for some lunch and whiskey. We reserved a snug and are going to play poker. If he's back in time, Zack's going to meet us there."

"I'll be back in a couple hours and we'll do something fun." His hands pulled at her behind. "You have no idea how fun I can be."

She giggled feeling his desire press against her and kissed him.

"I'm wondering what kind of fun you had in mind, Mr. Kelly."

"Drayson," he laughed.

She laughed and kissed him. He moved to kiss her deeper when there was a tap at the door.

"John?" Max stuck his head in the room, "our escort is here."

John stepped back from Alex. While holding her eyes, he kissed her hand, then followed Max into the entry way of Max's law office. Max hugged Alex then followed the soldiers out the door. Standing at the door for a moment, Alex watched John, Max and two soldiers walk to the elevators. With a sigh, she closed the door and raised her eyebrows.

"Gentlemen," she said. "Let the drinking begin."

Troy held up a deck of cards. Matthew jingled his keys.

"We can go to my house," Matthew said.

"Yeah, Erin would flip the fuck out," Alex said. "She can't stand cigar smoke."

Alex pulled her handgun out to check to see if it was loaded. She was digging around in the pockets of her jacket when her cell phone went off.

"It's probably my buddy Eleazar," Alex said. She began rifling through her purse.

"You're not going to answer it?" Troy asked. "It could be something important."

"You can," Alex said. She threw the phone at him. "Tell him I said, 'Hi'. I have to fix my eyes. I'll be right back."

"Captain Troy Olivas," Troy said answering Alex's cell phone. "What?"

Alex was humming in the small half bathroom off Max's office. As a partner in the law firm, Max had a plush set up. She changed from her dress into comfortable jeans and a long sleeved T-shirt. She was leaning against the sink putting her contacts in when Matthew came to stand at the open bathroom door.

"Your Sergeant's on the phone," Matthew said.

Alex moved to press past him and he grabbed her arm. Standing face to face, he said, "It's bad."

Alex nodded. Walking out of Max's office, she stopped. Troy was bent over with his hands on his knees. He looked up when he heard her come out of Max's office. Their eyes held for a moment. He shook his head and gave her the phone.

"Fey," Alex said.

"Sir."

"Yes, Sergeant," she said.

"There's been a plane crash. Captain Jakkman is a confirmed hit."

"What?"

"Captain Zack Jakkman is dead."

CHAPTER TWENTY-SEVEN

"Where?"

"Afghanistan. His U-2 crashed in the mountains."

"When?"

"Nine minutes ago," her Sergeant said. "Sir, it's a total loss. The Air Force says that it will be days before they can even get to the wreck. They had feed from him just prior to an explosion on board."

"And what exactly did Captain Jakkman say? Word for word, Sergeant."

"'Oh crap, that sucks' then the plane exploded and plowed into the mountain. The Air Force confirms that Captain Jakkman is dead by terrorist sabotage."

"Zack," Alex said as an out breath. She closed her eyes.

"There's more, sir. I received a priority email regarding the event. I tried to trace the email but I am unable to."

"How is it signed?"

"With a Vivaldi scripted 'F.'"

"What color?"

"Sir?"

"What is the color of F?"

"Black," her Sergeant said.

"Fuck. Can you move it to my secure area?" Realizing that she no longer had a secure office to view the document in, she added, "Scratch that. We have to come there."

"Sir, I do not advise that you return to base," her Sergeant said.

"Why?"

"I cannot explain."

"All right. Can I call you back?"

"Yes sir. Sir?"

"Yes?"

"I'm sorry about Captain Jakkman."

"Yes, Sergeant. Me too."

Alex's head bowed to her cell phone. Her fingers flew across the keys.

She texted this message: 'z-m?' then stood staring at the phone. Within seconds, she received a four letter text message: 'hvhm'.

Alex dropped to her knees and wept with relief. Matthew moved forward to comfort Alex but she blew out a breath and wiped her face. This was not the time for emotions. Eleazar's plan was in motion. Killing Zack was his first move.

"As far as you are concerned, Zack Jakkman is dead." Alex pointed to Troy then Matthew. "Got that?"

Troy and Matthew nodded their heads. They had heard stories about the Fey but never seen their sweet laughing friend, now boss, Alex turn into the Fey. Like a flick of the switch, she was the completely cold intelligence officer.

"We have work to do," Alex said. "We need to break into my Dad's office. Can you guys pick locks?"

Troy and Matthew, both a little intimidated by her, shook their heads.

"Eoin can," Alex said. "They are supposed to meet us here. Come on."

She walked out of the suite and down the hall. Troy and Matthew followed behind her. Alex stood with her head down thinking as they waited at the elevator.

"Shit," Alex said.

"What?" Matthew asked.

"We don't have a car," Alex said. "Eleazar has made every single thing so fucking hard. God damn it."

"I have Erin's bug," Matthew held up the key to Erin's lime green 1964 VW convertible.

Alex looked at the men and shook her head. "Weapons?"

"There's a baseball bat in the trunk," Matthew said.

"Come on Fey," Troy said. "We'll do it low tech style."

She shook her head. When the elevator bell rang, Cian and Eoin stepped off the elevator to meet up for an afternoon at the Irish Snug. Cian took one look at Alex then stepped back on the elevator. They took the elevator to the ground and poured into Erin's tiny car.

Pressed against the back window, Alex tried to remember what security was installed at the hundred and fifty year old building which housed her father's office. She shook her head. Guess I'll find out. She made a quick call for her Sergeant to run interference with the security company. Stepping out of the car, she saw the latest security addition—a US Army soldier? Standing next to the door of the office, carrying an M-16 machine gun, was Sergeant Lawrence Flagg.

"What the fuck are you doing here?" Alex asked. She pointed Eoin to the door of the office.

"I was assigned here, sir," the young man said. "I wanted to help and there was a concern about... What are you doing?"

Eoin had dropped to his knees to begin working on the door. Cian reviewed the security. Cian pointed to a video camera and Troy knocked it down with the bat.

"Sir, I'm sorry, but I cannot let you do that," Sergeant Flagg said. He nudged Eoin with the machine gun.

Alex nodded her head toward the young Sergeant and Troy raised the bat to him.

"Ok, I changed my mind. It's your father's office after all."

"Thank you Sergeant," Alex said. "Who assigned you here?"

"I was assigned at the last minute by Colonel Gordon, sir. I just got here. I was on site at Fort Logan when I was reassigned."

Alex smiled. "You don't happen to have a vehicle do you?"

"Done." Eoin opened the door.

"Yes sir, an armored Expedition."

"Weapons?"

"Just this M-16."

"What are we doing?" Troy asked.

"I need a secure computer," Alex said. "I set Maria up with a secure node about a year ago. I had a feeling I might need it some day."

The men followed her through the office to a small office near the back. Flicking the light on, she moved around the desk and turned the computer on. Alex opened a closet door.

"Cian, would you mind sweeping the office for listening devices?" She gave him the device.

"How does it work?"

"Just turn it on," Alex said. "It makes a loud noise when you find a device. Thanks."

"What do we do when we find them?"

"Use Troy's bat."

Cian and Eoin began in Maria's office then worked their way through the suite. The device screamed every two or three minutes as they found a listening device. Each siren was followed by the sound of the baseball bat smashing the devices to pieces.

"Jesse? Do you know her logins?" Alex asked. She tapped away at Maria's keyboard.

"Of course," Jesse said. He stood near the corner of the room.

"Who's Jesse?" Sergeant Flagg asked.

"He's right there," Troy said pointing to the corner. "Hey Jesse."

"How is that fair?" Matthew asked. "You can see Jesse?? Fuck. I loved Jesse and I can't see him. Jesse hated you."

"I made some mistakes when we were in training," Troy said. "But Jesse knows that I'm very sorry."

Alex looked up from the computer. "You can't hear him. Can you?"

"No," Troy said. "What did he say?"

"You're still a motherfucker," Alex said. "Can you hear him Mattie?"

Matthew wagged his head side to side.

"Ok, I am in. Troy, can you call my Sergeant and give him this series of numbers—01 486 99, no sorry, 909 43, um, 64."

"Shouldn't you write that down?" Sergeant Flagg asked.

"0148690943 64," Troy said. "What is your name again, G.I. Joe?"

"Larry, just call me Larry."

"Use this phone." Alex threw her cell phone to Troy.

Alex looked up at Troy and he nodded. Clicking through to the Internet, Alex logged onto the Homeland Security site. Clicking and typing as fast as she could, her fingers flying over the keys, she pulled up the email signed with a black scripted"F".

In the last month, she beat every bush, looked under every rock, trying to answer the question—was Joseph still a target? The answer was an overwhelming, "No." But Alex thought the data was too uniform. Everyone seemed to say the same words. Raz thought she was understandably paranoid.

"Don't make mountains out of molehills, honey. We've got enough on our plate," Raz said.

Before going to bed last night, she sent one last email. This email was his response. Alex fell back in the chair and swore. Joseph would be killed at the ceremony today.

"Mattie? I need you to do something for me."

Matthew nodded. Cian and Eoin returned to the office from their destructive mission.

"Would you mind calling, Raz? I need you to repeat to him what I say word for word."

"Sure Alex. Word for word."

"Tell Raz, 'Chocolate crepes are better outside of Notre Dame but only after two in the morning.' Ask him to repeat it. Then tell him: 'Majorca is wonderful in the spring.' He should reply by saying, 'The summer is more romantic.' If he does not say those exact words hang up the phone. If he says those exact words ask him why."

Matthew nodded. Spies. Codes. He would make a joke or roll his eyes but the whole thing was so damned cool. Under lowered eyebrows, he glanced over to see what Cian and Eoin thought. They watched the interactions with rapt attention.

"It's like a movie," Eoin said. Cian nodded with wide eyes.

Matthew laughed and called Raz.

"Oh Mattie, can you also tell him that: Sergeant Jakkman is a confirmed casualty. Thanks," Alex said without looking up from the computer.

"The Jakker is dead?" Larry asked.

"Yes," Alex replied.

Her complete focus on the computer in front of her kept her from slipping into panic. She began opening files on the Homeland Security server.

"Isn't that your friend Zack?" Cian asked.

"Yes, my friend Zack," Alex said. "Troy? Can you ask my Sergeant for F0810FL1230 and all of its linked documents. It looks like there are four, maybe five documents."

"He has already sent them to the port. I just turned on the printer and they are printing," Troy said.

"That's perfect. No one will know we looked at them. Thanks Troy. Mattie?"

"Raz said… wait," Matthew looked at the piece of paper in his hand and read: "The best part about summer in Majorca is getting to see you in a bikini."

"Really? Were those his exact words?" She smiled. Raz apologized for doubting her.

"Yes, I told him about Zack," Matthew said. "He did this weird thing. He kind of laughed then said, um," Matthew read again, "I like to see the diamond in your belly button flash against your black bikini."

"He said, 'your'?"

"Yes, he said 'your' twice," Matthew replied.

Alex clicked through the computer to her secure area at Homeland Security and opened a sub-folder in the area where Raz left her documents for her. She clicked open a document to find a note from Raz. In case he was wrong, and Joseph was still at risk, he outlined four possible scenarios. She smiled.

"Troy would you mind…"

Troy handed her a stack of warm papers from the LaserJet next to the door.

"Thanks. I need three minutes of silence, then we'll meet."

CHAPTER TWENTY-EIGHT

Digging around in Maria's desk, she pulled a yellow pencil from the drawer and began flipping through the stack of papers. Making notes on the edges of the documents, she made a face.

"Sir, I'd be happy to input the data into the intelligence server." Larry said.

Alex was humming Seether's "Gasoline" when Larry touched her arm. She looked up at him.

"Sir, the intelligence server?"

"Intelligence server? Yeah, people use the server." Turning back to the pages, she added, "I don't. Silence?"

Matthew and Troy stood at the end of the desk watching Alex work. She seemed to shuffle the pages back and forth. Transfixed, they watched her rifle the pages, tap her pencil on the table and hum. After a few minutes, she circled a word on one page, then underlined a sentence or another.

They had each worked with a variety of intelligence officers. But they had never seen anything like what Alex was doing. After more than a decade of saying, 'Yeah, I'm a good friend of the Fey,' they saw, for the first time, what made the Fey so special.

"Troy? Can you get my Sergeant on the phone? I need to speak with him. Thanks."

She worked on the computer for a minute only looking up when Troy gave her the telephone.

"I've sent you some documents. Yes, that's correct. Yes, can you transfer me to his line? Thanks," Alex said. "Howard? Can you confirm… No paper. Right."

Alex closed her phone.

"Mattie, I'm sorry, would you mind calling Raz back? Tell him that… uh… " Alex flipped through the stack of papers then read her note. "All right, tell him that you bought the tickets for Valencia and we are leaving in a half hour. But, he has to wear his… crap, what's a men's swimming suit?"

"Speedo?" Matthew asked. "Swim trunks?"

"No something larger…"

"What does he usually wear?" Troy asked.

"We skinny dip," Alex replied. She looked up to their wide surprised eyes. She shook her head. "Spy stuff. What do you wear Troy?"

"TYR board shorts," Troy replied.

"Ok, I bought the tickets to Valencia and we are leaving in a half hour," Matthew started.

"But he has to wear his TYR board shorts. He should say," Alex scratched her head. "'I can't wait to make sand castles.' Go."

"Do you really skinny dip?" Cian asked.

"Not in Ireland," Alex said under her breath. She continued working with the documents.

"Alex, Raz said 'Your sand castles will not win the competition this year. My sand castles will win this year.'"

"That makes me so sad," Alex replied.

Alex let out a breath and looked from face to face. How could this possibly work? For a moment, she yearned for the familiar comfort of Charlie and her team. She bit her tongue against the rising bile from her nervous stomach. There was no time for panic.

"Eleazar is making the first moves in what looks to me like a major offensive."

"Against you?" Eoin asked.

"Against all of us. He has killed Zack." Alex shook her head. "He thinks he killed Zack. He won't know for at least three days. That's the soonest the Air Force can get there. Sadly, there will be a lot of delays."

"Then your friend's body will have been eaten by wolves," Cian said.

"Something like that," Alex said.

"This is like a movie!" Eoin said. Alex rolled her eyes but smiled.

"I'm sorry. We must act as if Zack is dead. Any fuck up on our part and we lose. Zack is dead."

She closed her eyes.

"Next on his list is Joseph," Alex said.

"WHAT?" Matthew and Troy asked together.

"Please, hear me out. After Joseph is Max and John," Alex said.

"Motherfucker," Cian said.

Alex held up her hand for silence.

"We have no time for emotion. There's a hit planned on the President. Some brain trust at the Secret Service decided that Joseph is going to kill the President."

"Max and John?"

"They will get in the way."

"Alex, that's a long way around to kill Joseph, Max and John," Troy said. He was unable to keep the doubt from his voice.

"Yes, it is," Alex said. She was tempted to have a major temper tantrum. Blowing her frustration out in a breath, she said, "But the Secret Service will do the shooting. Plus, they will kill the President today. No one will give two shits about Joseph, John or Max after the President is killed.

"Keep your initiative moving AND make it seem like the government is behind it. That's real psychological warfare," Cian said. "I wish I had thought of something like that."

"I'm glad you didn't," Alex said. "Anyway, Raz said that he can cover Joseph, Max, and John. We," she pointed to Matthew and Troy, "need to save the President."

"I want to save the President," Larry piped up.

"I need you to do something else," Alex said. "These guys can't drive."

"I can drive," Cian said at the same time Larry said: "Who are these guys?"

Alex looked from one to the next.

"Sergeant Flagg, you are delivering the news that Captain Jakkman's plane has crashed in Afghanistan. He is presumed to be dead."

She flipped through the stack of pages and gave Larry the official notification of Zack's demise.

"Where did you get this?" Matthew asked.

"My Sergeant was thinking ahead."

"Sergeant Flagg, you'll drive us to Fort Logan then drop the three of us near the event. Use your identification to get into the event and go to the front with your paper. The President will announce Zack's death at the Ceremony. Cian and Eoin will sneak out of the vehicle and be on hand to help—only help. We don't want you to get deported. When it's over, blend in with the crowd then find my brother Colin."

Cian and Eoin nodded.

"We need a faster ride," Matthew said.

"No Zack. No chopper. And my Sergeant is confirming some details for me. I don't have time to…"

"Let me make some calls. You authorize…"

"Of course," she said. "If we can get a Black Hawk, we can parachute in before these guys get there."

"I'll see what I can do, sir." Matthew began making calls.

"Let's see if we can find the weapons locker here," Alex said. "My Dad showed me the locker when I returned to Denver but I was pretty out of it."

Alex's eyes went wide when she remembered that Colin was just here. Six weeks pregnant, Julie told him to get rid of his guns. Colin immediately removed the weapons and placed them in his father's gun locker. Such a good boy. Chuckling, she dialed his number.

"I'm so fucking bored," Colin said. "Why is it that you always miss these crappy political ceremonies?"

"I'm not the Golden Child?" Alex asked. "Plus, I'm either dead or never born."

"Very funny. What do you want?"

"Where's Dad's gun locker?"

"Why?"

"Col…"

"If you believe for one minute that you are doing something fun and I'm not involved…" Colin spoke in a terse whisper into his cell phone.

"You're a civilian."

"Fine, then I won't tell you." He hung up his cell phone.

Alex tried to call him back but he refused to answer. She let out a stream of curses. Then looked up when Troy's cell phone rang.

"Your little brother says that you are a big fat pig."

"That's very mature of him," Alex said. "Gun locker?"

She looked over while Troy spoke with Colin. She knew a lot of Majors who would be insulted at Troy's laughing conversation with Colin. She simply could not afford the time or the energy for anything more than a dark look. Glowering at Troy, he nodded to her.

"It's in the floor of your father's office behind the desk. The code is your nickname."

"Fey?"

"Pumpkin," Troy said.

"Great."

Alex stomped into the office and found the space where her father left his weapons. Kneeling down behind his desk, alone for the first time since all of this began, she closed her eyes and felt a wave of exhaustion and hopelessness. She rested her head against her knees and sank into complete defeat.

She never felt this way in the field. Never. Everything that happened was another opportunity, another chance to do something fun. Charlie would look at her and say, 'What's next missy?' But Charlie was dead. And there was no one to believe in her now.

With a sigh, she pulled up the flooring and pressed the code into the key pad. Turning the handle, she pulled open the vault to find a piece of paper.

P U M P K I N ,

S O M E   T H I N G S   Y O U   J U S T   K N O W .

I   L O V E   Y O U ,

Daddy

That's what he said when they finally sat down to talk about her parentage. Standing in the nursery, waiting for 'Rebecca's bastards', he planned his return into the field and away from the mess of his life. But the moment the nurse placed Alex in his arms, every thought of escape evaporated.

He had expected a boy.

Yet the nurse set a tiny baby girl in his arms. Before he could ask about the obvious error, the nurse whispered, "The whole nursery is in tizzy, sir. You have a boy and a girl, General. Identical twins."

At that moment, Alex opened her eyes to him. Looking in her eyes, he just knew that she was his girl. By the time the nurse returned with Max, his plan had changed, his whole life rearranged around being their parent. He felt as if he was put on the planet solely to be Alex and Max's father.

Some things you just know.

"What's that?" Troy asked peering over her shoulder.

"A note from my Dad," she said.

"What does it mean?" Troy asked.

"It means that he thought we might be here today. It also means that I need to stop feeling sorry for myself."

Troy nodded his head. Looking in the vault, he sucked in a breath, "May I? Your Dad let me take the Henry target shooting a few times. It's quite a weapon."

"Here's the ammo," Alex said. She gave him the Henry rifle and a box of shells. "You also need a handgun. Mattie? Do you still use a Smith and Wesson?"

"Forty-five," Matthew said coming behind the desk.

Alex smirked at him.

"What?"

"Nothing. Get what you need. Don't forget silencers."

"Raz called to tell you that the Air Force has delayed the fly over," Matthew said. "They're waiting to hear from you."

"Thanks. I'll take care of it," Alex stood with another handgun, two loaded clips and a different holster.

Moving past her, Matthew bent to pick out a handgun and ammunition while Alex dialed her Sergeant. With her back turned to the men, she closed her eyes and held her breath. Twenty-five military intelligence officers were reviewing the documents trying to affirm her scenario. What if she was wrong? Her stomach turned over. She almost laughed out loud when her Sergeant verified that she was correct. They were released for duty. She asked him to release the Air Force confirming that Zack's death would be properly announced.

With the phone pressed into her ear, she stepped into a Black Hawk helicopter. Troy pulled the door closed.

Ready or not, her little band of soldiers were on their way.

CHAPTER TWENTY-NINE

Twenty-five minutes later
October 8 – 12:25 P.M.
Near Fort Logan National Cemetery, Colorado

"Can we get Secret Service feed?" Alex asked the pilot.

"Ma'am," the co-pilot said. "We'd prefer for you to stay in the passenger compartment."

"Oh sorry, Captain Jakkman usually talks to me while he flies."

"Ma'am, Captain Jakkman is dead."

Alex stared at the co-pilot. Her mouth dropped open and her eyes went wide. Even though she knew that Zack was all right, she simply could not believe this young Sergeant's lack of sensitivity. She had known Zack since she moved to Denver when she was ten years old. They went all the way through Catholic school together. And this little snot-nosed Sergeant was going to blithely tell her that her friend was dead?

"What's your name?"

"Ma'am, we'd prefer for you to return to your friends," the co-pilot said.

"Your name, Sergeant."

Furious, she blinked her eyes and smiled slightly. Matthew came up behind her. He looked at the co-pilot then at Alex.

"Sir, can you remove her from the cockpit?" the co-pilot asked Matthew.

"You're asking me to remove Major Drayson from the cockpit?" Matthew asked. "I've been held hostage... twice. This face," he pointed to Alex's face, "is the face you want to see. Sooner rather than later. Pilots get picked up all the time. You better make up because the Fey never forgets. Come on, Major."

Alex raised her eyebrows and returned to the back of the helicopter where Troy had laid out their parachutes.

"Body armor?" Alex asked.

Troy gave her a flak jacket. She was tightening the sides of the jacket when the helicopter engineer came to the compartment.

"Major?"

"Yes, Sergeant," Alex said. Looking at Troy, she said, "Is there a smaller one? This one is too big. I usually wear a medium but sometimes a small. I'm tall but I'm not very big around."

"That's a medium," Troy said opening a compartment.

"Then a small. I think these Air Force jackets are made for fatter people."

Handing her a small flak jacket, Troy took the medium from her.

"Sir?"

"What Sergeant?"

"Permission to speak, sir."

"What do you want, Sergeant?" Alex asked. "This is perfect Troy. Thanks."

"I wanted to apologize for the co-pilot. We didn't know who you were. We thought you were, um, that guy's girlfriend." He pointed to Troy.

Troy looked up and said, "I wish."

"Let's get our chutes on," she said.

"Major?"

"It is unbecoming for any soldier to be that insensitive... to anyone but particularly a fellow soldier." Alex's face flushed. She looked down at the flak jacket to keep from venting her frustration and rage at the engineer. "He has no right to speak to anyone like that. You can guaran-fucking-tee that I will speak with his superior and... "

She was going to add "the Jakker" knowing that Zack would make certain that the co-pilot's life was hell. Matthew caught her eyes and shook his head. She let a breath out.

"Let's just say that the Fey doesn't forget."

"Yes, sir," the engineer said. "Your Sergeant left this backpack for you and the pilot would like to speak with you."

The engineer gave her a backpack.

"Thank you, Sergeant. Now go away."

Alex opened the pack and smiled. Ah, my Secret Service feed. She slipped an ear bud into her ear and listened to the Secret Service agents speak to each other about some woman's amazing behind. Digging in the back pack, she found communication devices for the three of them. She passed ear buds and microphones to Troy and Matthew then checked to see if they could connect Larry. Listening, she heard Eoin and Cian argue with Larry about a united Ireland. She found three Snickers candy bars, a present from Colonel Gordon, in the pack. Troy laughed when she threw him a Snicker's bar. Matthew looked up from putting on his parachute when Troy laughed. Alex gave him a Snicker's bar.

"Get ready and I'll see what these jerks want," Alex said. She walked to the cockpit again. "What do you want?"

"Sir, we would like to apologize again," the pilot said.

"I understand that," Alex replied. "We need a connection to command. While I realize Captain Jakkman is dead," she glowered at the co-pilot, "he usually serves as our connection. It is my understanding that this is standard for most pilots. Will you be able to assist us or shall I find another way to connect with command?"

"Sir, I have your command on the radio. They're waiting to speak with you."

"Thank you, Sergeant. Can you put them on speaker?"

"Yes Major," the pilot said. "We are three minutes out."

The co-pilot flipped a switch connecting Alex with her Sergeant.

"Major?"

"Yes Sergeant?"

"I sent our latest intel to the pocket computer in the backpack."

"I didn't see a pocket computer," Alex said.

"It's in the front pocket. Also, Colonel Gordon has spoken with the Air Force commander regarding the interchange between you and the co-pilot. The Air Force commander said to tell you that he wears an 'F' and will deal with it as soon as they return to base."

Alex looked at the co-pilot. "Forgot to turn your mic off?"

"Sir, I am very sorry."

"It's not my problem now," Alex said. She rubbed her eyes, then added, "Listen, we all make mistakes. Get us through this alive and I'll speak with your command."

The co-pilot nodded, "Thanks."

"Major?"

"Yes Sergeant?"

"We've got you on satellite. And sir?

"Yes?"

"There's a wind out of the west."

"Thank you Sergeant." Turning to the pilot, she said, "I need you to patch in on our frequency. We aren't sure what we are walking into. We need access command."

"Yes sir," the pilot said.

She moved to the back of the helicopter and put on a parachute. Digging the pocket computer from the pack, she reviewed the information then slipped the computer into her back pocket. She went from Troy to Matthew checking their body armor, communication units and parachutes.

"We've got a westerly wind," Alex said. "Let's try not to die."

"Good plan," Troy said.

"We're there," pilot said. "We will meet you at the entrance."

"Go," Alex said and Troy jumped.

"Go," Alex said and Matthew jumped.

Alex stood at the door of the helicopter for a moment watching the world below. This was her first real mission without her team. God, she missed them. She blew out a breath then jumped from the helicopter.

They fell fast in a straight military free fall dive with Troy laughing the entire way down. Pointing at the target, he pulled his chute and landed. He rolled out of the way and Matthew landed. He rolled and Alex landed. They ran toward the cover of the trees.

"Let's go," Alex said.

Dropping their chutes, they ran two miles toward the Memorial. They stopped a half mile from the ceremony.

"Any word?" Matthew asked.

"Nothing," Alex said. "Secret Service missed the drop. Troy, what do you see?"

Troy scanned the cemetery with binoculars. "Politicians talking."

"Let's spread out and see if we can find the shooter," Alex said.

"And if we don't?" Matthew asked.

"We notify Larry and get the hell out of there," Alex said.

"And hope their body armor holds," Matthew added.

"Well that too," Alex said. "You have your DOD badges?"

Troy and Matthew nodded.

"Major?" the pilot called from the helicopter.

"Yes?"

"There's a unit at the entrance," he said. "Your command requested Police and SWAT back up."

"Can you still land?" Alex asked.

"I'll need clearance," the pilot said.

Letting out a breath, Alex never missed Zack more. 'Fuck the police,' he would have said. 'Let the brass work out the paperwork.' Then he would have landed. Alex was the brass who ended up filling out all that paperwork. She sighed. She would give anything for that stack of paperwork right now.

"Can you patch me to my command?"

"Your Sergeant is on the line," the pilot said.

"Sergeant?"

"I'm on it. Go ahead."

"All right, we're going to find our shooter."

They split up around the ceremony. The fastest runner, Matthew took off to the corner farthest away from where they were standing. Troy set off to the west. Alex took the side closest to where they stood.

"I've got one," Matthew said. "Longrange rifle… looks like maybe a M-

21… in the trees here."

"I've got another in the trees," Troy said. "AK-47 about 300 meters from the ceremony."

"G.I. Joe Team? This is your commander and I'm in place," Larry said.

They laughed.

"There's nothing but people here. And, damn, there are a lot of people. I'm set to disrupt the ceremony."

"Go ahead Larry. We need the cover," Alex said.

"Yes, Major."

"Ok, I've got a third shooter. Another longrange rifle, M-21," Alex said. "He's standing behind a tree. Just a second."

She crept noiselessly behind the armed man. Reaching around his neck with her arm, she held him in a choke hold while pressing her other hand to his mouth. He punched her with his elbow and she brought her knee into his kidney. She held steady until the shooter went limp then she dropped him to the ground.

"Got him," Alex said. "Let's see what we have here. Uh, Male, Arabic, mid-twenties… We've got a sleeping non-national…"

The man moved and Alex punched his temple. He dropped unconscious again.

"Syria looks like. Let's see…what's in his bag? We've some C-4 and lunch. Nice. Anyone hungry?"

Troy and Matthew laughed. "What do you want us to do?"

"Hang on for a second. Sergeant?"

"Sir, your Sergeant is off line," the pilot said.

"Can you check with my command and see if we have any Federals or law enforcement in the trees here?" Alex asked.

"Got it," the pilot replied.

"Sergeant? The emphasis is on ANY Federals or law enforcement."

"Yes Major."

"Matthew?" Alex called. "Did you bring a silencer?"

"Yes," he said.

"Put it on," Alex said. "Troy? Do you have a handgun?"

"Yes, but I wanted to use the Henry," Troy said.

"Your command says no Federals, no law enforcement in the trees," the pilot said. "I repeat, no Federals, no law enforcement."

"Take 'em down," Alex said.

There was a burst of machine gun fire followed by the distinctive sound of the Henry. Across the cemetery, Alex heard shots fired in succession in the area of the ceremony. Three shots? Four? Then a shot answering in response.

As people's screams echoed through the monuments and white grave markers, Alex dropped to her knees gasping in pain. She clutched her chest. Max was letting her know that he had been shot.

"Alex, are you hit?" Matthew asked.

"No. Max. Broken rib. Troy?"

"Sorry about that," Troy said. "He saw me and pulled off a few rounds."

"How many?" Alex asked.

"Three," Troy said.

"Did he fire into the Memorial?" Alex asked.

"No. He fired at me," Troy said. "I'm coming back."

"I'll meet you at the bird," Matthew said.

Troy ran to Alex and they set off toward the entrance. Larry was waiting for them near the edge of the ceremony. They ran toward the entrance. The helicopter was running when they got there. Alex opened the door for Larry and Troy to jump in. Alex turned to look for Matthew when he ran up behind her. He stepped in and she followed closing the door.

"Get us out of here," Alex said to the pilot.

Alex turned to Larry. "Sergeant? Your report."

"Joseph was shot by a Secret Service agent. Then, I'm sorry, sir, the agent shot your brother and your husband," he said. "Agent Rasmussen fired on the agent. I left after that."

"Cian and Eoin?"

"They are with your brother and husband."

Alex opened her cell phone and called Raz. No answer. While Troy and Matthew told an enraptured Larry about the shooters, Alex sat down by herself.

Staring into space, she worked up the courage to do what needed to be done. Once she set this train in motion, there was no going back. Swallowing hard, she dialed Ben.

"Max Hargreaves and John Drayson were killed at the ceremony today as was Captain Joseph Walter."

"Got it," he said. "Jakker?"

"The same."

"Will do." He clicked off.

"Major?" the pilot called from the cockpit. "Your commander is requesting your report."

The co-pilot moved out of his seat. Leaning over her, the co-pilot plugged in a headset. Alex took the headset and put it on her head.

"This is Major Drayson," Alex said.

"Colonel Gordon here." His voice was tense and formal.

"Yes sir," Alex said.

"I need a report, Major Drayson."

"This channel is not secure, sir," Alex said.

"Don't tell me what I already know," he said.

"We found three shooters, two in the trees and one on the ground. I knocked out the first shooter. The shooter was a non-national carrying C-4 in a backpack. We checked with command and were told that there were no Federals or law enforcement in the trees. My associates took out the other two shooters. We returned to our meeting location and are now in the air."

"Confirm AK-47 fire," the Colonel said.

"Roughly three rounds were fired at my associate from a shooter about 300 meters west of the Memorial. The shooter was eliminated."

"Were shots fired toward the ceremony?" the Colonel asked.

"No sir," Alex said. "There was no fire from our direction into the memorial area. We cannot confirm information outside of our direct experience."

"Major, I expect a detailed written report," Colonel Gordon said and clicked off.

Alex stood, moving toward the back of the helicopter when her cell phone vibrated. She opened the phone.

"Howard, what is going on?" she asked.

"A Secret Service officer shot Captain Walter, Max Hargreaves and John Drayson before being neutralized by Agent Rasmussen," Colonel Gordon said. "Our guys picked up the shooters after you took off. The Secret Service is saying that they were responding to shots fired by Captain Walter. They say that Max and John got in the way. You'll be interested to know that Captain Walter is not armed."

"What are their conditions?" Alex asked closing her eyes.

"We have report from Homeland Security that all three are confirmed fatalities."

"That's correct."

"Captain Walter is in route to the hospital but he's fine. We're dropping him in route where his wife is waiting for him. Max and John are on their way to St. Joseph's Hospital. Both received minor injuries. They will be pronounced DOA at the hospital."

"And Captain Walter?"

"Pronounced at the scene," Howard said. "You're sure about this."

"Yes sir. This is a major offensive. Eleazar must believe that he is succeeding."

"He will be left with only one option."

"Yes sir. He has only one option now."

"And Captain Jakkman?" Colonel Howard Gordon asked.

"Sir?" Alex asked.

"How…"

"Sir?"

"Never mind. I need full details on my desk tomorrow. And Alex? Dot every single 'i'."

"Yes sir. And sir? Agent Rasmussen?"

"He's Homeland Security," Howard said. "He didn't kill that little weasel. They'll release Agent Rasmussen."

"And the President?" Alex asked.

"He's bruised up from the Secret Service, but he'll live."

"Thanks," Alex said.

"I'm proud of you guys. Tell your associates that they'll get a Presidential commendation."

"Thank you, sir," Alex said then closed her phone.

She looked into Troy's face, then Matthew's face.

"As far as we're concerned they are dead. Joseph died at the scene. Max and John will be DOA at the hospital."

"What about your parents? Erin?" Matthew asked.

"Would you mind calling Colin? Tell him everything. I need to take care of a few things. Then become the grieving widow."

When Matthew's attention turned to his telephone call, Troy asked, "Alex, what is Eleazar's only option?"

"He's coming for me."

CHAPTER THIRTY
Five hours later
October 8 – 6:30 P.M.
Near downtown Denver, Colorado

"Would you like some more?" John asked. He held a bottle of Cristal champagne.

Alex rolled onto her stomach and held her glass out. They were laying, naked, wrapped around each other in a tiny CIA owned boutique hotel room near downtown Denver. After being checked and bandaged in the emergency room, John and Max were whisked through a series of tunnels into Homeland Security vehicles. Ben arrived to escort Max, and his broken rib, to a family home outside of Montreal, Canada.

But John refused to leave Alex so they compromised with this hotel. John planned to write up his research project for the Journal of the American Medical Association. Alex and Raz had bets that he wouldn't make it a week. Alex had already arranged for his escort to Scotland.

"First," John said.

He grunted. The bullet caught the edge of his body armor bruising his shoulder. He was bruised and sore. Yet for a man who was pronounced dead only a few hours ago, he was remarkably fit.

She crawled across the bed to kiss him. He pressed her onto her back as their passion caught. They had been laying in the bed celebrating the two year survival anniversary with champagne and love for the last three hours.

"I think the news is on," Alex said.

"Oh by all means, I'd love to see your show," John said rolling to his back. Plucking the remote from a side table, he flicked on the television. Alex rested her head against his chest while he flipped through the channels.

"Here we go," he said. He kissed her head.

"Three dead as a day of remembrance turns deadly," the FOX news reporter said.

"I think that's a little dramatic," Alex said.

"Lots of dead in that. How about this one?" John asked.

"A family's tragedy deepens as Senator Patrick Hargreaves loses another son on the anniversary of his son Alexander's death."

"That's a good picture of my Dad," Alex said. "Oh look, I missed this."

Patrick, supporting a weeping Rebecca, moved into a limousine while surrounded by Secret Service officers.

"She looks very sad," John said.

"She's good," Alex said. "Look there I am."

The camera showed a picture of blonde haired, blue eyed Alyssa collapsing in the hospital waiting room. Alyssa sobbed into Erin's arms while Matthew pushed the cameras away. The announcer said in a solemn voice, "They were to be married in less than two weeks."

"How did I do?? Very convincing?" Alex beamed.

"You were brilliant," John replied kissing her. "Where is Zack?"

"Zack's dead, John, you know that," Alex replied in the same tone he used when he "reminded" her that Jesse was dead.

John squinted his eyes at her sarcasm and she laughed. Rolling over, she moved on top of him so that her mouth was next to his ear.

"He's with his girlfriend."

"Bestat the dragon?"

"Mmm... She sent me a text when they arrived in Cairo. They'll stay at her family's home near the Valley of the Kings until this is over."

"And when do we think this will be over?"

"This week," Alex said rolling onto her side. He rolled onto his side so he could look at her. "He's had success so he will keep moving forward. We are in place to move at any time."

"Hmm," John said. "Dare I ask? What's next?"

"We aren't sure," Alex said. She rolled onto her back to cover her lie.

"Hey." John touched her shoulder. He misinterpreted her lie for sadness. She looked over at him.

"At least it will be over at some point," he said.

She nodded wishing that she had his confidence.

"I have something for you," she said.

"A diamond?"

"Something better," she said. Standing Alex went to her suitcase and pulled out the box she found in the cabinet in the vault.

"We got this for you," Alex said. "It was a team present. Everyone was involved. Dwayne found it at one of those shops with junk stacked from the floor to ceiling in Abidjan, you know the Ivory Coast. He took Tommy and Jesse to see it but the shop wasn't open. I think Paul finally purchased it like a month later. Charlie had it cleaned. Mike made sure it was authentic.

Anyway, everyone had something to do with this including me." She smiled. "Close your eyes and hold out your hand."

She set a heavy cylindrical object in his hand. "You can open your eyes."

John opened his eyes to an antique fountain pen with an intricate snail detail in gold overlay the black enamel body of the pen. The gold cap continued in the snail detail. Opening the pen, he made a small noise reading the inscription on the gold nib–ALCO.

"Oh my God."

"Mike said that the pen was made 1884 or 1885 but the nib is newer," Alex said. She pointed to the date–1915. "I thought it was cool to think about someone using this pen for thirty years then replacing the nib. The eyedropper to fill it is in the case."

She passed him a pen case marked Aiken Lambert.

"I've never seen anything like this."

"We were going to give it to you when you finished your General Surgery certificate, but we were stuck somewhere," Alex said. "We were going to give it to you for Christmas but…" She shrugged. "We wanted to get you something special and we knew your love for fountain pens."

"I use my green fountain pen every day," John said.

"The one I gave you for our one month anniversary?" Alex said.

"I write my notes with it every day. I even wrote my first prescription with that pen," John said. "Alex, this is the most thoughtful gift I've ever received. Your team… they were truly great men. I will treasure this."

"Everyone felt involved in you becoming a doctor then a surgeon. We were proud of you. I am very proud of you."

"Thank you," He smiled at her and touched her face.

"You're welcome," she said. "Dinner?"

"I had something else in mind first," he said.

She giggled when he pushed her onto her back for another round.

One day passed, then another.

They began to believe they were on vacation. The hotel had secure connections to every major computer system with video conferencing. Alex wandered down the hall to work on the maps of Afghanistan then wandered back for lunch. Her Sergeant and his wife came for dinner one night. Raz moved into a room down the hall. For the first time in over two years, Alex and Patrick played pool with Raz for an entire afternoon while John worked on his paper. She played poker with Max via video conference between his morning fly fishing on the lake and his afternoon fly fishing on the river.

The constant pressure of pretending to be Alyssa, covering who she was, and looking over her shoulder, slipped away in this twenty room CIA created oasis. Two days passed into three days.

They were deliciously happy.

⚜⚜⚜

October 12 – 9:30 A.M.
Downtown Denver, Colorado

"Ah shit," Alex said as her cell phone rang. "Do you mind?"

She and John were eating a late breakfast in a courtyard tucked into the middle of the hotel. The waiter had just set their meal on the table when her phone rang.

"Go ahead," John said opening the Denver Post. "I have this important newspaper to keep me company."

Alex smiled. Surrounded by CIA operatives, government employees, and various spies from a variety of countries, she didn't worry about being overheard. Plus, she was fairly confident they were taping her calls anyway. She hoped they enjoyed their hotel room videos. Smiling slightly, she thought, better than porn.

"Yes?"

"Your friends wish to see you now," a voice said on the phone. "We're waiting for you in the front of the hotel. Tell him: 'Sorry, I have to go.'"

Alex clicked off the phone. Standing, she slipped on her leather jacket.

"Sorry, I have to go."

Smiling, John looked up from the newspaper. She kissed his lips then shook her head slightly.

"You know, he always says 'friends'."

John's eyes caught hers. She seemed a million miles away. Better to just let her do her work. She'll be back soon, he thought.

She smiled slightly and touched his chin, "I love you."

He smiled in response. Without another word, she walked out of the courtyard and through the front of the hotel.

Raz pulled out a chair from the table.

"Where's Alex?" he asked.

"She got a call and had to leave," John said behind his newspaper.

"Then she won't mind if I eat her... She left her coffee?"

John looked up and nodded.

"It was quite strange, really. She said that she had to go, then said that 'he always says friends.'"

Raz jumped from the table and ran through the hotel. Alex was sitting in the back of a cab that was pulling away from the hotel. She turned to look at him then pressed her hand against the window of the cab. Her brown eyes were round and hollow, as if he could see straight to her soul. He moved forward to catch a cab but a hand held him in place.

"Sir, we need to ask you to return to the hotel," the CIA doorman said. "There's been a confirmed major threat against this facility."

"But..." Raz said. He watched the cab move into traffic.

The doorman all but pushed Raz back into the hotel. The doors shut, then outer doors, designed to protect against car bombs, clanged shut. Looking down at his cell phone, he saw what he expected. 'No Service.' He threw the phone into the brick wall.

In that moment, Raz understood what Alex had told John. Furious with himself, he missed the fact that in every call, Eleazar said the word 'friend.' His mind clicked through a series of commands and sounds from the calls. Eleazar planted the word for the moment he would use it to control her. Walking back to the table, Raz felt his entire world crumble around him.

"John," Raz said.

"Hmm," John said from behind the paper.

"Eleazar has Alex," Raz said.

CHAPTER THIRTY-ONE
A half hour later
October 12 – 10 A.M.
North Denver, Colorado

When Alex came to herself, she was sitting in a chair with four men standing around her. Wrapped in rope, her hands were tied to her sides and she was tied to a chair. She wasn't sure what released her from the semi-trance state. She was just here. Closing her eyes, she remembered waking up, the feel of John's hands across her skin, the warm burst of water from the shower and the rich coffee at breakfast. God damn it, she left her coffee.

Opening her eyes, she looked from face to glowering face and smiled.

"Hello."

"How dare you speak to us? Filth!" A medium sized man stepped forward and hit her across the face with his open hand. He began screaming Islamic slogans at her in Arabic. His head was wrapped in a white turban and his beard was peppered with black and white. His eyes glowed with insanity.

"Do I know you?" Alex asked. Her eyes blinked at the sting of his slap. She looked at each face. They looked familiar but she had not met them before. "Oh right, you guys are on the Homeland terrorist list."

"You insolent little bitch," turban man said.

The man with the turban hit her across the face with the back of his hand. He spat at her face.

Alex closed her eyes against the burst of pain, then rubbed her bleeding lip against her shoulder. The man's discharge dropped from her cheek to her shoulder. Alex shifted her shoulder and the spittle dropped to the ground.

She had no idea what they would do to her. Eleazar was a sophisticated psychological terrorist. But these guys? These men were thugs, sadists so damaged by their delusions that they were willing to do anything to get what they believed they deserved.

She knew these men and men like them. She trained, from the time she was ten years old, for the eventuality of meeting them in a room like this. She negotiated with them for the release of thousands of hostages. She knew what they were capable of. She opened her eyes to look from face to face again. Yes, she knew them.

But they did not know her.

With a slight nod of her head, she began singing songs in her head. She smiled slightly when the first song that came to mind was "Somewhere over the rainbow."

"What can I do for you?" she asked in Arabic.

"You can get our property," a second man came forward. He spoke English with a clipped British accent. British born Islamic extremist. He couldn't have been more than twenty years old. Looking into his eyes, she saw his terror match his resolve.

"I am not sure what property you are referring to," Alex said.

The Brit hit her face with his fist. Alex saw stars as her brain smashed against the back of her skull. She nodded her head slightly.

She heard her father's voice echoing through the years.

"Stage One, is the 'terrify you' stage. They don't want information. They want to set the stage, destroy your hope, and make you more compliant to what would come next. They're going to beat you up, give you something to think about, then leave you alone to think. The real torture and raping will come much later after you've had time to think."

A third man came forward holding a knife with a gleaming ten-inch blade. He held the blade in front of her eyes then pressed the razor sharp blade against her throat. In one swift movement, he sliced into her left arm.

Alex ground her teeth together to keep from gasping and returned her focus to her songs, now "Hello Dolly." She wondered idly why these old musicals always came up first.

Squeezing the muscle and sinew, he used the knife to dig out the standard issue tracking device from her forearm. He held the device in front of her eyes on the end of his bloody knife. Dropping the tracking device on the floor, he crushed the tracking device with the heel of his shoe.

"No one will find you now," he said.

He ripped a filthy piece of cloth into a long strip then wrapped the strips around her wound.

"We want to keep you alive for a while."

The men laughed in unison, reminding Alex of the Pirates of the Caribbean ride at Disneyland. One more to go before the leader calls it off... for now.

"Hello Fey," the fourth man came forward. "You probably remember me."

Alex squinted her eyes thinking then nodded. British Intelligence. Collected by mistake in a raid, he had been tortured at Abu Graib. She and the team rescued him then helped him return to his family. British Secret Service believed that he still worked for them. Looking at the rubber pipe he held in his hands, they were wrong.

Letting out a breath, Alex turned the sole focus of her mind to "When you wish upon a star" playing in her head, the love in her heart, and a silent message to her twin. She felt the first blow, as the fourth man began beating her with the rubber pipe, then felt nothing else.

Her mind slipped into dreams and memories.

"Why Alex? Why do you have to be a Green Beret?" John, her husband of five days, asked.

He had just learned the origins of the scars on her back, her wrists and ankles. He was furious. Unable to even look at her, he stood at the hotel window staring out at Santa Monica beach.

"It's who I am. I've always wanted to be a Green Beret," Alex said moving to him. She kissed his neck and slipped her arms around his waist. "I made my Dad pinkie swear, when I was five years old, that he would help me become a Green Beret."

"Your father is behind this? My God," he said. He turned away from the surf to stare at her.

"I don't think he had much choice. I would have done it with or without his help. I think he just wanted to give me the edge."

"Pumpkin, you have to remember that they want you to be afraid. The only way to get an edge is to never show your fear. How will you do that?"

They were standing in the kitchen of their Sixth Avenue Parkway home in Denver. Patrick set the dirty dinner dishes in the dishwasher while Alex cleared the dining room table after dinner.

"Songs in my head," said a fifteen-year-old Alex. "I do that now when I'm at finishing school."

Patrick laughed. "I wondered how you were getting through that. What else?"

"Put the fear in a box?"

"That works. What else?"

"Don't get ahead of myself. Deal with each situation as it comes."

"Rest when you can," Patrick added. He poured dishwashing detergent into the machine.

"I have to believe that I can endure everything that comes my way."

"And then some." Patrick closed and started the dishwasher. "Ice cream?"

"Of course," Alex laughed.

Four hours later
October 12 – 2:00 P.M.
Olde Town Arvada, Colorado

Alex awoke with the taste of ice cream in her mouth. She was lying face down on a concrete floor. Before moving, her mind ran down her bones to see what was broken, what hurt, what damage was done. She felt the sharp pain of the knife wound. Nothing seemed broken. Rolling over, she groaned in pain at the knots, lumps and bruises which covered almost every inch of her body. Gritting her teeth, she moved to sit up. Her hands ran down her body. At least nothing was broken.

She felt the hair stand up on the back of her neck. Someone was watching her. Sniffing, she couldn't smell anyone close. There must be a video monitoring in this room.

With a grunt, she pushed herself to standing to check her surroundings. Three brick walls and one cement wall in a twenty by twenty foot storage room. While three florescent bulbs hung from the ceiling, only one bulb was lit. The light was dim in the bare, dusty room. She could see daylight from two thin basement vents. One door. Pressing her head against the brick, she heard nothing. One wall at a time, she listened. She heard a mechanical hum behind the concrete wall possibly from a heater or water system.

Maybe the door was unlocked. Pressing on the door, she saw that there was no inner handle only a key opening for a deadbolt. She pressed her shoulder against the door but the wood held. She wasn't getting out that way anytime soon.

Someone had placed a relatively clean empty bucket by the door and a sealed gallon of water. Clearly they planned on leaving her here for a while. She picked up the water, she looked around the top and edges for a puncture. What her eyes did not see, her fingers felt. The water was drugged.

Alex turned the bucket over and stepped up to touch the wood ceiling. Pulling on a loose plank, she peeked into the space between the wood planking and the floor above. There was eighteen inches of insulation before the underside of wood flooring. No one would hear anything that happened in this room but she would be able to hear people coming and going. Just enough noise to make her feel completely alone yet no one would hear her scream, call or beg. Eleazar was good.

The light shut off.

Feeling with her hands, Alex went from hanging bulb to hanging bulb pulling on the chains. Nothing came on. Someone set up the lights to give her hope only to snatch hope away when she couldn't turn the fixtures on. Yes, Eleazar was very good.

They had taken her shoes, her handgun, her new engagement ring, but left her fully clothed in a pair of blue jeans, a T-shirt and a sweater. She smiled when she noticed that they left John's simple gold band on her right hand. The ring wasn't worth much to them, but to Alex the ring was a precious connection to John. Slipping her hand under her T-shirt, she touched the diamond in her belly button and smiled. She was glad to have something from Raz.

When the lights were on, she had seen her leather jacket crumpled near the door. Feeling her way toward the door, she picked up the jacket then dropped it. The jacket was wet with urine. Her only possibility of warmth was fouled. Knowing that she wouldn't smell much different in a few hours, and not willing to risk getting too cold while she was injured, she put the jacket on. Feeling along the wall in the pitch-black room, she sat down in the corner farthest away from the door.

Alex stuck her hands in the pockets of her jeans. Her fingers felt along the stitching of her right pocket until they found the loose string. Making certain that her movements were hidden from any night vision video camera, she tugged on the loose string opening the cotton pocket to inside of her blue jeans. Her fingers worked along the jean fabric until they found what felt like an extra stitching. Unraveling the stitching, she felt a thin piece of plastic.

Relief coursed through her. She broke the piece of plastic in half to turn on the GPS locater imbedded in the ball of her hip.

Letting out a breath, she forced herself into the sleep that her body needed to heal.

❧❧❧❧❧
Northern Scotland

Once again, John Kelly Drayson was on his way to the farm Scotland to avoid being killed. Within fifteen minutes of learning that Alex had been taken, he was sitting in the back of an armored vehicle on his way to Buckley Air Force Base. A jet to Iceland then a commercial plane to Edinburgh under the name John Rasmussen. He was escorted by British secret service to the train station in Northern Scotland where Tom Drayson waited for him.

Stepping off the train, John felt exactly as he had when he was fifteen years old—terrified and very alone. Tom Drayson touched his arm then caught him as John collapsed, weeping like a child. His sister Rita prepared his old room for him and her boys tiptoed around him. No one knew quite what to say.

John tended sheep, mended fences and cleared out stalls during the day. The hard physical labor helped sooth his anxious mind. The days passed without memory but the nights were awful.

Unable to sleep, he worked on his research paper because it was the only thing that reminded him of who he was, who he had been. He dreamed of Alex every night. His eyes bounced open every morning, his heart racing with the hope that she was laying right there under his arm.

The last time he was in Scotland, he had so many big plans. He would study hard, move to America, become a doctor, make lots of money, and find her, the woman from his dream. He dreamed of her the night his father died. Then, after acknowledging his roommate's sister's first visit in more than two years with something intelligent like: 'That's cool, Max,' he fell into bed. Closing his eyes, he watched the same dream over and over again until he awoke exhausted for class. He stumbled, barely awake, through his morning then barged in on her in the bathroom. She had just stepped out of the shower. One look into her laughing eyes and his life changed forever.

He had achieved every dream the moment he met Alex and lost it the moment he failed to keep her from leaving the hotel. He knew it was irrational, but he blamed himself. He could have stopped her. He could have said something to break the trance. He could have… but he didn't. And, in that one moment of inaction, he lost every single thing that he had worked a lifetime to achieve.

And the only thing that mattered—Alex.

Staring at the familiar ceiling of the room he lived in more than a decade ago, he had come full circle. Starting with nothing, he returned with nothing.

Nothing but a fool's hope that he might see those laughing eyes again.

CHAPTER THIRTY-TWO

October 12 – 3 P.M.
Buckley Air Force Base, Colorado

"Sir, I have a signal," Alex's Sergeant said.

He pointed to the computer screen. Alex's friend worked in her small office under Buckley Air Force Base.

Raz looked over his shoulder, "Thank God."

"What does that mean?" Matthew asked.

"It means that Alex is alive and able to turn on the tracking signal in her hip. It means that we can determine her location and what to do next."

"If she's alive, we have hope," Colonel Gordon said.

"Let's go get her," Troy said. He was ready get into action. The sitting around worrying and wondering was almost more than he could handle.

"I'm sorry," Raz said. "We can't do that."

"Why? We know where she is being held. We'll just go and kick some ass."

"They will kill her before we even get close," Colonel Gordon said. "Alex knows that. I'm sorry, Captain. We need to work our plan and trust Alex to endure what is to come."

Matthew made a noise then sniffed his nose to hold back his emotion.

Troy looked over at Matthew, "Hey man, remember S.E.R.E.?"

Matthew stiffened. His mind flashed to the memory of laying on the cold tile, sobbing, while Alex sang children's songs to him. He could almost hear her sing "intsy wintsy spider." Matthew's brown eyes shifted to look at Troy, "Yeah."

"I mean you were with her, but I heard that the staff was completely freaked out by our Alex."

Matthew nodded his head. "She didn't bat an eye. She told me once that they have asked her to annotate her S.E.R.E. tapes to explain how she managed to never show fear. She refused. She said living through it once was enough."

"If she wasn't affected by S.E.R.E. then why would someone try to break her down by holding her captive now?"

Raz looked up from the computer screen to Troy.

"I'd be surprised if any record of Alex's S.E.R.E. exists. Her fathers probably destroyed the file," Raz said. "I've looked for it and I can't find it."

Troy laughed. For the first time since he learned that Eleazar had Alex, he felt like everything was going to be all right. He caught Matthew's eyes and Matthew started to laugh.

"Why?" Raz asked.

"They'll be lucky if they make it out alive," Matthew said.

Raz looked from Matthew to Troy. Shaking his head, he returned to Alex's computer hoping to find something that would help him to decide what to do next.

✒✒✒✒✒✒

October 12 – 7 P.M.
Olde Town Arvada, Colorado

Alex opened her eyes in the pitch black. She had no idea how long she had been in this room. The dark silence was disorienting. She might have been there a few hours or a few days. If she wasn't in so much pain, she'd think she was dead. She closed then opened her eyes. Either way, she saw the same darkness. Grunting with pain, she moved her hand in front of her face. She saw the movement, a streak of light in the black, more than her hand.

Sighing, she heard the sound that awakened her. Rain was dropping onto the street. Accustomed to the silence, her ears could almost hear individual drops of rain dance on the street above her. She thought she heard the sound of water moving through the gutter drains.

As her ears reached toward the symphony of sound, her tongue expanded in her mouth. Her throat constricted with thirst. She licked her dry lips.

"Jesse," Alex said as more of an out breath than a word.

"Don't speak to me, Alexandra. They can hear what you say," Jesse said in Spanish.

She looked toward the sound of his voice and saw a spark of light beside her. She sighed. She wanted to talk to Jesse. The idea that she couldn't speak to Jesse was bone crushing disappointing.

"Tommy taught you sign language," Jesse said.

Alex signed: "You don't speak sign language."

"I only have to understand it," he said laughing. "They can't hear me talk."

"I need water. I'm very thirsty. The water they left is drugged."

"It hasn't been that long," Jesse said.

"It feels like days," Alex signed. "How long has it been?"

"I've never been good at that," Jesse said," and I'm worse now. Less than a day, I think."

"They will most likely leave me alone for three days," Alex signed. "It's probably the rain, but I'm incredibly thirsty."

"You're injured," he said. "That can make you thirsty."

"Can you get me some water, Jesse?"

"I have no idea," he said.

"I can hear water in the gutter drain. There's a basement vent right there and the gutter drain is just on the other side. I'm certain it's intentional to get me to drink the drugged water."

"It rains almost every day this time of year," he said.

Jesse went to the wall and looked through the two inch high and eight inch wide space that served as a vent for the basement. Someone had placed razor wire over the inside and outside of the vent. Reaching through the vent and the razor wire, he could touch the drain. Alex was right that this was intentional.

"I'll be right back."

Alex rested her head against the brick again. As time went on, she was getting more swollen and more sore.

Rubber hose. The gift that kept on giving.

She smiled and wondered what her mother would say about the bruising. Maybe Claire could add sleeves to her wedding dress. Remembering the beautiful silk dress, she drifted into memories of John.

After a day of ignoring him, she was dancing with her arms around Max's roommate's neck at a beach party. How did she get there?

John asked her to dance when Max left to dance with some girl. She was dancing a couple feet from him, but this man was like a planet. Drawn by his gravitational pull, she drifted closer and closer to him until he put a hand on her waist. She was a bundle of sensations: the cool sand between her toes, the sound of the pounding surf, the music's rhythms compelling her hips to sway, and a rising heat in her belly.

Her mind focused on the list of reasons why she was not interested in this man. First, he was not American. Second, he was her twin's best friend. Third, he was a bed surfing slut. Fourth, he was just off limits. That's all. O-F-F limits. Her mind was convinced but her body burned under his hands.

"Will you marry me?" John asked.

He said something. What did he say? She slipped back a foot or two to look up at him, "What?"

"Marry me Alex. Marry me tonight."

She shook her head, "What are you saying?"

"I have this overwhelming feeling that I cannot live another moment without you in the center, the very center of my life."

"You're drunk."

"I am that. Marry me."

Stepping forward to him, she felt a yearning for him that she had never known. Her heart ached just looking at him. His beautiful blue eyes were framed by his black curly hair. Her fingers touched his full lips.

He looked away, embarrassed by her close scrutiny.

She opened her mouth to speak. She'd tell him exactly how they should not, absolutely should not get married. He was O-F-F limits after all. But, no words came out. She closed her mouth.

Trying again, she opened her mouth. Just opened her mouth. And the words rose from the very center of her being.

"Yes."

"What?" he asked. He shook his head as if he hadn't heard her.

"I'll marry you."

"Tonight?"

"Why not?"

♉

"Alex wake up," Jesse said.

Alex opened her eyes.

"I think I can do it. Did you use the bucket?"

"No," she signed. "I don't care if they have a mess to clean up. Plus I might need it."

"Good girl," he said. "Get your bucket."

Alex felt around the walls until she reached the door. Bending down, she picked up the gallon bucket and felt her way back to the spark of Jesse.

"Hold the bucket above your head. Right there," Jesse said.

Holding the bucket above her head, just under the basement vent, Jesse moved the razor wire tearing a hole in the thin aluminum gutter drain. Jesse moved his hand, creating an electric wall, which forced the water through the basement vent and into Alex's bucket. She stood with the bucket over her head until the rain stopped and the gutters had completely drained. There wasn't a lot of water, four inches, maybe more, but it was enough to keep her alive. Being careful not to spill the precious water, she took one small drink.

"Jesse?"

"Yes?"

"Will you stay with me for a while? I've never really been alone."

"I'm always with you, Alex."

✧✧✧✧✧✧

October 12 – 8 P.M.
Buckley Air Force Base, Colorado

"Sir," Alex's Sergeant said.

"Yes Sergeant," Raz said looking up from Alex's computer.

"Senator Hargreaves is here and wishes to speak with you. Also, we received a message from British Intelligence. One of their agents is traveling with Ben. They should arrive in a few hours."

"Thank you Sergeant."

"And sir?"

"Yes, Sergeant?"

"Captain Mac Clenaghan and Captain Olivas went home. I will stay until Ben arrives then I'm going home for a few hours. Sir, no offense meant, but Major Drayson would insist that you to go home."

Raz's face flushed with emotion. Raz nodded then returned to look at the computer.

There was no way for the Sergeant to know or understand what he had said. Raz never had a home before he met Alex. He lived in a tiny apartment in Queens with his mother until her death. He stayed in the apartment through the Police Academy. When it was time to get married, he bought a house. Even though he signed the documents and made the mortgage payments, he was always a guest in his wife's home.

Alex made a home for him. Alex was home.

He had to fix this. He had to sort it out.

He had no idea where to even start. Alex left a plan but it didn't make any sense now that she sacrificed herself to Eleazar.

That's what got him the most. Eleazar was supposed to come for him next. He should be beaten, tortured and locked in some cold dark cellar. He was ready. It was his turn. But Alex stepped forward instead.

Raz rubbed his hand over his head ruffling his short hair.

"Sir, Senator Hargreaves?" Alex's Sergeant escorted Patrick into the office.

Raz stood, "General. I'm very sorry, sir. I don't have any news for you."

"I didn't come here for news, Josh," Patrick said. "Do you mind if I call you Josh when we are alone?"

"No sir," Raz said. For some reason, he felt comforted hearing this great man say his name. "Why are you here?"

"I came to help," Patrick said.

"Sir?"

"My guess is that you know where she is but you don't really know what to do next. Go to get her by force? They will kill her. Leave her and risk her being tortured. Yet you still have no idea what they want. Is that accurate?"

"Yes sir," Raz said. "But..."

"She left a plan but it doesn't make any sense?"

"Yes sir. But..."

"I'm a little softer and a lot older than I was when I was a Sergeant in the field, but I'm still that guy, Josh. I even still have the security clearance. Let me help. Do you know what to do?"

"No sir."

"Then let's start at the beginning. Where are Alex's journals?"

"Alex doesn't keep a journal. Not since her team was killed."

"Alex always keeps a journal. Why don't you see if you can find it? I bet it was either on her computer or... is there a super secure place where Alex kept things?"

"Yes sir but I don't have her passwords."

"Lucky she has a twin. He's outside. Shall I get him?"

"Sir?"

"Max flew to Denver when he knew Alex was in trouble. He's talking to her Sergeant."

"Max is a civilian."

"Only sort of. He's a twin first. He'll know the passwords. Can you get me the tapes of these phone calls? And do you have her database?"

"Database, sir?"

"It should look like a spreadsheet or maybe an address book. She might have kept it on the computer, but I doubt it. She liked to work with a yellow pencil. She would have worked with the transcripts of the calls, cross checking every word, in an effort to determine what he was after. I can recreate her work from the tapes but Alex has a real talent for understanding what motivates people, especially terrorists. That's one of the reasons she was so good at extraction."

Raz raised his eyebrows and rubbed his hand over his head.

"You have no idea what I'm talking about," Patrick said shaking his head.

"No sir," Raz said.

"You're her partner. Right? You never saw her database? Alexandra..." Patrick shook his head and let out a breath. "She's not really over the loss of her team. Is she?"

"No sir," Raz said.

"We have work to do then," Patrick said.

"Sir, she had an address book at home. She said it held all the phone numbers of everyone she'd extracted."

Patrick nodded. "In Navajo code?"

"I believe so," Raz said.

"Good. We'll be able to keep those details private while working with her database. Unless you speak Navajo?"

"No sir," Raz said.

"Where is this address book?"

"She asked Maria to keep it for her when the house came down."

"Great. I'll take care of the address book," Patrick said.

Raz stood next to the computer not moving. He wasn't sure what to do.

"Josh?" Patrick asked.

Patrick put his hand on Raz's arm. Breathing out, Raz broke down. With his hands against his face, Raz let a few tears fall while blowing his overwhelm out in breath. Standing beside him, Patrick waited for the storm to pass. With a slight smile, Patrick gave Raz a handkerchief then patted his back.

"Don't worry, Josh. I've done this before."

✌✌✌✌✌

October 13 – 3 A.M.
Olde Town Arvada, Colorado

"Alex?" Troy whispered through a basement vent. Cutting the razor wire off the outside, he lay down across the wet sidewalk to pressed his face into the hole. "Alex?"

He would do what the spies said—don't go get her. That's fine. But leave her there? By herself?

She'd never slept alone. Not even one night. She went from sharing a room with Max to military life to being married. Even when she traveled with Raz, Alex always had someone close in the dark.

Troy teased her about her lack of independence. He told her that she was a child. She would laugh. She would tell him that he was terrified of commitment. And really wasn't that childish? They would laugh. He could only imagine what how awful she must feel to be alone now.

After staring at his bedroom ceiling for hours, he decided that the least he could do was go by the building. She was only fifteen miles East of his house. Practically on the way to... some grocery store somewhere. Once there, he followed Jesse Abreu to the basement vents. A little razor wire was nothing for the needle nose pliers in his Leatherman Mini-tool.

"Alex?"

"They are monitoring me—don't talk ok?" Alex asked.

From this position, he could only see the flash of light from her blonde hair. He closed his eyes when she grunted in pain. Reaching his hand through the vent, he clipped the inside wire. He slipped a Snickers bar through the basement vent. She chuckled, taking the candy from him, then stretched her fingers into the space. For a few minutes, he lay on the wet concrete feeling the soft tips of her fingers rub against his fingertips.

"Go," she said.

He slipped a leather glove through the space to help protect her hand from the razor wire. Together, they put the wire back. He sat back on his heels, then, almost by instinct, he pulled his Mini-tool from his pocket and slipped it under the razor wire. He heard her chuckle again. Her hand waved 'good-bye' to him and he backed away from the vent.

Looking up and down the deserted wet streets of Olde Town Arvada, he turned to walk back to his car. He was two feet from the building when he was jumped. Laughing, Troy fought with two scrawny Arabs. When the last man dropped unconscious to the ground, Troy pulled out his cell phone and dialed 911. He waited for the police to arrive then told them that he was jumped. Of course, his newly minted Military Intelligence Department of Defense identification kept the Arvada police from asking too many questions. Anyway, Homeland Security wanted the men on charges of terrorism. Troy was doing his civic duty, that's all.

Troy whistled as he walked to his car. At least those two weren't going to hurt Alex anytime soon. Honking his horn as he drove past the building, he thought he saw Jesse wave good-bye.

Maybe now he could get some sleep.

CHAPTER THIRTY-THREE

October 13 – 8 A.M.
Olde Town Arvada, Colorado

"You need to move, Alex."

Alex opened her eyes. She wasn't sure who had told her to move around but just straightening her leg brought waves of pain. With force, she pushed herself to standing. She had to be ready for them when they came. She glanced at the basement vents. The light turned from halogen orange to yellow.

Was that daylight? Had she been here one day or two?

Not three days.

Surely, not three days. The silent pitch-black night continued in this room.

Feeling for the wall, she began stepping around the edge of the room. When her body loosened, she walked faster then ran with her hand along the wall. As her body warmed the tightness and pain began to ease. Slipping off her jacket, she went through a Sun Salutation yoga routine to stretch her whole body. She dropped to the ground to stretch.

She thought she knew pain. The sharp pain in her forearm was familiar, almost comforting. But the swollen, bruised sensation between her skin and her muscles was a whole other beast. She felt as if the space between her muscles and skin was filled with aching, swollen lumps.

She walked the room ten more times. Ten was probably enough. She promised herself that she would repeat the routine tonight.

Dropping back to her sitting position, she ate another bite of the cherished Snickers bar. She never noticed all the textures and flavors in this candy. Captain Gordon loved these bars and sent them with people on missions. Troy used them when he trained for marathons. Snickers bar. She pushed the rest of the bar into its wrapper.

Only Troy would bring her a candy bar. He didn't think of bringing water or a weapon. Troy knew that she didn't really need those things. He brought her something she needed, something for her heart.

Her hand wrapped around the Mini-tool in her jacket pocket. Less than three inches when it was folded closed, the Mini-tool opened to seven inches of stainless steel with a needle nosed pliers in the center. Alex folded the steel arms open in her hand and ran her finger across the well used bottle opener. Touching the blade of the knife, she noticed the blade was very sharp. Troy had this tool when she met him in basic training. She had never seen him without his Mini-tool. Just holding it made her feel less alone. She folded the arms back in and tucked it into the pocket of her jeans.

She was loved.

She fell asleep with a smile on her face.

October 13 – 10 A.M.
Buckley Air Force Base, Colorado

Patrick rubbed his eyes then looked from face to face in the small conference room. Matthew, Troy and Raz sat along one side of a table while Ben and the British Intelligence Agent–what was his name?–sat on the other side. He hadn't led a meeting like this in over twenty years. He almost forgot how much he enjoyed leading competent, talented people. And Alex certainly surrounded herself with smart, talented people. He looked up as her Sergeant gave him a piece of paper. He nodded then set the sheet down.

"Let's begin," Patrick said then waited for the men's attention.

"Sorry, I'm late," Colonel Gordon came into the room. "Patrick, how are you?"

The Colonel held his hand out which Patrick shook.

"Thank you for being here," Colonel Gordon said. He sat next to the British Intelligence officer. "We are lucky to have someone of your experience to help us out. You won't mind working on a few other cases while you're here, would you?"

Patrick laughed.

Matthew and Troy looked at each other then at Patrick. They attended this meeting out of respect for Alex. They knew her father had been a General and was a hell of a poker player, but they knew next to nothing about his service record.

"First, what is your name?" Patrick asked the British Intelligence Officer.

"Sean Hudson, her Majesty's Secret Service, MI-5, sir. It's an honor to meet you, General Hargreaves."

"Sean? Every British person I meet is either a Sean, John, Tom…"

"Alex said the same thing when I met her," Sean said.

Patrick nodded. Alex knew it was a fake name too.

"Thank you for coming," Patrick said. "Anyone know where Trece and the White Boy are?"

"Sir," Matthew said. "They are attending to a security issue in Los Angeles. They left right after the ceremony and we..."

"They don't know this is going on," Patrick said. "That was wise. Troy?"

"Sir?"

"I apologize for keeping you inactive for so long. I'm wondering if there is anything you'd like to tell us."

Troy flushed bright red. Matthew shot him a look.

"Matthew, you are an excellent leader. You'll make a great General, if you're interested. However, when you keep people like Troy inactive for too long, they end up acting on their own."

"Troy?" Matthew turned in his chair to look at Troy.

"Um..."

"I have an Arvada police report about a mugging in old town Arvada. It says that Captain Olivas was... er... doing his civic duty." Raz looked up from the piece of paper in his hand. "Your civic duty?"

"What did you expect me to do? Just sit on my hands while Alex sits in that awful room all by herself. Fuck," Troy said. He crossed his arms and leaned back in his chair. "I'm not cut out for this work."

"Alexandra thought you were," Patrick said. "And I second that. What did you do?"

"I went by the building. I followed Jesse to these basement vents. They are just at sidewalk level... maybe two inches high and eight inches long. They had razor wire on the outside and on the inside. One is covered by a new gutter drain. It's probably not to code..." Troy looked up at Patrick who nodded and smiled encouragingly.

"And the other vent?"

"I cut the razor wire. I couldn't talk to her because she said she was being monitored. She touched my fingers then told me to go."

"Did you give her anything?" Raz asked.

"A Snickers bar and... my Leatherman Mini-tool. Oh, and a leather glove."

"Outstanding Troy," Patrick said. "Candy to give her hope and something for her to use. Well done. Now, don't go back."

"Yes sir. I was jumped by those guys by the way."

"Also good to know,"

"Is she injured?" Raz asked.

"I could only see a flash of her blonde hair. The room is very dark. But she grunted like she does when she's in pain. So yeah, I think she's injured."

Matthew made a small noise, which he covered by coughing. Raz looked away from the table.

"We must stay focused on the issues at hand. I'm sorry but our emotions won't help her now." Patrick looked from Raz to Matthew. "It's hard for me as well."

The men nodded.

"Sean, what have you come to tell us?" Patrick asked.

"We have an operative deep within this group. He's been with Eleazar for almost two years. They are from the same neighborhood in Jerusalem. This man was in Abu Graib."

"What does he report?" Patrick said.

"They are following a standard protocol. They beat her up then will leave her alone for a few days. The room is set up for sensory deprivation with some extra goodies."

"Goodies?" Raz asked.

"The gutter drain Troy spoke of? They left her with only a gallon of water laced with LSD and laxatives. If she drinks the water, she will hallucinate and have diarrhea. She will know this but..."

"She can hear the water in the drain," Raz said. "That's ..."

"Torture, yes," Sean said. "There is a high-end chef's table directly above where Alex is being held. The room is not used very much but there is a large dinner scheduled tonight."

"We've tried to get a seat at that dinner but so far, we've been unable to," Ben said.

"Our operative believes they will come for her tomorrow. They are instructed to follow a fairly standard torture plan."

"Does he have any idea what they want?" Raz asked.

"No. That's the strange thing. Eleazar is very vague about what they are after. He believes that he can break Alex. He's confident he'll be able to achieve his goals because she did what he asked her to do. We believe he needs her to do something but we have no intel on what that might be."

Sean looked at Ben who shrugged.

"How did he get Alex to do what he asked her to do?" Matthew asked.

"It's an assumption to believe that he did," Patrick said. "Let's get back to that in a moment."

"Is Eleazar here?" Raz asked.

"Not yet. He is expected tomorrow," Sean said.

"They may start working on her before he arrives?" Patrick asked.

"Yes sir. Their orders are clear. Keep to the schedule. He will be there when he can."

"It's my opinion that he does not want information. He wants a compliant, controllable Alex," Ben said.

"I agree," Patrick said. "This is what I recommend. I'd like Troy, Trece and the White Boy to collect Captain Jakkman and bring him back to Denver. I spoke with him about an hour ago. He is on his way to Rome. Sergeant? Can you make arrangements for Troy to collect Trece and the White Boy then meet Captain Jakkman in Rome? I'd like them back here by tomorrow evening at the latest."

"Yes sir," Alex's Sergeant left the room.

"Zack Jakkman is alive?" Sean Hudson asked.

"No," Patrick said. "Raz, tell me exactly what you saw when Alex left the hotel."

"I wasn't there when she got the call. I noticed she left her coffee and asked John about it. He said she answered her phone. She told him that she had to go and that 'he always says friend.' I ran to the front of the hotel and saw her leaving by cab. Her eyes were saucers—dark and round. She held her right hand up to the window. I was forced back into the hotel by the CIA operative. There was a major threat against the hotel."

"And was there?"

"Yes," Ben said. "There was a credible bomb threat. As a safety measure, cell phone, electronic signal, Internet access and telephone lines wereautomatically shut down. There was no way for Agent Rasmussen to contact the police or anyone to stop the cab."

"They knew where she was staying. Do they know about John? Max?"

"No," Sean said. "According to our operative, Eleazar believes he has murdered Zack Jakkman, Max Hargreaves, John Kelly and Joseph Walter."

"Captain Olivas?" Alex's Sergeant poked his head inside the conference room door. "I have your travel arrangements. You will leave in ten minutes. Does that work?"

"Oh thank God." Troy hopped to his feet and exited the room.

"General, do you believe that Alex is under Eleazar's control?" Colonel Gordon asked.

"Yes and no," Patrick said. "She clearly did what he asked. She should have only said what he told her to say. Which was," Patrick shifted through a few sheets of paper, "'Sorry, I have to go' according to the cell phone transcript. The video record from the restaurant shows that she kissed John and told him that she loved him. She also would not have put her hand on the glass to Raz if she was completely under his control."

"Are you certain, sir?" Matthew asked. "I mean no disrespect but I think we all want to believe that Alex didn't succumb to him. Yet she's in his control now."

"Matthew, General Hargreaves is one of the world's experts in psychological programming," Ben said.

Matthew looked at Alex's father with surprise. Patrick shrugged.

"It's a long story," Patrick said. "It's my opinion that she let it happen. I cannot imagine what it would be like to watch your entire team killed before you. Then she lost her home, her friends were almost killed, her twin shot, her husband... It goes on and on. She knew Eleazar wanted her. I think she didn't want anyone else to be hurt or killed. She probably just wanted to get it over with."

"She knew he'd torture her? Rape her? And just went along with it?" Matthew asked.

Patrick nodded. "When I look at the video, I see her saying good-bye to John. She had already arranged for him to go to Scotland where she knew he'd be taken care of. Yes, she knew what would happen. Now, Matthew, can you hear Jesse?"

"Not well," he said. "I'm too skeptical."

"I can," Ben said.

Patrick raised his eyebrows at Ben and laughed, "Really?"

"I heard him in the tunnels. He told us where to go."

"We need to remind Alex that they will blind her with the lights. I doubt we can get close again, like Troy did. She also needs to know that Eleazar is not here. If she can hold them off until he gets here, we will get somewhere. I wondered if we might send her that message."

"Sir, you are talking about speaking with a dead person," Raz said. "Isn't that a little..."

"Alex believes she sees and talks to him. Why shouldn't we? Now how do we get his attention?"

"I'll work on that, sir," Matthew said. "I think I know a way."

"Great. I'll work with Ben, Raz and Sean to see if we can come up with what Eleazar wants."

Patrick watched Matthew leave the room then turned to Ben.

"What do you have?"

"Are you all right?" Max asked.

He was walking down the hall carrying Alex's address book when he ran into Matthew. Matthew was standing in the hallway with his head against the wall. He looked up when Max spoke and shook his head.

"Come on, man. Let's get some coffee," Max said.

They walked down the hall to Alex's office. Max tilted his head sideways, then opened a cabinet and pulled out the coffee maker. He passed the pot to Matthew who filled it at the water cooler. With a flick of his hand, Max turned the coffee pot on.

"How did you know that was there? You even found her secret stash of French coffee."

"I just looked where I would put it," Max said. "It's not true for all twins, but Alex and I have always been very close."

"Is that why you can stay so calm?" Matthew asked.

"I guess. I look inside, to the place that Alex lives inside me, and I know that she's all right... asleep, I think."

Matthew nodded.

"What's wrong?" Max asked.

"What's not?"

"Have some coffee. Alex can't have coffee right now, so we should double up for her."

Max poured Matthew a cup of coffee then went to Alex's desk. Kicking a corner of the desk, the bottom drawer opened.

"Whiskey?" Max held up a bottle of Red Breast Irish Whiskey.

Matthew laughed and nodded.

"Don't tell her I showed you her private stash." Max poured himself a cup of coffee and added some whiskey.

"Your Dad... He just sat there talking about his daughter getting tortured... I..."

Max nodded. "It's just a reality for him. I think he's prepared himself for the possibility since she begged him to help her become a Green Beret. He was... crazy... when you guys were in S.E.R.E.... Absolutely crazy."

"I'm supposed to talk to Jesse," Matthew said. "I don't even know if I believe Jesse exists."

"He's right there." Max pointed to the door. "Did you call for him?"

"Just before you came down the hall. Then I just felt stupid and hopeless."

"Why did you need him?" Max asked.

"I'm supposed to tell him to tell Alex that they will try to blind her with the lights and that Eleazar isn't here yet. She's supposed to hold them off until he gets here but ... I mean, how can I ask Alex..."

"Jesse, remind her about the slit glasses," Max said.

Jesse nodded then disappeared.

"Well that's taken care of. Is there a shooting range here?" Max asked.

"Two floors below us, why?"

"The spies will be sorting out what their real names are and what not for a couple hours. Why don't we go shoot for a while? Blow off steam."

Matthew nodded.

"Do you really shoot a forty-five?"

"Yeah, why?"

"Oh nothing."

CHAPTER THIRTY-FOUR
Thirteen years earlier

Intelligence officer in training, Sergeant Alexandra Hargreaves, walked down a dim hall in the bowels of Fort Bragg. After shaking her awake at two in the morning, the two Military Police officers, one on either side of her, kept a clipped pace through the halls. She had no idea what was going on. She only knew that they wanted her to come with them.

They reached a door at the end of the hall. Unlocking the door, they held the door open and instructed Alex to enter the room. Alex stepped inside the small room and turned just in time to see the MPs close the door. She was locked in this room.

There was a battered table in the middle of the room with a chair on either side of it. Alex dropped into a chair at the table while she looked around the room. A white board filled one wall and the other walls were bare cinder block. The room was more like an austere closet than an actual meeting or training room.

Hearing a sound, she turned to see the door open.

"I was lying in my hospital bed," Ben said. He leaned against the closed door. "They told me that some Sergeant aced the intelligence exam. What should they do? I said, 'Give the Sergeant the test again'. How stupid can they be?"

Using a cane, he moved with obvious pain. Alex rushed to his side.

"What did you expect? They gave me situations I could have solved when I was a child," she said.

Tucking an arm under his shoulder, she helped him to the table. He dropped into the chair she vacated.

"That may be true, but you have now tested out of Special Forces Intelligence training. Alexandra, they test you at the beginning of training so that they have something to compare to at the end of training."

"Oh, I was supposed to blow the test? Why didn't you tell me that? I'll take it again. Can I take it again?"

Ben laughed.

"Are you here to take me home?" Alex asked.

"Not a chance. The CIA has dibs on anyone that does well on those exams. The Director himself is salivating over your scores."

"I want to be a Green Beret not a CIA agent."

"You sure you want to do this? You are moving into a world of elite intelligence. They will call you from your hospital bed and make you work."

"I'm sorry, Ben. You know I'd never…"

"Sit down," Ben said. He tapped a cigarette against the table. "I can't smoke in the hospital."

While Alex made faces at him and his habit, he bowed forward to light the cigarette.

"Tonight, you and I are going to run scenarios to make certain that you didn't cheat on that exam. We are monitored—video and sound. If it is determined that you did cheat, you go home. If you didn't cheat, you will join three seasoned Special Forces Intelligence officers in a class taught by me."

"I get to take a class from you? Well… That's great!"

"There's a condition."

"What?" Alex crossed her arms over her racing heart. She hadn't been this excited since she received her acceptance letter to Special Forces training.

"You will be attached to the CIA. If we need you, and you're available, you will work for us."

"Work?"

"I will arrange for you to work under me. The work will be anything from strategy to actual field work."

"But I still get to be a Green Beret?"

"Yes, Alexandra. You will still be a Green Beret. That is, if you can prove that you didn't cheat on the test."

"I didn't so that's easy…"

"You have to prove it. We'll run scenarios tonight. Depending on how well you do…"

"We get to run scenarios all night?" Alex cut him off. She was positively bursting with excitement. "Then I get to take a class with you! That's wonderful! Ok, go ahead."

"You are a sick, sick girl. You will join your group tomorrow morning on no sleep."

"That's all right. I can go at least ninety hours without sleep, easy. Can you make the situations really hard?"

Ben laughed.

ℱℱ
October 13 – 7:30 PM

Olde Town Arvada, Colorado

"Ben?" Alex whispered opening her eyes in the dark.

She could have sworn she heard him laugh. She listened as feet walked across the wood flooring above her. There was a scraping sound, a chair across the wood, and people laughing. The smell of Gitanes cigarettes, the brand Ben smoked, came through the floorboards. She heard serving ware clink against china as what sounded like a dinner party began. The room above filled with people until every chair was filled. Her mouth watered and her stomach rumbled as the smell of garlic and warm bread lifted from the table above to torture her senses.

Someone upstairs was tapping their feet. Crap Ben, you know my Morse code sucks. She looked up at the ceiling as Ben tapped 'I know your Morse code sucks'.

All right.

All right.

Ben says that it's been two days. Alex flushed with relief. Simply knowing how long she had been in this room grounded her in the present.

John was in Scotland. John. Alex smiled at the thought of John.

Max was with Dad at MI. Dad is… she cocked her head. What? There was a scraping sound and the tapping stopped. That was probably as much as he would risk.

With a sigh, she pushed herself to standing. Taking another drink of water, she ate a tiny bite of the Snickers bar, saving the last piece for tomorrow. She rubbed a finger across her teeth as a modified toothbrush.

Distracting herself from the laughter, garlic and cigarette smoke of the party she started her workout. She walked the edges of the room, then worked her way through running, yoga, and deep stretches. She tried a few burpees, but crunches were more than she could bear. She was certain she had never been in as much pain.

Bending over her left leg, she felt the sharp edges of a piece of shrapnel move toward the surface of her hip. Unzipping her jeans, she could feel the hard lump under her skin. Another thing she couldn't do a damn thing about. She sighed and pulled her pants up.

There was a clap of thunder, the dinner party overhead cheered, and the rain dropped to the streets below. The spark that was Jesse moved over to the vent. Alex held her bucket above her head while Jesse helped move the water into the bucket.

One more day. They would come for her tomorrow.

Then what?

She succumbed to terror. Tomorrow the real torture and raping began.

Hyperventilating, she dropped to her knees. The bucket fell from her hands. Panic consumed her. Her life-giving water spilled onto the cement floor.

Laughing people, less than twenty feet above her head, ate their gourmet meal oblivious to Alex's struggle for her breath and sanity. Looking up, she saw the sparkle of Jesse.

"You are ahead of yourself," he said.

She nodded. She slammed the panic and fear into a tight box in her head. Feeling in the dark, she found the bucket and held it above her head. Jesse helped the water fall into the bucket. They filled the bucket with five inches of water before the rain stopped. Taking a drink of precious water, she moved to sit down.

Drowning in the cold pitch black, she allowed her mind to return to her memories.

✧✧✧

October 14 – 2:33 A.M.
Olde Town Arvada, Colorado

Alex opened her eyes.

She was shivering. Pulling her knees up to her chest and wrapping her hands around her bare feet. She pressed her face into her knees in attempt to stop shaking. Nothing seemed to help. Standing near the basement vents, she realized that she was sweating. She opened her jacket to allowed the cold wind from the basement vents to cool her body. Looking up, she saw snow and rain drop onto the street above. The wind whipped through the streets and blew flakes of snow onto her hot body.

"I have a fever Jesse," she said out loud.

"Shh, Alexandra," he replied. "Your wound is infected. You need to scrape it."

"With what?" she mumbled.

"Use the drugged water and your knife."

"Did you lose your lighter?"

"You have my lighter. Alexandra, do not speak."

"Hmm, where's my lighter?"

"That's an interesting question. I'm going to leave if you speak again. Sign to me."

Alex stumbled around the room until her hand felt the door. She tapped the floor with her foot until she felt the bottle of drugged water. She slipped off her leather jacket. Setting her jacket next to the wall, her body continued to shake with cold and fever. She pulled off her sweater and placed it on top of her jacket. Letting out a breath for courage, she took off her T-shirt. She cut strips from the bottom of the T-shirt with Troy's Leatherman Mini-tool. Feeling for her sweater, she placed the strips onto her sweater. The room was so dark that she would lose them if she wasn't careful.

Taking two steps forward and one step toward the center of the room, she pulled the filthy piece of fabric from the knife wound on her left forearm.

"Ugh."

Jesse was right. She needed to scrape the wound to remove bacteria and dead skin. Singing the first verse of "Home" by Breaking Benjamin, she pulled the lid off the bottle and poured the water onto the wound. The ice-cold water on her inflamed burning skin sent a chill down her back. Shivering, she splashed water onto her bare feet before finally wetting the Mini-tool knife. With a gust of breath, she inserted the blade into the wound. Another deep breath.

That wasn't too bad.

She scraped the blade across the wound. Every motion brought waves of pain and nausea. She yanked the knife from the wound. Falling to her knees, she panted against the blinding pain.

"Get up," Jessie said. "NOW, Sergeant Hargreaves GET TO YOUR FEET!"

Alex jumped to her feet at Jesse's imitation of their Special Forces training instructor's voice. Weaving and shivering, she splashed more water onto the wound.

"Once more," Jesse said in his normal voice. "You have to do it again."

Alex's head turned toward his voice. She weaved.

"NOW. SCRAPE IT NOW!" Jesse imitated their training instructor again.

Alex fell forward to the ground in a faint. A pool of blood formed under her left arm.

"Wake up, Alex," Jesse said.

Alex blinked her eyes.

"You have to scrape the wound again. You'll die if you don't. Twice. You have to do it twice. Alex." Jesse's voice rose in anxiety. Not sure what else to do, he said the one thing he knew would make her respond. Imitating their bastard training instructor's voice, he sneered, "I knew you didn't have it in you to be a Green Beret."

Alex jerked alert. Pushing herself to her knees, she scraped the edges of the wound with the knife. The knife stuck on something in her arm. She tugged and pulled. Letting out a breath, she jerked the knife from the wound. Holding the bleeding wound away from her body, she mumbled, "Green Beret my ass."

Jesse laughed.

Wiping the knife on her jeans, her numb fingers fumbled with the Mini-tool. The wet steel bounced in her hand. She caught the Mini-tool just before she lost it forever in the dark. With greater care, she tucked the Mini-tool into her pants pocket.

"I'm a Green Beret, asshole, and you were court martialed for conduct unbecoming of an officer." Her voice slurred and was inaudible. "I'm a Green Beret and you're not. Ha, ha, ha, ha."

In a whoosh, she threw up on the floor. Her empty stomach heaved.

"You have to pee on the wound to disinfect it. You will die if you don't," Jesse said. "Alexandra, do not pass out."

Alex swayed then fell forward to the ground.

"Women are WEAK, insignificant CREATURES." Jesse repeated what the training instructor said over and over again. "Good that you are laying down, Sergeant Hargreaves. Now spread your legs and show us what you are made for."

Alex jumped to her feet at attention.

"Pee. NOW."

Vibrating and swaying, her frozen fingers pulled at her jeans. Her fingers fumbled to pull her panties down. Sticking her forearm between her legs, she let go of a stream of urine onto the bleeding wound.

Her head jerked up. She heard an animal suffering, screaming and howling. Where was the kitty? Who's torturing the kitty? Why would someone do that to a poor creature?

"Honey, that's you." Jesse's voice was kind and soothing.

Alex clamped her hand over her mouth. But the howl refused to end. The sound crept past her closed mouth in the form of a moan.

"Get dressed."

She pulled up her pants.

"Good girl," Jesse said. "Let it bleed for a while."

She held the wound away from her. Her blood dropped to the cement. Over her own moan, she heard the drops of blood hit the ground.

"Ok that's probably enough," Jesse said. "I wish you paid more attention in medical training."

"Jax..." she started. Between her pain and desperate longing for her dead friend, she couldn't finish the statement.

Her frozen rebellious fingers managed to create a tight bandage from the T-shirt straps. Shaking with cold and fever, she pulled what was left of her T-shirt on. Her sweater, still warm from her body, dropped warmth onto her shoulders. Slipping into her jacket, she realized that she vomited on the jacket.

In that moment, her loneliness, anger, and pain spilled forward and Alex began to wail. Moving back to her sleeping spot, she slid down the brick wall to the ground. She hit the floor with a thud bruising the one place on her body that wasn't bruised. Shaking with cold and sobs, she pressed her knees against her filthy chest. Her fever began to rise.

Everything was gone. Her home was destroyed. Her husband was not who she thought he was. Her father wasn't her father. Her teammates were dead. She tried to reach for Max but he was asleep or distracted somewhere.

Alone, yet somehow alive in this pitch-black purgatory, she howled like a wounded animal.

As her fever continued to rise, the LSD from the drugged water entered Alex's system. She fell into a delirium. A hundred times more extreme than her recent Ketamine hallucinations, her pain and loss surrounded her like cruel, taunting ghosts.

Without moving his lips, a demonic mime spoke in Eleazar's laughing voice. He pointed toward her lost husband, her lost father, and her lost home. He took her lighter and burned her Green Beret. The burning pieces of fabric grew to burning ropes that held her in place. She could only watch in horror.

Laughing, he launched a fireball. Zack, Matthew, and Troy screamed and writhed as they burned. As Trece and White Boy screamed in horror, he shrank the enormous men to spider size then squashed them under the ball of his foot. He pointed his index finger toward Max.

A bullet flew out of the end of his finger to catch Max in the forehead. Turning his finger, the demonic mime shot Joseph then John. Laughing, the mime executed Raz with a bullet behind his ear. He pushed her parents, Rebecca, Patrick and Ben, into blood red quick sand. Screaming and begging for Alex to save them, her parents sank to their deaths.

Standing at the memorial, the mime called to the zombies of her dead friends. They rose from their graves to chase her through Fort Logan Cemetery until they trapped her in the limestone vault. The laughing zombie Charlie closed the limestone door leaving her inside surrounded by dead bodies and blood. She pounded on the door begging Charlie to let her out. Slipping on the blood slick floor, she fell face first into her own rotting dead body.

And then, Alex lost her mind.

CHAPTER THIRTY-FIVE
October 14 – 9 A.M.
Olde Town Arvada, Colorado

Alex opened her eyes in the dark room and wondered where she was. Remembering the hotel room, she looked for the light under the door. Seeing nothing, she puzzled. She patted the space next to her to see if John was there. Nope.

Her face pinched instinctively against the odor of urine, vomit, sweat, stale cigarettes and garlic. Pushing her greasy hair out of her face, she realized that she was the smell.

"Heya Jesse." Alex smiled at the apparition of her best friend.

"Shh, Alexandra. They are monitoring you," Jesse said. His apparition moved to sit down next to her. "Use sign language."

"Lucky you're a ghost because I smell pretty bad," she signed. "Where am I?"

"You were taken hostage, beaten up then stuck in this room," Jesse said.

"Ah shit. That sucks. I thought the whole beat up and stuck in a dark room thing was a dream. Did you use the Captain's voice last night?"

"I did," Jesse said. "I'm sorry."

"It worked." Alex shrugged.

"Did he really get a court martial?"

"Yep," Alex signed. "He's been working basic. After humiliating this poor girl in front of her team, he assaulted her… pressed himself against her, jumped on her… that stuff he used to do. Remember Jason Smith?"

"JS? He was in training with us? Why?"

"He's a big deal now. Caught the Captain in the act. Court martial city! He asked me to testify but I… I didn't want to leave the house," Alex said. "I always tell you Jesse. Bad guys lose. It's inevitable. Hey, why can I see you?"

"Light reflected off the snow."

"Oh look! It snowed." Alex pointed to the snow on the street above. "At least the snow will block some of the wind."

"I guess your fever broke," Jesse said.

"I had the most amazing dreams," Alex signed. "I don't know Jesse. It's like everything fell apart, then cell-by-cell, I came back together again. What's next?"

"Today is rape and torture day."

"Well we can't have that," Alex signed. She pushed herself to her feet then slipped back to sitting. "God damn. I hurt. If I ever see that fucker and his rubber hose again..."

"You can't be too angry. He's kept British Intelligence informed about what's going on here. His handler is working with your father."

"Which father?"

"Both," Jesse said. "Remember Eleazar doesn't know that you know."

"There's a lot of things Eleazar doesn't know," Alex signed.

"Your father asked Matthew, who asked Max, to tell me to remind you that they will try to blind you with the light. Max said to remember the slit glasses."

"That's a lot of asking," she signed. "I can make them while I wait. When do you think they'll get here?"

"Three, maybe four hours," Jesse said. "Eleazar isn't here yet. I heard Ben say that he's due here this evening."

Smiling, Alex nodded.

"I'm so glad you're my friend," Alex signed.

Jesse wasn't sure what to say. She used to say that. She'd smile her bright smile and thank him for being her friend. She hadn't said anything like that since the team died.

"You'll let me know when they get here?" Alex signed.

Jesse laughed. Looking at her smiling face, he felt like his best friend had returned from a long journey. And he was the one who was dead!

"Of course."

⌀⌀⌀⌀⌀⌀
October 14 – 5 P.M.
Northern Scotland
(9 A.M. in Colorado)

John Drayson was standing at the top of a small hill working on a broken fence. Pulling the broken barbed wire from the wood post, he had the sense that Alex was near.

Maybe she's thinking of me.

He hadn't heard a word from her or her family since he left Denver. Leaning against the post, his hand instinctively wrapped around her dog tag. He wondered if he would ever see her again.

Moving to the back of the truck, he unwound a length of barbed wire from the spool and smiled.

He wouldn't even kiss her until Father Seamus said they were husband and wife. Standing at the beach party, she suggested they 'test out the works.' Then she smiled that crooked smile. Oh God. Sand, crowd, party be damned, he almost jumped her right there. Everything in him longed to connect with her, but he... somehow he managed to step away. John shook his head. To this day, he had no idea how he resisted her.

Clipping a length of barbed wire, he remembered the electric charge that ran through him when he finally kissed her. He still felt that spark sometimes. She ignited the very core of him.

Overcome by the idea of being married, he took his bride-of-ten-minute's hand. He gained control with each step toward the street. When he raised his hand for a cab, he already had a plan in place—bed her, quick annulment, no feelings hurt, back on track. He even smiled at his brilliance. Of course he had to marry her. How else could he bed his best friend's sister?

Sitting in the back of the cab, he brushed her lips in a kind of "kiss the wife" way then could not stop kissing her. Every thought of retreat vaporized in that cab ride. He would have had her, right there in the back of the cab, if... If what? If she wasn't his wife. She became his wife on that cab ride.

John's laughter echoed off the Scottish hills.

He was so drawn by her lips, tongue and teeth that he didn't notice that the cab slowing at the apartment until the cab driver hit him on the back of the head.

"Pay up. Jeez, get a room," the cabbie said.

Certain that Alex would be offended, he started to move toward the cab driver when his eyes caught Alex. She was beaming. Seeing the look on his face, she began laughing.

"Yeah, very funny lady. Get out of my cab."

She scooted out then waited for John. He had never carried a person before and had certainly never carried a woman. Everything is a first with Alex. He scooped her up simply to give him better access to that supple mouth. He carried her up to the apartment then found himself in front of the locked door, keys at the bottom of his tight pocket, and his arms filled with his beloved. He wasn't going to set her down.

She laughed when he kicked the door open. Setting her inside, and somehow managing to close the door, he ripped her silk blouse open. As her buttons ricocheted off the entryway, he dropped his mouth to her captivating mouth. Pulling at his tongue with her teeth, she worked his T-shirt from his body. They ripped their way through jeans, underwear and bra to plush naked skin.

She stepped back from him. They stood in front of each other. Naked. Neither moved. They just looked at each other.

When her lips turned upward, he responded.

"JOHN." Tom Drayson touching John's shoulder.

John raised his eyebrows.

"I've been calling you from down the hill. Where's your head, boy?"

John shrugged.

"You're almost done here," Tom said. "We need to get to the North end."

"To look for the fox?" John asked.

"Right, he comes out this time of day. Fox and chickens. You can't have one without the other."

John nodded and moved toward the fence with the barbed wire. Tom took the other end of the wire.

"Rita won't let us kill the fox."

"That's what we used to do." John tacked the wire to his post. He moved to tack the wire Tom held.

"She won't have him in her chickens either."

"What would you like to do?" John asked. He bent to pick up his tools and they walked toward the truck.

"I have a plan."

John nodded and stepped into the passenger seat.

Turning the key in the ignition, the old truck caught with a roar. Tom caught the goofy look on John's face and laughed.

"She must be some girl."

"She is."

✄✄✄✄✄✄
October 14 – 10 A.M.
Buckley Air Force Base, Colorado

"You guys worked a lot with the Fey?" Sean Hudson asked.

The British intelligence officer, Raz and Matthew were working on their laptop computers in a small conference room. Matthew was tracking Eleazar as well as running interference for the gathering team. Raz worked with Alex's database. Sean compared the information Raz came up with from Alex's notes, journals and database with what British Intelligence had on Eleazar.

"Sure," Raz said. "I've worked with her for… five, almost six years? I'm her Homeland partner. Matthew just started working with her as her second in command here at Military Intelligence."

"We've been friends for twelve years," Matthew said.

"How do you know Alex?" Raz asked.

"She appeared in my bed," Sean said.

Raz and Matthew looked up at him.

"I was sound asleep and I roll over to find this... tasty woman was lying in my bed. She's just lying there wearing this tank top and tiny panties."

Sean fell quiet remembering.

"And?" Matthew asked.

"I thought, 'If this is an enemy agent, I may as well show her a bit of hospitality.' I'm smooth, you see. So I slip on top of her to have a go. She smiles and puts her arms around my neck. Her mouth is right next to my ear when she says, 'You have a leak in your department. Your entire team is targeted for elimination.' I move to kiss her and she says, 'If you think you're going to use that, you should think again.' She slips out of bed and is gone before I'm awake enough to follow her."

Sean laughed.

"Was there a leak?" Matthew asked.

"Oh yes. Very big, very messy. My boss, actually. If she hadn't warned me? I'd be dead.. and everyone on my team, as well. Nasty stuff."

"When did you see her again?" Raz asked.

"How did you know?" Sean laughed.

"It just had to happen," Raz said.

"A couple years later. I'm bored and frustrated, sitting, in a meeting. We've got this impossible hostage situation. We've tried everything we know to do and... Nothing. We're fucked. I figure the hostages are dead. Behind our backs, the PM rang some Yank expert. And the great expert is late. We're sitting in a conference room like ripe old buffers when her team arrives. Did you meet those guys?"

Raz nodded.

"Bloody hell. They were huge guys. Tall, at least six feet, every one of them. Testosterone everywhere. Bulging muscles. Very macho. They push their way into the room with machine guns and dark glasses," Sean laughed.

"Ten guys stand around edges of the room. Alex wags her hips across the room with this tawny pit bull looking guy by her side. That was THE Jesse that General Hargreaves was talking about?"

Matthew nodded his head.

"She sits down at an empty chair in the middle of the table. We're so taken back that no one speaks. She smiles then says, 'Next time? Call me before you fuck it up.' She stands up to leave and my Unit Chief sputters, 'What about the hostages?' She looks at him, puts her dark glasses on and says, 'They are waiting for you in the hall. MI-5 saves the day' and leaves the room."

Sean blushed bright red.

"Uh huh, what else did she say?" Raz asked.

"Every person in the room is watching her bum as she swishes toward the door. She gets to me. I'm sitting near the door. She raises her glasses and says, 'Heya Sean. I didn't recognize you with your clothes on. While there's a certain element missing,' she looks straight at my crotch then raises one eyebrow. 'It's very nice to see you again.' I was so embarrassed that I think my face bled. My team went wild to find out what that was about."

"Did you tell them?" Raz asked.

"Not a chance. You think I want them to know that I had her in my bed and let her go? The tape shows her team laughing about me. They joked, in Irish Gaelic no less, the entire way out of the building."

"The hostages?" Matthew asked.

"Outside the door," he said. "I have no idea how she worked their release. The hostages never said a word."

Sean fell silent and the men went back to work. After a silent hour, Sean looked up. He watched Raz and Matthew work. While Alex lingered in his mind somewhere between fantasy and dream, these men were her friends. If he didn't ask them, he would never know.

"Have you spent time with Alex?" Sean asked breaking the silence again.

Raz furrowed his brow, "All over the world. Why?"

"Have you ever noticed that she has a smell?"

Raz pierced his brow, then looked at Matthew.

"Cinnamon rolls," Matthew said. "Troy says she smells like cotton candy."

Raz raised his eyebrows and laughed.

"Oh come on, you've noticed it."

"Warm chocolate lava cake," Raz said. "I thought it was because we've eaten so much chocolate together. She loves warm chocolate lava cake."

Raz and Matthew looked at Sean who blushed and looked down at his laptop computer.

"Well?" Matthew asked.

"Christmas pudding," Sean said.

Raz made a disgusted face.

"It's wonderful stuff. We'll have it the next time you're in London."

"I'll take your word for it," Matthew replied.

"The very smell of her is intoxicating. She's still married, right?"

Matthew nodded his head.

"That guy would have to be a complete idiot to fuck that up. There's a guy at SIS who is absolutely obsessed with her. I guess she rescued him from somewhere in Eastern Europe. He swears she smells like rain. Do you think everyone experiences that?"

Matthew smiled. "I think it's only men. Her team used to tease her about it."

"Is it a perfume?"

"No," Raz said. "It's just the way her skin smells."

Sean shook his head then returned to his laptop. The men worked in silence for more than a half hour before Sean had to ask one last question.

"Why do you think it's different for different people?" Sean asked. "My unit head says she smells like a sweet shop."

"She's a fairy, Sean. You're smelling fairy dust," Raz said under his breath.

Matthew remembered Alex standing over him on the martial arts mat at Special Forces training. She had just kicked his ass. Beamed at him in greeting, not pride or achievement, just greeting, she held her hand out to help him up. He hated this woman for daring to be a Green Beret. But looking into her smiling face, he knew he'd made a friend for life.

Matthew nodded. "Fairy dust."

"Fairy dust?" Sean asked

"Fairy dust."

⚘⚘⚘

October 14 – 12:30 P.M.
Buckley Air Force Base, Colorado

"Sir?" Matthew asked.

He walked into the conference room to find Patrick and Ben arguing. In all the years of knowing Alex and dating Erin, he had never seen Patrick Hargreaves angry. At this moment, Patrick's face was flushed bright red and the soldier–hard, driven and deadly–emerged on Patrick's face.

Standing with his face an inch from Patrick's face, Ben punched Patrick's chest with the index finger of the hand holding a lit cigarette. They were speaking French in terse whispers. When Matthew spoke, Ben whipped around and glowered at Matthew. He walked away from Patrick puffing on his cigarette.

"Max says that Alex is doing well."

Patrick put a hand to his face. Ben fell toward the wall catching himself with the hand that held the cigarette. Not sure of what to do next, Matthew kept talking.

"Jesse said that she was really sick last night but when she woke up this morning she was better. Max says that she's really better, like before all of this happened, like two years ago."

"And what does Jesse or Max say she plans to do?"

Matthew smiled, chuckling a little, "She's going to kill them then wait for Eleazar."

"How will she do that?" Ben asked. His desperation seeped into his voice.

"I'm not sure exactly. Max said something about razor wire and the Mini-tool? Does that make sense to you?"

Patrick laughed and patted Matthew on the back.

"Wire around the leather glove?" Ben said in French to Patrick then laughed. "They won't miss the wire because of the snow."

Matthew made no indication that he understood Ben. There was no way he wanted Ben to think he spoke French. No way. Working with Alex was one thing but Ben? Not a chance.

"Max says that we need to get moving. He's not sure where but he says that Alex thinks they will move her."

Patrick nodded. "Thank you Matthew."

"And sir?"

"Yes?"

"Jordanian Armed Forces have Eleazar's mother in their control as Alex planned. Also, UN Security Forces have surrounded Eleazar's home in Jerusalem but they have been unable to enter."

"Guards?" Patrick asked.

"No sir. The PIRA is in the house. They responded to the death of John Kelly. Raz said that they seem to be waiting to hear from Alex."

Patrick raised his eyebrows and rubbed his forehead.

"Thank you, Matthew."

"Yes sir."

As Matthew walked toward the front of the room, he heard Ben apologize to Patrick and Patrick laugh. Turning to close the door, he saw the men hug.

For the first time in days, his dear friend Alex was in real, serious danger.

He was glad her fathers were on edge.

✥✥✥✥✥

October 14 – 12:45 P.M.
Cherry Hills Estates, Denver, Colorado

"Mom," Erin said.

Rebecca looked up to take a cup of chamomile tea from Erin's hands. Dressed in their warmest clothing, they were sitting on Patrick and Rebecca's deck looking out toward the snow capped Rocky mountains.

"It's been three days," Rebecca said letting out a breath.

"I know," Erin replied. "We have to believe that Alex is alive and doing all right because the alternative is just too awful to contemplate."

"Every time. I worry about her every single time. I keep thinking that I will get used to it, but I never do. And I always know when she's in danger. I always know," Rebecca said.

Erin put her hand on Rebecca's arm.

"It's been wonderful having Alex back," Erin said. "I don't think I knew how much I missed her."

Rebecca smiled a little, "I'm sorry I made her go away."

"You did what you thought was best. I know that, so does Alex. Even Max says it was good. After all, that's how he met John and how Alex met Jesse. John and Jesse were Max and Alex's first friends."

"And how Alex met Matt," Rebecca said.

At the mention of his name, Erin smiled. Her face flushed and her eyes shone with love.

"And Matt."

"He's a wonderful man, Erin. I am very happy for you," Rebecca said reaching over to hold Erin's hand.

"Yes, he is. Who would have thought? Me and Matt. I dreamed of being with Matt, you know, day in and day out, when I was sixteen years old. It seemed impossible. I mean, he's on a twenty year contract!" Erin shook her head at the impossibility. "The last months have been a dream come true. He says that too. Can you believe it? And it's all because of Alex."

Rebecca turned from Erin to watch the mountains. They sat in silence.

"Even though I know the sun will set tonight... Even though I know that what happens today is absolutely out of my control, I still wish..."

"Me too."

CHAPTER THIRTY-SIX
October 14 – 12:53 P.M.
Olde Town Arvada, Colorado

"They're coming," Jesse said. "Three men, guns."

Alex stopped running in place. She was warm and loose or as warm and loose as her battered and bruised body could be in this frigid room. Sitting with her back to the camera, she had made leather shoes out of bottom of her leather jacket then set to work on the slit glasses. Cutting a long strip, she sliced a thin slit down the middle of the leather. These slit glasses would act like dark sunglasses and shade her eyes from the worst of the light. She left the arms, shoulders and chest of the jacket intact for warmth and protection. Trying to gauge space in the absolute dark, she positioned herself where she thought the men would stand after coming in the door.

She also had no idea if the British Intelligence agent was working in her favor. No matter. She was prepared for any possibility.

Closing her eyes in preparation for the blinding light, she heard the men move down the hallway. Her heart pounded in anticipation when the key scratched into the lock. With a click, the dead bolt moved. Light blazed from every light fixture. Even shaded by the slit glasses, her eyelids flashed bright red.

The door moved open a crack then stopped. The bottom of the door caught on the dirty bandage set there to make them force the door. As precious seconds passed, her eyes adjusted to the light behind her eyelids.

One man rammed against the door.

Alex waited.

Two men threw their weight against the door. Jesse moved the bandage and the men fell into the room.

Alex exploded off the concrete floor. Jumping straight up into the air, she kicked her feet outward in a wide V. Her kick knocked both men backward. Still in the air, she heard someone throw what sounded like broken glass on the floor. Laughing, she landed on one covered foot. Rotating sideway, she kicked the British national in the chest. He slammed into the cinderblock wall.

She punched her right fist, covered in the leather glove and wound in razor wire, forward at turban man. He ducked her fist. He moved to punch her. She sliced the razor wire through his beard and across his throat. His face flashed shock. His hands clutched at the deep wound. Choking on his own blood, turban man fell to the floor. Before Alex could finish him, the Brit jumped her.

Rotating back, Alex punched the Brit in the face with her left fist. The Leatherman Mini-tool's needlenose pliers, held between her middle finger and ring finger, tore at the man's eye. Rotating her fist, she exposed the knife. With her forearm in front of her face, Alex slashed at the Brit. The young man screamed with fury. She cut his arms. When he rushed her, she let loose a powerful sidekick. Her foot smashed his larynx. He dropped to the ground.

Turning, she saw the man she had rescued from Abu Graib. He stood just inside the door with the piece of rubber hose.

"You fucker!" She rushed him.

With her left arm under his throat, she pushed him toward the brick wall. They hit the wall with a thud. Holding the knife less than an inch from his face, she said, "Where's your boss?"

"Stupid bitch," the man replied in Arabic. Rotating his arm, he hit her exposed ribs with the rubber hose.

Alex slashed his forehead. The five-inch flesh wound bled profusely. Breathing hard, they stood less than an inch from each other. Blood spilled into his eyes. Alex had to decide whether to kill him or trust him. Closing her eyes, her heart said trust. As if he heard her heard, he nodded. He pushed her chest and she stepped back. She rotated her right hand and the razor wire in a wide arch and he slipped from under her.

They were locked in a delicate dance. She had to fight him for the video cameras but she could not truly injure or kill him.

He had to take her to Eleazar.

Moving behind her, he batted at her back with the rubber hose. She rotated, jumping into a butterfly kick missing his face by less than a half inch. He raised the rubber hose nearly missing her head. Her front kick pushed him off her.

He pulled her Glock 9mm handgun from his pants. He pressed the muzzle of the gun against her forehead. Alex raised her hands but did not let go of the wire or knife. She let out a breath as if defeated, then raised her right knee sharply crushing his genitals.

Leaning forward into her knee, he screamed, "You think a little bruising is anything after having my nuts burned in Abu Graib?"

Cocking the gun, he fired the gun. Alex moved her head out of the way of the bullet, then punched her left hand forward. The point of the needlenose pliers stopped less than a millimeter from his face. He slapped a handcuff on her left hand. Using her momentum, he rotated her left arm behind her.

"Just stay there," he murmured closing the second cuff over her right hand.

Stepping away from her, he pulled the leather slit glasses from her eyes. Alex closed her eyes against the light. Protected from the video cameras by his body, she folded the Mini-tool and tucked it into her back pocket. The man pulled the leather glove and razor wire from her hand. Taking a handkerchief out of his back pocket, he pressed the wound on his forehead then made a modified bandage.

"Get on your knees." The man pushed her to the ground.

Dropping to her knees, she gasped as the glass on the ground cut into her blue jeans. The man dropped a black fabric hood over her head. Yanking her to standing, he pushed her in front of him. They went up seven creaking wooden stairs, then turned left down a corridor or tunnel. They walked what felt like an entire city block. With the handgun at her back, he pushed her up a series of wooden steps. He unlocked a door, then pushed her out into the snow.

The cold hit Alex with the force of a truck. Her feet froze through her modified shoes. She shivered in the cold while he slowly opened the van door. He pushed her inside. Falling forward onto a bench seat, her chin hit the seat. Hearing him lock the door, she rotated to sitting. He stepped into the driver's seat. Without warning, he punched her face. Her head knocked against the seat. His hand dropped two pills into her lap. He pulled the fabric off her head.

"Antibiotics."

She picked up the pills with her tongue. To cover her motions, he hit her with an open hand. Alex spat at him. Wiping her spit off his face, he laughed then started the car. He turned the stereo to blast Arabic music.

Alex had been in that dark room for so long that every sound, every sensation, every sight assaulted her senses. Closing her eyes, she dropped her head to her lap. Every inch of her body hurt. Even the follicles of her hair ached.

"Sick?" he said under his breath.

"Yes," Alex replied. "Need to eat."

"Just make you sicker. Rest while we drive. It'll be a couple hours."

A couple hours? Then what?

Alex smiled.

Whatever happened, she was ready.

✧✧✧✧✧

October 14 – 2 P.M.
Buckley Air Force Base, Colorado

"Sir, Arvada Police are on scene. As you know, they responded to reports of gun fire." Alex's Sergeant came into the conference room where Patrick, Ben, Matthew, Raz and Sean waited. "There are two men down. As we expected, they are non-nationals on Homeland's terrorist list. Sir, the room? They said there is blood everywhere. There is a pool of blood near the door. It looks like... well, their forensics is there. I'm sorry."

Patrick searched the Sergeant's face wondering what he wasn't telling him.

"And the gun shot?"

"They found a 9 mm shell in the brick wall. They do not believe the bullet hit anyone."

"Sean, have you heard from your guy?"

"No," Sean said. "According to Agent Rasmussen, they are driving west on the interstate. My operative has been staying at a remote cabin in the Pikes Peak National Forest. I assume he is taking her there."

"Satellite?" Patrick asked.

"I have a picture of them leaving the building, sir," Raz said. "She's wearing a hood. He pushes her in the car. We can't tell exactly but I think he gives her some pills."

"He was going to give her antibiotics," Sean said.

"Probably. They slap at each other in the car then he takes off. We are following them by the transmission in her hip."

"And Eleazar?"

"He is in the country," Ben said. "He's taken a private jet from New York State. We believe he will land at a private air strip near the cabin."

"What's his travel time?"

"Three, maybe four hours."

"So your guy will take her to the cabin, then they wait for Eleazar?" Patrick asked.

"That's our assumption," Ben said.

"Will you hear from your guy, Sean?"

"I might. He's fairly safe since the other people are either dead or in Arvada City Jail awaiting transfer."

"And the rest of the team? Matthew, when do they arrive?"

"They will touch down around four o'clock. I have spoken with the pilot and he is going to fly them to Fort Carson. They should be at the cabin by five o'clock, give or take a half hour."

"Shall we go?" Max asked walking into the conference room.

Matthew and Raz looked up at him then Patrick.

"I can't," Patrick said. "US Senators don't mobilize on targets. I'll stay here. Sean?"

"He's my guy. I'm going."

"I'll go." Matthew stood from his seat.

"Ben?"

"I'll stay here."

"Sergeant?" Patrick asked.

"I think Major Drayson and the team will need me here. I can keep track of movement and the satellite. I mean no disrespect, sir, but should Max go? He's a civilian."

"I don't think we can stop him," Patrick replied.

"Then we're leaving?" Max asked.

Raz stood, stretched and walked toward the door. Max's face was set in an expression he recognized from Alex's face. Max was done talking. Putting a hand on his shoulder, Raz said, "Shot gun."

Matthew laughed and followed them out of the room leaving Sean to speak with Patrick and Ben. They were standing at the elevator when Sean caught up with them.

"Weapons?" Sean asked.

"We're set," Matthew said. He pulled a handgun from the holster.

"Got your forty-five?" Max raised his eyebrows at Matthew.

"Yes. You made that face at me yesterday. Why does every fucking Hargreaves make that face about my handgun?"

Raz put his hand on Matthew's shoulder. He opened his mouth then laughed. Stepping onto the elevator, he pressed the button for the garage.

"Hargreaves family saying," Raz said. He looked at Max.

"We're just concerned for Erin," Max said. Raz laughed.

"What?!? Just fucking tell me."

"Patrick says that weapons were like penises. If you know how to use your, uh, weapon, it doesn't matter what size it is. People only need large weapons when they can't... well..."

Sean burst out laughing looking from Matthew's indignant face to Max's laughing smile.

"That's great. That's just great," Matthew said as the elevator doors closed.

*

CHAPTER THIRTY-SEVEN

Alex stumbled on a branch covered by a layer of snow . Her captor pushed her forward under the trees. They arrived at a small cabin. Rather than taking her inside, he pushed her around the cabin. Stumbling and walking, they reached the river about two hundred yards from the cabin. He pushed her against a pine tree.

"Turn around," he said. "I'll unlock them."

Alex jumped through the handcuffs so that her hands were in front. He laughed and unlocked them.

"The entire house is monitored with video and audio by everyone including British Intelligence. No one can see or hear you here." He pointed to the trees. "No satellite either. We can speak freely here."

"Thanks Sumit." Alex smiled.

"I'm sorry Alexandra," Dr. Sumit Roy said. "You are at risk for clotting from your injuries. You need an ice bath and I cannot give you one in that monitored bathroom. The river will have to suffice. I'm sorry."

"Sumit, what is the plan?" Alex asked.

"Eleazar will be here in two, maybe two and a half hours. In the meantime, we will dress you like a proper woman. Of course, I'm going to rape you first."

Alex raised her eyebrows indicating that she'd like to see him try. He laughed.

"We will pretend," he said. "I know you find me irresistible but I am married."

Alex laughed. "How is Dalal?"

"Very well. Excited to lose a child. My eldest boy was admitted early to Harvard. He will attend next fall."

"I can't believe he's old enough for college."

"They grow up fast," he said. "Alex, I have to stay with you while you clean up. Do you mind?"

"No."

"You were so kind with me." Sumit stopped talking for a moment as the memory came to him. "You gave me a warm bath, warm clothing, even held me while I shook... I cannot repay the favor."

"I'd be grateful for some food."

"We'll eat a proper meal when we go inside. Rice for you. You will throw up anything else."

Alex nodded.

"How is the wound?"

"Infected." Alex looked at her left forearm.

"We'll take a look at that as well. I have bandages in my pockets."

Alex nodded. She peeled off her filthy clothing. The cabin was located over nine thousand feet. It was very cold. Taking a deep breath, Alex walked naked into the three foot high river. The frigid water shocked her to the core. Moving through the river to a deep pool, she sat down and rinsed her body with her hands. Sumit threw her a cloth and a small bar of soap. Using the cloth and soap, Alex did her best to clean up. She lay back in the pool letting the cold water numb her bruised and broken body.

"I need to burn this clothing," he said. "I'll set this here."

Sumit held up the Leatherman Mini-tool then set it on a rock by the river. While Alex soaked, he built a large bonfire. One piece at a time, he burned her clothing.

"It's time," he said.

Moving to the bank of the river, she set the cloth and soap down. Sumit threw her a small towel. He pointed to a spot by the fire where she could warm up.

"Raping?" Alex asked.

"Ah yes," Sumit said. "God, you are bruised. Is that from me?"

"Fucker," Alex replied.

"Let me see the arm."

Alex held her left arm out to him. He unwrapped the wet strips of T-shirt away from the gash and made a noise.

"Did you do this scraping?"

Alex nodded.

"Probably saved your life," he said.

Tearing open a small packet of disinfectant ointment with his teeth, he smeared the injured area. He bandaged the arm with gauze and tape. He checked her pulse then her temperature.

"You won't take aspirin," he said.

She shook her head. He shrugged.

He gave her a black abaya, robes that covered her from head to toe. He gave her a black niqab, a scarf covering her face and a scarf to cover her head. Only her eyes were seen.

"Would you like me to bandage your forehead?" Alex asked.

"No, I will do it for the cameras. You need these." Sumit gave her a pair of long black gloves.

"Sexy," she said.

"You are not a Muslim man," he said.

"Not today. Shoes?"

"I don't have any," he said. "You need to know... I will do what I can for you but... I've been informed that my placement in this organization is of greater importance..."

"Than my life?"

"I'm sorry."

Alex shrugged. "They're probably right. I will do what I can for you as well."

"It is what we can do. Remember you have just been raped."

Alex nodded. While Sumit put the waning fire out, she tucked the Mini-tool into a seam of her right glove.

"Shall we?" Sumit asked.

Alex nodded and they began their dance of distain.

Sumit grabbed her arm and pulled her toward the cabin. They moved from the cover of the trees. Alex stopped half way, bending at the waist and pressed her hand to her crotch as if in pain. He yanked her arm and pushed her toward the cabin. She fell forward, catching herself with her hands, then glowering at him.

He unlocked the cabin door and they moved into the one room cabin. Alex limped to a chair next to a tattered Formica table. She plopped herself into the chair while Sumit began making a mid-day meal. Resting her head on her hand, she was asleep by the time he finished cooking. He shook her awake then threw a plate of rice at her. Glowering at him, she stuffed rice into her mouth. He ignored her while he ate his meal. Standing over her, he pressed his hips toward her face, covering her from the cameras. His hand slipped more antibiotics into her mouth.

After the meal, he pulled her into the main living area where he handcuffed her to the couch. She fell asleep to the sound of soccer on television.

It would be over soon.

✧✧✧✧✧✧

October 15 – 1:07 A.M.

Northern Scotland

(October 14 – 5:07 P.M. Colorado)

"Wake up John," Alex whispered.

They were backpacking through Yosemite National Park. Opening his eyes, he stretched his sore body. He blinked. Alex was naked surrounded in an almost neon blue light.

"We must rest, love. We have twelve miles uphill tomorrow" He turned over in his down sleeping bag.

"You'll never believe what I found," she said. "Come on."

"And if I say 'no'?"

"You'll miss out." Her words were mixed with laughter.

John unzipped his sleeping bag and worked his way out of the tent. Alex smiled at him.

"You won't need these," she said.

His clothing disappeared. The cold air blew across his warm skin and he shivered wrapping his arms around himself. When he opened his mouth to ask her what was going on, she smiled.

"Come on."

Seeming to float a few inches off the ground, she took off down the trail. Even running full speed ahead, he was unable keep up with her. She waited for him like a bright blue beacon in the dark night.

"It's here," she said pointing to the river.

"Oh love, this water is very cold. Let's go back to bed" He reached for her.

She laughed and stepped into the water.

"Join me," she said. The laughter in her voice rose above the sound of the river like the tinkling of crystal bells.

Stepping into the ice-cold water, he walked along the sandy river bottom.

"This way," she said. "Come over here."

His skin became numb in the frigid water. A bright yellow moon moved from behind a cloud to light the way to her. He slipped into the deep pool where she was swimming.

"You'll catch your death, love. Come out of the river with me."

Giggling, she said, "Come to me."

Moving forward, he felt a flush of warm water. His face must have registered shock because she laughed.

"It's a hot spring," she said.

The water warmed as he drew close to her. She slipped her arms around his neck. He kissed her deeply, savoring her touch and flavor. Under the bright moon, they lay wrapped around each other. Her close, naked contact and the warm water awakened his longing for her. Laughing, she moved on top of him. With the moon shining over her blue shoulder, she kissed his lips.

When he shifted to join with her, she disappeared from his arms. In a breath, her weight, warmth and closeness vanished. Certain she was teasing him, he turned to look for her in the river.

His empty arms felt the cold first. The warm flushed out of the river. He lay in ice-cold water. Storm clouds blew over the bright moon. He called her name into the wind. His eyes searched the dark for her blue light. Snow fell as he ran down the path toward their tent. He found tent windblown, empty, and cold.

Standing at the tent opening, John called Alex's name and strained his ears for her response. The cold wind and snow finally drove him into the tent. Reaching to zip the tent, he heard voices. Still naked, he jumped from the tent and ran in the direction of the sound.

Breaking through a circle of pine trees, he came to a clearing. With her hands tied behind her back, Alex kneeled on the ground. She was dressed in black robes, the traditional dress of a Muslim woman. A man stood behind her holding a handgun to the back of her head.

John screamed her name and the man fired. The front of her skull exploded and pieces of her brain and blood splattered onto the pine needles. What had been Alexandra "The Fey" Hargreaves fell forward to the ground.

"Alex!"

John's scream awakened the sleeping house. Jumping out of bed, he paced the length of his room. What he could possibly do? Tom pushed the door open.

"What is it, boy?"

"Alex is going to die."

*

"You will get on your knees," Sumit said. He pointed her gun in Alex's direction.

Eleazar arrived at the cabin with two machine gun welding guards. After making certain Alex's hands were handcuffed, Eleazar punched her to the ground. Alex lay face first on the ground with Eleazar's Gucci shoe on her back. Sumit gave an embellished report on the valiant efforts of the men and Alex's trickery. He exaggerated her easy capture. Eleazar laughed at Sumit's elaborate description of 'raping the infidel.'

Alex bided her time. She heard Trece's whistle about ten minutes before Eleazar arrived. Her friends were close. They would intervene when she gave them the signal or they knew she was in danger. Right now, she was listening.

"Alex," Jesse's face materialized next to hers. "We still don't know about Sumit."

Eleazar mashed his foot against the wound on her left arm.

"I don't like him."

Alex blinked to indicate that she understood.

With his hands clamped around the knife wound, Eleazar pulled Alex to standing. She wobbled on sore battered legs and knocked into Eleazar. He stepped back to keep from falling. His guard slapped Alex's face but caught the edge of the niqab instead. The scarf and head covering slipped from her head. Sumit moved forward, pressing himself between the guard and Alex, to replace the niqab.

Eleazar sneered at Alex.

As a way of displaying her submission, she bowed her head. Covered in scarves, Alex smirked. For a year and a half, this tiny man, at least five inches shorter than Alex, terrified her. Peering at him from her submissive gestures, she felt a cloud move away. Eleazar was merely a little man behind a green curtain. She survived his dangerous parlor tricks and games. She will survive him today.

Sumit and the guards were another story.

"What do you want from me?" Alex asked.

Eleazar hit her across the face. "Insolent woman. How dare you speak to me?"

Alex closed her eyes for a moment. Her tongue ran across her teeth. Nothing loose. She would have spit at him but her mouth was covered by the niqab in front of her face. She swallowed the blood that pooled into her mouth.

"What is this?" Eleazar asked holding up a Zippo lighter.

Sumit pressed the muzzle of her handgun to the back of her head.

"You will answer when spoken to."

"It's a lighter," Alex said.

"How does it work?" Eleazar asked.

"Unlock me and I'll show you," Alex said.

She returned to her submissive stance. She felt Eleazar's eyes scour her skull. Her only chance was if Eleazar believed that he could control her. When she felt Sumit unlock the handcuffs, she knew that she had won the first battle of deception. Rubbing her wrists, she moved the Mini-tool to a more accessible position.

With her eyes lowered, she held her hand out for the lighter. Eleazar dropped the Zippo into her hand. Flipping the hinge top off the Zippo, she flicked the round thumbwheel a couple times without success. She shook the lighter to see if it had fuel.

"I cannot work it with gloves on."

"You may remove them, my dear," Eleazar purred. "I'm certain you are tired. Please sit down."

She set the lighter on the edge of the small Formica table. Pulling on one finger at a time, Alex moved the unnoticed Mini-tool toward her palm. She moved in slow deliberate movements working to keep the Mini-tool from falling onto the floor. She dropped the glove, with its hidden prize, onto her lap and picked up the lighter.

Turning the lighter over, she said, "I wondered where this was."

"My associate took it from you after he shot you."

"How did he manage that with my bullet in his brain?" she asked.

Eleazar's hired gun raised his hand to hit her but Eleazar raised his hand to stop him.

"You remember?"

"I remember," she said.

She flicked the lighter but was unable to get a flame. Something nagged at the back of her mind. Jesse appeared behind Eleazar.

"Your lighter is broken," Jesse said. "You broke it a couple days before we were shot."

Alex shrugged, "The lighter's broken."

"I am aware of that," Eleazar said.

"How can I help?" Alex asked She bowed her head in mock submission.

"It is my understanding that this item controls an area where my property is stored."

Alex puzzled. What is he saying? She felt movement in the room and peeked out above the niqab. Eleazar motioned the men away from them. Sitting down across from her at the table, he changed his tack.

"Listen, Alexandra, all I want is my property. It's nothing personal. Over the last months, we've become such good friends. I know that you want to give me what I need." His voice was kind and loving.

Alex nodded. Here we go. He's trying to control me. Fucker.

"How can I help?" she asked.

"That's the spirit. Good girl."

Eleazar's voice was like a caress. His hand reached across the table to hold her gloved left hand.

Alex forced herself not to show her revulsion to him. She was grateful for the robes and niqad for they covered her automatic responses. No wonder women loved wearing these things. Alex blinked.

"I wonder how your mother is doing," Alex said.

Eleazar's hand jerked up.

"She's in the custody of the King of Jordan." Alex gauged her voice for neutral keeping her eyes on the lighter. What had she done to this lighter? Something specific, she remembered that.

"My mother is dead," he said. He stared at her bowed head.

"Not yet," Alex said. "But execution by hanging is automatic for terrorists in Jordan. Your children, however..."

Eleazar reached across the table. Grabbing Alex's shoulders, he shook her with force. She looked him in the eye.

"What are you talking about?" he asked.

"Maybe you should call."

Speaking in rapid Arabic, Eleazar requested a cell phone from one of the men. They informed him that their phones did not receive cell service in this area.

"We can get service in the clearing in the back," Sumit said.

Alex slipped the Mini-tool up the left sleeve of the abaya and pulled the right glove onto her hand. She reached for the lighter but Eleazar snatched it from her hand.

"This is mine," he said.

She blinked. Feeling the muzzle of a machine gun in her back, she stood. The guards pushed her out of the cabin. She stumbled, falling face first onto the ground and the guards began kicking her. In the dust and flying pine needles, she slipped the Mini-tool into the palm of her hand.

"That's enough," Eleazar said. "We don't want to kill her yet."

By the time they pulled her to her feet again, she had opened the steel arms of the Mini-tool exposing the needle nose pliers. She heard Trece's bird whistle asking if they should respond. She shook her head slightly.

"On your knees." Sumit pushed her to the ground.

Falling to her knees, she knew she was going to die. Sumit was going execute her in this clearing. Her life was over.

Letting out a breath, she longed for a kiss from John, a hug from Matthew, a chance to listen to Trece's verbal diarrhea, an argument with Troy, a smoke filled conversation with Ben, a sweaty workout with the White Boy, a rolling of her eyes at her mother, a strategy session with her father, a shot of whiskey with Colin, a chance to hear Erin laugh, another moment nestled in Raz's safe arms, a shopping trip with Samantha and more than anything, she longed for Max. Then, like a short life, the longing was gone. She resigned to her fate.

Bowing her head, she made the sign of the cross and began to pray the rosary.

Eleazar stood with his back to her. He spoke in forceful Arabic into a cell phone. He became more and more angry as the conversation progressed. Turning around, almost spinning in place, he nodded to Sumit.

Sumit cocked her handgun.

Alex closed her eyes and waited for the bullet.

Sumit pulled the trigger.

Thwook.

An arrow shot Sumit through the shoulder, rotating his shoulder back. The shot went wild.

Startled, the guards looked around for the shooter. Eleazar screamed "Kill her". The men raised their machine guns, clicked off the safety, but never got a shot off. They fell forward with arrows through their hearts.

Silence. A slight wind blew a tree limb to creak against another limb. Eleazar's head jerked toward the sound. Sumit pulled the arrow from his shoulder and moved back to Alex. Eleazar stood looking around him.

Rotating out the knife of the Mini-tool, Alex popped to standing. In two quick steps, she held the knife against Eleazar's throat.

"You don't want to do that." Eleazar used the voice he was certain controlled Alex.

"Yeah, you know, I really do." Alex scratched the sharp knife against his throat. A bead of blood dropped to the collar of his expensive suit. "That's going to stain."

Sumit's right arm was covered in his blood. His left hand held her handgun. He fired in Alex's general direction before another arrow shot him through the left shoulder. Screaming, he fell backwards. Alex's handgun flew from his hand.

They heard the sound of someone walking toward the clearing. Zack Jakkman appeared through the trees. He picked up Alex's handgun. Clicking open the magazine, he checked for bullets then cocked the gun.

"Oh. I just realized that you don't know who I am," Zack said to Eleazar. Holding his right hand out as if he was going to shake Eleazar's hand, he said. "Hi. I'm Captain Zack Jakkman. They call me the Jakker."

Eleazar jerked with surprise, "That is impossible."

"You're the one who thinks that friends are such a big deal." Zack shrugged.

"You're not going to kill me, Alexandra. You can let me go now." Eleazar continued to work on Alex's mind.

"No she won't kill you." Max stepped into the clearing with a compound bow. "But, I'd be happy to."

"You're dead," Eleazar said.

"As dead as I am," Joseph Walter said walking to Sumit. He placed his foot on Sumit's chest. "Just stay there, asshole."

"John Drayson or, sorry, I mean John Kelly would be here," Troy melted from the trees with a compound bow in his hands, "but he's with his PIRA family in Scotland. The people on the phone would be very happy to know that. Go ahead."

Eleazar raised the cell phone to his ear then held the phone out to Max.

"This is Max Hargreaves," Max said in Irish Gaelic. "Yes, thank you. We have him. Thank you for your help." Max laughed then looked up at Eleazar, "Did you decide whether they should kill your oldest son or the baby?"

Eleazar let out a stream of curses.

"Yes, that's correct. John Kelly is in Scotland. Yes, she will phone you as soon as she's free," Max said continuing in Gaelic. Max closed the phone. Looking at Eleazar, he said, "You must have realized that the PIRA takes care of their own. They will turn your family over to the UN Security forces."

Trece and the White Boy appeared from the pine grove to stand beside Alex.

"You can let him go," Trece said.

Alex turned her head to whisper in Eleazar's ear, "You'd have to have friends to be able to control me with the idea of friends."

As if he was a snake ready to strike, Eleazar wound back.

"Patrick Hargreaves is not your father."

Alex laughed, kissed his cheek then let go of him. Turning away from him, she beamed and held her arms out to Max.

In one fluid movement, Eleazar pulled a small handgun from the pocket of his pants. He fired at Alex.

Trece's hands went around Eleazar's chin and broke his neck. He tossed Eleazar's body to the ground.

Alex coughed, working for breath, then fell onto her back to the pine needles carpet.

Everyone moved at once.

Max dropped to the ground to hold Alex's head. Seeing his face, she reached her hand out for him. Matthew moved her robes to find the injury. Finding her naked under the robes, Matthew slipped off his jacket to cover her hips.

"I'm a doctor," Sumit said.

"Shut the fuck up," Joseph said.

"He's... a... doctor." Alex pushed one word out at a time.

The White Boy lifted Sumit to standing and pushed him over to Alex.

"She has a punctured lung," he said. "There is plastic wrap in the kitchen of the cabin. It will help. I assume the helicopter is near? We heard a helicopter a half hour ago."

"I'll get it," Zack said. "Raz is entertaining your handler at the helicopter. He wanted to be here, but we wanted to kill you."

Matthew ran from the cabin with a roll of plastic wrap. Tearing a strip, he placed the wrap over the bullet wound. Max helped her sit up and Matthew placed a piece of saran wrap at her back.

"You have to leave a space for the air to get out," Sumit said pointing to Alex's ribs. Matthew shifted the piece of saran wrap.

Alex worked to catch her breath. When she was able to breathe, she began to laugh.

"How did you...?" she asked.

"We saw the signal, the sign of the cross, but Max fired before you made the sign," Trece said.

Alex shook her head and looked at Max.

"Tom Drayson called Ben. You were right. They know each other. John had a dream that you were shot by that guy in this clearing. John was so adamant that you were going to die that Tom thought he should call."

"Nothing that an arrow can't fix?" she laughed.

"Nothing that a friend can't fix," Trece said. "Homeland's on the way to clean up this mess. We'll leave that kid here, you know the G.I. Joe kid?

He's in the chopper."

Alex made a face.

"Don't ask," Troy said, "or you'll find out that he's assigned to us."

"Does she need a stretcher, prick?" Trece asked

"I do." Sumit dropped to the ground.

With Max at her head and Matthew holding her hand, Alex knew for the first time in a very long time, that everything was going to be all right.

CHAPTER THIRTY-NINE
October 22 – 2:45 P.M.
Northern Scotland

"Yes Father. We will be there right away," Rita Kelly Drayson said into the telephone. "Thank you, Father."

Setting the phone down, she turned to her sons.

"Get ready for church. Tomás?"

"Yes Rita, I'm going," he said from the other room.

John sat in the living area reading a novel. He had been in a foul temper all day. Today, he was supposed to get married again. Today was his thirteenth wedding anniversary. Today, he was sitting on this couch reading some moronic adventure novel. Alone.

Why wasn't he with Alex?

"It's not safe." Alex said that twice a day when they spoke on the phone. "Wait until we can come and get you."

Protected like a Goddamn child. He tried to leave twice but was blocked at every turn. Tom just shook his head at him.

"John, you know that we are needed at church this afternoon. Father Callum called to say that we are needed earlier than he thought."

"Have a great time," John said.

"John Kelly, you get up and get ready for church." Rita's face was bright red and her finger pointed like a dagger at his chest. "I don't know where you have been or who you think you are, but our priest called and asked specifically for our help. You get your arse up and into the shower. Johnny, you smell like a tramp."

"But Rita! God damn it. I can't do it... Not today."

"You will not take the Lord's name in vain in this house."

"Get ready, boy," Tom said coming out in his Sunday best.

"If Johnny doesn't have to go," Will, the youngest boy, whined, "why do I have to go?"

"John has to go," Tom said. He pushed Will back to his bedroom. "John, get off that couch and into the shower. NOW."

With a sideways smile, Fionn, the second son, scooted into the bathroom.

"It's occupied," John said.

"Use our bathroom," Rita said. "GO NOW! You are worse than a four year old."

John stomped to the bathroom. While they went to Mass every week in Denver at the Cathedral of the Immaculate Conception, they weren't connected to the parish. If he was in Denver, no priest would call their house and disrupt their day. If he was in Denver, he would be with Alex. He sulked through a quick shower.

He had let himself go since coming to Scotland. His hair was a long curly mess and he had grown a beard. Wiping the steam off the mirror, he made some effort to comb his hair finally giving up. Who cared? He didn't need to look like anything for anyone. He certainly wasn't going to be kissing anyone. They should be glad he didn't smell. He pulled clean clothing over his wet body then followed the family out of the house.

"Will you get in the car?" Rita yelled from the front door.

"What are we doing?" John asked.

John slammed the door shut and stalked to the Range Rover.

"Does it matter, John?" Rita said. She was still angry with him. "I'm glad our mother died before seeing what an elitist jerk you've become."

John watching the Scottish highlands pass outside his window.

"I'm sorry Rita. You are absolutely right. I've been a complete arse," John said.

Danny, the oldest son, looked at John then at his mother. He had to look away to keep from laughing.

"Yes, you have," Tom said.

They drove in silence to the church. There were no vehicles in the parking lot. The family fell out of the Range Rover and walked toward the small chapel. The building was quiet.

Tom pulled the door open, then by plan, John walked first into the chapel. In the dim light, he saw a familiar figure standing near the door.

"It's about time," Max said. "I thought you'd never get here. And you look like crap. Come on, we have a lot to do."

"Max?" John asked. He looked at his best friend then at Tom and Rita. Max hugged the confused John.

Tom winked at John.

"Love you Johnny." Rita kissed his forehead. They hugged.

"Where's your mum?" Tom asked Max.

"She's in there. My father, Patrick, is waiting for you and the boys. Rita, your dress is in with Alex."

Max nodded his head toward a door near the back of the entryway.

"Alex is here? Where is she?"

John ran to the door Max had indicated only to find himself nose to nose with the massive Trece. Trece held a machine gun and wore dark glasses.

"Get out of my way," John said.

"I can't do that, John," Trece said. "It's bad luck for the groom to see the bride before the wedding."

"Groom? Bride?" John fell back. "Wait. What? We're getting married?"

"I will not marry you, John. Not now. Not ever. Stop asking." Trece raised his dark glasses so that John could see his intense dark eyes. "She's been through hell to make this happen."

"We all have," Raz said coming out the door. He hugged John.

"Let her have this." Trece dropped the dark glasses over his eyes. "She deserves it."

"I... but..." John started.

"Come on, John," Max said. "I have your tux. But you're a mess. You know that Alex won't kiss you with that beard. If you want to marry my sister, we've got to get you cleaned up."

Raz put his hand on John's arm. John looked at Raz then at Max and laughed.

"Our area is over here." Fionn pointed to a door on the other side of the entry. "We have tuxes too! There's a big guy inside called the White Boy."

"Everyone knew?" John looked at Tom.

Tom nodded. "Come on, boy, let's get dressed in our monkey suits."

John shook his head. Opening the door to the men's dressing room, he felt like he was walking back into his life. No, not his old life but a whole life, his whole life, a place where Tom and Rita and Alex and Max could live together.

Matthew raised a hand to John but did not look up from his card game with Troy and Colin. The White Boy was flexing his biceps for an entranced Will. Cian and Eoin were laughing at something Danny said.

Raz pushed John into a chair and trimmed two weeks of curly hair from his head. Looking a little more like himself, John took the clippers from Raz. Going into the small restroom, John shaved his beard with the clippers. Fionn gave John the razor and shaving cream he swiped from the bathroom. With special care, John shaved off the rest of his beard.

He was going to kiss Alex today.

John smiled at himself in the mirror. He had been such an ass.

"Will you get dressed?" Tom laughed. He gave John a shot of Irish Whiskey.

While the men talked or played cards, Max passed John the tux one piece at a time. Adjusting the cummerbund, John realized that this was the tux he had altered in Paris at least forty years ago… three very long weeks ago. Without looking up from his cards, Colin threw cuff links to John. Once they were dressed, Tom Drayson made a toast and passed out cigars.

John was excited, breathless with anticipation for the ceremony, and to simply look at Alex. Laughing, John joined the card game.

✑✑✑✑✑✑

October 22 – 4 P.M.
Northern Scotland

Rebecca stood outside the bridal changing room watching the guests arrive for the wedding. There weren't many, certainly not as many guests as she had invited to the Cathedral. Only family or very close friends could be trusted to attend this wedding since most of the wedding party was supposed to be dead.

She nodded her head in greeting to John's biological father and his wife. He stopped for a moment to introduce Rebecca to his wife. Rebecca blushed when he kissed her hand. That is a very attractive man.

Joseph and Nancy Walter stopped for a hug. Joseph said they were taking a second honeymoon. Nancy beamed at Joseph and he laughed. Freedom of movement was a wonderful side effect of being legally dead.

She never would have picked this place, this ceremony or these people, not in a million years. After all, it wouldn't look right for her daughter to be married here. But this tiny church in the middle of Northern Scotland waswhere John and Alex should be remarried. She felt this in her soul.

Rebecca closed her eyes for a moment in a silent prayer of gratitude.

Rebecca smiled as Zack Jakkman and his alluring girlfriend Bestat Bahur came in the church. Bestat always reminded Rebecca of the John Singer Sargent painting called "Egyptian Girl." Rebecca made a mental note to ask Bestat about the painting. Zack blew Rebecca a kiss, and she nodded. They were a beautiful couple.

Rebecca returned to her musing. Alex's face and body were so badly bruised that Rebecca had to research makeup to cover the welts. Claire had a combination of foundation colors created for Alex by some makeup artist in Paris. Alex wouldn't look like she had been beaten and tortured. Not today.

Today she was a bride.

Maria Abreu and her children stopped to chat. They were spending the week in touring the United Kingdom. Rebecca watched Maria's eyes cloud with grief and knew how much she must long for Jesse. Rebecca held Maria to her until Maria straightened her shoulders and tucked her grief away.

Rebecca kissed her cheek before they were escorted to their seat by some soldier.

They called him G.I. Joe. What was his name?

Claire and her children worked day and night to add sleeves and finish the beading on Alex's gorgeous wedding dress. They put together lovely dresses for the four bridesmaids—Erin, Samantha, Julie and Helene. As a surprise, Claire created the most beautiful dresses Rebecca has ever seen for herself, Rebecca and Rita.

"Blue to match our eyes, Becky," Claire had said.

Rebecca smiled remembering Claire's use of her childhood name. Only Benjamin called her that… Benji. She was surprised at how good she felt when Claire said 'Becky.' Underneath all the pretense, Rebecca knew that she was Becky at heart. Alex and Max healed another relationship.

Rebecca let out a breath. Everyone stretched. Everyone worked. Seeing Alex's beautiful beaming face just a moment ago, she knew that everything was worth it. This celebration was going to be wonderful.

Rebecca's breath caught and her heart stopped. For the first time in decades, she didn't care that something didn't look right. Maybe her mother was finally dead. She smiled at the thought.

Looking over the small chapel, she realized that the guests were seated and waiting. Rebecca tapped on the men's room then went to see Alex one more time. Her strange and beautiful daughter, the one she had been so ashamed of, hugged Rebecca and told her that she loved her. Rebecca's eyes filled with tears.

Alex loves me.

The organ began to play the wedding march and the wedding party lined up in the church pre-chamber. Matthew held an elbow out for Claire then escorted her to the front where Frederec and Eugene waited for her. Troy held his elbow for Rebecca and escorted her to the front. Claire smiled at Rebecca when she sat down next to her. Rebecca reached for Claire's hand. Holding hands, the mothers waited for their Alex.

Matthew escorted Rita to the front pew on the other side where she sat beside her sons. Matthew returned to the back to stand next to Troy. Drawing their handguns, Matthew and Troy walked to the front of the church. Matthew moved across the front of the church to the left while Troy moved across the front of the church to the right. They would guard the ceremony from the front.

Colin started the procession. His blonde hair standing straight up, he escorted Julie and her tiny baby pooch to the front of the church. They separated at the front. Raz followed with Samantha on his arm. Cian laughed down the aisle with Erin. Beaming from ear to ear, Max, the best man, came down the aisle with Helene, the maid of honor.

Tom Drayson walked John to the front of the church. Tom hugged John then sat with his arm around Rita and the boys. John turned to look down the aisle into the church pre-chamber.

He did not want to miss even one moment.

Alex stood in the bridal room alone.

"You are beautiful," Jesse said in Spanish.

"Thanks. It's amazing what a little makeup can do," she said.

"My Maria looks so beautiful today," Jesse said with noticeable longing.

"She does," Alex said. "Jesse? I wanted to…   I don't really know how to… Thanks."

Jesse laughed. "We're a team. You need to get going."

Alex nodded.

"I'll be around," he said disappearing.

Holding Camille's hand, Ben came into the room. Camille carried a white basket full of pink rose petals. Her dark ringlets were held out of her eyes by a small white barrette. She wore a dress that matched Alex's bridal gown. Another tap on the door and Patrick joined them. Patrick kissed her cheek.

"Shall I put the veil down?" Patrick asked.

"I guess so," Alex said.

He lifted two layers of the veil and covered her face.

"Oh, you have to unhook me." Alex held her arm out to Patrick. "Just pull on the fitting."

Patrick lifted her cream silk sleeve to reveal the tubes, which connected Alex to her IV antibiotics.

"You won't tell, will you?" She pleaded with Patrick and Ben not to tell John that she should wear the IV. "I'll put it back on when we're done."

"I won't tell," Patrick said. With a firm tug, he disconnected the fitting to the IV.

"You know I won't," Ben said.

"Camille? Will you tell anyone about the IV?" Alex asked in French. She crouched down to look into Camille's eyes.

Camille looked at the fairy princess called Alex and batted her huge blue eyes. She nodded then wrinkled her nose.

"I have one right here," Alex laughed. She held an orange Tootsie Roll pop in her hand. "Your Maman said you could have this when you get to the front of the church."

"Oui. Ne dirai pas." Camille wasn't going to tell either.

"We'll put this in your basket." Alex slipped the candy into Camille's white basket.

Holding her rosebud bouquet in her hand, Alex took Ben's arm then took Patrick's arm. They walked into the pre-chamber of the church.

Ben gave Camille a little push and she started down the aisle. She threw a handful of petals on one side then weaved forward to throw a handful of petals on the other side. She threw another handful of petals and picked up some petals in her hand. Noticing Helene at the front of the church, Camille ran forward, the petals falling unnoticed from her basket and her hand.

"Look what I have," Camille said in French. She held the orange Tootsie Roll pop out to Helene. Turning to her mother, she pleaded, "Maman?"

Laughing in the front row, Claire said, "Oui."

Helene lifted Camille into her arms. Throwing the wrapper on the floor, Camille stuck the candy in her mouth.

"Please rise," Father Seamus said.

Everyone stood. Turning toward the church pre-chamber, a gasp went through the crowd. Alex was absolutely stunning.

Moving slowly down the aisle, she nodded, winked and smiled to the friends and loved ones in the pews. She shyly lowered her head when they approached John.

Stopping at the front, Alex turned to Ben who raised one layer of her veil then kissed her cheek. Turning to Patrick, she smiled as he raised the last layer. He touched her chin, then kissed her face. He slipped into the pew after Ben.

Alex turned to John. The blue of his eyes was all but consumed by his black pupils and his mouth was slightly open. Blushing at his reaction, her lips turned upward.

Before her lips could form the crooked smile, Father Seamus began the service.

✧✧✧
October 23 – 1 A.M.
Northern Scotland

"What is it, love?" asked John as he came up behind her.

Alex was standing in her pajamas at the front window of the cottage. Somehow escaping John's notice, Rita and Tom converted a sheepherder's cottage to a honeymoon escape for them. Turning, she reached her arms around his warm naked body.

"I like to see out," she said, "especially at night."

John put his hands around her face and kissed her.

"When we get home, I'll build you a porch off our bedroom where you can watch the stars."

"We'd need to get a home first."

"Max, didn't tell you?"

"Tell me what?"

"He found an old boarding house about a block from our old house. It is very large and dilapidated. The building is in foreclosure and has been vacant for most of the last year. We've been negotiating with the bank this week. They are thrilled to be rid of the building and gave us a great deal if we close in two weeks. We should be able to move into at least one area of the building by New Year's. We'll live together."

"Are you all right with the loss of space? You wanted your own space, your own house. It's why we bought the other house."

"My priorities have shifted quite a bit in the last few months," he said. "When remodeled, we'll have two separate living spaces with a common kitchen, living area and dining area. The basement will be contiguous with it's secret office, entertainment room and guest rooms. Don't tell Raz, but we're planning to convert the carriage house into a loft apartment for him. It's a bit of a surprise."

"How do you know all of this and I don't?"

"Max didn't want to bother you. You've been in the hospital. Christ, Alex, you're still on IV antibiotics. You should still be in the hospital."

"Kiss me again."

Melting at his touch, she buried her head in his arms.

"I'm sorry about losing the ring," she started.

John laughed, rocking her in his arms.

"I don't care about that anymore," he said. "Would you like another one?"

She kissed his neck.

"Honestly?"

He nodded looking into her dark eyes.

"I love this band." Alex pointed to the thin gold band she had worn every day for almost thirteen years.

He smiled then hugged her again.

"Why don't I stay up with you?" John asked. "I can tell you everything you would like to know about mending fences and cleaning sheep stalls. If you're nice, I'll flex my muscles for you again."

"Oh Mr. Kelly Drayson your biceps are huge," she said in a mock Betty Boop. She kissed each arm.

"Two lonely weeks working on the ranch," he said. "Wait here. Just one second."

John went to the bedroom and pulled on a pair of pajamas. Bringing a wing back chair and a blanket from the sitting area, he opened the blinds and sat down in the chair.

"Please sit with me," he said.

Alex sat on his lap and he covered them with the blanket. He kissed her neck then held her close to him. They sat watching the night.

"Are you sleeping?"

"Not at night," she said. "My mind has so many other things to work out in the dark." Leaning against him, she sighed. "God, I've missed you."

John smiled.

"I dreamed of you every night." Overcome with emotion, he stopped speaking. "I thought I'd never see you again."

"I thought I'd never see you or anyone again," she said. "When I knew he was going to kill me? The first thing I longed for was you, kissing you."

"That's very nice," he said. He kissed her lips. "I don't know how long we'll have. I'm just grateful to have one more moment with you."

She nuzzled his neck under his chin.

"I'm different, you know. Everything is different. And yet…" she said. "I mean it's weird. We went through so much, such difficult times and…"

"Yet we learned so much," John said. "Yes. You know, being a doctor, having lots of money, is really not so important."

"Being a Green Beret or a super spy is not so important," she added.

"What's important is family, friends…"

"And love. Yes."

"All of these secrets. Your fathers. My history. They were stupid. I'm so sorry I hurt you, didn't trust you. I was foolishly trying to control you, control your opinion of me. I never realized I actually kept myself from loving you fully."

"Loving fully. I thought a lot about that when I was in the room," she said. "I've hidden myself away from you so that you would never know me, all of me. I never realized you knew me all along."

He kissed her head and held her tight. They watched the night together in silence.

Alex sighed.

"What is it, love?"

"I'm so very glad I survived… to sit right here… with you."

*

5207793R0

Made in the USA
Charleston, SC
14 May 2010